Elite: Legacy

by

Michael Brookes

An Elite: Dangerous Novel

The right of Michael Brookes to be identified as the author of this book has been asserted by him in accordance with the Copyright, Designs and Patent Act 1998.

Elite © 1984 David Braben & Ian Bell. Frontier © 1993 David Braben, Frontier: First Encounters © 1995 David Braben and Elite: Dangerous © 2012, 2014 Frontier Developments plc.

'Elite', the Elite logo, the Elite: Dangerous logo, 'Frontier' and the Frontier logo are registered trademarks of Frontier Developments plc. All rights reserved. All other trademarks and copyrights are acknowledged as the property of their respective owners.

Discover the Elite: Dangerous Video Game

http://www.elitedangerous.com

400 Billion Star Systems
Infinite Freedom
Blaze Your Own Trail

Elite: Dangerous © **1984 - 2014**
Frontier Developments plc. All rights reserved.

DEDICATION

Writing Elite: Legacy presented a unique opportunity for me as a writer, a developer and as a fan of the game. Back in the mid-eighties Elite was the game that first made me realise the scope of what computer games could be. Since then I've been a huge fan of computer games.

I became involved in Elite: Dangerous during the Kickstarter campaign and during that process I first encountered the amazing community of fans all eager to see this new game made.

Combined with my life long love for science fiction it took no time at all to accept when David asked me to write a tie-in novel for the game. And here is the fruit of that labour!

So firstly thanks to David Braben for the opportunity, thanks to all the dedicated team who are putting together an incredible game.

Thanks also to the community for your support and encouragement for both the game and this book.

And not forgetting of course my good friends and family who's support is invaluable.

Keep up to date with my writing on my blog:

http://thecultofme.blogspot.com

OTHER ELITE: DANGEROUS NOVELS

Published by Fantastic Books Publishing

Elite: Reclamation by Drew Wager
Elite: Mostly Harmless by Kate Russell
Elite: And Here the Wheel by John Harper
Elite: Tales from the Frontier by various authors

Published by Gollancz

Elite: Wanted by Gavin Deas
Elite: Nemorensis by Simon Spurrier
Elite: Docking is Difficult by Gidean Defoe

Published by Writer and Author Press

Elite: Out of the Darkness by T. James

OTHER BOOKS BY MICHAEL BROOKES

The Cult of Me
Conversations in the Abyss
Faust 2.0
Sun Dragon

An Odd Quartet
An Odder Quintet

- 1 -

Even at this great distance from the Artemis system's pale orange star, the light sliced sharp shadows between the asteroids hanging seemingly motionless as the small freighter passed. The once-pristine white livery on the Lakon Type 7 exposed its age with blemishes, darkened under the harsh radiation of many suns during its long life.

In contrast to its stern, almost box-like lines, the vessel moved with an easy grace through the dense cluster of asteroids. The belt had formed from the remnants of a celestial collision, recent in cosmological terms yet still long before the species which created the ship existed.

The small freighter bore the name *Twin Vipers*. A curiously aggressive name for a ship more used to safe trade runs, such as the food they'd delivered to the mining colony of Freeholm. Like the fragments of rock around it, the name was a marker to history, albeit one of a much shorter time frame.

Although the ship's two-man crew spent most of their time travelling to and from different star systems, they considered Freeholm their home.

The previous day Freeholm's population, including the two pilots on the ship, had celebrated two different ten-year anniversaries over the past two weeks. For the station, they celebrated their hard-fought freedom.

Once the station was a penal colony for the surrounding system with the mines worked by prisoners, most of whom were imprisoned for their opinions rather than their crimes.

For the pilots now accelerating out of mass lock in the asteroid belt, it marked the end of the violence which dominated their lives and the start of something much more fulfilling.

As bounty hunters, they'd both piloted Vipers and hunted pirates and other criminals along the borders of Imperial space. The lines on their faces reflected the hard life and many battles they'd survived. Those lines had softened somewhat since their decision to retire from the life of hunting bounties.

Freeholm held the distinction of being their first trade run. Being so soon after the rebellion, they'd made a tidy profit, although at considerable risk. At the station they'd also found a home, one that welcomed them, and they returned there whenever they could. A circumstance which benefitted them, as over the years they became favoured traders. As such they enjoyed significant discounts when purchasing the refined ores and minerals the station produced.

On this run they filled the cargo hold with some of the more exotic minerals. They could have made a quick, but more modest profit by transporting the materials to the populated planet Laphria which orbited nearer to the star. By travelling to more distant systems, they stood to make a larger profit. That would come in handy as they'd discussed trading in the Type 7 and upgrading to a Type 9 and that required a lot of credits.

"We're approaching the edge of the belt," Darius, the elder of the partnership, reported. Not that much separated the two in age. Both he and Simeon possessed the same lean physiques, ideal for and born from a life inside a cockpit.

"Nothing on the scanner," Simeon replied.

"I'm not surprised, I expect everyone's still sleeping off last night's celebrations."

"I wouldn't have minded a bit more time in bed myself."

"You were putting that Lavian Brandy away a bit last night. Do you realise how much that stuff costs? I thought we were supposed to be saving up for a new ship?"

Simeon at least had the decency to look a little guilty, even if he didn't feel it. "You have to let your hair down sometimes."

"I've no problem with that, but the bar bill was a bit much."

"Nag, nag. You sound like an old woman sometimes and besides, I didn't hear you complaining when we returned to our quarters."

Darius reddened. They'd been together for ten years and he hadn't overcome his embarrassment when talking about sex, even when it was just the two of them. He'd been raised with the attitude of what happens on ship, stays on ship. An attitude that remained common in certain parts of human space despite all the passing centuries.

"I'll admit you were a little athletic," Darius coughed and then changed the subject. "I've locked in the first jump to Kappa Fornacis. Once we're clear of the belt we'll jump."

"We should be clear in a few minutes. And anyway, I wasn't the only one being a bit over the top last night. What was all that with you and Julia?"

"It was only a joke. She laughed, didn't she?"

"She did, but her father didn't. You know how protective he can be. We really don't want to piss of the head of security."

"He was there?"

"Oh yes."

"Oops."

"Oops indeed. Wait a minute. What was that?"

"What?"

"I'm not sure. I thought I saw something at the edge of scanner range."

"Well if it's that far out we should be okay, we'll be jumping in a minute."

Simeon kept an eye on the scanner. With Darius flying the ship, he didn't really have much else to do. There wasn't often much traffic out here, maybe the odd trader like them heading to or from Freeholm. Occasionally you saw a Laphrian Navy patrol, but usually it was quiet. The momentary contact worried him, or maybe the Lavian Brandy still fogged his thoughts. A hot breakfast had helped, but his head still ached.

There it was again. A brief burst of heat, enough to register for a moment on the scanner. Not enough to resolve into an identified target though.

"There's someone out there and they're trying to keep quiet about it."

Darius glanced at the scanner and saw nothing. He trusted Simeon's instincts though. "We're clearing the belt now, so we should be able to jump at any moment. Let's warm up the drive and be ready."

"All right. Putting more power into the engines."

"We're approaching supercruise velocity. I'm now matching the jump vector."

On the front of the cockpit, a holographic marker highlighted their jump destination.

"We're aligned," Darius continued. "Activating frame shift drive."

The powerful engine that bent space and allowing them to travel impossible distances whined into activation mode and then faltered.

"What the hell was that?" Simeon demanded. He had never heard the frame shift drive sound like that before.

"I've no idea, maybe we're still mass locked?"

"No, we're clear. The system isn't showing us as mass locked, it's reading unknown error."

"Are we being interdicted?"

"There's no sign of device being used."

"Has it malfunctioned?"

"Not that I can tell. I'm checking the diagnostics now."

"I'll maintain course and get us further away from the belt. Maybe it is just a mass lock malfunction."

"I don't think it is. The computer isn't showing any error either. Still no trace of an interdiction wave. Wait a second. Our friend's back. Scratch that – friends."

On the scanner the fresh contact appeared on the edge of the scanner's range and divided into four.

"They're picking up speed," Simeon reported.

"Okay, this stinks. Anything on the drive?"

"Nothing. Should we run back to the station?"

"They'll be on us by the time we've turned round. You need to get that drive working!"

"How? I don't even know what's wrong with it. The system just shows the same unknown error message."

"I think this is one of those times I wish we still had our Vipers."

"You and me both. All right, we're going to have to do this the hard way. You get on the comms and let them know we're in trouble. I don't like it, but we need their help and they'll scramble their alert fighters."

"They're at least two hours away," Simeon pointed out. "This thing will be over by then."

"Get the word out. Maybe the planet's navy has something close by?"

"On it. They'll outrun us, but don't make it easy for them."

"I have no intention of it. I've got everything I can in the engines."

On the scanner, the three nearest targets formed a loose line, ready to counter any escape event. Simeon thought that the fourth target looked larger, but he couldn't be sure.

"Freeholm station, this is *Two Vipers*, we have unknown

targets on the inner edge of the belt. We could do with some help out here."

"Anything?"

"You're on the same channel, did you hear anything?"

"Freeholm station, this is *Twin Vipers*. Can you hear me?"

Nothing.

Simeon cycled through the displays on the communications panel. The radio channels all registered intense jamming and even the hyperspace channels reported no carrier wave.

"We have a problem here."

"I'd noticed. What's going on with comms?"

"Everything is down."

"Everything? Even the hyperspace links?"

"Everything. The laser system seems to be okay, but we don't have any friendlies near enough to align with."

"Could you relay something from the nav beacon?"

The navigation beacon still displayed brightly on the scanner, but the approaching ships would cut them off before they could get close enough.

"Probably, but only if we survive that long."

"That's the spirit!"

Sometimes Simeon wondered how much Darius missed their old lives.

"We can't stay out here," Darius continued. "I'm heading back into the belt and see if we can get close enough to the beacon to get a message through."

"All right. The nearest contacts have resolved. We have three Sidewinders on our tail. I can't tell what they're equipped with yet, but my guess is that they'll be in weapons range in less than five minutes."

"What about the fourth contact?"

"Nothing. He's keeping behind the Sidewinders for now. He doesn't seem to be having any problems holding station though and they're coming in at full burn."

"Do you think they're after the cargo, or us?"

They weren't carrying the most valuable cargo in the galaxy, but it was worth enough credits to be worth the heist. On the other hand, they'd also made some enemies over the years, so it was possible that someone was after payback.

"We can dump the cargo and find out?"

Neither of them liked that option, since the cargo in their hold represented a major investment in their future for them. With the profit they planned to upgrade to a larger ship, and a bigger ship not only meant bigger trades, it also meant better-appointed quarters while they were on long runs.

However, losing the cargo would be a more palatable option than losing the ship.

"I guess we don't have a choice. As soon as you drop the cargo I'll head back into the belt. It's not much, but at least we'll have a bit more cover."

"Dropping the cargo now."

A string of cargo pods ejected in a loose line behind the ship. When the last pod dropped, Darius banked into a tight turn. The main engines trailed exhaust crystals as they raced back towards the asteroid belt.

Darius kept his attention on the ship's course while Simeon monitored the contacts on the scanner. They hoped the Sidewinders would slow and scoop up the discarded cargo and then they would all get on with their lives. Poorer, but at least alive.

"They've ignore the pods and changed course, and they're following us in," Simeon reported.

"Damn it. Well we're not going to be able to outrun them. We can't fight them either, but we'll have to try."

"Activating defensive systems."

The Type 7 wasn't designed for combat, especially compared to the Vipers they used to pilot. The three Sidewinders wouldn't have stood a chance against two Vipers, but the bulky freighter was another matter. Despite its disadvantages, the ship wasn't without teeth and Simeon activated the four auto-turrets. Although they were designed as point defences against missiles, they could also engage smaller ships.

"The turrets are online. I'll switch some power from the engines to them once the Sidewinders are in range." He looked at the heat sink launcher. The all-out run from the initial contact had generated a lot of heat and that gave him an idea.

"Can we hide from them?"

Darius understood what Simeon intended and he shrugged. "Maybe. It's a better option than running or fighting so let's try it." He checked the scanner. "We've got a small cluster of asteroids coming up. Maybe we can squeeze in between the closer ones. Get ready with the heat sink and launch on my mark."

A tense minute passed as they charged towards the clump of asteroids. The three Sidewinders chased after them. The fourth contact remained unresolved on the edge of their scanner range.

"Now."

Simeon launched the heat sink. The glowing disk spun off into space, glowing hotter than the ship. In the same moment, Darius cut the engines and buttoned up the radiator vanes so that they no longer emitted any of the vast quantities of heat generated by the ship.

They couldn't remain buttoned up for long, as even in low power mode the heat build-up would quickly begin to damage the ship's systems. Darius feathered the thrusters, using as little power as possible to arc the ship between the massive asteroids.

Simeon watched the Sidewinders on the scanner. He hissed in relief as they thundered past the asteroid and followed the heat sink.

"They've taken the bait."

"It won't fool them for long. I'll drift for as long as possible. Keep an eye on them and when they start to turn we'll boost again and give them a new target to chase. What's the fourth contact doing?"

"He's in the same pattern, bringing up the rear. We have two heat sinks left."

"We'll have to make them count."

Stating the obvious wasn't Darius's most endearing trait. In fact Simeon hated it, but he also knew that it was one of his lover's defence mechanisms, so held his tongue and watched the contacts on the scanner. He also timed how long the diversion worked.

If they could hide and sprint enough to build a decent gap between their pursuers, then maybe they'd get out of this.

"They're starting to turn."

Darius reacted as soon as Simeon spoke and poured everything the ship had into the engines.

He opened the heating vents and the rear of the ship glowed as it dumped their excess heat.

"They see us," Simeon told his partner.

"How long until they reach weapons range?"

"It's difficult to be sure, but probably no more than ten minutes."

The tactic had gained them five minutes. Not much but maybe enough if they could make the last two runs count.

"Let me know a minute before they reach weapons range."

"Will do."

The ten minutes burned by all too quickly.

"They're in range."

"Dump the next heat sink."

Simeon launched their second heat sink as Darius fired the lateral thrusters, changing their course while hidden by the bloom of the heat sink. He shut the engines down again and buttoned up the ship so they vanished once again from their pursuers' scanners.

"They're not falling for it this time."

"Shit."

"One of Sidewinders has broken off to follow the heat

sink, the other two are following our original course. They'll have visual at any moment now."

"Damn it."

"Weapons lock. Raising shields and activating turrets."

"Keep some power in the engines so I can manoeuvre. Put the rest in the shields, although I don't know how long they'll last."

Their shields hissed as the first Sidewinder swooped in, firing his burst lasers. The enemy hadn't expected the return fire from the defence turrets and had to take evasive action as his shields drained from the rapid laser fire.

"He'll be a bit more cautious on his next run," Darius quipped.

"I think they all will be, look."

The Sidewinders took turns to nibble at the Type 7's shields. They split up so that they could hit the evading freighter from different angles. They kept their distance as well so the point defences caused little damage.

"They don't seem to be in any hurry," Simeon remarked.

"That's what worries me, and I still can't raise anything on the comms."

"We could try to surrender?"

Darius pulled a face in response.

"I don't like it either, but we're not going to get away from them. Those Sidewinders can outmanoeuvre us easily and they outgun us. And who knows what the other contact is."

As if to reinforce his point, a fresh fusillade of laser fire slashed into the shields. The shields were already darkening around the ship. Both of them recognised that they wouldn't last much longer. Darius swerved the ship and the second burst missed by mere inches. He wasn't so fortunate with the third salvo.

"Damn it! You're right, we can't out-fight them. Try

contacting them with the laser comms."

Simeon tapped on the communication console, aligning the tight-beam communications system with the still unresolved target. It lurked farther back from the more energetic Sidewinders who continued their assault on the Type 7's shields.

The laser pinged back indicating that it had located a receiver. The shields collapsed as the system initiated a handshake with the unknown ship. It all happened too slowly for Simeon as he willed the computer to work faster. As soon as the connection established, he spoke.

"Attacking ships. We surrender. Halt your attack. We surrender."

The ship shuddered as laser fire smashed into the hull, their shields now fully collapsed. The connection indicator blinked off on the console as the unknown ship severed the connection.

"Missile lock!" Darius shouted in concert with the alarm in the cockpit.

On the scanner, Simeon watched the unknown contact blossom into several smaller contacts that streaked towards them. Darius swung the ship in a tight turn. The *Two Vipers* couldn't turn tightly enough and the missiles tore the ship apart.

- 2 -

Darik Cavus ran through the pre-flight checks in the cockpit of his Eagle fighter. As head of security for Freeholm he could have, in fact should have, sent the alert fighters. The colony's command centre had received a distress signal originating from the edge of the asteroid belt.

Darik liked to fly and the mission had a personal edge. The signal contained the ship registration. He knew Darius and Simeon. They were one of the first independent traders to visit the station after the rebellion.

His daughter, Julia, didn't appreciate him pulling rank to respond to the call. In fairness, as lead pilot and on alert, she should have been the one to respond. She argued that she should escort him in her own Eagle, or at least take the alert two Sidewinders with him.

He denied her requests as he didn't know what situation awaited him. He intended to approach quietly and ascertain what had happened. Ships from the station could respond quickly enough if there was trouble or if he needed support.

The signal concerned him. The pair were experienced pilots and Darik knew of their past lives as bounty hunters. He also knew that the distress signal would have triggered on a delayed response. Experienced bounty hunters often programmed a delay into their escape pods so that they didn't broadcast their location while the hostiles who had just destroyed their ship were still in the vicinity.

Whatever had happened on the outside of the belt was most likely over, but it didn't answer the question of why there hadn't been any other communications. As he mulled over the likely scenarios, he realised that going out on his own might not be the best move. He opened a channel to his daughter.

"Julia."

"Yes Dad."

"You and the alert fighters follow me. When we reach the nav beacon, hold position until I call for you."

"Roger that."

He heard the relief in her voice. At least if there was trouble he'd have backup to hand. Julia would have preferred to accompany him to the signal source. Darik appreciated that he should be used to including her on missions by now. They'd flown together for years, but even so, when he sensed trouble he chose to face it alone.

Perhaps that wasn't the wisest choice for someone who was supposed to be responsible for the defence of the whole station and the surrounding belt.

He shrugged. When it came down to it, the choice and the responsibility belonged to him. Opening a channel, he contacted flight control. A rather grandiose name for what was really two technicians monitoring the colony's systems.

"We're ready for launch, Eagle Two and the two alert fighters are coming with me. Get hold of Talia and Lev and get them on the pads. It's probably nothing, but I want to be ready in case I'm wrong."

"Understood, Commander."

The title came with the job, he'd never get used to it though.

"You are cleared to launch, Commander."

The clamps holding Darik's fighter released and a gentle magnetic pulse lifted the ship off the pad where the ship's thrusters took over. The colony had invested in rotation correction assist to make take-off and landing easier for visitors. But Darik knew the station's motion well and always insisted on full manual launch.

He looked at the scanner and even though it displayed no contacts, he glanced around the ship to be certain. Designed for combat, the Eagle's open canopy provided good all-round visibility.

The docking bay was a vast, almost cavernous expanse. Its cylindrical shape allowed efficient use of the available surface area, and at maximum capacity the station could dock up to twenty ships. Those could be as large as a Panther Clipper, although Darik had never seen a ship so large visit Freeholm, or seen all the pads in use at once for that matter.

Darik kept the power to his thrusters low as he moved through the dock. A mistake before departure wouldn't do his reputation or the colony's finances any good. Julia and the two Sidewinders waited in the bays behind him. Directly above him he saw Lina Mater's Cobra Mk III. She was another independent trader who considered Freeholm her home, so much so that she tended to keep to short runs with the neighbouring systems.

Confident that all was clear, he increased his vertical ascent and rolled to match orientation with the docking port. He increased speed as he approached the port and added some roll to match the station's rotation. The station spun so that the living areas on the upper levels of the station experienced a gravitational effect from the centripetal force.

The docking port was lined with several powerful energy shields, similar to the ones that protected ships from attackers in space. On their own, shields wouldn't provide an airtight seal, but layered as they were enabled the docking bay to be pressurised, although at a lower level than the rest of the station.

It always felt good to depart from Freeholm. As much as he loved it, his love of flying stretched further back, all the way to his childhood.

The colony was constructed inside one of the asteroids that formed a dense cluster within the belt. This was a common rocky asteroid, the other more valuable ones had been moved into position for easier access. They also provided a defensive ring around the station, although it hadn't needed to defend itself for over a decade now.

A navigation beacon signalled the right vector to avoid the shuffling orbits of the asteroids being mined and their debris. The defence force for Freeholm was small, just Darik, Julia and four Sidewinder pilots. Their work primarily meant keeping the approach lanes free of the larger chunks of debris that occasionally found their way near the colony.

On a few rare occasions, they'd intercepted rogue miners who attempted to set up operations within the belt. The co-existence treaty with the Laphrian government meant that all exploitation rights for the belt belonged to the former penal colony. The inhabitants of Freeholm had to defend those rights for themselves though.

A subtle course correction set Darik on a path towards the beacon. He couldn't use the frame shift drive while in the belt, but it wasn't a long journey. He made use of the time by reviewing the limited information they received from the signal.

The location of the signal had been pinpointed some distance away from the traffic lanes provided through the belt. Except for a few patches the belt wasn't dense, but encountering even small debris at speed could be problematic if a pilot wasn't prepared. Darik knew Simeon and Darius, they were both experienced pilots and wouldn't have left the transit corridor unless they had a good reason.

The reported location made even less sense when Darik considered that they were heading to Kappa Fornacis. They should have jumped as soon as they left the belt, unless they had been prevented somehow.

And there lay Darik's foremost worry. This wasn't the

first ship to go missing in recent weeks, although no trace of the previous two had been found. They weren't regulars either so he couldn't be certain that they hadn't just headed elsewhere. The galaxy was a big place. Still, it didn't feel right and Darik had learned at a young age to listen to his instincts.

As he reached the navigation beacon, he called in to update Julia.

"I'm passing the nav beacon now. I'm going to follow the corridor to the usual jump point at the inner edge. That's where I think Darius and Simeon were heading. I'll then sweep along the belt until I'm in line with the transmission and then move in from the edge.

"You hold position at the beacon. I may need you to sweep directly through the belt towards the transmission. I'll let you know when I'm in the final approach."

Julia acknowledged his instructions and he closed the channel. He'd maintain radio silence from now on. He powered down his shields and other systems to reduce his heat signature. It wasn't full stealth, but it would make him harder to detect, especially at long range.

The journey took longer at reduced power and his focus remained concentrated on the scanner for the entire journey. His Eagle was well equipped with passive and active sensors. Using passive sensors reduced the information flow from his surroundings but, as with the lowered heat generation, made him harder to detect.

The Eagle was an old design, one that had been popular throughout human space for decades. It remained one of the few ships that had been used by both the Federation and Empire and still operated for both navies as a long-range interceptor.

For Darik it had been the ship he'd learned to fly in, although he didn't like to think about his life with his old family. There were too many bad memories from that time and the guilt from the action that changed the course of his life. They were memories best left buried, but in one of the jokes that life enjoyed playing, his love of flying had sparked from the training from his father.

Before even becoming a man he'd mastered basic and advanced flying and was a capable fighter pilot. Of the four siblings, he had been considered the one with the most potential. Even his father had judged him a natural talent and he'd been a hard man to impress.

The solitude of silent running in space wasn't the best place for such thoughts. The dark and the absolute cold of space centimetres from his face provided an all-too-willing accomplice for descent into those years. With an effort he focused on the matter at hand, along with a repeated mental promise that Julia would never have to make the choice that he had at her age.

All through the journey through the belt he watched the scanner closely. He saw no indications of anything untoward, only the ghosts of the giant rocks around him displayed on the scanner. After an hour's flight, he reached the edge of the belt and angled his ship towards the source of the transmission.

He still saw no signs of life on the scanner. In the far distance towards Laphria, the ship's sensors detected the usual confusion of EM signals from a habited outdoor world. Now that he flew outside the belt, he felt exposed. Technically the act breached the treaty between the planet and its former colony.

There was no point in starting an incident so he curved the ship's course back into the belt and followed the edge along the inside. Sometimes it was these long and boring flights that created the most nerves. He held faint hope that he'd surprise whoever had attacked the freighter. It was a large assumption that they'd been attacked at all. There might well be another explanation for the distress call and subsequent lack of communication.

As he headed back to the belt, his sensors detected the low-level locator beacons built into most cargo pods. The legally transported ones anyway. The ID tags matched that of Darius and Simeon's Lakon Type 7 and that confirmed something had happened. Although why was the cargo so far away from the distress signal? And if the freighter had been attacked by pirates then why hadn't they collected the cargo?

He didn't want to break radio silence yet, so he marked the point on his system map. He would arrange for the canisters to be collected by one of the traders at the station, buy the contents and use the credits to fund funeral arrangements or just transfer the credits into the pair's estate.

Another hour's flight picking through the asteroids and a sudden flare of electromagnetic energies blossomed on his scanner. He recognised the pattern almost as quickly as the ship's computer as the energies coalesced and a large ship popped into existence.

The ship's silhouette looked familiar and Darik cursed. He didn't hold anything against the planet's patrols, indeed they were part of the agreement, but he had hoped to investigate on his own before any interference. Not that the Laphrian Navy had any jurisdiction within the belt. More annoyingly, the arrival of a warship from supercruise and pinging with military-grade active sensors destroyed any hope of a covert approach.

Captain Belin's ship, the *Demeter*, was an Anaconda frame, but there the similarity with the well-known trading vessel ended. The ship had been outfitted in a light cruiser role, the most valuable export from the Artemis shipyards in past years. It looked bulkier, mostly because of the extra armour fitted to the ship, and extra weapon mounts had been fitted giving the ship impressive firepower.

An incoming audio communications request highlighted on his comms panel. With a voice command, he accepted it.

"Captain Belin," he greeted the Laphrian officer.

The captain's clipped tones went straight to business.

"Commander. I'm responding to a distress call from this part of the belt."

"As am I."

"Have you ascertained the situation?"

"Not yet. I was taking a covert approach."

"May I ask why?"

"I know the owners of the ship the call originates from, they would have used a delayed transmission."

"Ah, I see."

Darik calculated the timings in his head. "If you're responding to the call, why did it take so long to get here?"

If Belin had reacted to the call promptly then he should have arrived here over an hour before Darik's slower approach.

"We experienced some trouble of our own. A pirate attack nearer the inner system."

"That's a bold move going up against the *Demeter*."

"I think we surprised them."

"Them?"

"Four Sidewinders, and they ran the moment we made contact. For some reason they kept taking pot-shots at us even as they retreated."

Darik agreed that seemed strange. The converted Anaconda's main weakness was its speed, so the Sidewinders would have been able to escape easily. "Where was the attack?"

"In deep space, between here and the planet. I'll send you a datacast."

Darik looked at the data that Belin transmitted. The location made even less sense than the attack. "That's in the middle of nowhere, who were they hoping to ambush?"

"I wondered the same thing. If they had stationed between the star and Laphria it would have made sense. They might have interdicted a transport from your station heading towards the planet."

Even over the compressed audio channel, Belin didn't sound convinced and once more Darik agreed with the Navy captain's assessment. "I didn't think you guys encountered a lot of pirate activity? I know we rarely see anything and we're a more likely target."

"Agreed. We haven't seen anything except for this attack. However there have been some occasional contacts along the belt, which could be someone sneaking about. You might want to increase your patrols just in case."

"I'll do that, but first I need to find out what happened to my friends."

"Understood. Let me know if I can help."

"Will do, thanks Captain." Then Darik remembered the canisters. "Actually Captain, I found discarded cargo from the attacked ship, can you keep an eye on it until I can arrange collection?"

"Of course. Send me the coordinates and we'll swing by."

"That's appreciated."

"No problem. Have a better one, Commander."

With the stealth approach now out of the question, Darik contacted Julia.

"I'm heading straight to the transmission origin now, at full burn."

"We saw the arrival, a Navy patrol?"

"Yes, it seems they had some trouble of their own."

"Did they catch the guys?"

"No, it may not be the same attackers, maybe we'll find out something new at the transmission site."

"Okay, what do you want us to do?"

"Head straight through the belt to the origin. I've not seen any activity on the scanner so I doubt there's anyone there. Unless they're keeping very cold."

"On our way."

"I'll see you there."

Darik increased the power distribution to his engines, pushing them beyond their normal maximum limit. At these accelerations you lost a lot of the ship's manoeuvring capability, although he didn't need them for now. He just wanted to get to the site as quickly as possible.

As he approached the region where the signal originated from, he switched the extra power into his shields and dialled back the throttle. He swept the area with his active sensors and found nothing lurking in the debris.

The lack of any large debris surprised him. There was enough to indicate that a ship had been destroyed, but few large pieces. The ship had been taken out with serious overkill. It looked like there was little to learn here and that frustrated Darik.

He did find the source of the signal, it was all that remained from an escape pod. Either the pod had been destroyed with the ship or it had been hit after ejecting. Darik wouldn't even be able to bring the bodies back to Freeholm.

- 3 -

In the darkened cockpit of a Fer de Lance, a lone figure watched. He had been there throughout the initial attack and due to the fortuitous placement of recon drones on previous visits, he'd watched the chase and the final kill.

For such a large ship, the Fer de Lance hid itself well in the cold of space. This ship had many upgrades to maximise its heat management, essential for any ship operating covertly in hostile environments.

Throughout the battle, he remained undetected. The pilot watched the engagement with a practised eye. The battle had been one-sided, although the freighter had done well to have survived as long as it did.

He saw the end of the battle through the drone's sensors. Two escape pods had ejected and were quickly cut down by the Sidewinders. Even for pirates that was unexpected. As he tracked their exit from the belt and saw that they ignored the ejected cargo, it became clear that these weren't pirates.

Clearly a deeper game was being played here. He didn't know what that game might be, although it might prove beneficial information for the future. He made a note of where the four ships jumped into hyperspace. Unfortunately he was too far away to be able to track the wake so he didn't know which system they jumped to.

The watcher remained in place to observe the reaction from the colony. He had expected a quicker reaction despite the jamming on both radio and hyperspace channels. The arrival of the Navy Anaconda surprised him.

Thankfully, operating with caution and the proximity of one of the asteroids hid him from the warship's powerful sensors.

Reflections of the Anaconda's scans also revealed a lone Eagle sneaking its way to the site of the distress signal. The watcher smiled, the head of security for Freeholm had been quick in his response. The communications between the two ships registered, but they were encrypted so he didn't know what they discussed, although he could easily imagine.

This was only intended as a quick visit to collate the drones' sensor data. The battle had distracted him and now the presence of the two ships meant he couldn't depart without attracting attention. He'd have to wait them out. That wasn't a problem, he was a patient man.

You had to be in his line of work.

He also thought that something big would occur in the area soon, and that it might be a good idea to place some more recon drones near the colony. That would have be done later though, the others were waiting and they would want to know what he had learned.

- 4 -

The news of Darius and Simeon's deaths hit the inhabitants of the community hard. Darik Cavus gained a sense of their mood as he walked to work the following morning.

The station had been constructed as a large cylinder around the docking bay through the central axis of the asteroid. The farther down you went, the higher the gravitational effect from the station's spin.

When the station had been a penal colony, the prisoners were kept in cells on the inner levels along with the workshops and maintenance areas. The outer levels were reserved for the officers and key personnel. When they returned to Laphria after the rebellion, the remaining prisoners moved into the upper levels and made them their home.

For those unused to living in starports, the arrangement of levels at first seemed counterintuitive. They soon learned that spin pushed them outwards, so when they left their ships they would climb down and as they did so the rotational effect increased their weight.

In some of the outermost levels of starports, a disorienting and spectacular effect could be created. For those who could handle the effect and afford the transparent materials, they would transform the floors of their quarters into windows and would appear to walk above the stars.

Unfortunately, as Freeholm had been constructed within an asteroid, no such window floors existed. Darik had seen such a sight once though, back during the travels in his youth.

Darik and a few other residents proved the exception and preferred the lower gravity so stayed in the inner levels. They were also popular with traders and other spaces used to living in little or no gravity. The lesser demand for these quarters also meant that their apartments were significantly larger than those on the outer levels.

As head of security he could have taken of one of the penthouse suites, once the exclusive domain of the officers. Sometimes he wished that he had. The walk to work would have been much quicker. He could have taken one of the lifts which provided rapid transit around the station. However, he'd established the routine soon after becoming the head of security after the regime change.

The walk helped keep him in shape. Prison food and constant manual labour had kept him trim. He'd allowed that to slip a little until he found sitting in the cockpit uncomfortable. From that embarrassing moment, he walked to the office on the top floor every day.

Freeholm formed a relatively small community, with only five thousand souls on board at any one time. Most were permanent residents, but there was also a large number of people like Lina, or Darius and Simeon, who used the colony as their home even if they travelled away a lot. His walk to work (and home again in the evening, or whenever he finally came off duty) took him through the main commercial district of the station. Passing though the lively bustle allowed him to keep in touch with the opinions and mood of the general population.

His role as head of security included law enforcement on the station as well as dealing with external threats. Darik preferred flying so he tended to let Jon Mayborn, the internal security chief, handle most of the day to day activities. Much as he'd like to, Darik couldn't leave it all to Mayborn.

Word of the traders' deaths had spread quickly

through the tight-knit community. Most people didn't know Darius or Simeon well, but they did know who they were.

The first indication of this occurred soon after he left his apartment. In many ways, the inner decks still held the memory of the old penal colony. The institutional colour scheme of the walls and bulkheads hadn't changed in ten years. The bland colour was broken up with flashes of vibrancy from posters and the odd graffiti from some of the station's youth.

Vandalism wasn't tolerated on the station. Any community in space had to be sure that everything remained in working order in case of emergency. The same applied to the safety signs and notices placed throughout the station. The council were well aware that people liked to publicly express their views and even minor rebellion, so designated wall spaces were provided to allow such artistic and not-so-artistic expressions.

One such piece appeared on the wall near his quarters. Julia used to live in an apartment on the same level, but as she didn't enjoy the low gravity as much as her father, she'd moved to an outer level apartment a few months ago.

Something people often found strange, if they were not used to being on a station, was that the rooms and walkways were upside down from their normal point of view. The station's rotation pushed things outward to create the gravitational effect, so the floor was placed where the ceiling would be on a planet. Most got used to it quickly, although a few never really became comfortable with it.

The effect was even stranger if you climbed up and down the stairs, especially if you moved between all the levels quickly. Some people took advantage of effect, running down the stairs as the effort needed increased the lower you climbed.

The term running was a bit of misnomer, for the

inner levels at least. Where the gravitational effect was minimal, magnetic footwear had to be worn to provide traction with the floor. However, you always had to have one foot planted for the magnetic effect to work. The convention on many starports was that people walked on the floor. Although often younger children would play on the ceiling.

Until an adult spotted them, of course.

On the second flight of stairs, Darik encountered the first person to comment on the attack. He could climb down the stairs all the way to the outer floors. However, the second floor led onto the first commercial deck. He usually took the long route to show his face to the people starting work at the same time as him.

He liked to start early so that usually meant he met people as they were setting up shop for the day. He nodded to the man on the stairs who had stopped to allow Darik to catch him up.

"A terrible business," the man stated after the initial exchange of greetings. Darik tried to remember the man's name without success, but did recall that he worked in one of the repair shops.

"Indeed, we're still investigating what happened, but we'll find the culprits."

"I hope so, we can't have any of our own attacked like that."

Similar sentiments were expressed by others he encountered while he walked through the lower commercial deck. Here the businesses focused on more exotic needs. There were repair shops, gadget stores and others took advantage of the lower spin effect for heavy and bulky items.

The deck had a much larger and open feel compared to the more claustrophobic accommodation levels. In the tight corridors, you could almost imagine you were in a ship rather than a starport. On the commercial levels it felt more open, and walking through the buzz of the early morning activity always buoyed him with a positive feeling for the day.

The smells of breakfasts from a dozen different cultures emphasised the harmonious feeling. Often he'd stop for a hot drink or light snack from one of the cafes or vendors. He tried to visit different ones as much as he could. Today he had the security briefing so kept his pace brisk.

Even so, people called to him to express their support, or to enquire when the memorial service would be held. Religion didn't form a large part of most people's lives on the station. Although many followed different beliefs, all wanted to be a part of remembering the two pilot's lives. Some of those people might have raised their eyebrows at the pair's antics; nevertheless, they would be missed.

Maria Teller, one of the cafe owners who also sat on the council, intercepted him as he passed. He politely declined the offered herbal tea and she asked if he had learned more since the emergency council meeting the previous evening.

"I'm on my way to the security briefing now to plan our response, but it will include the measures we discussed last night."

"I know you didn't want to go on the record in the meeting but do you have any suspects for the attack?"

"I'm afraid not. Not yet at any rate. We are investigating."

He managed to extricate himself after a few minutes and was caught by other curious members of the public. He normally enjoyed these encounters, but not today. Today he found the interruptions annoying as he wanted to get to the briefing, so in a break from his usual routine, when he reached the stairs he took them straight up to the outer level without visiting the intermediate commercial and accommodation levels.

For the outer level, the entrance was kept sealed and guarded. This level formed the core of operations for Freeholm. The security within the public areas of the station were deliberately kept low-key. Many of the residents had once been prisoners here and an effort was made to provide an open yet safe environment for all.

Even so, key areas of the station were guarded. The mining operations and trading generated a reasonable level of wealth that needed protecting. The guards knew Darik personally but he still underwent the biometric scans to confirm his identity before being allowed access.

After acknowledging the guard's greeting, he entered the main control centre, where he proceeded through another security checkpoint. The operations area was divided into four main sections, and administration occupied the most space. This provided a large open-plan area with clusters of desks for the day to day running of the station.

A smaller area along one wall contained the flight operations crew, who controlled and monitored flights around the station and within the belt. He nodded to Dee Callum, a recent recruit to the team. The docking bay was managed from a secondary control tower situated on a spindle in the docking bay itself on the far wall. In an emergency docking, systems could be controlled from the flight operations centre as well.

On the opposite wall lay the council chamber and private offices for the senior staff. Darik had an office there but spent most of his time in the security office. Like the much larger admin section, this followed an open plan with a large briefing room along with a few smaller rooms. As expected he found everyone waiting for him in the briefing room.

Everyone stood as he entered. As with the salutes and rank, he wasn't comfortable with the military behaviour. It was expected of him so he had learned to accept it with good grace. He waved everyone back into their seats and started the meeting. Although the meeting primarily concerned the external defences of the station, Jon Mayborn the station's internal security chief joined the discussions. His team might need to be involved at some stage and Darik had always thought it best to keep everyone in the loop.

As senior pilot, Julia was present. Darik had been resistant to her joining Freeholm's modest defence force at first. She loved flying as much as he did and her skills couldn't be ignored so he'd eventually given in.

In truth he'd cultivated her skill at flying at a young age, so he only had himself to blame.

Lina Mater also joined the team for the meeting. While she wasn't part of the defence force, they did rely on resident traders and trusted allies for intelligence gathering and support. She was an experienced trader and knew many of the major players in their region of the galaxy. Her contacts had proven useful on many occasions.

"Good morning everyone, sorry I'm late. I'll start by reviewing the situation as it stands."

Everyone around the table nodded and murmured their agreement.

"At 11.59 UST, flight control identified an automated distress signal near the inner edge of the belt. No other sensor readings or transmissions were received."

He activated the room's holographic projector. The lights dimmed and a schematic of the asteroids around the station was displayed.

"I deployed along with Julia and the two alert Sidewinders in support. I made a covert approach through the main lane and then along the inner edge of the belt. I detected no intruders or signs of anything amiss until this point here."

The hologram shifted to show the contact point where he had found the canisters and a red line indicated his course.

"Unfortunately, Captain Belin charging late to the

rescue blew my approach. In fairness it doesn't look like there was anybody waiting anyway. If they were there then the presence of his Anaconda probably kept them in their hole.

"We swept the area and found only debris. I'm suspicious that they didn't collect the cargo pods, whoever did this didn't care about covering their tracks."

"Maybe they didn't have time?" Julia suggested.

"That's the other odd part. Captain Belin informed me that he was attacked by a small group of Sidewinders who apparently were lying in wait between Laphria's orbit and the inner edge of the asteroid belt."

"That's a big open space to be loitering."

"Indeed, and other than the timing there's nothing to connect the two incidents. It is a bit too convenient that they prevented Belin from responding. Although he responded to the same signal we did, so why didn't they call out for help sooner?"

"Maybe they couldn't?"

"Some sort of jamming seems likely, but we should have detected that level of jamming. And why didn't they contact us through the hyperspace link? Beyond that, if they were after the cargo then why did they continue to chase them into the belt? Or at least not collect the cargo on the way back?"

"I guess the cargo wasn't the target, Darius and Simeon were."

"That was my conclusion as well. Unfortunately that doesn't explain the other disappearances. Although I grant you that we don't know if they've been hit or have just travelled on. Even if it was just this incident, there is another aspect that concerns me and that is why Darius and Simeon didn't jump?

"I can accept that they couldn't call for help, jamming equipment is readily available. Heck, you can buy it two floors up from this room. Not being able to jump should only occur if they'd been mass locked, but the position of the pods indicates they'd crossed the jump line.

"Even if they'd been interdicted, the smart move would have been to run for long enough to enter supercruise."

He looked at each of them in turn to see if they had a suggestion. None of them had and that didn't surprise him. A thought about what could have happened had kept him up until late into the night. Interdiction technology had been available for several years, almost as long as the frame shift drives. However, the interdiction effect was quite localised and generated a very distinct energy signature. It could also be escaped.

If a new form of interdiction had been developed then that was a truly frightening thought. Even if the technology just prevented supercruise, that would be a devastating advantage.

He kept that thought to himself for now. He needed some evidence before bringing such an extreme idea out into the open.

"We conducted as thorough a search as possible and all we know is that Darius and Simeon's ship was taken out with some serious firepower, it was overkill for the job. We also think that the escape pods were destroyed after they were launched."

That sparked a few curses around the table. Firing on an escape pod was considered one of the lowest acts in space.

"I met with the council last night. They agree that we have a potential situation on our hands and that even if the attack is a lone hit then we cannot tolerate such actions within our area of control. This belt cannot become a free fire zone for assassins and pirates."

He was satisfied to see the nods of agreement around the table; he hadn't expected any other response.

"So we have three immediate priorities. The first is to ensure that the space around Freeholm is secure. The second that all traffic to and from the station is kept safe. The third priority is to determine who attacked Darius and Simeon and bring them to justice.

"After much discussion, the council agreed that we don't have the resources to achieve the goals and to be honest, growth in our defence forces has been a long time coming. We don't need a navy, but we do need to be able to react to situations without being shorthanded if something else comes up at the same time.

"That's obviously something we can't deal with in the short term, but I will be following up on longer term plans in the next few days. To tackle the first priority, we'll no longer hold the fighters on alert. Instead they will conduct patrols close to the station and along the main transit corridor into and out of the belt. They'll also lay a string of sensor packages tight-linked to operations here on the station. They'll provide us more warning if something come sniffing around."

"How are we going to cover all this activity, we don't have enough people?" Julia asked.

"For now I'll provide escort for traders arriving and departing."

"You can't cover that on your own. I can help you."

"I have a different mission for you, Julia. You're right, we don't have the ships or the manpower to keep this up for long. The council have agreed a budget to hire some temporary help while we recruit additional pilots."

"You're sending me away? You're going to need me and my ship."

This had been the other problem that Darik had wrestled with throughout the night. He hadn't wanted Julia to join the defence force in the first place. After she did and then proved her ability, he realised that she was ideal for the job. Over the months he'd come to believe that one day she would replace him as head of security. She wasn't ready yet, not by a long shot. There was more than flying to the job that she needed to learn.

Building a network of contacts would be a start. She

might be well known in the station and also to some of Freeholm's friends in nearby systems but she would need more. This mission would help cultivate some of those contacts and the skills she would need in maintaining them.

He also couldn't deny to himself that having her away from the station helped calm the feeling in his gut. Darik suspected that there was something else going on with this attack and didn't want her involved more than she had to be.

In the end the choice was between sending Julia or him going himself, obviously out of the question. Lina Mater would have been a good choice, she certainly knew the right people, however having her Cobra handy provided a bit more flexibility. They had the monthly deliveries to Laphria coming soon and she would be needed for that.

"Yes, you have two missions. The first is to hire pilots and ships that can provide escort and patrol duties. You know what and who we need. I'll provide you with some profiles and places to start. You should also keep your eye out for people capable of taking part in a strike mission if, no when, you find out who killed Darius and Simeon."

"Me?"

"Yes. Hiring additional help is important; we need the extra ships and pilots as soon as possible. It's also a cover while you dig for information on what happened and if there's anything more brewing out there. Mayborn will provide you with contacts that you can speak to, you know a few of them already."

"I have a dossier we can go through before you depart," Mayborn told her.

"When do I leave?"

"As soon as possible. We're almost done here."

"I have a question," Lina said. "You can't provide any escorts beyond the belt, how will they be protected from there?"

"I'll contact Captain Belin later this morning to arrange a handover protocol. It's in their interests to keep traders safe in the system as well as ours."

- 5 -

The *Demeter* continued its patrol in the gulf of interplanetary space between Laphria and the asteroid belt. Most of the system's population lived on the outdoor world. In orbit around the planet was the Artemis shipyard. For fifty years the shipyard provided light cruiser and frigate upgrades to freighter hulls. The last of which was the *Demeter*. She had completed her refit in 3294 and was the youngest vessel in Laphria's small navy.

The Laphrian system lay in a small isolated cluster of independent systems between the Imperial and Federation borders. Their shipyard provided the most advanced starship engineering facility for thirty-odd light years in every direction. For many years, the economic advantage of the penal colony providing cheap materials had undercut any of the local competition.

Captain Belin had been a lowly ensign at the time of the rebellion on the colony. Almost a third of the fleet had been regularly deployed around the belt back then. Now only a single ship enforced the planet's jurisdiction.

In the quiet of his own quarters, Belin contemplated the map of the Artemis system. Unlike the massive Majestic-class vessels operated by the Imperial Navy and their allies, Belin's ship operated in zero-gravity. The ship was simply too small to spin effectively without causing motion sickness and providing an unstable platform for its regular operations.

The lack of gravity did have its advantages, the first visible from the layout of his quarters. Compared to the quarters he was assigned at the shipyard they were small, although still substantially larger than those assigned to his officers and crew. The lack of gravity meant that every surface could be used and that created a larger volume of open space in the centre of the room to allow large projections such as the system map he now scrutinised.

Naval regulations assigned each wall a specific purpose, and that same pattern was reflected throughout the crew and officer quarters to reduce disorientation when entering another person's room. The use of magnetic footwear (usually boots, although when off duty many wore lighter and more comfortable socks that provided the same grip) enabled any surface to be used as a floor.

Because he'd grown up planetside, it had taken Belin some time to become used to moving around with the mag-boots. You could also wear gloves that provided the same grip. Walking in magnetic boots required a different gait to walking under gravity. It proved tricky at first. Once he'd mastered it he preferred the feeling and convenience of weightlessness from that point onward.

From the perspective of the ship's natural orientation, the floor of the room held his bed and downtime furniture and effects. He'd discovered the joy of sleep in micro-gravity early in his training. The lack of weight made sleeping in any position unbelievably comfortable.

Pirate encounters had been rare for many years and the few that did tended to be hit and run around the K-class star at the centre of the system. The Navy maintained regular and more substantive patrols in that region so these rare incursions were usually dealt with swiftly.

The incident with the Sidewinders still puzzled him. The traders from Freeholm were a fair target for pirates, but waiting for them in deep space made little sense when there was a choke point that would provide better ambush opportunities.

To reach their position, they would have had to travel from the central star and then out past Laphria where the Navy had an even stronger presence to protect the shipyard and the home planet. The Navy's overall strength had declined considerably since the rebellion, however it remained more than sufficient to control the inner system.

Out here they were stretched, or rather as the only ship on patrol, he was stretched. That provided the other aspect that struck Belin as strange. The group of Sidewinders were assumed to be lying in wait for traders heading from the belt, yet they also happened to be in the path of his patrol.

That wasn't a welcome thought. He had relative autonomy in his patrols although regulations required him to register his planned course and any changes with Fleet Command. He deliberately changed his patrol route at regular intervals, although those intervals were differently spaced to prevent ambush.

More than that, they were positioned in the right time and place to prevent him responding to a more serious attack. He hadn't known the two pilots personally, but in his duties he'd encountered them on a few occasions. He knew they were both bounty hunters. He'd read their details in the Navy Intelligence files, so maybe the attack was simply revenge for something from their previous life.

The attack required a lot of planning and resources, a lot of effort to kill two ex-bounty hunters. Nothing in their files indicated that they'd made that level of enemy. It wouldn't have been the strangest thing in the galaxy though.

Belin didn't buy it. If the two pilots were the target, they could have been ambushed more easily elsewhere. On the projection in his cabin, he replayed the incident. The four Sidewinders took care not to overextend their attack, as the *Demeter* would have destroyed them.

They could have escaped easily, but didn't, instead they continued to harass the much larger ship.

When Belin reported the incident, he'd expected to be granted permission to chase the Sidewinders when they jumped. Unexpectedly he had been ordered to stand down and resume his normal patrol. Fleet Command informed him that Navy Intelligence would follow up on the attack, another strange decision added to the already long list of oddities.

The holographic record of the attack comprised the bulk of his report to Fleet Command on the incident and he added his own recommendations before sending it. He hoped they would be considered more rationally than his request for pursuit clearance. Belin closed the hologram and initiated the encryption. The report would be automatically sent once that process completed.

Despite the late hour, he decided to surprise the night watch crew currently in command of the ship. It probably wouldn't be that much of a surprise to them as he tended to split his time between both watches. Some captains preferred to spend most of their time with one or the other of the watches. In Belin's opinion that led to favouritism within the crew.

Before the advent of the new and quicker hyperdrives, ships tended to have three watches which each covered an eight hour watch. The Laphrian Navy (and others) had switched to two watches as the ships no longer had to fly on extended cruises to patrol the same volumes. Jumps to nearby systems took minutes rather than days, and with the frame shift drives they could reach anywhere within the system in less than an hour.

That also meant that they returned to port more often. This helped improve morale, especially for those with families. It enhanced the maintenance schedule for the vessels; they could be spread over multiple visits, rather than the ship being dry-docked for an extended period.

It also encouraged the government that took over

after the rebellion on Laphria (one that Belin had actively supported) to downsize the Navy and the personnel who crewed it. With more active ships, fewer were needed. Not having to support the penal colony also reduced the deployment requirements, although on this front Belin considered that the politicians had gone too far. The co-existence treaty had specified that the colony owned no jurisdiction beyond the belt, a tricky situation for an independent station reliant on traders. Up until now that hadn't proved too much of an issue, even so Belin believed that the Navy should bolster its activity near the belt.

That might become possible with the election of the new president. His campaign promised to invest in the planet's shipyard, an industry that had declined somewhat since the rebellion, mostly due to the downsizing of the Navy. The promises made also condemned the *Demeter*, a bittersweet prospect for Belin.

He'd been captain of the *Demeter* for three years, and she'd been a dependable ship all through her service. Service in the Laphrian Navy wasn't as exciting as some of the larger navies. They weren't deployed into other systems and most of their operations were simply patrols and the occasional pirate action. Still, she had been his ship and his first command.

The Cutters required a smaller crew to operate than the Anacondas. According to a colleague in the Planning Office, the spare crews would be used to help expand the Navy. From a force of a dozen Anacondas plus several fighter squadrons, the Navy would expand to twenty Cutters.

On the positive side, the light-cruiser-outfitted Anacondas were due to be replaced with Cutters from the Imperial Gutamaya shipyards. The deal had been signed with the Empire and the ships had already started to arrive. The first Laphrian Cutter had just entered its initial shakedown cruise.

The Cutters represented an order of magnitude of improvement over the old converted Anacondas. They were sleek and quick, much faster than his current ship. They packed the same punch as the Anacondas and were as well protected, but many times more versatile.

Another advantage would be the two Imperial fighters that could be deployed from the Cutters. Before its conversion, the *Demeter* had hanger space for a single small fighter. That space was converted into ammo storage for the extra missile launchers and sensor arrays. Some of her sister ships maintained the hanger, but for deployment of naval infantry via a dropship.

It would be fair to say that Captain Belin looked forward to commanding one of the new ships. He'd miss the old girl he currently captained. He'd been informed that he would take command of one of the new ships within the next two weeks. In the meantime, he had a patrol to finish and a crew to keep in top shape.

After making sure that his uniform was properly presented, he wiped his face with a moist cloth that both cleaned and refreshed. As commanding officer, he provided an example for the discipline he expected to see in his crew. Running water wasn't practical in zero-gravity, although specially designed showers did allow proper cleansing.

Once you got used to it, moving in zero-gravity was amazing. Providing you timed your pushes and pulls, you moved easily along the corridors. Before he'd actually experienced zero-gravity for himself, Belin had shared the common planetsider misconception that it was like swimming. He'd quickly discovered the truth and revelled in the freedom it provided.

When you floated in water, it buoyed you, but you still felt your weight. In zero-gravity you had no weight, so it didn't feel like floating. A strange experience at first, also one that felt liberating once he'd adjusted to it.

The biggest danger was forgetting that while you

didn't have weight, you still had mass. The fractured wrist in basic training taught Belin that lesson early on. Now he was more experienced and travelled through the ship with ease.

At the door to the bridge he encountered the two Navy infantry guards. A squad of them were assigned to the ship for internal defence duties. Although in the case of repelling a boarding action, the whole crew were expected to defend the ship.

The two guards saluted and opened the door allowing him entrance.

"Captain on deck," the watch officer announced.

"At ease," Belin responded. This was more for the watch officer's benefit as the other crew and officers were all at their posts and standing to attention was a bit pointless in zero-gravity.

They were also a distraction. Thankfully it was only required for ceremonial occasions like the arrival of an admiral or dignitary. Belin had heard of some officers who were a stickler for officiousness. He didn't approve of anything that hampered the efficient running of the crew.

"Anything to report?"

"Nothing out of the ordinary, Captain. We're running the listed patrol pattern along the inner border of the belt."

"How's the review of the sensor logs progressing?"

Belin had ordered a review of the sensor logs as well as those from Fleet Command to see if they could trace where the Sidewinders had come from. They must have entered the system near the star, and Navy and police patrols kept that area under constant surveillance.

A jump generated a lot of energy, too much to be hidden, especially in a system with a naval presence. Skilled pilots could remain hidden from that point on. That would have taken a long time to travel in normal space; the same journey in supercruise would have been more likely, although that should have generated an entry and exit wake.

"Nothing so far, sir. We have them when we encountered them and all the way to their exit point."

They had the analysis of the hyperspace cloud, so they knew which system the Sidewinders had jumped to. It seemed certain that would have been the first in a series of jumps to hide their eventual destination. Even if Navy Intelligence had despatched a unit immediately, they wouldn't have arrived in time to track the subsequent jumps.

There was an idea there, the shape of something obvious that Belin knew he was missing. The watch officer observed him closely, awaiting his next command.

"Do you have the supercruise logs?"

"We have ours, sir."

"And have you reviewed those?"

"No sir."

Yes, that had to be it. Ships in frame shift didn't register on sensors until they re-entered normal space. However, while in frame shift other ships also supercruising could be detected and from much larger distances (when compared to the real space equivalents).

The *Demeter* entered supercruise whenever it changed its patrol pattern. Their area of operations was much too large to be covered in normal space effectively. To compensate for this and to cover larger volumes, they supercruised to a new focal point and then continued the patrol in the new volume in normal space.

Throughout their patrols, they recorded all of their sensor data. Following standard procedure, they also shared it with Fleet Command.

"Who's conducting the review?"

"Lieutenant Harris in tactical."

"Carry on, Commander. I'll join the Lieutenant and we'll review the sensor logs while we were in supercruise."

"Yes sir."

Belin pushed himself through the air to the small cluster of command consoles to the right of the bridge. The bridge was divided into four areas. At the centre was the command chair where the captain or watch officer sat. From their console, they could access any of the ship's systems.

To the front and centre lay flight operations, where the pilot sat. To their left was navigation officer, who also handled comms. On the pilot's right was the tactical officer who managed the ship's sensors and weapons. All sat in sturdy seats that used gel to help protect their occupant from high-G forces while the ship manoeuvred.

The bridge was spacious, but lacked seating for more than the assigned crew. Another advantage of zero-gravity was that the seats weren't needed and Belin floated beside Lieutenant Harris while he explained what he needed from her. At strategic locations around the bridge, secondary consoles were clipped with folding brackets to the wall. He pulled one of those free and it lit up, ready for use.

Together they loaded the sensor data for all of their periods in frame shift and reviewed it. The murmur of conversation faded into the background as they checked and rechecked the data. The watch officer took over responsibility for monitoring the current sensor readings. They hadn't finished when the day watch took over the bridge. Belin continued the search while the tactical officers swapped over and Harris went to enjoy some downtime.

The new watch officer interrupted him after another hour had passed. They had received a communication from Darik Cavus from Freeholm.

"I'll take it here," Belin instructed while indicating the console with the latest sensor recordings. Only one jump remained to review and so far he'd seen nothing to indicate how the Sidewinders had entered the system.

That disappointed him, although was not unexpected. Besides, the ship's records didn't cover the whole timeline of when he thought the ships had entered the system, just the time the *Demeter* was in supercruise.

Commander Cavus's face appeared on the holographic screen before him. Belin fitted an earpiece so he could hear the Commander without disturbing those around him.

"Good morning Commander, what can I do for you?"

"And to you, Captain. I wanted to update you on our investigation and preparations that you need to know about and to see if you'd learned anything useful in your investigation?"

Belin thought that his counterpart looked tired. It appeared that Belin had not been the only person working through the night.

"I have nothing of note as yet, Commander. I'm currently reviewing the frame shift sensor recordings to see if I can isolate who attacked us and if there is any connection with your attack."

"It seems to be too much of a coincidence for there not to be."

"I agree, but I need something substantial to give Navy Intelligence. They're already looking into the incident, but the more local information I can provide them the better."

"Checking the logs is a good idea. Our frame shift coverage is patchy at best, but I'll see if we have anything useful."

"I will do the same with Fleet Command. I'll let you know if I hear anything that might help you."

"That's appreciated, Captain. In the meantime I'm organising escorts for transports departing and arriving at the station. I obviously can't provide any support beyond the belt so would you be able to provide support from that point?"

Captain Belin considered the request. His mission was

to patrol the whole zone, however in practice the traffic to the station would present the only real targets in the area if they were developing a pirate problem.

"I can do that. I assume that most will hyperspace as soon as they can upon leaving the belt anyway?"

"That should be the case."

"Okay, for departing vessels let me know when they are due to depart and we'll rendezvous on the inner border near the main transit corridor."

"That's appreciated, Captain."

"No problem, although do give us as much notice as possible, I have a large volume to patrol and I can't permanently station at the transit point."

"Understood Captain, what about arriving vessels?"

"They'll come out from the inner system, providing they supercruise I can meet them at their arrival point when they are mass locked by the belt and escort them to the belt where you can meet them."

"That sounds good, Captain, again the help is appreciated."

"I'll contact Fleet Command and let them know I need to be notified of any ships travelling to Freeholm. Is there anything else?"

"No, we'll be in touch."

"All right Commander, I'll let you know if we learn anything more about the attack."

When the transmission closed, Belin turned to the watch officer and instructed him to send a request to Fleet Command for the supercruise sensor data from other ships in the system over the past few days and to provide notice of any ships travelling to the belt.

From past experience, Belin knew that the requests would take some time to process, so in the meantime he would sleep for a few hours.

– 6 –

The universe snapped back into place as Julia dropped out of hyperspace near Kappa Fornacis' yellow sun. The lurch was an optical effect from the collapsing spatial dimensions that enabled faster than light travel. Even though no actual deceleration occurred, she couldn't help but brace herself whenever it happened.

She'd visited the system twice before. On both occasions she'd been with Lina, who happily let her ride along when she traded in nearby systems. Kappa Fornacis provided most of Freeholm's food imports from its extensive farms on the surface. She didn't expect to find many, if any, pilots here. The system wasn't known for its mercenary market.

Julia's main purpose for visiting was to try and find some intelligence on whoever had murdered Darius and Simeon. Julia had liked the pair, they were always fun to spend an evening with. She'd known them since she'd been a little girl.

She had been ten when the rebellion ignited on the station. Both her mother and father were involved in the fighting. Julia knew that she had been part of the reason they had fought alongside the other prisoners. They'd wanted a life for their daughter. A life that wouldn't include growing up in a penal colony only to become a prisoner herself when she came of age.

Her mother had died during the uprising. Shot in one of the skirmishes as the prisoners battled their way through the colony. The guards had not given up willingly and the fighting had been fierce, with many casualties on both sides.

Julia felt sure that her father blamed himself for her mother's death. He tried not to show it, but there were times when she caught him brooding. Those times became less frequent over the years as time brought the gift of acceptance.

The glow of the holograms displaying the key systems bathed her in a pale orange light, almost drowned out by the glare from the star. She locked her navigation system onto Harvestport, the planet Panem's single orbital starport. With her destination selected, she initiated the frame shift drive to enter supercruise.

This journey away from home resurrected her desire to explore. She listened to the tales of the traders when they visited and she liked Darius and Simeon's stories of their bounty-hunting days most of all. Freeholm was a quiet starport in a dull system, and her father might be content with that, but she wanted to see the places she had heard about.

As a girl she'd even dreamed of being the first pilot to discover Raxxla. Her father disapproved of such tales when she'd been a child. Even so, the desire to head into deep space called to her.

With just the six of them to defend Freeholm, there had never been time or the opportunity for her to venture far from the station. She didn't begrudge that, she enjoyed flying the Eagle. It was the same model as her father's and a fine ship. She wanted to see more of the galaxy and maybe if they were really expanding the defence force then she could broach the subject with him.

Julia didn't expect him to be happy about the idea. He'd never told her why he had been a prisoner at the penal colony. Unlike most of the prisoners there, he had actually committed a crime to be sent to the prison. Most had ended up there for expressing the wrong political views.

Her father had never told her the details of his crime. She knew it involved murder, but he always explained that he had been a different person then. He was so well-respected at the station that no-one was willing to tell her details about it. She'd gone through a curious period during her early teens, but now considered the matter history.

She still hoped that one day he would tell her about it.

Her memories of the station as a penal colony were indistinct. A blend of the confused and stark detail. She could remember the cells and the guards but only as vague impressions. There were still signs of its previous incarnation around the station. Everyone who had stayed on at the colony made a concerted effort to make it their home.

In truth that was their real victory.

Yes, maybe the time would come soon to talk to her father about leaving the station. She wanted her own life, but to travel she would need her own ship. Julia hoped that keeping her Eagle would be possible, as she'd become used to its idiosyncrasies and it was a joy to fly. Whether it was a suitable ship for travelling all the way to Alliance space was another matter.

The desire to travel had been her dream for too long now. What she would do while she travelled remained an unresolved question. As a skilled fighter pilot, she felt sure that work would be available, but a life of combat wasn't something that attracted her. When she talked with Lina, the thought of becoming an independent trader appealed. If she followed that path then the Eagle would most definitely not be a suitable ship.

Exploration enticed her with its mystery, again not really a suitable role for the Eagle, but maybe as part of a larger group. Julia decided that the time was coming to stop dreaming and make it a reality. In fact, she would put together a plan before speaking to her father. Yes, that made a lot of sense.

As the distance to Harvestport reduced, she brought her attention to more immediate matters. She hailed the station and requested docking clearance. While she waited for the response, she used the scanner to see what traffic there was around the system. Apart from the patrol of Sidewinders that transmitted local authority IDs, she saw only three other vessels.

The first was a Cobra, currently making its way through the docking port.

The Cobra Mk III was an old and still popular design, operated by independent traders all through human space. It balanced a reasonable cargo capacity with the ability to defend itself. With plenty of upgrades available from shipyards across most systems, it was easy to keep maintained.

The other two ships loitered near the approach to the station. They were much larger Lakon Type 9s, presumably here to pick up the latest of Panem's bountiful harvests. These paled in comparison to the mega-freighters which transported the bulk of the harvest to the industrial systems of the Federation. They were almost the largest vessels for independent traders, only the famous Panther Clippers could transport greater loads.

Julia had seen one those massive ships dock during her first visit to Starport Darmen in the BU 741 system. That system would be her next port of call after finishing her business here in Kappa Fornacis. She had been next in the docking queue after the Panther Clipper and discovered a newfound respect as she watched the ship's pilot steer the vessel through the docking port. Lina had told her that the size of the Panther Clipper was such that it only just fit through. It wasn't for the faint-hearted though; there was no margin for error if there was a mistake.

After a few minutes, the docking clearance displayed on her HUD and Julia headed towards the docking bay. The interior looked very similar to the docking bay at

Freeholm, since most were built using standardised components. Visiting traders told tales of Imperial and well-appointed stations whose interiors were said to be magnificent to behold.

The key difference compared to Freeholm was that Harvestport lacked the correction assistance system. The station authorities promised that they would install the system soon, although they had said that for a few years now.

The lack of assistance didn't concern Julia too much. Her father insisted that she learned full manual docking in case the system ever broke down or she was visiting starports like this which lacked the modern conveniences. Her Eagle compensated for the rotation easily.

Flight Control assigned her a pad positioned in the middle of the rows. A bit more lateral thrust pushed her ship in line with the pad. She accelerated a little to bring ship closer. The station authorities didn't appreciate loitering here, despite the low levels of traffic.

When she approached the pad, the scanner on her dashboard blinked out and was replaced with the docking view. It showed a holographic schematic of her ship in relation to the pad. A few minor corrections brought her to the centre and a gentle thrust put her down. The clunk of the docking clamps reverberated through the ship. She powered down the ship's systems and prepared to leave.

Mayborn had provided her with a contact she was to visit. She'd first been to Dusty's Bar on a previous visit with her father and on another occasion with Lina on a trade run. The second visit had been a lot more fun than the first.

Dusty's Bar was situated on one of the inner decks, and its lower gravity made it a favoured haunt for spacers. Usually traders, but sometimes you encountered bounty hunters and mercenaries there as well. Dusty (Julia didn't know her given name, everyone just called her Dusty) had been a prisoner at Freeholm. She had left the colony soon after the rebellion. She still valued her ties with Freeholm and kept her original home up to date with the latest gossip and information she picked up from patrons of her bar.

Julia didn't intend to stay here long, as the chances of finding suitable pilots here were slim. She was more interested in any rumours Dusty might have heard regarding the pirate attack in the belt. It didn't take long for her to travel via the mass transit system from the docking bay to the bar.

The difference in lighting between the main corridor that ran along the circumference of the level and the bar was striking. Her eyes took a few seconds to adjust to the gloom after the brightly lit passageway. The bar contained only a few customers who she looked at casually while walking to the bar. She walked with the curious rolling gait common amongst spacers and those used to walking in low gravity with mag-boots.

Dusty welcomed her with a warm embrace when she recognised Julia. She was a tall woman and reed-thin, indicative of having spent so much of her formative childhood in zero-G – a true spacer. She stood taller even than Julia who was noted for her height. That was a trait she'd inherited from both of her parents.

"Julia, it's been too long! Come here."

The older woman enveloped Julia with a welcoming hug.

"Hi Dusty, I don't think I've recovered from the last visit."

On her last trip here, she'd come for a quick drink with Lina. They only intended to say a quick hello to Dusty before returning to Freeholm. That flying visit morphed into an all-night celebration where they'd tried to sample every exotic spirit and liquor Dusty's Bar possessed. Julia remembered vaguely that there had been a party for a young bounty hunter having claimed his first bounty.

It had been a fun night, but even just the memory of it hurt her head. Two days passed before Julia and Lina recovered sufficiently to fly the Cobra back to Freeholm. Her father hadn't been best pleased having to cover her patrols and ready times for her. He vented, but as he usually did, he forgave her quickly.

"I did warn you against the optic chaser, but you didn't listen."

"Well, I've learned my lesson."

"If I had a credit for every time I've heard that..."

"I know, you'd own the station by now!"

"Exactly. Now what can I get you?"

"Just an iced tea and I'm starving. Do you have anything to eat?"

"Just the usual snacks, or I can print you off a burger?"

"We're in orbit around an agricultural planet and all you can offer me is a processed burger?"

"People don't come in here for the food, honey. If they want food, they go up a level. They come here for strong drink and no-one listening to their business."

Julia lowered her voice. "About that..."

"Let's get you fed, there's a free booth over there." Dusty indicated a dimly lit section set into the wall at the far edge of the room.

"You get comfortable. I know what it's like for a spacer. Take the weight off your feet while I get your order." Dusty bustled off behind the bar, chuckling over her own joke.

While Julia waited, she observed the other customers. There were only three others in the bar. The first drew her eye immediately, since he was huge. Her father had told her tales of the old gods of Earth, and in the gloom of her cell they seemed larger than life. Here, sat at a table in the middle of the room with his back to her, was a giant of a man. He looked like one of the old gods from the northern mountains, enjoying a break far from Earth.

When he raised his glass she saw the side of his face.

57

He sported a fine reddish beard that blended with the mass of long hair bunched into a loose ponytail. In the low gravity, wisps of it floated behind his head.

Across the room in a booth similar to her own sat two men. They chatted together although in the few minutes she watched them, they didn't touch their drinks.

"Here you go," Dusty interrupted Julia's observation. "I know you're a fan of loud music, so I'm sure the other customers won't mind a bit of lively music to accompany their drinks."

"That's fine with me," the giant's voice boomed. The other two looked at their drinks, but didn't say anything. Loud and pumping music slammed into everyone's ears. Dusty touched the control panel hidden in the shadows of the booth. The deafening volume of the music lessened.

Julia noticed the big man move his head in time with the pounding rhythm, his hair flowing in a trail behind the motion.

"What was that about?" Julia asked, keeping her voice low.

"We have unfriendly ears, we're secure in here. The noise cancellation reduces the volume of the music, not everyone likes the loud music, or prefers to talk. The cancellation allows us to speak and also hampers any remote listening device."

"The two on the far wall?" Julia guessed.

"Indeed. They and others like them have been hanging around the bars all over the station."

"Who are they?"

"I'm not sure. I've not seen them in here before."

"Can you ask around?"

"I already have done, and nobody knows. Or is willing to talk about what they know. I've even tried a friend in the police and he said nothing came up on a scan."

"Where are they from?"

"I was able to find that out, they're not local that's for sure and they're a long way from home."

"Which is?"

"Ross 629. It's another agricultural world."

"I've never heard of it."

"There's no reason why you should, however they have been hiring local pilots."

"For what reason?"

"That I don't know. Maybe just to protect some trade route, but if they're setting up a trade route halfway across Federation space to our little world then it's most definitely not your usual agricultural products."

Julia bit into the burger, it was warm but that was about all it had going for it. She pulled a face and put it back down. The electrostatic charge in the packaging swept up some of the crumbs – something intended for when the burger was consumed in zero-G to stop them floating in the air. The rest spiralled downwards into small vents built into the table's surface.

"Smugglers?"

"If they are then they're not very discreet ones. What's strange about them is that they don't seem to care who they're hiring, as soon as someone becomes available they snap them up. They're offering good money as well from what I hear."

"So there's no-one left to hire?"

"None, except the big man there."

That sounded promising. "Who is he?"

"Calls himself Hammer. I've no idea why. He came in this morning. I saw one of the others spoke to him but he didn't seem interested. When they left these other two came in. I think they're keeping an eye on him."

"I'll have to have a chat with him."

"You do that. If you don't have any joy, you could try Caleb's place on the level above us. He gets the occasional bounty hunter in there. Usually the posh ones who think they're better than everyone else in orbit. You never know though, you might get lucky, but they'll be expensive."

"What about pirate activity? Have you heard any rumours?"

"Not a peep. I did ask a few people. Quietly of course, but nothing. Which is a bit unusual, as there's usually some gossip floating around. Although that might have something to do with the big fella."

"Okay, why?"

"He might not be very chatty, but his ship is distinctive. I had my friend run the ship registration through the system. He flies an Anaconda and apparently he was jumped as he passed through one of the local dark systems, LHS 142."

"How do you know that?"

"My friend tells me he claimed the bounties on them."

"Interesting, and that's the only pirate activity recently?"

"Apart from the attack in the belt. How's your dad doing with that?"

"He has a plan."

"He always did." A group of four mechanics entered the bar. "Looks like I have customers. Watch your back and we'll talk before you head off."

Julia forced the lukewarm burger down before walking over to the big man sitting on his own. The moment she left the booth, the music pounded her at full volume. She flinched at the sudden noise. One of the mechanics noticed her discomfort and laughed, she shrugged her shoulders and he looked away as she reached the table.

"Hi, may I join you?"

She had to shout to make herself heard over the din. He grinned at her, or at least she assumed it was a smile under the beard. In any case he indicated to the seat opposite and said "A pretty lady is always welcome at my table."

His voice indicated joviality rather than a come-on so she nodded her thanks and sat. The volume of the music reduced a little, enough to conduct a conversation, but still loud enough to create a wall of background noise.

"Would you like a drink?" she offered.

"Of course."

Julia indicated to Dusty who acknowledge with a nod.

"I'm Julia."

"You can call me Hammer."

"Hammer is an unusual name."

"I'm an unusual person, now what can I do for you Julia? Unless this is a personal visit?"

She blushed a little at his generous wink and he roared with laughter. Dusty saved her with the arrival of drinks.

"Don't let this great ox worry you."

Hammer laughed again, "It appears that I'm gaining a reputation." To make sure of that he drained a huge swallow from the local brew Dusty had placed in front of him. Julia waited for Dusty to return to the bar before speaking again.

"I'm looking for pilots."

"Okay and why do you need pilots?"

"The station where I am based may be developing a pirate problem."

"So place a bounty on them. There are always bounty hunters looking for fresh scores."

"It's not as simple as that, we don't know who the pirates are."

"That would be a problem, although again a bounty hunter could help you track them down."

"Yes, they could. However we also need to protect the trade vessels that visit our station."

"That might be something I can help with. Why don't you buy me a fresh drink and tell me more."

Hammer drained the beer in a second swallow and placed the empty glass on the table. Over the next drink, Julia told him about the attack and the little they knew.

"It sounds like you have more than a pirate problem and maybe I can tell you a little something more than what you know."

"Another drink?"

"Of course, business is always best conducted with suitable lubrication."

When the beer arrived, he continued after another huge gulp. Julia wondered how much he could drink. He didn't seem drunk in the slightest and Dusty had indicated that he'd been here all day. More customers had arrived and Dusty appeared to be busy behind the bar.

"Very nice, this is good beer. Now, where was I? Ah yes, well, you are not the only people hiring." His eyes flicked towards the two men in the booth behind her. "I was approached this morning about a job, I refused. I do not sign up for jobs without knowing who I work for and these people did not smell right."

"What was the job?"

"They didn't say, but what should be of interest to you is that they told me that others would come looking for pilots and that it would be bad for me to accept the job."

"Do you know who they are?"

"No and I don't care. I do jobs, but not in secret. I also don't like being told who I do or don't work for."

"Would you fly for us?"

"Maybe. We can talk terms later. In the meantime if we are going to work together then we first get drunk together. You need proper drink."

So much for promises of no more all-night drinking sessions.

- 7 -

Darik guided his Eagle in a lazy orbit around Freeholm; he'd just completed a patrol along the flight corridor through the belt. Five days had passed since the attack and yesterday they held the memorial service for Darius and Simeon. It seemed as if the entire station had turned out to pay their respects to the two pilots. The wake had lasted until long into the night.

As he was scheduled to fly the next day, Darik had withdrawn from the wake early, although he had spoken at the service. He'd done this before and it never became any easier. Three pilots had lost their lives in the service of Freeholm, two to accidents and one two years ago while engaging a rogue miner.

What did you say about people who had lost their lives like this? He'd known Darius and Simeon. Despite his popularity, Darik preferred his privacy so didn't know them as well as many others. He spoke of their popularity, how they were known and their friendship. He told anecdotes of their encounters over the years.

They had been friends with and loved by many in the station, even if a few of them disapproved of their relationship. The aftermath of the celebration of their lives was visibly evident in the faces of the crew in the docking bay. Lina should have already flown out of the belt on a trade run.

While he waited, Darik took the opportunity to inspect the exterior of the station. The bulk of it sat in the centre of the asteroid. Set into the face of the huge rock was the docking port, a slit mouth of grey metal and ceramics that blended with the grey rock.

Other signs of habitation were visible with clusters of antennas and sensor arrays dotted over the surface. The asteroid had been chosen as one lacking in valuable minerals and metals. The sturdy rock also provided a solid block of armour beyond that provided by its composite structure.

After several orbits of the rock, Darik's mind turned back to the call with Julia. She'd called after departing Harvestport to inform him about her first hire, who would arrive at Freeholm within three days. She was now heading to BU 741 where she hoped to have more success.

She'd also told him about the mysterious group hiring pilots. He'd passed that to the rest of his security team. He decided to share the information with Captain Belin when they met up later for Lina's transfer, assuming that she ever launched.

Julia sounded more evasive when he asked her why she had stayed in Harvestport. He already knew the details, Dusty had contacted him to let him know what had happened. The heads-up also provided him with the time to vet Hammer before he arrived at the station.

Freeholm licensed data from one of the large independent security corporations and while it wasn't as comprehensive as the Imperial or Federal databases, it was enough to learn some details of their new pilot.

Hammer wasn't a bounty hunter, although with his list of claimed bounties he certainly could be one if he wished. Details of his personal life were sparse in the database, but as well as numerous bounties he also had a long list of offences of his own. None of it too serious, but he certainly liked to get drunk and fight, something Dusty had already told him.

Darik wasn't amused that Julia had spent the night drinking with the man and even less happy that they'd started a fight with some of the local pilots. However, he couldn't deny that Hammer would be an asset.

One aspect of Hammer's profile seemed odd and that was the fact he flew an Anaconda, yet rarely traded anything. Not according the database at any rate. Darik knew the Anaconda was a fine ship and was a dangerous foe if suitably equipped, it wasn't ideal for hunting pirates though.

As he dug deeper, he discovered that Hammer had dedicated most of his adult life to hunting pirates, mostly in the rimward border of the Federation. The volume of operations widened in recent years as Hammer had meandered his way along the border until his encounter with Julia. From the records, it seemed that Hammer's purpose was to fly onward and kill pirates. Not a bad goal, Darik thought, but he felt sure there was a deeper story to learn.

When Hammer arrived, Darik would meet him and weigh his intentions. Hopefully he would be an asset. If not, he could continue along his way.

He checked the time on his dashboard HUD. Lina was now almost an hour late. If she wasn't flying out today then she could have at least told him. He activated the control panel and contacted Flight Control for the station.

"Is Lina coming or not?"

"Yes sir, she arrived at her ship about ten minutes ago. She's not in a good mood, sir."

"She's not the only one, can you patch me through to her?"

"Yes sir."

There was a moment's pause until Lina's voice came on the line.

"I told you last night I don't need an escort."

"And I told you that for the time being you don't have a choice in the matter. I'll fly with you to the edge and then Belin will watch over you until you jump."

"I've flown this route a thousand times and never

needed a babysitter."

"I'm not having this argument again, Lina, and besides, you don't normally mind me watching your rear."

"It's too early for your flirting, you know I'd break you in half anyway."

"So you keep promising, now let's get this thing going."

"All right, requesting docking clearance now. I'll be with you in three minutes."

Darik flipped the ship over, accelerated to the front of the station and waited for Lina's Cobra to clear the docking port.

"I have you on visual," he told her.

"Yeah, I see you too."

"You are in a grumpy mood today."

"I'm always grumpy in the morning."

"We're well past morning."

"Whatever."

He laughed and let her fly in peace. They followed the usual course through the traffic lane; it wasn't a long flight, just a direct course to the edge of the belt. The route remained reasonably stable over time, although on occasion an asteroid would stray into the path.

When this happened, the asteroid would be redirected. The colony had a special ship that was all engines and fuel, which would clamp itself to the asteroid and push it into a new orbit. For most of the ships visiting the station, dodging the asteroids wasn't a real hassle, even so Darik liked to keep the routes clear.

Over the past few days, the routes had been lined with sensor drones. These small devices used passive sensors to keep watch on the surrounding area. They were supplemented by more active recon drones that followed patrol patterns. The data from both types was transmitted using a tight-beam line of sight system which reduced the chances of being detected. They could also support laser transmission and act as a relay network.

Darik had instructed the maintenance team at the

station to upgrade his dashboard systems so that they now supported command and control functions. In essence this enabled him to combine the sensor data from any source in Freeholm's network. It also allowed his ship to act as a node in the line of sight network. Over the next few days, the same upgrades would be applied to the Sidewinders and to Julia's Eagle when she returned.

An hour later, they approached the edge of the belt. Darik had expected to see Captain Belin's *Demeter* waiting for them. The Captain was normally punctual to a fault.

"Lina, I'm not seeing the *Demeter* on the scanner, he must be running late. We'll hold here until he arrives."

"I'm not waiting, I have..."

"Lina, I didn't copy your last."

Silence on the comms channel.

"Lina, can you hear me?"

He then tried contacting the station, and received no response from them either. He connected to the tight-beam network from the surveillance array, again he received no response. He checked the scanner, nothing was showing except Lina's Cobra who manoeuvred in front and waggled at him.

He couldn't remember if Lina's Cobra was equipped with a laser comms system, but it was worth a try. He also patched into the array. He only had the single laser transmitter so couldn't maintain two active connections, but the computer could switch between the two links quickly enough to seem like they were both active together.

"Lina, can you hear me."

"I read you, I've lost all regular comms channels."

"I've connected with Flight Control on Freeholm. They're not seeing an incursion anywhere."

"Could this be natural?"

"Unlikely, we're not close enough for any solar storm to knock out radio channels this completely."

"So what's going on?"

"I don't know. Keep an eye on your scanner. We should head back to the station."

"I can't Darik, I have a schedule to keep."

"Lina, we don't know what's out here."

"The sensors are clear, even if someone is lurking I'll be in supercruise before they have chance to catch me."

"Let's not risk it. Lina listen to me, we have to go back."

He watched as her Cobra swung past in a tight arc and the engines flared as she powered towards the belt.

"Damn it! Flight Control, scramble the Sidewinders I think we have a problem out here. I'm following Lina and try and make sure she's not getting into trouble."

He banked the Eagle and accelerated after her. The Cobra's engines were more powerful, but had more mass to push. He should be able to catch her by the time she reached the edge of the belt. It would be close though.

A few minutes later and he was only a klick or so behind her. He'd misjudged and she was now beyond the inner border of the belt. If he followed her past the line without agreement then he'd be violating the co-existence treaty.

"I can't follow you out there, Lina."

"You don't need to, I'm leaving the mass lock zone now and powering up the frame shift drive."

He banked to keep his ship within the belt and powered back to circle in a tight arc. He kept a close eye on the scanner, but the surrounding space still appeared empty.

"What the hell!"

"Lina, what's going on?"

"My frame shift drive just failed."

"That can't happen. Are you still in the mass lock zone? Maybe an asteroid has drifted and still in mass range?"

"No, the computer is showing an unknown error."

"Get out of there, Lina. Let's return to the station, we can figure out what's happening from there."

"No, I can reboot the system. It's probably just a software malfunction."

"When have you ever heard of drive software failing? I'm ordering you to return to Freeholm."

"You can't order me to do anything, I have a trade to complete and I'm a woman of my word."

"Damn it Lina. What the hell?"

His own words echoed Lina's as his connection to Freeholm shut down.

"What's happening, Darik?"

"I've lost the laser link with the station, we're going back now. No argument."

He willed her to listen to him and actually do as she was told for once.

"The system is rebooting now, it'll be up in thirty seconds."

"We need to go now."

"Twenty seconds."

Darik cursed as he saw two spots appear on his scanner. They were behind him, farther into the belt. Had they taken out some of the array and was that why he couldn't link with Freeholm?

"We've got company."

"Ten seconds."

Four more targets in two groups of two appeared on his scanner. From the infrared range and vector, he knew they were outside the belt and were heading towards Lina's position. The first two targets glowed brighter as they generated more heat and powered towards his position.

"You're out of time Lina, there's four contacts heading in your direction."

"I see them. The drive controller has rebooted. I'm initiating the drive now. God damn it! All right, I give up. I'm returning to base."

Darik hoped it wouldn't already be too late. All too slowly, she turned her Cobra back towards the belt. In the meantime he had his choice to make: should he help Lina, or tackle the two ships racing towards him?

He activated his shields and deployed his weapons. The Eagle had three weapon mounts, and beam lasers were his weapon of choice. They required extra skill with their fixed mounts, but were devastating against shields and hull. Their main drawback was their high power consumption and extreme heat generation, but he wasn't planning on sneaking anywhere so that shouldn't problem.

The beam lasers occupied the mounts under the wings, and in the centreline hard point he carried HE seeker missiles. These provided a heftier punch when he engaged a better-armoured target, although he'd need to bring down the enemy's shields first.

Engaging the two ships heading towards him would have been an easier choice, but that would have left Lina alone against four opponents. If he helped her then he'd leave his rear exposed, but his job was to escort her so without hesitation he increased to maximum thrust and diverted everything he had into the engines.

Lina continued her turn and now faced towards the belt, she also powered to maximum thrust. The targets on his scanner resolved into six Sidewinders. They'd pose a problem, but between the two of them they should be able to handle them. As long as they closed the gap so they could support each other. Although Lina's Cobra lacked the Sidewinder's manoeuvrability, her greater acceleration meant that she could outrun them if she chose to.

Darik doubted that she would.

The first group of Sidewinders reached weapons range and fired their pulse lasers at the Cobra. The impacts flared on her shields, but at extreme range the lasers lacked any real punch. Darik adjusted his approach vector to intercept the second group. He tried to communicate with Lina, but their manoeuvring made maintaining the laser link difficult. He hoped that she'd continue her straight line dash until he reached weapons range.

He now approached visual range of the Cobra and the chasing Sidewinders. He lined up on the nearest Sidewinder, and dropped the extra power from the engines and into the weapon systems. He fired both beam lasers at the locked target. Even with the extra power, the beams overheated and ran out of energy within seconds. Seconds where he needed to strip the shields from the Sidewinder, which jinked to avoid a second salvo. The pilot banked away from the fight to allow his shields to regenerate.

Darik resisted the temptation for the easy kill. Lina's rear shields were now taking a battering, that increased as her retros fired and her speed crashed to near zero. The Sidewinders hadn't expected the move and overshot her at full velocity. Her beam lasers stripped the shields from one of the targets and scored through its hull.

With his own weapons ready to fire again, Darik targeted the Sidewinder Lina had just hit. His lasers sliced through the rear armour and destroyed one of the Sidewinder's engines.

The two Sidewinders chasing Darik now entered the fight, their multicannons beating a rapid tattoo on his shields. He dropped his thrust into the sweet spot for tighter turning and arced to engage them.

Lina chased the remaining two who had overshot her. The other Sidewinder that Darik had first hit now dived in above her. The pilot held his fire until at point blank range to inflict the most damage. His first pass failed to penetrate her shields, she jinked in response and her fire missed the target she was chasing.

Darik lined up one of the two ships long enough for a missile lock and fired two missiles that streaked hungrily towards the locked target. They wouldn't do much damage with the Sidewinder's shields still active, but they did fulfil their purpose as it began weaving to dodge the incoming missiles.

He now found himself locked in a turn war against the other Sidewinder. As he chased the ship in a tight bank, he saw that Lina was now in trouble. Three Sidewinders chased her and their superior agility kept them on her tail despite her attempts to dodge them. At such close range, her shields wouldn't last much longer.

Darik's pulled out of the turn and transferred some of his power into his shields. He hoped that they'd absorb the shots from the two Sidewinders he was leaving in his wake. He increased the throttle to close the gap and for a few brief seconds the laser link established a connection.

"Run Lina, and I'll pick them off your tail."

"What about you?"

"When I take one out you can come back around and engage the two on my tail."

He didn't know if the last sentence got through or not as the link failed again. Lina dodged more incoming fire by mere metres. Her rear shields flared as they failed and laser fire strafed the back of her ship. She pulled a violent manoeuvre to try and escape the hits but the chasing Sidewinders out-turned her and kept her in their sights.

Darik admired their skill, but their focus on the kill proved their undoing. He held his fire until the last moment and put all of the ship's power into the lasers. The targeted Sidewinder's shields disintegrated and he fired two missiles at the unprotected ship. At that range, the target had no time to evade and the missiles impacted by the engine ports, tearing the ship apart in a large fireball.

The ship's computer warned him that his own shields had failed and cannon shells tore into his port wing. The same calm voice informed him that his port weapon mount had malfunctioned. He cursed into the dead comms channel.

He transferred energy back into his shields so that they would regenerate more quickly. He would now have to dodge or die. The Eagle was a fine ship, but not particularly tough. He took a snap shot at one of the two ships still chasing Lina. The shot scored little damage, but at least put the pilot off his aim.

Lina must have realised that Darik was in trouble and that he wouldn't be able to stop the other Sidewinder chasing her, as she stopped jinking and poured on the power. The red flare of the engines indicated that she was pulling a zoom and boost, trying to escape the slower chasing ship. The move put her in line with the two Sidewinders chasing Darik and his sensors detected the opportunistic shot she took, although it failed to penetrate their shields.

His shields system had discharged the overload and were now filling the capacitors so that the shield could be restored. Glancing at his controls, he guessed that they wouldn't be up for another thirty seconds.

The Eagle shuddered as more cannon shells ripped into the fuselage and then a pause. He jerked the ship using his lateral thrusters and started a fresh turn. A glance at the scanner indicated that the Sidewinders were re-aligning for a massed attack on Lina's Cobra and then he felt a burst of hope as he saw a new target appear on the scanner.

The new target resolved into a Cobra. As he completed his turn and followed the Sidewinders charging Lina with all their lasers blazing, the hope that this might be a trader or someone who could help them vanished as Darik's ship's computer warned him of a missile lock. His shields wouldn't restore before the missiles hit and he had only one chance.

He turned off flight assist to gain more precise control over the ship's thrusters and flipped the ship on its central axis. He now travelled backwards and faced towards the incoming missiles. For the first time, he wished that he had gimbal-mounted weapons as the missiles raced towards him. His port beam laser was still out of action so he feathered the trigger gently to only trigger a short burst.

The first missile exploded as the intense energy focused on it.

Then the second.

The third detonated just in front of his ship and peppered the cockpit canopy with debris. Less than a second later, the remaining three missiles tore into his ship and in three massive explosions ripped the ship apart.

His hand didn't even reach the escape pod release.

- 8 -

The *Demeter* travelled in parallel to the asteroid belt in line with Laphria's orbit. The data Captain Belin had requested from Fleet Command took longer to arrive than he'd expected. There was usually some bureaucratic overhead, but that meant a few hours. In this case it had taken three days. He now pored through the data with the help of his first officer on the bridge.

They had already sent notification for their move to the belt to Fleet Command. All vessels in the Laphrian Navy were required to log their supercruise journeys in advance. It was an open secret that the fleet always had a single ship in supercruise at all times. Its sensors provided an overview of most of the system and could track any other ship (or a large part of it anyway) that was also in supercruise.

Knowing this sparked Belin's request for the records. He considered it a reasonable assumption that the group of Sidewinders had travelled in supercruise to the point where he had encountered them, or at least nearby. When he reviewed the received data he noticed an issue: a six-hour window leading up to the encounter wasn't included in the records.

When he requested the missing data, he was simply told it wasn't available and further requests for clarification yielded no other response. The computer ran a preliminary scan of the data and returned no tracks near the encounter's location. He and his first officer had also tried a manual search through the data. The sparse traffic between Laphria and the asteroid belt made such a task possible, if a boring one.

Their own search resulted in the same lack of any contacts. There had to be something within the missing six hours that explained how the ships reached such an isolated place without being spotted.

Maybe they had been seen?

Now that was an unsettling thought.

If they had been spotted then why was he not allowed to see the data? That was clearly a question he had no concrete answers for, so he turned his search elsewhere and examined the ship's log for the same time period. An item just before it caught his eye. They had filed their planned supercruise travel to the next part of the patrol zone, near where the encounter happened.

That had to be a coincidence. He hoped so, at any rate. If it wasn't then the encounter had been deliberate and someone had wanted him to be distracted while the attack in the belt took place. That was an even more worrying thought. If such a thing had happened then it was someone who had access to secure Navy communications.

So far the attack appeared to be an isolated incident. There had been no further encounters and for that Belin was grateful. He had a lot of space to patrol and the rendezvous protocol for each arriving and departing ship took up a large amount of time. He hoped that if no further events occurred then they could stop the handovers and resume regular patrolling.

The first officer reminded him of the next transfer, due in an hour. They could reach the transfer point easily within that time. Even so, Belin liked to be punctual. In fact that was one of his sore points. He tolerated many things from the crew, but lax timekeeping wasn't one of them.

He ordered the ship into frame shift. The ship entered the alternate spatial dimensions and flew towards the meeting point. Flying in supercruise felt very different to normal space. Rather than moving through space, in frame shift space moved around you, somehow. It was as if space had shrunk dramatically. This meant that you felt some of the usual forces as the ship manoeuvred, but nowhere near what would otherwise have been the case – and clearly much better that you didn't end up as a stain on the cockpit walls with any change in direction or perceived speed.

It took some getting used to and Belin still experienced the sense of disorientation as the frame of reference changed so dramatically. Some people couldn't handle it at all, and some three per cent of the Navy's training intake had to be discharged because of severe reactions to the jump. The convenience of being able to travel so quickly anywhere within the system, mass locking permitting, more than outweighed the side effects.

The journey to the rendezvous would only take ten minutes. As they passed the seven minute mark, their speed crashed to normal space levels and they exited supercruise without any warning. Belin looked at the system readouts on his console, which said the frame shift drive had performed an emergency stop. This occasionally happened if the pilot had miscalculated an approach to a planet or other large body. Out here in the middle of nowhere, there was no mass to cause such an event.

First he checked with the pilot for more information.

"Sorry sir. We've just stopped. Normal space engines are fine."

"Continue at best speed and prepare to re-engage frame shift drive."

Best speed in normal space wouldn't get them to the rendezvous in time by a large margin.

"Engineering, this is the Captain. What just happened?"

"We don't know sir; we're checking the system now.

No malfunctions have been reported."

"Can we enter supercruise again?"

"Unknown at this point. We're checking the systems, but no problems reported as yet."

"Okay, prepare to jump on my mark. Tactical, do you have anything on the scanner?"

A thin hope – a large enough ship could drag a passing vessel out of supercruise. This occasionally happened when one of the mega-freighters travelled through the system.

"Nothing on the scanner, sir."

"Any sign of an interdiction event?"

"No sir. The scanner is clear."

"All right, let's hope it was a transient glitch. Lock destination."

"Destination locked," the pilot confirmed.

"Engage frame shift."

For their class, the converted Anacondas were equipped with very powerful frame shift drives. What they lacked in thrust in normal space they more than made up for in supercruise. The drive powered up and Belin experienced the usual lurch, but the feeling didn't complete and neither did the switch into supercruise.

"Frame shift failed," the pilot reported.

"Engineering. What's going on?"

"Unknown, sir. The drive started to build the connection to establish the frame shift, but it slipped and failed."

"What do you mean it slipped?"

"I'm not sure sir, as part of the diagnostics we had the energy flow model active and we saw the anchor points coalesce for the dimensional shift, but the anchors collapsed and the switch failed."

"What caused it?"

"Sorry sir. We don't know that either."

"What could cause the problem then?"

"In theory, not much. A sudden energy surge within the field effect might do it, although no such surge was detected. A large mass, but the systems would recognise that."

"What about a failure in the drive itself?"

"That's the only thing that would make sense, sir, however the diagnostics should alert us if that was the case."

"Understood. Start a deep diagnostic and manual review of the system. How long for you to complete that?"

"Sir, that sort of thing is usually performed while in dry dock. We can run a deep diagnostic easily, that's automated and will take six hours. The manual inspection will take longer, probably twice as long."

"Get started, we'll continue in normal space for now and I had better inform Commander Cavus that we'll be late."

Belin switched the console to his contacts list. He didn't see Darik's Eagle listed, or Lina's Cobra.

"Tactical, do you see any contacts near the handover location?"

"Nothing at the moment sir, we are too far out. We should be in range within fifteen minutes."

He nodded. On the contacts list he selected Freeholm station. They would be able to patch him through to their head of security. He received no answer to his initial hails. He tried again, without success.

"Tactical."

"Yes sir."

"There's no response from Freeholm, are the communications channels clear?"

"They should be... Wait, there's something strange."

"What?"

"Some sort of interference, it's all around us."

"Why wasn't it detected?"

"Sir, it's not showing up on the threat board."

"Is it natural?"

"I don't see how it could be. The nearest magnetic field capable of generating this level of interference is the sun, or the gas giant on the other side of the belt and even so it would still register on the threat board."

"All right, I'm trying the hyperspace channels."

He tried hailing Freeholm through the hyperspace channels, again without any response. In case the problem was at the other end, he tried contacting Fleet Command. They received no reply from them either and Fleet Command never ignored contact from one of their ships.

It had to be equipment failure. The hyperspace communications used the same technology, although on a tiny scale, as the frame shift drives.

Two related failures couldn't be a coincidence, so perhaps the failures were connected in some way.

"Engineering."

"Yes sir."

"We have a failure on the hyperspace communications system. We're not connecting to Freeholm or Fleet Command."

"We can check the system immediately, although that will slow down the review of the frame shift drive."

"Understood, focus on the drive for now."

"Yes sir."

On his screen, Belin ran the high-level diagnostics, and the results came back quickly. The system appeared operational but wasn't able to establish a connection. As with the frame shift problem, the system reported an unknown error.

"How long until we reach the meeting point on normal thrust?"

"Approximately two hours, sir."

Belin kept his frustration from his face. The timing of all this stank. He needed to get to the rendezvous now, but had no way of doing so, or contacting anyone.

"Sir?" The tactical officer interrupted his thoughts.

"Yes, Lieutenant."

"We've registered a few contacts at extreme scanner

range."

"Pipe it to my console."

"Yes sir."

The upgrades to the Anaconda's systems included extensive refits of the ship's sensors and command and control systems. As he looked at the readings displayed in 3D on his console, he checked the sensor profile. They were operating in full active mode. The contacts appeared as a tight bundle towards the asteroid belt.

At this range they couldn't distinguish the individual targets, so he cycled through the sensor filters to gain some hints. On the passive infrared, he saw tight flares of heat and movement. Their direction indicated they were probably the ships heading for the meeting.

Minutes crawled by and the contact separated into two. One flared brighter and headed out from the belt, that had to be Lina Matar's Cobra. Belin had never met her in person, although he'd encountered her ship a few times over the past years of his command.

The brighter contact exited the belt and Belin saw several other contacts appear on his console.

"Sir, I'm reading more contacts."

"I see them."

He watched the new targets vector onto the two existing targets. They flared as engine output increased. Whatever was happening included some sharp manoeuvring.

"Weapons fire!"

"Confirmed. Lieutenant, can you resolve the individual targets yet?"

"Not yet sir, almost everything we're getting is in the infrared, not enough for identification of ship type."

"Keep trying. How long until we reach them?"

"One hour, thirty-eight minutes."

Too long, the engagement would be over long before they arrived. "Understood. Make sure we're capturing all the sensor data."

"Yes sir."

He suppressed the temptation to call engineering again. He knew his crew, they would be working as fast as they could. Bothering them over the comms wouldn't change that fact. All he could do was wait and watch in frustration as the battle unfolded on his console.

One of the targets bloomed and then vanished from the scanner. Belin swore under his breath. He didn't know what was going on and could do even less to intervene. At first the two ambushed ships appeared to hold their own. They had even scored a kill, but now the attackers moved in concert against their prey.

"We have ship identities."

"Thank you Lieutenant."

The contacts on his console now displayed the ship IDs. He recognised Lina Mater's Cobra and Commander Darik's Eagle. The other ships were all Sidewinders, although no registration data was displayed.

"Lieutenant, I can't see any registry data for the Sidewinders."

"It looks like they're being masked, sir."

That took some organising and a ship without pilot registration shouldn't have been allowed to travel within the system. It was one of the trigger signs that attracted attention from the Navy and police patrols near the star. With the numerous patrols near the system's entry point, they must have been spotted.

Belin couldn't even report the battle.

A fresh target appeared on the scanner and a flurry of missiles leapt at Darik's Eagle which then vanished from the display.

Belin stared at the screen waiting for the distress beacon on Darik's escape capsule to transmit. He'd known Darik for years. While they weren't friends, he did share a respect for their respective roles.

Nothing showed for a minute and in that time Lina's Cobra ran deeper into the asteroid belt, chased by all of the remaining attackers. Four fresh contacts appeared on the scanner. From their vector, Belin calculated they were Freeholm's defence force.

The distress beacon still hadn't displayed and Belin now feared the worst. It was possible that Darik used the old bounty hunter trick of not sending the distress call until the battle was over.

Belin hoped that would be the case.

Lina turned her Cobra to re-engage the attackers. The reinforcements from Freeholm swept up to her. Although the attackers had the advantage of numbers, they changed course and headed out of the asteroid belt. The new Sidewinders gave chase, along with Lina. They were too far behind and Belin knew that the attackers would depart the belt before the defenders caught up with them.

That gave him some hope.

Whatever prevented the *Demeter* from entering supercruise would surely affect them as well. In truth he didn't know what volume of space was affected by the disruption. He hoped that it would include the transit point for the belt. It seemed a reasonable guess, if it hadn't then Lina would have had time to escape.

She wouldn't have left Darik on his own to fight the ambushers.

Belin knew that was probably true.

The attackers had now cleared the belt. The reinforcements continued their chase, but were several minutes behind. Lina's Cobra had stopped in the vicinity of where Darik's Eagle had been destroyed, no doubt searching for his escape pod. The pod's distress beacon still hadn't sent a signal.

Following the fleeing ships' vector, he saw that they were heading into interplanetary space. He ordered his pilot to adjust course to intercept them. He now watched the pursuing Sidewinders carefully, as by treaty they weren't permitted to follow the escaping ships out of the belt. The same was true for Belin, he couldn't enter the belt even in pursuit either.

To his relief, the chasing Sidewinders turned and reduced their speed as they approached the inner border. He liked the inhabitants of Freeholm, he didn't want to have to engage them just because they were a little hot under the collar.

On the scanner, the escaping ships all started to increase their heat output. There was no indication of weapons fire and this thermal profile usually indicated the frame shift driver powering up for a jump. At the same time, his console indicated that the hyper-communications carrier wave had been established.

"Tactical."

"Yes sir."

"It looks like we have comms again. Contact Fleet Command and apprise them of the situation, we have hostiles and are in pursuit. Then contact Freeholm and advise them we are engaging hostiles fleeing their zone."

"Yes sir."

"Engineering. Are we able to enter supercruise?"

"We haven't completed the low-level diagnostics yet, sir."

"Hyperspace communications are now up and I'm willing to bet we'll be able to jump now."

"It will take a minute to exit diagnostics mode."

"As quick as you can. Helm, as soon as engineering are ready, enter supercruise and lock on the fleeing ships."

"Yes sir."

If the ships were preparing to jump then the *Demeter* wouldn't arrive in time to prevent them. However, it should arrive in time to be able to analyse their jump trail and determine their location."

"We're entering supercruise now, sir," the pilot reported. "Estimated time to intercept is eleven minutes."

"Thank you."

"Sir," the tactical officer reported in.

"Yes Lieutenant."

"I have Fleet Command on the line, sir, they wish to speak to you immediately."

"Patch them through."

"Yes sir. Connected."

"This is Captain Belin."

"Captain, this is the watch officer for Fleet Command."

"It's good to hear you, sir. We've been out of touch for a short while, do you know anything about it?"

"We've received the initial report from your tactical officer and an investigation will be assembled. We understand that you're also in pursuit?"

"Yes sir, several ships engaged the Cobra we were due to meet as it transited from the belt. We were prevented from arriving in time due to the interference and in normal space we observed an attack from several ships displaying no registry or pilot identification. We are currently in pursuit of those ships, although I believe they are preparing to jump."

"Will you reach them before they jump?"

"Unlikely, sir. We should arrive in time to retrieve their jump destination from their trail. I'm requesting permission to pursue."

"Denied, Captain."

"Sir, they have attacked and destroyed at least one vessel from Freeholm."

"Another unit will handle the pursuit, Captain. You are to continue to the belt and offer aid and recovery. All data from the encounter is to be marked as code access only and sent to Fleet Command."

"Sir, I..."

"You have your orders, Captain."

"Yes sir."

"Fleet Command out."

Belin took a moment to suppress his annoyance. They could have followed the attackers. The ships might have greater acceleration and manoeuvrability in normal space, but in hyperspace and in supercruise the *Demeter* had the advantage. He considered disregarding the order, but only for a moment.

"Helm, change course and take us to meeting point by the belt."

– 9 –

The old man waited in the apartment for his children to arrive. Rex's eldest son Mervan had summoned them all for an emergency family meeting. The family owned discreet apartments like this one all over this sector of space. As with all the others, this was owned by a network of shell corporations and fake registrations intended to stall any investigation into their owners.

This location had been chosen as it was approximately equidistant for the family. Rex had been the first to arrive even though his journey had been the longest. A lifetime of operations in space provided acclimatisation to life in low gravity. Outposts like this were too small to spin for gravity.

These days Rex spent most of his time planetside, taking care of the communications and management side of the family business. He'd never been one for the intricacies of paper trails and intelligence gathering, but now as he approached 120 years, his reflexes were no longer what they once were. He'd lived a dangerous and successful life as an assassin, following in his parents' footsteps in the same way that his children had done.

Most of them anyway.

For the past five years he had remained at the family home, located far away from their area of operations. There were many opportunities on the Federation and Alliance border. Power plays with the independent systems and the constant covert operations kept the family busy and well fed. It never paid to be too complacent though.

His daughter, Seline, arrived after he had waited for three hours. In that time he'd rediscovered the comforts of low gravity. He'd resisted the urge to continue his work. This might be one of their safe houses but he took communications security very seriously.

The pressure doors hissed as they opened, announcing her arrival. Rex had seen her at the door through the miniature surveillance camera. Even though he recognised her, he held his pistol ready and out of sight under the table.

She pushed herself into the room and her gaze swept around, checking to make sure she wasn't entering an ambush. The room was sparsely furnished, just the table and four seats. Off to one side were two bedrooms and on the opposite side was a small open-plan kitchen and a bathroom next to it.

"Father," she said.

Not for the first time, Rex considered the differences between his daughter and her mother. They shared the same looks, lithe-limbed and tall. She kept her dark hair long much as her mother had done, and in some ways it was like looking back in time when he saw Seline. So much so that it resurrected painful memories for him.

The similarities, though, were physical only.

Her mother had been full of life, even considering the business that they were in. She was efficient on the job, but still maintained a more welcoming personality when not. Seline was very different, although she hadn't always been. As a young girl she'd shown the same love of life and had been quite affectionate. Competition with her brothers seemed to have removed that side of her and of the four siblings, she was by far the coldest.

Rex often wondered if the fact that Seline had been born into the life of a contract killer, where her mother came into it later in life, had also made the difference.

"Seline, I take it the business has been handled?"

She nodded as she took one of the seats at the table.

The nod indicated that an independent trader with a sideline in weapons smuggling was now drifting in deep space somewhere. She handed him a tiny data chit. The secure data on the chip would provide the proof the client required for the hit and payment would be forthcoming.

The family had provided their services for many years, although their name wasn't a publicly known one. That was for the best. In their business reputation provided advantages, although not as much as anonymity.

"Would you like a drink?"

She shook her head in response, pulling a flat pack carton from her belt. She swallowed a mouthful and didn't offer any to her father, who would have declined anyway. He no longer drank. The death of his wife had also killed his enjoyment for anything other than his work.

"Will my brothers be here soon?"

"Yes, any minute in fact. They docked some time ago, but are just completing a sweep of the area."

She nodded. "Do you know what this is about?"

"I don't. Mervan sent the summons, but didn't provide any details."

She nodded again.

They waited in silence until the two brothers arrived. Lee entered first, scanning the room carefully as he did so. He took after his father with his stocky build, but shared the same dark hair as his sister. Rex's hair was now silver, having lost the rich blond colour a long time ago.

Mervan's remained. He possessed a blend of features from both parents. He stood tall, with short blond hair. Of the three siblings his face appeared the most open, with a ready smile usually in place.

Today though, his expression lacked any warmth.

When both had taken seats at the table, Rex offered drinks. Both refused and then he took charge of the meeting, even though he hadn't called them together.

The whole family, or those that remained in the

business, rarely met. Rex usually provided the conduit between the siblings and while they visited home every so often, they usually did so at the convenience of the jobs he had taken for them.

"So, Mervan. Why have you called us together? And why couldn't we meet at home?"

"Darik's dead."

"How do you know this?"

"I discovered where he lived a few years ago."

"And you didn't tell us?"

"You ordered us not to communicate with him, Father."

That was true. He had instructed his children to not speak to the son who'd left some twenty years ago now. By the code they lived by, the expected decision would have been to kill Darik. It would probably have been a sensible decision as well. For the first time in his life, Rex had balked at issuing the kill order. So soon after the death of his wife, he lacked the resolve to kill his son as well.

"I did and yet you did so anyway."

"No Father, I located him, but I didn't make contact."

"So how do you know he is dead?"

"I saw him die."

"Where?" Seline demanded.

Rex held up his hand for her to be quiet. "Tell us from the beginning."

"Passing through Crevit six years ago, I stopped in a bar while hunting Dale Redem. Do you remember? The crooked bounty hunter?"

Rex nodded. His memory hadn't faded with age and he remembered all of the contracts he had been involved with.

"Well, the lead turned out to be useless. While in the bar there was a news item about an ex-penal colony in the nearby system called Artemis. I wasn't really paying attention, the bar was quiet but we kept our attention on the people around us. Anyway, I caught a picture of Darik on the screen. I instantly knew it was him, even though I hadn't seen him for over fifteen years."

"How could you be sure?" Seline scoffed.

"Have a look for yourself."

Mervan removed a small holo-projector from an inside pocket and placed on the table between them. A screen popped into view and they all examined the face. Darik had aged since they last saw him, but the expressions on their faces confirmed that they recognised him too.

"I take it you checked to be certain?" Rex asked.

"Of course."

"How did you check? Did you involve anyone else?"

"No, Father. I did it all remotely, through data scans and public newsfeed data. He's not really kept a low profile. He led a revolt at the penal colony."

"What was he doing there anyway?" Lee wanted to know.

"Well, that took a bit of figuring out. It seems that the prison was more for political prisoners, although some criminals were held there. The records are all sealed now, but I did locate an old court transcript. Apparently he was ambushed and killed the attacker who turned out to be a well-connected bounty hunter. They gave him life for murder and a few years later he led the rebellion."

"So he didn't lose the will to kill after all." Of them all, Seline had been hit hardest by her brother's desertion.

"It doesn't seem like it, he was instrumental in the fight to overthrow the guards and is quite the hero."

Mervan couldn't help but grin as he said that, much to his sister's annoyance. Rex cut into the conversation, all too quickly he was remembering how peaceful not having the siblings together was. "What did he call himself?"

"That's the strange thing, he didn't change his name."

"He should have known better than that," Seline sniped.

Lee responded to her with a laugh. Of the three, he

was the most cavalier. Happy to take unnecessary risks, something that brought him into conflict with his father on a regular basis. "Maybe he wasn't ashamed of the name after all."

"Well, we're ashamed of him."

"You might be," Mervan responded to his sister. "I feel differently."

"That's clear, after all you have disobeyed Father's instructions."

"I didn't make contact."

"Enough," Rex intervened again. The siblings took the signal and leaned back. "What happened?"

Mervan called up a fresh display on the projector. A section of space containing many large asteroids popped into view. A battle could be seen between the rocks with flashes of energy.

"After the rebellion, he became the head of security for the colony, which they renamed to 'Freeholm'. Over the years I've deployed recon drones in the area around the base and kept an eye on what our brother has been up to. As you can see, he still has a fondness for Eagles."

"It never did him any good against my Viper," Lee joked.

"When I visited the system a week or so ago, I caught an attack that took out a Type 7 freighter."

Another sneer from Seline. "So you saw a bunch of pirates. The galaxy is full of them."

"This was no pirate attack. They weren't interested in the cargo and took the time to destroy the escape pods."

"A hit?" Now she sounded interested. "What has this to do with Darik?"

"The same group of Sidewinders killed him."

"The hell you say," said Lee.

"Are you certain they were the same group?" Rex asked.

"As certain as I can be. None of the ships had any

registration data, which isn't unusual for operators, but in a backwater system like this it's rare."

Rex nodded his agreement. "Do you know who they are?"

"No. I made some discreet enquiries, but no-one seems to know a thing."

"Are there any known pirate groups in the area?"

"Not of any significance and these don't look like pirates to me. If they are then they're highly skilled and equipped ones, but also the most useless pirates I've ever seen."

"How do you know they killed Darik?"

"One of my drones recorded the engagement. Here, take a look."

The battle filled the room as it replayed in holographic form. They watched in silence until Marven paused the recording as the Eagle disintegrated under a storm of missiles. Although the recording had been taken at long range, it was clear that no-one could have survived the hits.

In answer to the unspoken question, Mervan also stated, "No distress signals were transmitted either."

"He could have been laying low until the end of the battle?" Lee suggested.

"No, the engagement ends with the Sidewinders from the station chasing the attackers away. A converted Anaconda from the local navy also shows up to secure the area. Although for some reason, it broke off its pursuit of the attackers. He wasn't playing possum."

"Are you certain it was him?" Rex asked again.

"As certain as I can be, the ship is his. It had his registration."

"I still can't believe he kept his real name," Seline said. "And I guess it doesn't matter know, but what does matter is why you've called us here, brother. Darik left us long ago and he's been dead to us since that time. Why does it matter that his body has finally caught up with that doom?"

"He was still one of us," Mervan replied.

"No he wasn't. He couldn't take the life and he ran away. He could have caused us no end of problems, especially as he was stupid enough to keep his real name."

"It didn't cause us any trouble though."

"So he got lucky, or we did. Either way, he was the one that deserted his family."

"What choice did he have? Maybe if he had known what he was getting into then he could have handled it better," With that statement, Mervan glanced at his father.

"It doesn't matter," Rex replied. "What concerns me more is knowing who killed him and why. Could the attack have been aimed at us?"

Mervan shrugged. "Maybe. We don't have enough information to determine that. He was head of Freeholm's security so it's more likely that the station was the focus of the attack."

Lee then spoke. "But what if someone did make the connection, the attack could have been a way to get at us."

"All the more reason for us to ignore it," Seline said.

"No, that would make us look weak and that is never an option," her father stated. "And neither can we ignore the death of one of our own."

"You exiled him!" Seline snapped.

"As Mervan said, what would he have done? He chose his own life. I was as disappointed as you when he fell apart after the job. He couldn't be part of our life as he couldn't contribute to it, but that doesn't mean I wanted my son dead.

"More importantly, if this is an attack on us we have to respond to it."

Both of the brothers nodded their agreement. Seline scowled, and offered one further protest. "If this is an attack on the family then they will expect us to respond."

"Naturally, but there is no way that we cannot respond.

We will have to be cautious though. You three should see what you can discover about the attack. I'm sure there will be a funeral, or some sort of memorial so Mervan will attend as the family's representative and act as bait. You two will be hidden close at hand if our unseen enemy reveals themselves."

"That's risky, Father," Mervan commented.

The old man nodded. "Yes it is, so make whatever preparations you need to remain safe. I don't want to see another of my sons killed in an unknown system in the middle of nowhere."

"Yes Father."

"What about our contract?" Lee enquired. The three siblings had been due to engage in another job in a nearby system.

"I will handle that," Rex replied.

"Father, you haven't been on a mission in years and it is a three-person job."

"I have a few friends to call on for support and I may be old, but I can still pilot my 'Lance well enough. This is a family matter and I want you three to focus on that, find out what happened to your brother. And no matter who killed him, whether they knew who he was or not, you will make sure they suffer the consequences. Is that clear?"

They all agreed that it was and then Mervan said, "There is a complication."

Seline laughed, "Of course there is."

Rex indicated for his son to explain further.

"Darik has a daughter."

"Interesting," Rex responded. "And her mother?"

"She died in the uprising from the newsfeeds I've seen."

"What do you know of the daughter?"

"Not much, she doesn't really feature in the local feeds. She's in her early twenties, she takes after her father and likes the Eagle. Apparently she's a skilled pilot and has seen some action, and flies as part of Freeholm's defence force."

Rex considered for a moment before replying. "Find out more about her, maybe she can be a part of the family that her father failed to be."

- 10 -

Piotr Vanchenko examined the data tablet. He preferred the physical feel of old-fashioned screens to the holograms favoured by almost everybody else. For a person in his line of work it was also rare not to have the implants that allowed viewing data without an external screen. For him it just didn't feel right and he'd never found himself at a disadvantage in his years as a bounty hunter.

On the screen, he read through the incident report for a failed bounty hunter engagement six years previously. Sahiba Mehta had been more than a friend. In a universe full of scum, she had provided the only ray of light he'd known.

Occasionally they allied to take on more dangerous criminals and on that occasion he wished she had teamed up rather than take the job alone.

At first glance, the job appeared simple. A well-to-do trader became a target after involving himself in local politics. She had accepted the job of shadowing him for a run into the system. Piotr watched the engagement as he had hundreds of times.

As they entered the system and prepared to supercruise away from the central star, a lone Viper, one of the new Mark IIIs, had attacked. Sahiba responded in her own Viper, the same model as the attacker's. The attacker then disengaged and retreated at maximum burn, with Sahiba giving chase.

A voice inside him screamed at the mistake. A Fer de

Lance and another Viper appeared, their heat signatures glowing as they powered up their systems and intercepted Sahiba. As they appeared, the fleeing Viper banked and curved back in to engage the mark's freighter. Neither battle lasted very long. Two minutes thirty-five seconds for the trader. Long enough for his shields to collapse and then for the Viper to destroy the cockpit.

Sahiba lasted twice as long. She at least had manoeuvrability on her side. She was skilled and her ship well equipped, but that counted for little as the two opponents destroyed her ship with contemptuous ease.

Piotr watched the engagement again. The attackers had destroyed her escape pod, obviously keen not to leave any witnesses. They'd also destroyed the wreckage. However, a forensic team had recovered some sensor memory buffer fragments from the site, enough to piece together the battle.

Tracking who had killed his friend proved much more difficult. He'd financed the bounty on Sahiba's killers personally. Without pilot identification or ship registry information, it had been impossible for anyone to take up the bounty. He didn't give up, unfortunately the recovered data didn't provide even a profile to work with to narrow down the suspects.

There were two types of bounty hunter in the galaxy. The first were simple opportunists. They watched the newsfeeds and looked for hotspots of pirate activity. The braver, more foolish or better equipped ones visited dark systems and known pirate bases to hunt.

The second group consisted of hunters with a more investigative mindset. They selected choice bounties from the law enforcement and Pilots Federation databases, then use their contacts and data mining to track down the bounty and claim the kill. Piotr belonged in the second group, although he wasn't adverse to opportunistic bounties he happened across.

With only the ship models to go on, he researched

attacks and looked for a pattern. He paid thousands of credits to hackers and inside data operatives to collate more and more data on attacks in an ever-increasing volume of human space. His investigation occupied more of his time and to finance it he had to take on ever-riskier bounties.

These generated larger pay-offs but also increased the risk to him and his ship. To compensate, part of the fees he earned were invested in the ship, improving its capabilities to beyond its factory specification. As his own Mark III Viper evolved so did his tactics, in part due to the change in weapons and defensive systems. A larger part stemmed from his investigation into Sahiba's killers. The ambush had demonstrated a high level of skill in stealth and ambush tactics and so did he as he delved deeper into their mindset.

Over the years his own skill grew. Despite this, he gleaned only the faintest of hints on the identity of the attackers. He isolated a few attacks in which the same three-ship configuration had featured. Far from comprehensive proof, but after so long without any progress it provided some small satisfaction.

That feeling didn't last long. When he investigated those attacks, he encountered a dismaying lack of accurate sensor records and in most cases tampering with what little evidence there was. Although he learned little from those encounters, he did come to realise that he hunted not only a trio of skilled pilots, but they operated a sophisticated support network.

Still, it was a big galaxy and the little he had learned at that point indicated that they roamed across a wide territory. He couldn't be sure that all of the attacks were perpetrated by the same team, although the next break he received did shine some light on that mystery.

Back in the early days of being a bounty hunter, he followed his ranking with the Pilots Federation religiously. Whenever he rose a rank, he celebrated. After Sahiba's death he lost the person he celebrated with and a reason to make merry. The Pilots Federation bureaucracy didn't care about his loss of interest, it continued to accrue his bounties and he continued to climb the ranks.

The day a pilot reaches the coveted Elite status is usually a proud one, but for Piotr it almost passed by unnoticed. Along with his official notification and invite to the Founders World, he received a private message – one that provided the next stage in his investigation.

The records kept by the Pilots Federation were extensive, even more so than those held by the intelligence agencies of the Alliance, Empire and Federation, some claimed. Even better, they covered all jurisdictions, in some cases whether the ruling authority recognised them as legal arbiter of bounties or not.

The increased data provided a better pool to hunt for the pattern Piotr had searched for. It also yielded a name, that of 'Cavus'. Details were still scant and the name wasn't an uncommon one. However, Piotr knew that someone of this calibre and cold-blooded capability had to be of a certain character. The profile he compiled thinned the numbers down somewhat, but there were still hundreds of names on the list. And that assumed that the people he hunted were registered members of the human systems on various databases.

The past few months had been spent crossing names off the list. In LP 98-132 he thought he'd found his man. A local smuggler with pretensions of becoming something more had the right name. He also had two friends with the right ships. Questioning him had proved to be unpleasant, and it seemed he was not the person Piotr hunted. Still, the galaxy now had three fewer pirate scum in it, and that couldn't be a bad thing.

The next name on the list brought him here, to BU 741. A small backwater system with three suns that just happened to be near the Federal and Imperial border. The system was corporate-run, but also a known haunt for bounty hunters. Piotr's ultimate destination was the Artemis system, but he figured that he would stop here first and see what information he could gather from the local hunters.

The databases hadn't provided much information on Darik Cavus, except that he was the head of security for Freeholm station. He'd featured prominently in the rebellion there some time ago. Apart from the occasional rogue miner engagement, the news on the head of security had been scant.

Piotr did learn that Darik had a daughter, although she was too young to be a likely suspect. Considering the man's role and history, Piotr thought it unlikely that Darik was the one that he sought. Still, he was a methodical man and this Darik was next on the list.

Making contact with the local hunters hadn't been difficult. They often met up in the imaginatively named Bounty Harbour Inn. Presumably someone's dim-witted idea for a pun. Business was quiet, or at least had been for the three hours that Piotr had been there. Unusually for this type of bar, it was on the planet, rather than in the orbital starport.

Piotr found the constant gravity more than a little uncomfortable. He spent most of his time in orbit and greatly preferred zero-gravity. He devoted time each day to exercising to maintain his muscle mass, and regular gene therapies and supplements helped prevent some of debilitating consequences of spaceflight that had afflicted the early explorers.

As the lack of business indicated, Piotr encountered only a few of the local bounty hunters and learned a few useful pieces of information. Darik apparently favoured the Eagle. While far from conclusive proof, it provided another indication that this wasn't the person he sought.

Despite this, Piotr needed to be certain, he couldn't imagine finding out at a later date that he'd let his prey slipped away. Freeholm now operated as a separate entity within the Artemis system, although free passage was permitted. Having some form of cover for the visit would be useful and an opportunity made itself known in the second nugget of information.

A brutal pirate attack had been reported near Freeholm. Apparently a rare event in the system. The Laphrian Navy operated some ageing ships but they were more than adequate to deal with pirates. The victims of the attack had made the subject a hot topic (if such a term could be applied to the quiet conversation in a dead-end bar), as they'd been two bounty hunters who retired from the life some years ago.

Nobody seemed to know who the attackers were and Piotr learned that Freeholm were looking for pilots to help hunt down the attackers. A perfect job for a skilled bounty hunter and one which would give Piotr good reason to visit the station. Even more usefully, they had sent an emissary to local systems to recruit pilots, and she was on her way to BU 741. That emissary was no less than Darik's daughter and Piotr intended to make the most of the opportunity to learn more about the man.

The bartender told him that she would arrive today and so Piotr waited. While he did, he searched through the local newsfeeds to see what he could learn about her. The results were disappointing. He learned little that he didn't already know but it filled the time. For Piotr, patience was a skill, one developed over the years. It rewarded him now as Julia Cavus entered the bar.

It wouldn't pay to seem too eager, however Piotr had laid the groundwork with the bartender. Piotr knew what Julia was looking for and it seemed a good bet that she would ask the bartender for information first, so he made sure that he would send her Piotr's way. In this case, the bar being almost empty worked in his favour.

Piotr worried that business would pick up as the day faded into night. He didn't want any competition to interfere with his plan. He recognised her immediately as she entered. When she approached the bar he folded his data screen and placed it away, drank from the glass of tox-free beer.

From the bar menu set in the table, he ordered the regular local brew. When it arrived he slipped a small tablet in the drink which transformed anything alcoholic (and three thousand other known intoxicants) into harmless sugars. Working off the extra sugar wouldn't be a problem, but slow reflexes could be. Many hunters relied on stims to give them an edge. Piotr preferred old-fashioned natural reflexes augmented by permanent medical enhancements.

He allowed his body posture to relax as he studied the young woman. He appeared at ease, an old hand relaxing between jobs. To his practised eye she appeared tense, and he wondered what might be the cause of that. She was undoubtedly young so maybe it was simple inexperience, perhaps something deeper. Her conversation with the bartender lasted longer than Piotr expected. The man had told Piotr that she had never visited the bar before and he now wondered if that was true.

After several minutes, Julia glanced over at Piotr. He kept his expression neutral and facing away from the bar, her movement noticed in his peripheral vision. She approached the table and he covered a glance with a long pull from his glass. He took care to drain the glass empty and provided her with the easy opening line.

"Can I buy you a drink?"

Piotr took a moment to look her over. He inclined his head to the affirmative and replied, "A drink is always welcome, especially from an attractive young lady." He felt no desire for the young woman, but he knew that a little flattery rarely did any harm. "Although I think you'll find my old bones a little dry for your tastes." He flashed a disarming smile, it helped put her at her ease. Yes he noticed her beauty but had no real interest in her.

Julia motioned to the bartender to bring a fresh drink

for her new companion and asked if she could sit. He agreed with a casual gesture. "And what can I do for you?"

"My name is Julia Cavus and I'm a representative from Freeholm in the Artemis system."

"I'm Piotr Vanchenko and I know of Freeholm. I've never been there. Your name does sound familiar though."

"You're probably thinking of my father."

Piotr's drink arrived and he carefully palmed the detoxicant into the drink, allowing a few seconds for it to work its magic before taking a large swallow.

"Why would I think of your father? Is he a well-known man?"

"Well, he's head of security at our station."

"So he's been in the news a bit then?"

"Yes, we're in a quiet volume of space, but we do have the odd incident."

"I know what you mean, villains everywhere. Still it keeps my ship well-maintained and pays for a welcome brew when I'm in port. Although a free one never goes amiss!"

"You're welcome, I wanted to talk to you."

"I thought you might, but about what, I wonder."

"We've had a significant attack within our space, something way beyond the few rogue miners we've encountered in the past."

"Aye, I've heard of the killing of two ex-bounty hunters."

"You have?"

"Of course, news like that is of interest in a place like this."

She blushed, realising she'd asked something obvious and to his surprise he tried to lessen the sting of her embarrassment. "It also helps I have plenty of time on my hands and I'm looking for my next job. The pickings on the board are pretty slim at the moment." And that was true, quieter than he would have expected, even for an out of the way location like this.

"Now that's interesting, and leads into what I wanted to talk to you about."

"You want someone to hunt down the attackers?"

"Yes, and to help secure visiting and departing traders until the threat has been dealt with."

"I'm not one for escort duty, although some investigation and hunting is my line of business. Do you know anything about the attackers?"

"Nothing at all."

"Well that's not a good start, but I've been dealt worse hands."

"I doubt that, how can it be worse than nothing?"

"Okay, maybe not worse," he laughed and she responded with the same. "Is there a Pilots Federation bounty on them?"

She shook her head. "We don't have enough data on the ships or their pilots to register one. We've issued a local jurisdiction bounty."

"No offence but they're useless unless we catch them within your jurisdiction, or way out in uncontrolled space."

"It's all we can do at the moment."

"I understand and agree we have to follow the legal niceties."

"I wasn't suggesting..."

"I know you weren't. I'm just thinking out loud." In reality he was probing her morals, always difficult in a quick meeting like this, but the blush more than the denial indicated that she wasn't used to bending the rules. By association that probably meant her father was on the level as well.

Still, the job intrigued him. Not only did he need to cross this Darik Cavus off the list, the thought of murderers of fellow bounty hunters getting away with their crime didn't sit well with him. And he was more than happy to bend the rules to make sure proper retribution took place, although this easily embarrassed young lady didn't need to know that.

"What's your security like?"

"We have a small squadron of fighters, enough to deal with the odd rogue miner, but we're overstretched for the current problem. Plus we don't have jurisdiction outside of our space."

"What about the rest of the system?"

"We've had reasonable relations since the revolt."

"Are they helping to find the attackers?"

"Yes, although my father doesn't think they're doing enough."

"He's your head of security as well?" She nodded. "How does that work?"

"What do you mean?"

"I mean what's it like working with your father?"

"Well..." She seemed about to say something more and caught herself before she did. Piotr filed that away for now.

"What bounty are you offering for the job?"

"We've set the bounty at 100,000 credits."

"That's a tidy sum."

"We'll also pay 2,000 per week for escort duties."

"As I said, I'm not one for playing babysitter, the bounty is attractive though. It'll need a lot of investigation. Was there even a forensic analysis of the contact site?"

"Unfortunately not, we don't generally have the need."

"Okay, I might be able to help. What do you say to the weekly retainer for some investigative work?"

"Only if you help with escort duties while you're in-system, if we're shorthanded."

"Not my favourite way to fly, but I'm happy to help out. Will your father need to approve the bond?"

"No, I have full authority to act on his behalf."

So they're a trusting pair, he mused. "It sounds like we

have a deal, I take it you want me to start straight away."

"Definitely, we need you there as soon as possible."

"All right, let me spend two days digging for information, hopefully I'll have something useful to report when I arrive."

"Sounds good, send me your pilot registration and I'll arrange the bond."

"I'll do that right now." He pulled out his data screen and transmitted his ID information. She obviously had implants as she responded immediately.

"Got them, combat bond sent."

The details for the bond appeared on his screen, and he spent a few minutes skimming through the details. It looked to be a standard agreement. Julia sipped her drink while she waited. He noted that she was happy to wait in silence, a good indicator of confidence. Most people seemed to feel the need to fill empty places in conversation. Or fidgeted if they couldn't.

"This all looks fine, I've sent my acceptance." She nodded indicating she'd received it. "Now then Ms Cavus, how about we seal the deal with a celebratory drink?"

He noticed that she blanched a little at the suggestion, but covered it quickly.

"I'm afraid not, I still have other places to visit, but thanks for the offer."

"No problem, where are you heading next? I can't imagine there are many places to find what you're looking for."

"Regrettably no. I'd hoped to find more than one interested pilot here, but you seem to be the only one available."

That had surprised Piotr as well. This might be a backwater system, but to have a bar dedicated for bounty hunters indicated that there were more than a few in the region. In fact he recognised the typical stance of low-level bounty hunters on the few patrons at the bar. A deal like this would have been snapped up, so he wondered why they weren't interested.

Perhaps he should talk to a few once Julia had left.

"Well, good luck with your task and I'll arrive at Freeholm in two days."

"Excellent, I'll see you then."

She rose and offered her hand, a strangely old-fashioned custom, but he took it anyway.

- 11 -

As Julia departed the Bounty Harbour Inn, a communication icon flashed on the priority screen projected within her vision. The message had arrived while she'd been talking to Piotr Vanchenko in the bar. Her hunt for pilots had come up far shorter than she had expected with only the bounty hunter and Hammer. She could swear that her head still ached from the night celebrating with Hammer. With any luck he would be arriving at Freeholm any time now. She felt sure that some of the deck hands would welcome a new drinking buddy, although she also felt sure that they'd regret it the next day as she had.

At least both pilots seemed more than capable, although she anticipated that her father would be disappointed when she returned with so few pilots. She perked herself up. She still had a few places to try, including some of the navy bars at the Artemis shipyard. There were some regular haunts for ex-service crews from the Laphrian Navy. Of all the systems in the area, that was the most likely bet for recruiting mercenaries and conveniently she had to pass by the planet when she returned to Freeholm, so she would make that her last stop.

The message was a short recording from Lina Maters. Its contents were terse, just a command for her to contact home immediately. Julia sighed inwardly. She'd known Lina for many years and while they were friends, sometimes Lina's stern attitude annoyed Julia. And the tone of the message didn't help. Julia decided that a reply could wait. The communications gear in her ship was more secure than her implants anyway.

Besides, she would be back in the ship all too soon and off to the next system. It had been two years since she last walked on a planet's surface and experienced real gravity. The sensation felt strange, as the rolling gait that marked most spacers who spent most of their time in low gravity wasn't really suited to walking planetside.

She could enjoy one benefit and that was a simple walk under a real sky as she returned to the spaceport from the bar. Most of the planet's space traffic was handled in orbit and through a larger spaceport to the north of the city. This port was designed to accommodate smaller ships like those used by the bounty hunters. Shuttles were the most common ships on the small landing pads. Her Eagle stood out amongst the transports and shuttles, apart from a menacing black Viper, one of the latest Mark IIIs she noticed with a little bit of envy.

Compared to her gunmetal Eagle, it looked squat and mean. The flat black coating seemed to suck the warmth from the light of the darkening sky. The Viper massed more than her Eagle and it dominated the assortment of smaller ships. This had to be Vanchenko's, it was the only one here that she could imagine him flying. The ship failed to respond to a ping request. This wasn't unusual to ignore identification requests while docked and she lacked the clearance needed to override the lockout.

A search of public databases revealed that Vanchenko did indeed fly a black Viper. That didn't prove that this was his ship, but it was good enough for Julia. The message reminder blinked on her inner screen, it was time to get back to work.

It occurred to her that it seemed odd that Lina had contacted her rather than her father. Maybe it wasn't related to the station at all. Lina had been due to head out on a trade run, although not in the direction of BU

741. Perhaps her plans had changed and she wanted to meet up.

That wouldn't explain the terseness of the message.

Julia sighed, she was back at her ship anyway so time to get in touch. As she climbed into the cockpit, she considered – and not for the first time – that the Eagle wasn't the best ship for these longer runs. It was a fine combat vessel, well armed and manoeuvrable, although definitely a lightweight compared to the more modern Viper Mark IIIs. However, it was lacking in the conveniences of home, in particular room to move.

Maybe she would need to rethink what ship she chose for her journey to the frontier. Something with a spacious cabin would be nice, or even better, maybe she could sign up with a large trader and still keep her Eagle while also having a berth on a mega-freighter. From a comfort perspective that was a fine idea, however that would then tie her down to a specific trade cruise. The mega-corps rarely sent their precious freighters into harm's way.

She still hadn't solved the problem of when and how she should tell her father of her plans. After the immediate crisis was a given. There hadn't been any further attacks since she'd left Freeholm so hopefully that was a good sign. If no new attacks materialised then maybe Darius and Simeon had been targeted after all. She cursed as she realised that she should have provided that information to Vanchenko. She could send a follow-on message later; it seemed a reasonable bet that they would be his first line of enquiry.

The ship responded as she settled into the seat. The holographic flickered into life, bathing the dull sheen of the dashboard around her. The comms panel opened in the top right of the screen with another message from Lina Mater, again instructing her to contact home.

Julia couldn't put it off any longer, although she was annoyed by Lina's constant badgering. She connected to the local comms net and activated a hyperspace link.

She was over ten light years from Freeholm but Lina responded within seconds, and a video screen popped into view. Julia realised that Lina appeared upset, but her anger overrode that and she demanded to know what the older woman wanted.

"Julia, I've been trying to contact you for hours, why didn't you respond?"

"I've been busy. You know, on the mission my father sent me on."

She regretted her petulance, although too late to stop the words being said in an aggressive tone. Lina ignored her anyway and now Julia heard a catch in her voice.

"Julia, I'm so sorry. It's about your father..."

- 12 -

The universe snapped back into focus as Hammer exited hyperspace into the Artemis system. He'd originally planned to arrive in the system the day after sealing the bond with the young Cavus woman. The girl had spirit although she didn't seem to handle them very well. He grinned to himself again as he recalled her accusing him of starting the brawl.

As if he would do such a thing!

He'd merely been protecting the lady's honour.

Hammer summoned the in-system map and located his destination. The station lay within the wide asteroid belt. The strident call of the proximity alarm disturbed his preparations. In the ship's heads-up display, a large interdiction warning preceded the shutdown of the frame shift drive.

Glancing at the scanner, Hammer saw a single target, which he assumed to be the welcoming committee. Most secure systems patrolled the region around the primary star of a system to challenge ships hyperspacing in. Usually they'd run an ID check and not interfere with a ship's passage, but sometimes they liked to take a closer look.

This looked to be one of those times.

Chromatic distortion flared across his vision as his ship dropped out of supercruise. Immediately an incoming comms request blinked on the comms panel. He activated the channel with a voice instruction.

"Vessel *Hammer,* this is the Artemis Navy Ship *Achilles.*

Continue along your current course and maintain velocity. Prepare to be scanned."

Like his own real name, Hammer had changed the name of the ship when he'd inherited it from his father. For a while he'd left it unnamed, but he discovered that people expected a ship of this size to have a name. As they had been partners together in their quest for revenge, it seemed only reasonable that they share the name that Hammer had adopted.

A name he now preferred to his old one.

He glanced around the bridge of his ship. Anacondas were designed to be operated by a small crew, but Hammer preferred to fly alone. He enjoyed company only when he drank and he never drank while in command. It had cost him a fortune to automate the ship enough that it operated at the same efficiency as that of a fully crewed vessel.

Expensive as those upgrades had been, they paled in comparison to the other, more fundamental changes to his ship.

The scanner displayed three targets. The first appeared to be a ship of similar size to his own. The scanner confirmed that this was the one that had hailed him. It also confirmed that it was the same hull type as his own – another Anaconda. At a glance, he recognised the changes on the Anaconda that shadowed his course at the edge of its weapon range.

Anacondas were fine ships, sturdy and with enough volume to be converted to fill a wide variety of roles. The one he now watched was a classic light cruiser conversion with additional weapons, extra armour and the capability of deploying two light fighters. Those fighters headed towards him now and Hammer cursed as the scanner identified the incoming fighters as the latest Imperial fighters and not the cold war era Ospreys he'd expected.

From the intelligence summaries he'd bought and

reviewed before flying to the Artemis system, he'd expected an ageing navy. Formidable for the local systems, but out of date. He looked more closely at the following Anaconda. Its silhouette indicated it was one of their standard upgrades, a class that provided the mainstay of the Laphrian Navy for decades.

Hammer monitored the signal emissions and heat output from the other Anaconda. Again he saw nothing unexpected. The sensors appeared less than top of the line, but more than adequate for its current role. Hammer enjoyed the thought that the Laphrian Navy captain would expect that his ship outgunned Hammer's and that was far from the case.

Hammer called his creation the *Trojan* class. A class which consisted of only one ship that continued to evolve as Hammer travelled along the periphery of human space. He lived for two reasons: the first to kill pirates and the other to develop his ship into the most deceptively effective combat vessel.

He'd put a lot of effort had gone into making sure that his ship's capability remained hidden from any aggressors. Bait didn't work if the fish discovered that it possessed teeth. Not that Hammer considered the Navy patrol a threat, however deception only worked if no-one knew about it. That was also partly why he followed a nomad's life since extracting his revenge on the pirate gang that murdered his father. Word of exploits quickly spread after an attack, so he kept moving to keep his method a surprise.

The trick was simple. He'd designed his Anaconda to look more vulnerable than it really was. The shields fitted were the cheapest he could find. A ploy that many inexperienced or greedy traders employed to maximise their profits – often to their peril. As a surprise to an attacker, the shields may be weak but the ship was extremely well-armoured.

Offensively, Hammer's ship was also deceptive. It

possessed a number of point defence weapons on its hard points. Appearing vulnerable wasn't the same as being stupid. The point defences had a serious limitation, namely that of range. They were designed to shoot down incoming missiles and harass any ship flying too close, not a threat to a skilled pilot in a decent ship.

The secret of the ship waited in the cargo holds, or rather the lack of them. Where once there had been vast empty spaces waiting to be filled with trade goods, now stood extra bulkheads. The entire skeleton of ship had been bulked up and armoured. Between these sturdy frames sat rack upon rack of missile-filled magazines.

Within the outer armoured hull, additional hard points had been constructed. Hammer hunted for months to find an outfitter capable of hiding the extra missile mounts within the hull. When pirates attacked, they tended to swarm the larger ship. They did so swiftly to overpower the shields and point defences. When the ship offered little resistance they usually became overconfident. Not always, many cannier pirates suspected something amiss although it was usually too late by then.

The first and least obvious part of the counterattack came from the underpowered point defences. Their weapons might have been weak, but their targeting systems were top of the line. Normally the turrets used the ship's main sensors for their targeting data, and they were more than adequate for that purpose. The more advanced system was only used in dire need and were slaved to the missile launchers.

Anyone scanning the ship would detect the point defences, but not the missile launchers. They were cunningly built into the hull and disguised with thick plating and active countermeasures. When deployed, they could unleash thousands of missiles within two minutes. A devastating barrage that could strike against a horde of targets simultaneously.

The weakness in the deception was the structural changes. The plating and countermeasures were adequate against the typical scanners used by pirates. It seemed a reasonable bet that the incoming fighters were equipped with better technology than that. Up until now he'd managed to avoid being scanned by modern military-grade sensors. The engineer who'd supervised the upgrades claimed that the tech used would withstand such scrutiny. Well, now the truth of those claims would be tested.

"Anaconda *Hammer*, this is *Achilles* patrol lead."

"Acknowledged." Hammer watched the lead fighter approach. Its partner held back, ready to strike if Hammer showed any signs of running or resisting.

"Drop your shields and prepare to be scanned."

The request struck Hammer as unusual, after all, shields weren't known to interfere with scans. It did, however, leave the ship somewhat vulnerable while being scanned. Perhaps it was simply a tactic to unnerve visitors and startle them into a rash move. In any case, Hammer's ship didn't rely on shields for its protection. The extra armour his ship was equipped with would be more than a match for the fighters' weapons.

The other Anaconda posed a greater threat, but Hammer didn't worry about that. He carried a legal combat bond for Freeholm and according to the Pilots Federation database entry on the Artemis system, the free travel treaty had held strong for a decade. It seemed unlikely that would change now.

His passive sensors detected the active scan. Hammer watched through the large windows of the bridge as the fighter swept past. It possessed an elegant form, the trademark of all Imperial ships. The small cockpit swept in a smooth arc to a ring of thrusters on the wing tips. It looked menacing and beautiful at the same time.

The database entry hadn't mentioned top-of-the-line

fighters from the Imperial Gutamaya shipyards. Hammer wondered what else had changed.

"Scan complete *Hammer*, thank you for your cooperation. Where are you heading?"

Now Hammer wondered whether the scan had detected anything. The tone in the pilot's voice gave nothing away. The conversion wasn't illegal, there were no armament restrictions in this system. However, knowledge of the alterations wasn't something he wanted available; surprise was as effective a weapon as the thousand warheads in what was once the cargo hold of his Anaconda.

"I'm going to Freeholm."

"And what is your business there?"

"Just that, business."

"There have been incidents in the area, you are advised to contact Captain Belin and arrange an escort as you approach the belt."

Hammer allowed some concern into his voice. "Incidents? What do you mean?"

"There have been a few attacks in the area, and we're providing escorts for traders to the belt. Contact Captain Belin on this channel and he will rendezvous with you."

"Is the journey there safe? The belt is half a system away."

"The incidents have been isolated and you'll be safe under escort. We can't provide protection once you enter the belt. Captain Belin will arrange for you to meet units from the Freeholm defence force."

"I see. What were these incidents?"

"I'm not an information service, *Hammer*, you can access the newsfeeds on the public channels."

"Understood, *Achilles* patrol lead."

"Safe journey, *Hammer*."

The fighter peeled away, was quickly joined by its partner and headed back to its parent ship. Hammer wondered whether the message was supposed to make him nervous or was just a friendly warning. Too many years of hunting meant he had developed a suspicious streak. It didn't really matter, he'd agreed to the bond so he sent a hail to Captain Belin. The Captain responded quickly.

"Commander Lamon."

Hammer winced as he heard his real name. By convention, pilots and ships' crew tended to be referred to by their rank and call sign, only the most officious used the real name. It seemed that this Captain Belin belonged in the officious camp.

"Captain Belin, I was told to contact you for escort to Freeholm."

"That is correct, there have been incidents in the region and the Laphrian Navy has deemed it best to escort travelling ships."

On his journey to Artemis, Hammer reviewed the Pilots Federation's data on traffic in the system. The data showed that a dozen ships travelled to Freeholm each month. Traffic seemed regular, the system was far enough from the main trade routes that the traffic comprised of mainly regular traders.

He'd also learned that pirate attacks in the system were very rare. The two incidents in the last few weeks totalled more than in the same number of years. He learned of the latest attack while reviewing the traffic data. He sadly wondered how Julia had reacted to the death of her father. He remembered all too clearly how he'd felt when he learned of the death of his.

"Incidents, Captain? Are there pirates operating in this system?"

"The attacks appear to be isolated and unconnected, Commander. However, we're not taking any chances. Now I see your position as just leaving the jump zone. Are you coming straight to Freeholm or going to Laphria first?"

"I'm going straight to Freeholm."

"Very well. I'm transmitting a waypoint, we will rendezvous with you there in one hour."

Hammer checked the location on his map.

"I can be there much quicker than that."

"I can't, so time your approach to arrive at the time I've said."

"What if I'm interdicted?"

"Don't worry Commander, the area is well-patrolled and all of the incidents so far have been in the belt."

"Understood, Captain. I'll meet you at the waypoint in an hour."

"We'll be there. I'll contact Freeholm and inform them you are coming; they'll provide your escort within the belt."

"Wait, you aren't escorting me to Freeholm?"

"The belt is their jurisdiction. I can only take you to the belt and they'll take over from there."

"Okay, thank you Captain."

The journey proved uneventful and Hammer travelled at less than half power to time his arrival at the rendezvous. The Captain was true to his word and arrived just before Hammer. Once again Hammer heard the Captain's voice over the channel.

"Commander Lamon, we will travel in normal space for the remainder of the journey."

"Wouldn't it be quicker in supercruise?"

"It would, but Freeholm won't be able to send an escort for another two hours."

"Why not? They should be expecting my arrival."

"They are, and they will be at the belt's edge in two hours."

"Didn't they say anything else?"

"No, Commander. They lost somebody important to them yesterday and things are a little chaotic for them at the moment. Belin out."

The Captain seemed a little upset. Hammer wondered if he'd mistaken his terseness for something else. Perhaps he'd known Freeholm's head of security. That seemed a logical conclusion, especially if the Captain patrolled this area on a regular basis.

The two hours passed slowly and Hammer used the time to try and determine if his supposition was correct. Unfortunately the Laphrian Navy didn't post their patrol schedules in the public feeds. Captain Belin's name did appear a few times in the records. The most recent related to the two reported attacks, but they didn't tell him any more than Julia already had.

In the next entry, also from the local newsfeed, he learned that Captain Belin had been promoted to captain only three years ago. Voices over the comms could sometimes be deceptive, but Hammer was certain that the Captain was older than he would have expected for such a recent promotion. The report confirmed his hunch, the Captain had been forty when given his first command.

Hammer wondered why he'd been promoted so late, and if there had been a problem with the Captain's past then why had they promoted him at all?

The final, and oldest of the returned results provided a clue to the mystery. Ten years previously during the revolt in the penal colony, the Navy had staged a coup. It had been a popular move and supported by the civilian population who had grown weary of the many injustices perpetrated by the planet's regime.

Probably not popular with those who lost the power, Hammer guessed. Even though he'd only been a young ensign, Belin had featured publicly in the coup, mostly due to being part of the team who arrested the ruling president. His fame hadn't lasted long, but those ousted from power no doubt had longer memories.

The arrival of two Sidewinders interrupted Hammer's reading. He thanked the Captain for the escort and safe arrival and then followed his new escort into the belt. Hammer watched his scanner as they travelled along the safe path through the belt. Unlike many asteroid belts he'd seen before, this belt had a high density of large rocks. Most were sparsely populated, with isolated clusters of larger asteroids and planetoids. In some places, this belt more resembled rings round a planet than an open belt in deep space.

Such a sight was rare and usually indicated great mineral wealth. With exclusive rights for the whole belt it meant that Freeholm possessed a fortune. Or at the very least, the ticket to one. Money was usually the reason for men committing violence, and it seemed a reasonable bet that the same held true here.

His escorts said little during the passage through the belt. With so much mass around they couldn't supercruise to the station, which meant another slow journey. Funny how even a short journey of a few hours had become an inconvenience since the invention of the new drives.

He remembered his father telling him of taking weeks to travel between stars, even journeys between planets could take as long. With the new generation of hyperdrives, powered by the frame shift technology, journeys took mere minutes. As well as a new generation of drives, a new generation of spacers had arisen.

A more impatient bunch, Hammer thought to himself.

Freeholm's flight control granted landing clearance as soon as he contacted them. The Anaconda was a tight fit through the docking port, but he'd performed the manoeuvre many times before. The design spec for the ports allowed passage for any ship up to the Panther Clipper's size, however as any pilot knew, it took nerves and skill to fly a ship with only centimetres of clearance through the gap. Especially when a station's automatic defences could sometimes mistake a collision for an attack!

For new pilots, the peril lay not only in collision, but being too cautious. Stations had ships coming in and out all the time and loitering in the port was an offence in most jurisdictions. Rookie pilots too scared to scratch their new ship sometimes fell afoul of the rules if they took too long, and were fined for loitering. Hammer remembered his first time flying the Anaconda, he'd been very young but his father had been there to guide him through.

A bittersweet memory.

He docked with economical grace for such a large ship and connected to the station services network. He refuelled, but didn't request a maintenance check. He preferred to do that himself, or at least with a team he could trust. His ship contained too many secrets to allow strangers to crawl across its hull.

Once Hammer had secured his ship, he decided to get to know the lay of the land more. After all, there was only so much that could be learned from newsfeeds and databases. He headed for the nearest and cheapest bar, that's usually where you found the local engineers and station crew and they knew the local news in better detail.

And he liked a drink.

- 13 -

Two days had passed in a grey fog. Julia couldn't remember flying back to Freeholm. She must have done, because here she was. She didn't want to accept what she'd been told. Her father had been her strength, more than that he'd been the centre of her life.

And now he was gone.

A bitter truth she didn't want to accept.

Yet...

This morning the dreaded moment would come. At the memorial service, the time would come for her to accept the truth. Speaking the words would solidify the reality she refused to accept.

For two days, she'd pushed her grief to the back of her mind.

She ignored all the preparations, and made it clear that she didn't want the service. A tiny voice within her argued that her behaviour was childish and in no way honoured his memory.

It was easier to ignore the voice and pretend that nothing had changed.

Except that it had.

Everything had changed and so did the grief that stalked within her. She certainly didn't want to share it with everyone. She sensed it lurking in the back of her mind. As a hero of the uprising, she wouldn't be allowed to mourn his passing alone, as so many people owed him their freedom and, indeed, their lives.

Everyone wanted to gather together and to remember

him and when they were done remembering, they would celebrate his life. And she would have to take part in every minute of it.

She hadn't slept, not since the message from Lina.

She couldn't sleep. She didn't want to surrender to the dark.

Julia wanted to leave, to fly far away.

They wouldn't let her leave. They'd locked out her ship.

For her own good, Lina had claimed.

The door chimed, it cut into the fugue, an unwelcome guest. It would be Lina. She didn't want to speak to Lina, or anyone for that matter. All she wanted was to be alone in her Eagle and heading into deep space.

There was a little bit of anger lurking around the edges of her denial. Anger at her father. Anger at Lina. Anger at everyone who asked her if she was okay.

Chimes from the door again.

Best to ignore it, and hopefully Lina would go away. It was better here alone. They could remember her father without her. Some of them had known him longer than she had.

He wasn't dead anyway. There couldn't be a universe without him in it. A small part of her accepted the truth, most of her still wanted to deny it.

As if her denial could change the universe.

The damn chimes again.

Safer in here, alone. The world could remain out there.

"Julia!"

The loud voice was even less welcome than the chimes.

"Julia, get up." Lina Mater's voice demanded acknowledgement.

"I'm going to stay here."

"I'm sorry, but you can't. Your father's memorial is in two hours."

"I'm not going."

Slender hands pulled her from her bed.

"You are going to attend." Lina's command was brusque, but then softened. "I know it's hard for you."

"How can you know?"

Lina nodded in response to Julia's question.

"I realise that you think that your pain is your own and you can't share it. Knowing you as I do, you probably don't want to share it, but you must. In two hours, people will gather to honour your father."

"I don't want to remember him. I want to see him."

"It's hard, Julia. I do understand, honey. If it were just you then I'd let you wallow in your bed until you found the energy to continue. You have no choice, you have to get up now. There's too much to do."

"I can't do it."

"Yes you can, just take it a step at a time. If you don't want to talk at the memorial then that's fine, but you do have to be there."

"I can't."

"One step at a time. The first step is to get out of bed. You can do that can't you?"

Lina had taken the mothering tone and that irritated Julia. It was the tone she usually took when her father had asked the older woman to speak to her whenever he thought a woman's touch was required. Her back straightened against the tone and she sat up.

"See. That wasn't so hard now was it?"

From there, Lina cajoled Julia into the shower. She found Lina patiently waiting there when she left the bathroom. Feeling clean did help Julia feel better, although she almost resented the fact. On this day she shouldn't be feeling better, even by the smallest amount.

"Let's get you dressed."

Lina searched through Julia's wardrobe for something suitable to wear.

"I want to wear my flight suit."

Lina stopped her search. It wasn't what she had in

mind, but with a moment's reflection it wasn't necessarily a bad choice. The Freeholm defence force wasn't a military unit so they didn't have uniform. Over the years they'd evolved something close, but nothing like a dress uniform. However, to Lina it seemed that the choice was more about a statement of intent.

Perhaps Julia was starting focus on what comes next.

"I really can't do this." Julia slumped back onto her bed, half-dressed.

"No you don't. Up you come. Finish getting dressed and let's get something to eat. I bet you haven't eaten since you returned."

"I don't want to eat."

"I know, but it will make you feel better. Get something warm inside you. You will need your strength."

More cajoling until finally Julia was dressed in her black flight suit. Without further resistance, Julia allowed the older woman to lead her to a nearby café. She didn't eat, instead she drank black coffee in silence. Lina tried to start a conversation, to encourage Julia to talk, without any success.

"It's time."

Julia nodded in reply. They took one of the transit cars to the public gallery where the memorial would be held. The gallery provided the only view into space for the inhabitants of the station. Its position just under the centreline of the station meant that it experienced none of the gravity effect from the station's rotation. By convention, everyone wore mag-shoes while visiting the gallery.

At the other end, a matching window looked out into the docking bay. It had been a favourite haunt for Julia when she was younger. She liked to watch the ships docking and leaving, imagining the far-off destinations they travelled to.

Now as she entered the chamber with Lina at her side, those memories seemed so far away. They weren't the first to arrive, far from it. The room was filled with people waiting. Despite the large crowd, a solemn quiet hung in the air. Soft murmurs from person to person heralded their arrival. Many turned as they entered. Julia felt the crowd's eyes holding her in their gaze. Their eyes full of sympathy, and wet with their own grief.

In response Julia's eyes welled up, and with an effort she blinked them clear. She hadn't cried yet and she wouldn't in front of all these people. A darkness within her invited her to collapse inside herself, but with Lina's strength beside her she resisted.

Julia recognised many of those who had come. She couldn't meet their eyes. A few spoke to her as she passed, delivering platitudes of sympathy and compassion. Their words meant nothing, although some part buried beneath the fugue recognised their intent.

At the far end of the gallery by the window looking out into deep space, a smaller, more select group gathered. Four of them wore flight suits like Julia's and she felt some relief at that. The statement had seemed a good idea at the time, but when she saw the crowd of mourners in their civilian finest she'd worried that she'd made the wrong choice. Seeing the four Sidewinder pilots in the same dirty black – well not too dirty, some effort had been made – provided some relief.

Along with the pilots stood the dignitaries of the station, the council members and the department heads. All were friends of her father's, and many of them had fought alongside him during the insurrection. More than that, they'd worked hard together to rebuild the penal colony into the thriving station it had since become.

For the first time since hearing of his death, Julia wondered who had killed her father. To have done so would have meant admitting that he was dead. It wasn't the best time to have the realisation. It caused an almost physical pain that washed through her. She'd almost reached the gathering by the window, her eyes drawn to the jet black of space beyond the transparent alloy.

Mayborn noticed her stumble and stepped forward, but Lina was already there supporting the young woman. The pilots also moved forward and screened her from watching eyes as Lina guided her into one of the seats. Mayborn waved away the other executives. They would give Julia a few minutes to gather herself.

"I can't do this."

Those around her comforted her, tried to lend her their strength. With their support she eventually calmed and they moved to the centre of the gathering. She sat and tried to keep her face calm as the president of the station council took position at the dais. The larger crowd below took note and stopped their own conversation as they took their seats in the rows laid out for the occasion.

"Ladies and gentleman, thank you all for coming on this most terrible occasion. Like many of you, I first met Darik when this station still operated under the rule of Laphria in a world very different from what it is today.

"Darik Cavus is the reason that we no longer suffer in that terrible state of affairs. He didn't do it alone of course. Through the strength and courage of those of you here today and those that are no longer with us, we attained our freedom.

"And our freedom hasn't been easy. Our relations with Laphria transformed as they underwent their own changes, but we alone had to build our future. Together we have turned what was once a prison into a home fit for our children to grow up in.

"When we won our freedom, none of us really knew what to do next. We had no plan, simply the desire for freedom. To become masters of our own destiny.

"We had to organise and first and foremost of our needs was establishing security. In those early days and with the withdrawal of the Laphrian Navy, we became an inviting target for rogue miners and even pirates.

"We didn't have a defence force back then and we were still licking our wounds from the desperate struggle. The Laphrian forces had left only a single ship, an old Eagle fighter barely capable of flight. Darik took up the challenge, even though at the time his wife had just died from injuries sustained during the fight.

"Of course he also had a young daughter, only ten years old, to care for. That lovely young lady is with us now to remember the life of her father."

He remained silent for a moment, although he glanced at Julia sat nearby. Her eyes misted from the memories in her own head. She managed a nod at the President to acknowledge his words.

"Julia, of course, is now the lead pilot of our defence force, and so following in the footsteps of her father. Before the formation of the force the only defender we had was Darik in that beaten-up Eagle. He fought against the rogue miners looking to steal our valuable minerals. He also engaged the pirates seeking easy pickings.

"Often outgunned, he formed the barrier which provided safety for the first traders to arrive at the station. It took time, as all things do, until eventually we'd earned sufficient funds to purchase a second Eagle. Even though the new ship was an improved model he kept his old Eagle, he said the old bird brought him luck!"

A few restrained laughs from the crowd as they remembered how often Darik cursed his old fighter, yet remaining adamant that it was his to fly.

"The station grew and as it did, so did our defence force. All through the years, the reputation gained by Darik's actions helped keep our home secure. I remember he all too reluctantly agreed to become our head of security even though he'd been filling the role for three years already.

"Beyond his talent as a pilot and his bravery as a fighter, he provided strength and wise counsel to those around him. He formed one of the pillars of our community and it is with great sadness that he is taken from our lives.

"On this day of remembrance, we will not dwell on the manner of his passing, as that is a matter for tomorrow. Today let us remember the man we knew, the man we respected and the man that we all loved.

"You're all quite used to hearing me speak, but there are others who have their memories to share. So let me express my condolences and sympathies to Julia, his daughter and for all of us here."

The President glanced at Lina as he stepped from the podium and she shook her head in response. Julia's stoic expression had crumbled, the truth of her father's death all too plain on her face. She wanted to speak and honour her father, but she couldn't. The President understood and motioned to one of the other notables who stood up and began to speak.

Throughout the afternoon, each of the dignitaries took their turn to reminisce about her father. His virtues were extolled and on occasion even his few vices. From the crowd below, sobs and the occasional laughter were heard. Julia managed to keep her tears silent, but they streamed openly down her face.

Whenever one of the personages finished their speech, they would glance in her direction and each time Lina discreetly shook her head. As the afternoon faded and the latest person to speak looked round, Julia gripped Lina's arm to indicate that she would speak. She almost faltered as she walked to the podium. She'd never felt as alone at that moment when she stepped forward.

Once at the podium, she summoned her strength and spoke.

"Thank you everyone for coming today. I wasn't sure if I would be able to speak and share my memories of my father. To be honest I wasn't even sure I could come to this memorial."

She turned and shone a wan smile at Lina. "It's only because of my dear friend that I found the strength to be here."

Julia turned back to the audience. "My father will be remembered for many things and I'm grateful that our council have granted him the honour of placing the memorial plaque here in this gallery. Whenever we come to look out to the stars, he will be with us, guarding us in spirit as he did in life.

"Some of you here remember my mother." A few nods from the people who'd been prisoners there. "She died during the uprising. I was only ten years old at the time and I didn't really comprehend what was happening. I'd lived my entire life here in the colony, so I didn't understand any other way of living.

"It seemed natural to me that a girl didn't go to school. Or have toys to play with. I didn't know that it wasn't normal for an entire family to live in a tiny cell. I was too young to work, so while my mother and father slaved in the mines, I remained locked in the cell alone. I had no form of entertainment except for a book, a single book about a young man's quest to save a princess from an alien dragon. My father must have bought it on the black market. He couldn't have got it from anywhere else.

"I still have that book."

She had to pause for a moment, the memory of her first and for many years her only possession threatened to overwhelm her. Everyone waited patiently for Julia to regain her composure.

"You all remember my father as the great hero. The fighter who battled alongside you and led you all to victory. And as the husband who sacrificed his wife to the revolution.

"He was all those things to me as well and yet so much more. During the fighting, he hid me in the ventilation system. At first I was there all alone, but every so often he visited with scraps of food that just about kept the hunger pangs at bay. He brought other children so I wasn't alone. There weren't many children in the prison and my father rescued all but one.

"I didn't learn about my mother's death until after the fighting had ceased. I didn't understand what he told me at first. I couldn't accept that the universe could exist without my mother in it.

"And now I have to accept the same truth about my father. He was the man who cared for me, taught me to read and write. And most precious of all, he showed me how to fly. You all know my love of flying, although some of you probably don't appreciate that as much as I do."

A few chuckles from the audience. Her antics in the cockpit were legendary in the station. The most famous had been the controller fly-by on her first solo flight at the age of twelve. Under manual control, she'd matched the docking bay's rotation and floated in front of the control tower waving at the duty crew inside. As far as she'd been concerned it had just been a silly prank, but apparently even approaching the control tower was a crime and she'd been lucky not to have been engaged by the station's automated defences.

There were other occasions, some sillier and others less stupid, but she always remembered that one. It wasn't the first time she had been shouted at by her father, it was however the first time he'd done so with a smile on his face.

She knew that her love of flying came from him. As she'd grown older, it provided the common bond that kept them together. In her teenage years she'd blamed him for her mother's death. It didn't seem a great deal at the time. After all, he'd blamed himself for her death as well. She'd grown up though and had realised that her blame was unfair. In the past few years they'd grown closer and now this.

"My father was at the core of every good thing I ever tried or achieved in my life. I can't imagine my life without him here to support and guide me. The universe is diminished without him in it and my life has grown darker without his light."

Julia paused. Her eyes weren't the only ones misted up.

Movement at the rear of the gallery attracted her attention. Three people, two men and a woman had entered. They were spacers, that much was plain from their gait. They also had a lean look to them and it was difficult to tell at that distance, but there was something familiar about them. Almost as if she'd seen their faces before.

"I do know one thing. The galaxy will be a better place without the sons of bitches who killed my father in it."

That might have not been the done thing to say at a memorial, but the whole crowd agreed with her anyway.

- 14 -

The memorial had been a quiet affair, and the siblings had intended to arrive long before it began. Unfortunately the need to maintain appearances with the Laphrian Navy required more time than Mervan anticipated. Of all the people to visit this backwater system, the three siblings were the last people to need an escort. Even more amusing was the fact that their escort was an old converted Anaconda.

They'd encountered similar vessels before. Typically they were operated by independent system navies who lacked the money or contacts to operate the newer and more capable vessels from one of the major factions. Mervan considered that a good thing, They didn't know the situation here or the circumstances of Darik's death. With so many unknowns, he considered it possible that they would have to engage one of these ships. With his extensively upgraded Fer de Lance, and Seline and Lee's top-of-the-range Vipers, they'd fly rings around one of these tubs. True, they were heavily armoured, but their weapons would be up to the task.

While that might be the case, Mervan considered the possibility remote. It was more likely that Darik had been killed by a pirate gang. Now that the siblings were here they would determine who and destroy every single one of them.

Mervan didn't believe that would happen, he was certain of it.

The memorial neared its end as the siblings arrived.

Although it was a private ceremony, they weren't challenged when they entered. He recognised Julia the moment he saw her, even though he'd never met her in person. She resembled her paternal grandmother more than her father. He hadn't recognised the resemblance from the newsfeed images. In person and even at a distance of a hundred metres it hit him hard enough to stir memories of his mother.

She too had died when Mervan was young. It happened when a job went badly in a tightly patrolled Federal system. A police patrol cut off their escape and she had sacrificed herself so that her husband could escape. Her death had changed their father. Since then he'd become colder and more distant.

He blinked and let the memories return to the depths of his mind. The young woman's grief appeared clear, even at this distance. However, with her final words he saw her bearing change to the same determined fierceness that he'd known in his mother. In that moment, Mervan decided that he would approach the girl and reveal more about her father's past. Whether he told her everything remained to be seen.

In the meantime, he instructed his brother and sister to investigate the station further. Seline hadn't been happy of course. That came as no great surprise as her temperament didn't suit investigative work.

The memorial might have been a private affair but the wake which followed filled the commercial levels of the station. It appeared as if the entire station's population had joined to celebrate and remember the life of their head of security. Mervan felt pride that his youngest brother had made a life for himself where he was loved by so many.

No such destiny could ever happen for him, or for Lee and Seline. While he didn't regret his choice, he did sometimes wonder what life might have been like if he'd possessed the same courage as Darik. Unfortunately such thoughts lacked substance. He enjoyed his work and the close bond he shared with his brother and sister. True, there wouldn't be an adoring crowd when he died, but his death would be avenged.

And despite Seline's disagreement, they'd do the same for Darik.

Throughout the afternoon Mervan wandered through the commercial levels. He mingled with the crowd and listened to their conversations. When they docked he'd purchased a secure link from the station's public network. Even with a custom encryption system, the connection lacked the security he would have preferred. He doubted anyone on this station would have the ability or the equipment to crack the encryption in time to be a threat.

The connection fulfilled two purposes. It provided a link to the ships and through them to his surveillance and recon drones positioned around Freeholm. Any ship movement near the station would be detected and he'd know immediately.

It also allowed him to keep in discreet contact with Seline and Lee. Between the three of them they pieced together an intelligence assessment of the station. Despite the large crowds drinking and celebrating, there appeared to be only around twenty uniformed guards deployed.

Mervan assumed that plain clothes security mingled amongst the crowd as well. Perhaps the data he'd reviewed over the years proved correct and this station was indeed a quiet and peaceful place to live.

Except for mysterious pirates that didn't seem interested in cargo.

The family had worked their network of contacts without learning anything about the attackers. That indicated that this was unlikely to be the work of a major player, although it didn't rule it out completely. It probably meant that the trouble was local or somebody new looking to gain some reputation. Or quite possibly both.

They didn't usually operate this far from the core systems so they lacked anyone on the inside to learn anything further. They'd have to do this the old-fashioned way with legwork and hacking. As the technical genius of the family, Seline would investigate the local data networks.

As well as assessing station security, the siblings watched the crowds. Their implants automatically scanned the people in sight and compared them to several local databases. They currently only had access to the public systems, but any unidentified faces were stored and would be checked once they gained secure access later that evening.

Mervan believed it unlikely that the attack on Darik formed the bait for a trap. Someone would have to be in deep to know that Darik had any connection with the family. It wasn't completely impossible, so they moved cautiously.

That assumption suffered a momentary blip when Lee identified the bounty hunter. The quick background check revealed that Piotr Vanchenko had quite an impressive reputation and an Elite ranking. The same data lacked any connection to the family's operations which put Mervan back at ease. Considering the situation and the death of the two ex-bounty hunters, it wasn't surprising that others of their ilk looked to gain revenge and earn some credits.

In truth the real surprise was that there weren't more bounty hunters at the station.

Mervan also played a hunch with these scans. He considered that whoever perpetrated the attack on his brother had inside help. That help could have come from a newcomer on the station. So they looked for strangers in a small city where they were strangers themselves.

The search revealed a few interesting possibilities.

The most likely candidate was a trader known to operate near the Federation core worlds. Nothing in the data indicated anything suspicious. It just seemed unlikely that a trader would travel all the way from his usual trade routes to a backwater system like this.

With the crowds as cover, Seline easily placed a tracker on the trader without being noticed so they could keep an eye on his movements. So far movement had been limited to walking to the bar and back in one of the watering holes on the lowest level. Whenever one of the siblings passed by, they watched him get more intoxicated. By the end of the afternoon, the old guy looked wasted so Mervan dropped him as a suspect.

Almost all of the businesses had thrown their doors open as part of the celebration. Even those shops that didn't sell food or drink provided places to stop and rest. The concourse filled with people from all over the station. Mervan guessed that most of the population had turned out to join the wake. As he filtered through the crowds, he heard much of the conversation centred on his long-lost brother.

He'd wanted to contact Darik rather than simply spy on him from afar. Unfortunately doing so would have provoked his father's ire. He'd watched though and felt pride in his brother's achievements. Mervan had known from an early age that his younger brother wouldn't last long in the family business. He was a skilled pilot, but lacked the ruthlessness needed to murder in cold blood.

Being amongst all these people who loved Darik provided a connection Mervan wished he'd had with his brother. For an hour he wandered from one shop to the next. He stopped in bars and cafes and listened as they exchanged stories. He drank like those around him. Unlike most of them, he nullified the effects of the free-flowing drinks with engineered bacteria in his gut. He could never enjoy the effects of inebriation, it posed too much of a risk for someone in his business.

His father had the bacterial culture implanted in all of his children at a young age and Mervan wondered if Darik had ever had his countered, or whether he maintained a life of sobriety for his own reasons.

Throughout the afternoon, Julia toured the commercial levels. Mervan took care to keep his distance from her group. He intended a more discreet meeting with her later, although he hadn't determined yet how he would manage that.

An opportunity rose as afternoon descended into evening. Naturally the distinction was artificial on a station like this without the light from the sun to mark the passing of the day. On the uppermost level, he noticed a bar that had been closed for the afternoon. This seemed an unusual contrast to everywhere else so he sent Seline to observe the situation.

He also tasked Lee with following Julia's party. She continued moving through the throng and stopped on occasion to exchange anecdotes or thank people for their sympathy. Lee reported that she wasn't drinking and neither were the people with her. Their clothing indicated that they were pilots. No doubt the members of the local defence force who'd failed to keep their commander alive.

Seline reported that access to the bar was possible, a small group had been admitted. She planned to charm her way in.

Mervan groaned as he heard her say that over the comms link. He knew all too well what her charm could mean. He called Lee and ordered him to find somewhere close to the bar and be available to provide backup. Lee confirmed the instruction and headed up to the upper limit. Mervan moved to Julia's current location at a seafood restaurant on the middle level.

"I'm in," Seline reported.

"Excellent, keep me up to date. And keep out of trouble."

"Of course, big brother."

For the next hour he tailed Julia's group. Everyone she encountered offered their condolences. She thanked them and Mervan couldn't help but be impressed by her calm. She dealt with the constant stream of well-wishers with an ease that belied her age and the visible grief in her expression.

The group worked their way to the top level where the crowd thinned considerably. That made Mervan's surveillance difficult. Before, he could blend with crowds even if there wasn't much movement. Lee reported that he suffered a similar problem, although he was now able to enter the bar so found himself a secluded seat inside. Two minutes later he called Mervan.

"I think we might have a problem."

"What's happening?" Mervan replied.

"Seline's got that look on her face."

"Shit. Why?"

"She's playing cards with a big trader and a couple of locals."

"So?"

"She's just got that look of hers."

"What happened?"

"I don't know, I'm too far away, but she looks like she'll blow any second."

"All right, I'm on my way."

He shouldn't be surprised really. Her temperament wasn't suited for this kind of work. In her cockpit she could rage as much as she wanted to relieve the tension. With people around, she preferred other amusements. Mervan had hoped that for this particular mission she'd maintain some control. In retrospect, she had been the most upset when Darik chose to leave the family. That anger hadn't mellowed over the subsequent years.

Mervan should have known better. He could have left her in her ship hidden in the belt. Which would have been the sensible option if anything went wrong on the station. Instead he chose the extra pair of boots on the ground.

A bad choice.

He found the argument in full swing by the time he entered the bar. A sight worthy of David and Goliath welcomed him. Mervan had encountered some big guys in his time. Sometimes the job required a close-up kill and they usually had protection. For some targets they believed that the size of their protection represented ability. With the availability of DNA manipulation and physical implants, becoming a man-mountain just required credits.

Mervan's little sister, who stood barely five feet tall, faced off against a bearded behemoth. It was clear from his stance that his size was natural. It also looked like he didn't take his size advantage for granted, as he watched the much smaller woman carefully. Neither of them spoke, but Seline never did. She did, however, prefer to let her opponents make the first move, but the big guy didn't look like he would oblige.

No words were spoken, but everyone had cleared enough space if things became physical. Mervan rushed to the pair, and as he moved he saw Lee off to one side.

Lee never did know how to deal with his sister when there was trouble, which was Mervan's job.

Or if things were really bad, their father.

Even Seline didn't dare disobey their father.

"What's going on?" Mervan asked as he reached the pair.

"I have it under control," his sister replied. Her flat tone indicated she was ready to go.

"I don't want any trouble," the big man said.

"It's okay, sorry about this. Seline, let's go."

"This guy cheated."

"I did not!" the guy boomed.

"Hammer," a new voice intruded. Mervan turned and saw Julia approach. Her escort fanned out behind her.

"Seline, this isn't what we're here for."

He grabbed Seline's shoulder which she shrugged off. She had to turn to do so and he slipped between her and the man-mountain.

"Walk away, Seline."

She flashed her eyes angrily at him, but after a few tense seconds stalked to the bar. Mervan sighed, she'd want to get drunk but wouldn't be able to. That would just make her mood worse. It was time to return to their ships, better that she rage out of sight. He couldn't leave without a plan. They were here for a reason after all.

First he faced the big guy and offered an apology. Hammer waved it away, seemingly as quick to cool as he was to start. Mervan nodded his appreciation and then turned to Julia.

"Miss Cavus, I'm sorry for the disturbance."

She glanced at Hammer, who shrugged in response. It was over as far as he was concerned.

"Do you know me?"

"Only by reputation. Please allow me to offer my condolences on the death of your father."

"Thank you, now who are you?"

Mervan noticed that the pilots had strategically placed themselves to be able to provide support at a moment's notice. This wasn't the circumstance in which he wanted to speak to his niece for the first time.

"Can we talk somewhere a bit more private?"

"I think here is fine."

Up close, he recognised the weariness on her face.

"Okay, can we at least take one of the booths?"

She considered his request. He noted the doubt in her eyes. She was on her own turf, but she didn't know him. He stepped back to add space between them.

"I'm not here to cause trouble. I'm here to help."

She paused for a few seconds and then agreed. As they sat in one of the booths that lined one of the walls, Mervan activated a signal suppressor to block any electronic eavesdropping. Lee and Seline occupied another booth several metres away. The pilots joined Hammer's table and the card game resumed. Even as they played, they cast glances at the booth to ensure that Julia remained untroubled.

"So are you going to tell me who you are?"

"Of course. Once again I apologise for the situation. I really wanted to meet under better circumstances."

"Who are you?"

"There's no easy way to say this. My name is Mervan. Mervan Cavus and I'm your uncle."

"No, that can't be true. My father had no family."

"I know it's hard to accept, especially out of the blue like this. There were good reasons why he wouldn't have mentioned his family."

"Us? Who else is there?"

"Well you've just met my sister. Your aunt, I guess."

Seline would explode with fury if someone called her an aunt. The thought made him smile.

"Her?"

"I'm afraid so."

"Her?"

"Yes and the guy sat with her is also your father's brother. There were four of us."

"I don't understand. Why wouldn't he tell me?"

"He couldn't."

"I'm his daughter!"

"I'm sure it was hard for him. There were very good reasons why he couldn't talk about us."

"Nothing should stop him telling me that we have family." She paused for a moment. "Assuming that you are who you say you are."

"I assure you that…"

"I'm sure that you do, but it's suspicious that you should appear now of all times. What is it that you want?"

"The same as you. We've come to find the people who killed your father."

144

"Why? You've had no contact with him, have you?"

"No. Not for many years."

"Then why now?"

"Your father chose to leave us and while it was hard for us, we respected that. Now his choice doesn't matter, but we will kill those responsible."

"So you've said, but why didn't you come to me earlier?"

"We didn't want to intrude and to be honest I wanted our conversation to be private."

"So you followed me around for the afternoon waiting for your chance?"

Mervan nodded his head in understanding. He'd obviously underestimated the security team here. "Yes. I can see how that would look."

"Why didn't you just come to me?"

"Well, we have our own reasons for wanting to avoid attention."

"That went well for you."

"There were people looking for your father when he left us and by association they hunted for us too. We had to be cautious. Those people could be connected to what happened to your father."

Mervan wasn't happy with telling Julia a distortion of the truth. He still hoped that she could join the family and become more than her father had. As his original plan appeared to have failed, he improvised.

"Do you know who these people are?"

"No and that's the other reason we had to be careful approaching you. We believe that it's likely that you have somebody here on the station that is providing information to the attackers."

"That's impossible."

"I'm afraid not. I've seen it all too often."

"I know everyone here and I can guarantee that no-one would betray us in that way."

"What guarantee would you provide? The life of your

145

father?"

"You son of a bitch!"

"I know. It's an awful thing to say and I'm sorry. I truly am, but I am not joking when I say with absolute certainty that someone here is providing your enemy with information. Now before you deny it again, it's an easy thing to test."

"How?"

"Set up a trap."

"What type of trap?"

He felt pleased that she adapted so quickly. She might not want to believe it was true, but she'd also do what needed to be done.

"The only type of value, an easy score for them. Something that would hit the station hard. Then let word leak out and see if anyone takes the bait."

"That doesn't prove anything. They could have remote drones or even a ship nearby."

"So sweep the neighbourhood."

"We do, but there's no way to be certain."

Indeed there wasn't. Mervan knew that all too well as he had several surveillance drones in the local volume. "You're right, but those drones wouldn't be able to tell the significance of a vessel leaving the station."

"Why should I trust you?"

"You don't have to. I see that coming here the way we did wasn't the best approach. We'll leave tomorrow. First thing in the morning. You should test my theory for yourself and see what happens. Contact me if something shakes loose. When you find out who it is, we'll take care of it."

"Not a chance. I intend doing that myself."

"I know how you feel."

"No you don't!"

"Listen to me…"

"No! You listen to me. You follow me around all day,

and then claim that you're a long-lost relative and that my father has a past that created enemies. You don't tell me anything of value and you accuse the loyal people on this station of being traitors. You are leaving this station whoever you are, we do not need your help."

"Julia…"

"Leave now, or you'll be forced to leave."

"That would be a mistake."

"The mistake was listening to you at all. Now take your brother and sister and leave this place."

Mervan stood, Lee and Seline cfollowed him from the bar.

Plan B it would have to be.

- 15 -

The memory of the discussion with her supposed uncle plagued Julia's thoughts throughout the following morning. She didn't appreciate the irony of actually having a full night's sleep only to find the day filled with turmoil.

It started well enough with a light breakfast under Lina's watchful eye. The downhill slope began at the morning's flight briefing. It had been the first she'd attended since her father had sent her looking for pilots.

The four Sidewinder pilots welcomed her back. They'd given her the strength she needed to make it through the day before. Julia recalled with some embarrassment her behaviour towards Lina and was glad that the older woman forced her to attend the memorial. While grief still clouded her thoughts, she had at least achieved some small release during the ceremony.

The subsequent wake and the constant stream of condolences proved harder to endure. Not so much because of the sentiment. She appreciated everyone's depth of feeling and sympathy. Not only for her father, but that directed at her as well.

Since her tenth year, her father had formed the core of her life. After the death of her mother, she'd retreated and she'd only allow herself to be alone with Lina or her father. When she entered her teens, her father introduced her to flying. Not only did she discover a joy undreamt of inside the cockpit, she also discovered a new family amongst the pilots and the maintenance crew who readily adopted her and became her extended family.

Rob Deacon filled the role of kindly uncle. For a fighter pilot he was huge, although not quite as big as Hammer (Julia doubted that anyone who hadn't been gene-engineered could be!), but big enough that Julia didn't know how he squeezed into such a small cockpit when they first met.

The youngest of the four defence force pilots became like a big sister to Julia. San Kira was only a few years older than Julia and at first they hadn't got along at all. Julia recalled that she'd been little brat at the time and San didn't tolerate fools. With hindsight it seemed that was probably why her father asked her to help with Julia's flight training.

The threat of not being allowed to fly soon mellowed Julia's temperament, and eventually they became firm friends. It always surprised Julia that San stayed at Freeholm. To Julia, the woman seemed larger than the life offered at the station. Young as San was, she'd lived a full life and possessed a seemingly endless list of anecdotes from her adventures around the galaxy. Although San didn't share the exact details of how she ended up at Freeholm until they'd been friends for a few years.

The turnover of pilots in Freeholm's defence force was low, but of the four pilots only San and Rob had been there as long as Julia had been flying. The next pilot with the longest service was the colourful Delvin Reese. The other pilots came from military or law enforcement backgrounds whereas Delvin came from the other side of the fence.

He'd grown up as a pirate on the frontier of Alliance space and his tales exceeded San's for sheer extravagance. How he ended up as a defence force pilot was a story in itself. He'd grown up as a pirate in one of the many gangs which lurked in the darker regions of human space. He described himself as an ex-pirate, but for the most part his gang had been nomads. Nomadic spacers weren't unusual, but they weren't welcome in core systems. As a result they spent most of their time on the frontier or beyond in unpopulated space.

Julia hadn't known that her father had travelled so far. In truth, she knew little of his life before his incarceration at the prison colony. He avoided questions about his past. On her fifteenth birthday, he'd told her that he'd been convicted of murder and sentenced to life imprisonment. He explained that he'd been attacked by a pirate who turned out to be an undercover police operative. He'd killed the operative in self-defence. Unfortunately for him, the local law didn't allow such a defence for the killing of one of their own.

The real kicker had been that the crime occurred in a different jurisdiction. According to her father it took place in deep space. Strings had been pulled and her father was tried and convicted. At the time she'd accepted the injustice, as she'd lived most of her life in a world built upon injustice. Most of the prisoners in the colony were political. They had committed no crimes, and they just needed to be silenced.

From Delvin she learned that there was more to that story.

Her father lived with the nomad gang for several months. His injuries were severe and his recuperation took time. They also helped him rebuild his Eagle. Not the same one that he died in. That one had been left by the Laphrian Navy when they retreated from the colony.

Delvin was too young at the time to know the details, his understanding of the gang's life being a vague impression of adventure that spiced up the long boring journeys. An adventure, of course, isn't exciting with peril. The peril came from the authorities who didn't welcome nomads who wanted to trade. For the most part they were simply moved along.

Other agencies proved less enlightened, however the real peril arrived after they robbed the wrong transport. Sometimes you got lucky with piracy. Like a fat corporate transport full of useful spare parts and real food. Real food from an actual farm was a treat compared to their usual diet of processed algae, or if they were fortunate, food cartridges.

Sometimes you got really lucky and stole a credit-rich cargo of rare metals or minerals, and maybe some luxury goods. And sometimes you hit a big score and your luck took a nosedive because the richest scores were usually owned by the most dangerous people. There had been elation when the Frankenstein ship pirated a cargo of fine meats. They thought they'd hit the jackpot and a decent meal for a change.

That realisation chilled into fear the moment they found the drugs hidden within the meat. They ran immediately but it wasn't quick enough.

The mercenary flight of six Core Dynamics Dropships caught up with them within twelve hours. The nomad ship wasn't equipped for combat. It could defend itself, but not against six top-of-the-line heavy attack fighters. The Dropships were designed to enter hot assault zones and deliver marines under fire. They were heavily armoured and carried a lot of ordinance.

On the nomad ship was an old Sidewinder. A common small ship which the gang used as a runabout and in this case a limited line of defence. Her father's Eagle also waited in one of the hanger bays. He joined the battered Sidewinder against the mercenary attack.

Outgunned and outclassed, they bought enough time for the nomad ship to jump out of the system. The old man piloting the Sidewinder was less fortunate and her father almost didn't make it either. As the nomad ship jumped, he caught their slipstream and they kept jumping.

For a week they jumped from system to system. The

reach of the cartel stretched, but space stretches forever and with each jump they slipped a little further from their grasp. On two further occasions, her father scrambled to engage their pursuers until finally the cartel stopped the chase.

Of all the stories about her father that Julia heard that night, Delvin's shone the brightest. Sure, the novelty of a new memory compared to all the ones she'd heard a dozen times before helped raise it, but it was more than that. Since a young age she'd seen her father as a hero, but on a personal level which somehow contrasted with the general acclaim everyone around her.

Delvin saw her father the same way. He had been saved by her father who had also provided a new life for the young man.

Julia recognised the false logic in her thoughts. Most of the people around her owed their lives and their freedom to her father's actions. Yet somehow it felt different.

The flight briefing started well, although Gimna Thorne, the newest member of the defence force, was missing in action. He arrived at Freeholm less than three months ago. He'd already gained a reputation for over-indulging in drink and other intoxicants. He'd never missed a flight or even a briefing before though.

No flights were planned for today, but the memory of the visit from Mervan and her supposed uncle and aunt changed that. Whether or not they were really her father's siblings she didn't know, and at that moment it didn't matter. It seemed an extreme tale to weave, but there was definitely something about them that made her wary. An instinct that they represented some danger and that gave her pause. She just didn't want to believe that her father could be one of their breed, whoever they turned out to be.

No matter who they really were, they would soon depart the station. She'd checked the outgoing flights, they weren't heading inward and they hadn't contacted the Laphrian Navy to arrange escort. Not that that meant anything. She'd identified their ships and the two Vipers and a Fer de Lance could tackle anything the Artemis system was likely to throw at them.

They planned to head outward towards the gas giant beyond the belt. Why they were heading there presented a mystery. Julia thought it likely they just wanted to jump with lower chance of having the jump tracked. Wherever their destination, Julia would feel better knowing that they had left the system and if she could discover their destination then all the better. So rather than a day of rest, Delvin and Rob would fly a sweep following the siblings' flight path after they left.

With that change in the day's flight schedule, she prepared to leave the briefing room to meet with Piotr and Hammer. As she did so, Jon Mayborn asked her to join him in his office.

"How are you doing?" he asked her as they sat.

What could she say to such a question?

"Okay. Well no, not really."

He nodded his understanding. "I wanted to leave this for longer. To give you some time, but I need to ask you something."

"What do you need?"

"The station is without a head of security. I'm filling in for now, but my remit is really just station security. Sooner or later, and preferably sooner, we need someone to take over your father's job."

"I understand."

"Whoever instigated these attacks is still out there."

"I know that and I'm just on my way to meet with the two guns we've hired to plan our next move."

"We need more than that. We need someone to take control of our defence force. Someone the team can respect."

She thought about that before replying. Her only focus was finding whoever had killed her father. "I understand.

I'll work with whoever you have in mind. As long as I remain part of the operation."

"You misunderstand me. I've discussed this with the station council and they want you to take over your father's position."

That surprised her.

"No. I can't do that. I'm not my father."

"Of course not, but you would be perfect for the job."

"The team would never accept me as their leader."

"They already have, Julia, and I know your father wanted you to take over from him."

Another surprise.

"What?"

"We never discussed it in any detail, but he did mention it on a few occasions. He couldn't have imagined it would happen so quickly. Even so, we need move forwards."

"No, this is impossible."

"I realise it's a lot to take on board and I really wanted to leave it longer before I spoke to you about this. Unfortunately time isn't a commodity we have in abundance."

"I can't…"

"However you don't need to decide now. I can stall the council for a few days while you hunt for whoever is attacking us. I do urge you to consider taking the role. I understand that it's not something you even want to think about right now, but we do need you. So will you at least think about it?"

She'd known Jon Mayborn for almost a decade and he was one of her father's closest friends, so despite her misgivings she nodded her acceptance.

"I'll think about it."

"That's all I ask. Now find the bastards who killed your father."

While she walked to meet with Piotr and Hammer, she thought about the brief conversation with Mayborn. She'd never considered following in her father's footsteps beyond sharing their love of flying. Learning that her father wanted her to take over came as a surprise.

The idea conflicted with her dream to fly to the frontier and seek her own adventure. She didn't want to follow her father, she wanted her own life. None of that mattered for the moment. She couldn't go anywhere until she'd killed those responsible for her father's death.

Piotr and Hammer waited for her in one of the meeting rooms in the administration level. Julia guessed that Hammer and probably Piotr as well would have preferred meeting in the bar. She hadn't met anyone who could consume beer like Hammer.

"Who were the people last night?" Piotr greeted her as she walked through the door.

"What people?"

For a moment she forgot the visit from her 'uncle' and now that she did, she recalled his warning.

"Hammer told me about the three strangers in the bar last night. Who were they?"

Julia thought about what Mervan had said. He claimed that there had to be somebody helping her enemy here on the station. She didn't want to believe that was possible, but she could test the suggestion.

"Well?"

She now wondered why Piotr was being so pushy about it.

"They were nobody, just some passing mercenaries." She knew it was a terrible lie the moment she said it and tried to cover it. "They were friends of my father's and just wanted to pay their condolences."

Using her father's name to compound the lie sank hard in her stomach. A tiny voice inside her mind pleaded the case for Mervan and the two others. What if they were telling the truth? It seemed unlikely, but she didn't know Piotr either.

"I see. How long are they staying?"

"They're not, they left this morning. Two Vipers and a Fer de Lance."

Piotr looked at her sharply. "What did you say?"

"They left this morning."

"No, what ships are they flying?"

"They're flying two Vipers and a Fer de Lance."

"Shit! I need to go."

Julia was confused. "Go? Why?"

"Those three might be connected to the attacks."

This time Julia smelled a lie. "How do you know this?"

"I received some information from a contact yesterday."

"And you're only mentioning it now?"

"Things were busy yesterday."

"I could have been doing anything and you should still have interrupted me if you had information about who killed my father."

"I wanted to be sure. The information isn't solid."

"Well, what is the information?"

"Just some ship registrations. I'll track down these visitors and will report if it comes to anything."

He pushed his way past her and left the room. The idea of calling Flight Control and stopping Piotr's departure tempted her, but what if his information was correct? That thought made her sick. She could have been sitting with the person connected to her father's death.

That thought seemed as strange as Mervan being her uncle. None of this made sense. Hammer's large hand touched her shoulder, and he shrugged to indicate that he found it all a bit crazy too. She smiled although there was little warmth in it.

"Okay then, I have a plan," she said to him.

- 16 -

Hammer loved being in a crowded bar. He also appreciated his opinion being listened to and Julia had listened to him when they'd spoken earlier in the day. In fairness, they'd discussed a possible plan on the night that he'd signed up to Freeholm's cause. Her memory of that evening remained fragmentary at best. It always amused Hammer when people tried to keep up with him during a drinking session. He'd known men who took narcotic suppressants to puke before he'd even slowed down.

Still, she'd given it a good go and even better she wasn't a mean or a sad drunk. Hammer liked a fight but nothing annoyed him more than people who couldn't control themselves when they were drunk. So in their meeting, once the cold fish Piotr had rushed off after the mysterious visitors, Hammer reminded Julia of his speciality.

His Anaconda formed both bait and a trap. It presented a juicy target for hungry pirates, although after talking to people on the station he wasn't convinced that's what they were up against. Pirates didn't usually leave valuable cargo behind. It wasn't unprecedented though, occasionally pirate gangs became strong enough or organised enough to try and muscle in to a system and take it over. A rare event and unheard of for a system with a half-decent standing navy like Artemis.

Another possibility was that a pirate gang was making a play for Freeholm itself. A risky gambit as treaty limited

157

Freeholm's territory to the asteroid belt. However, it was valuable real estate considering the mineral wealth located here.

Hammer's gifts related more to tactical advantage than grand strategy. Over the years since his own father's death, he'd battled many pirate gangs and defeated them all. On every occasion he had done so on his own. This would be the first job working with others, for the preparation stages at least.

The train of thought returned him to when his father had been killed. A gang of pirates operating on the Federation-Alliance border ambushed his father's Anaconda (the same one that Hammer now operated) in a dark system he used as a waypoint for one of his trade runs. The pirates had been a ruthless gang.

In the past, piracy usually included murder. That practice had evolved over the years. The pirates finally learned that they could harvest traders more than once if they didn't kill them. Combined with the increased law enforcement presence throughout human space, this both moderated pirate behaviour and pushed it out to less populated regions.

Things changed once again with the invention the new hyperdrives. They could now jump between systems almost instantly. This required navies and law enforcement to change their tactics. Although the new drives did give them one advantage: jumps arrived within the gravity well of a star. Or a massive enough planet if it was isolated enough, such as in many dark systems. The volume was still huge but at least more manageable than a volume filling an entire system.

Most pirates now followed a code. Admittedly not one understood by most of the population but at least a trader could generally expect to survive an act of piracy, as long as they submitted to the their demands. New devices like the limpets also enabled pirates to steal cargo without destroying their target.

Not so with the scum who'd attacked his father's ship. They'd disabled the engines and weapons and then boarded the ship. Once inside they murdered his father and the crew, leaving their bodies to rot while they transferred their booty from the cargo hold.

Two weeks later, a bounty hunter discovered the wrecked ship and called it in. Hammer had a real name back then and guilt had pushed him on the quest to kill those who'd murdered his father. A typical story for many sons and daughters of independent traders, most followed their parents' paths. Others, like Hammer, rebelled and went their own way.

For Hammer, rebellion meant a life planetside on one of the bountiful outdoor worlds. He's grown up in the old ship and while the Anaconda was a large vessel, it always seemed small to the young Hammer. He dreamed of living on a world and working with the land with a blue sky above his head.

And when he reached adulthood, that's what he did.

He signed up for a ten-year contract with a corporate farming facility. Most of the work was automated but even so he loved every minute of it. The work was hard, but he thrived under the open sky and he'd found his place in the universe.

Naturally the choice disappointed his father, although he'd still supported his son's decision. When Hammer learned of his father's death, the choice he'd made tasted bitter. The thought lurking in the depths of his soul was that he should have been there.

The common sense part of him knew that it wouldn't have made any difference. After all, he hadn't been a fighter. Not then.

He brought himself back to the present and the bustle of the bar around him. This wasn't his usual type of place. Almost every orbital had one. They called them 'Zero-G Bars' although technically it was extremely low gravity rather than zero-gravity. They were positioned on the centre line of a station to avoid the gravity created by a station's spin.

These places were usually the centre of any underground or counter culture in a station community. In Freeholm's case that meant practically naked teenagers with the latest fashion in magnetic boots. The new fad placed repulsion at the core of the gloves and boots worn by these youngsters. They used these to perform all manner of acrobatics.

Sitting amongst these overactive youngsters made Hammer feel old. He admitted to himself that they were a delight to watch. He wasn't such a fan of the music though. A loud din of discordant notes assaulted his ears with anti-instruments. He'd heard about this music trend on the newsfeeds. Apparently you take a perfect tone for a note and then subtract the same note from the chosen instrument. It created a shadow of the original sound and as far as Hammer was concerned, a headache-inducing mess.

He could have suffered the loud noises with better grace if only he could order a decent drink. Without gravity you couldn't properly enjoy a decent glass of beer. In an upmarket zero-G bar he'd once visited, they had these amazing glasses. They appeared solid, but were actually an engineered foam. The smart material detected when it was tipped and when lips touch the rim. When that happened, nanoscale pumps pushed the liquid into your mouth.

It still didn't taste or feel quite right, but Hammer thought it pretty clever all the same. So much so that he stole one of the glasses and it now owned pride of place in his galley. In this dive they lacked anything quite so sophisticated. Here the drinks were pouches with straws. A technology that had barely changed for a thousand years.

You couldn't drink beer through a straw.

Well you could, but it just wasn't right.

Hammer gave it a damn good try anyway. There was no way he would drink whatever manufactured rubbish the kids around him were getting high on. Besides, he had to make it clear to everyone around him what a good time he was having. This formed the first part of the plan he discussed with Julia earlier.

To be the bait, they needed to make sure that the bad guys knew who to target. They didn't know how the enemy were gathering their information and Julia remained adamant that it wasn't anyone on the station. Even so, she asked him to get drunk and tell everyone that he was departing the station tomorrow with a cargo hold of refined precious metals.

He'd already registered his departure with Flight Control. It wasn't a requirement but often Flight Control preferred large ships to pre-register to avoid congestion or accidents. The list could also be accessed by the public. He also registered his transit into Laphrian-controlled space with Captain Belin, still on patrol near the belt.

Hammer happily agreed to the bar crawl. He tended to do that when visiting a new station anyway. In his opinion, if you knew the bars then you'd also know the people of the station. Well, the people he'd likely interact with.

This first bar of the tour was this loud and excitable pack of kids. He wouldn't stay long, just enough for a few drinks. The bar did have one gimmick, hardly an original one, but one that aided his purpose. It was completely automated, a hub of activity at the centre of the large space. With no gravity chairs needed, it was far more comfortable to float in mid-air.

Tables were also superfluous as people let their drinks float beside them. The youngsters formed organic clusters that shifted as people moved from one group to the next. Inbetween them, people showed off their tricks with crazy displays of acrobatic dance. Guests were each assigned a serving drone, a small sphere that responded to voice input and fetched drinks from the bar.

Hammer noticed that the regulars ignored theirs and summoned them as needed. Hammer quite liked the attentive ball, especially the way it bobbed away when he bellowed a drink order at it.

"Another and quickly. I'm on a special run tomorrow and I'm enjoying my last night in port!"

He guessed that the unsubtle words fell on deaf ears in this venue. It was the first of many so he didn't mind too much, although he hoped he'd be able to get bigger drinks at the other bars. Besides scaring his serving drone, the bellows disturbed the young drinkers around him. At first a few had mocked, quietly of course. An eyebrow-framed stare cowered them into silence and now they flinched whenever his voice boomed.

They only served small drinks in this bar, so he bellowed an order every few minutes.

While his silver-plated drone buzzed off to retrieve a tiny and overpriced beer in a pouch, he thought about Julia. He'd been in the same situation Julia now found herself, and like her he focused on revenge. When it finally arrived it felt as if a great weight lifted from him, unfortunately it left a hollowness in its wake.

Strange that he'd not realised it before. He travelled from one system to another acting as bait to draw out and kill pirates. Not a bad living, some would say. Maybe even a noble one. But years ago he hadn't even wanted to be in space and now he spent more time in the ship than his father had.

He drained the pouch of beer in a single swallow and like the seven before, it failed to satisfy. The reflection of Julia's loss highlighted the rut his own life had fallen into. The loud binges provided a contrast to the lonely life in space. He looked at the crowd around him, they looked like they enjoyed life.

Well most of them did anyway, a few of the nearest kept glancing at him nervously. He didn't mind that too much.

He'd avenged his father and he'd help Julia avenge hers. Hopefully if they succeeded quickly enough then she wouldn't end up on the same course that he had.

After so long, the memories of his life working the land resurfaced. They felt alien, like somebody else's memories. He bellowed for another drink, there was plenty for him to think about but first he had a job to do. This would be his last drink in this bar, he hoped that the next served proper beer and maybe some food.

- 17 -

Captain Belin reviewed the action board. They only had one rendezvous listed. Traffic to Freeholm had been light over the last week, not that it was ever that heavy. There was usually a ship or two a day. The recent attacks had clearly frightened trade away and while it made his life easier, he worried about the effect on the station.

The station had been visited by three ships that he assumed to be more bounty hunters coming to help with their own investigation. Unlike the other ships they refused an escort to the belt, politely but also emphatically. Two Vipers and a Fer de Lance represented a decent combat capability so they probably didn't need the escort.

As a matter of course, Belin had his intelligence officer conduct background checks on the pilots. Nothing came back beyond the bare minimum required by interstellar treaty for identification. If they were bounty hunters then were secretive about it. Such secrecy wasn't completely unheard of in the business, but it was unusual enough to notice.

Following the same hunch, he ordered a trace on the ship registrations. Such searches were less reliable than a personal identity check, it was much easier to disguise the registrations of a ship. In reality it was relatively easy to do the same with a personal identity, it just cost more money and came under more scrutiny.

An instinct tempted Belin to hold the three ships even though he had no real pretext to do so. To have done so would no doubt have resulted in more trouble with Fleet

Command.

The investigation into the attacks hadn't revealed anything new and more frustratingly, Belin thought he was being marginalised in the investigation. Scratch that, he'd been shut out completely. Something wider appeared to be at play here. All information gathered on the attacks had been restricted. Even the data collected by his own ship. Which also seemed a bit odd and pointless considering they had local backups of the same data.

He'd made several requests for updates on the investigations. So far they'd all been denied. This morning an angry captain from Navy Intelligence ordered him to drop the requests. His office would handle the investigation and any interference would not be welcome. Belin continued, this time through his fleet commander who repeated the same message.

A life in the Navy prepared Belin for some of the idiosyncrasies of bureaucracy. Certain departments guarded their areas of responsibility jealously, but he'd never encountered active resistance like this before.

Those obstructions alone annoyed him, but the events in conjunction with the technology demonstrated on the encounter before Commander Cavus's death worried him. Belin believed that the malfunctions in the frame shift drive were caused deliberately. He didn't know how as any form of interdiction technology released identifiable traces.

Belin knew that technology capable of disrupting the frame shift drive undetected and on a large scale would provide a significant advantage for those that possessed it. The frame shift drive had caused the biggest shift in naval strategy for centuries. The ability to nullify it at will would provide a huge advantage.

He knew it seemed farfetched and, considering the issues he'd encountered with his command of late, he decided to be more circumspect with his inquiry. He contacted an old friend from the academy who now worked in the special weapons division. He doubted that he'd learn anything concrete but perhaps he'd at least receive some indication if he was on the right track.

"Captain," his executive officer interrupted his thoughts.

"What is it?"

"We've received a priority mission alert."

"And?"

"Well, I'm not sure. We've been tasked with responding to a distress call."

"That's unusual, but not unknown. Where's the call originating from?"

"The position is two AU east along the belt."

"Who's in trouble?"

"Unknown. The squawk identifies them as a corporate freighter. That's not what's strange though."

"Don't make me guess."

"No sir. It's the signal, we haven't received it."

"So?"

"A distress signal is always sent in the clear and in wideband so we should have received the signal."

"So we don't have a confirmation on the signal?"

"No."

"Did you confirm with Fleet Command?"

"Of course and they repeated that it was a priority tasking."

"What about our rendezvous with the Anaconda from Freeholm?"

"We can't cover both, sir."

"Understood. See if you can find out anything more about the distress call. Set course for the signal source and contact Freeholm and provide them with a new time for the handover."

"Yes sir."

"Carry on."

"Sir, there's an incoming message for you."

"From Command?"

"No, Commander Sterling."

"Patch it through."

Miles Sterling studied in the same class as Belin in the academy, Belin was surprised that he'd responded to the message so quickly. He waited for his first officer to leave before accepting the call.

"Miles, how are you?"

"Good evening Stefan. This isn't a social call I'm afraid."

"What's going on?"

"The message you sent me earlier."

"Do you have something for me?"

"I do, but it's not what you're hoping for."

"Well?"

"You have to stop this line of enquiry."

"Why? What do you know?"

"I don't know anything, but I do want to give you a friendly warning."

"A warning for what?"

"Stefan, you have to drop it."

"I can't, something very strange is going on out here."

"I don't know what's going on."

"Yet you know enough that you have to warn me."

"I'm trying to help you here, Stefan. We've been friends for many years and I know you've had a hard time of it because of your actions in the coup."

"I'm fine."

"No you're not. You're a captain of a border patrol vessel. You should be in command of the whole area of operations. You stuck your head above the parapet and your career has suffered for it."

"I had to act."

"I know you did, but as you know there have been consequences. If you continue your current path then at best you'll end up captaining a desk."

"Who is this coming from, Miles?"

"What do you mean?"

"You don't know anything, yet you're warning me off. Who told you to speak to me?"

"Stefan, no-one told me to speak to you. I looked into what you sent me and the level of security I encountered was enough to warn me off. There's an operation in progress and one with the highest security clearance. I wish I did have something to give you. Something to make you drop whatever it is you're looking into."

"I can't."

"Well then be careful. Be very careful."

"I'll try."

His friend vanished from the screen as the call ended and Belin sat back in his chair. He wanted to believe that his friend had been sincere in his warning. Miles played the political game better than he did although he'd always been honest before. Miles didn't scare easily, so something big or at least very well connected was going on.

The warning wouldn't make a difference though. Three people were dead. One of whom Captain Belin respected. The problem now was how to continue his investigation. His old friend had been his hope for a discreet line into what was going on.

Miles was correct about one thing. Belin's career was restricted to line duty which meant that he lacked the range of contacts he needed in something like this. He'd followed the rules throughout his career, except for the coup. Over the years he noticed that his progression seemed slower than that of his colleagues.

Officially his involvement in the coup hadn't resulted in any censure. The coup had been popular with the civilian population, even those who'd benefitted from the old regime had publicly supported the change. The coup enjoyed little support from the military's upper echelons at the time, although they were sensible enough to go with the flow of public opinion.

As well as being marred by his involvement in the coup, Belin suspected another cause of his stifled career. It often appeared that it was a case of who you knew rather than your performance ratings. Belin had never been willing to play the politics game, he just wanted to do his duty and he believed that he did that well.

The same duty compelled him not to give up on his investigation.

He called up his personal contacts list to see if any names sparked inspiration. The list was long, but heavily weighted towards fellow combat officers. He lacked significant intelligence and security or, more importantly, command staff level contacts. He highlighted and reviewed their files of few that he had. It wouldn't be sensible to just contact them all, he would need to be more circumspect.

He was still reviewing his contacts when the first officer contacted him over the internal comms system.

"Yes."

"Captain, we're approaching the distress signal."

"Have we identified the source?"

"Not yet."

"All right. I'm coming to the bridge now."

The *Demeter* re-entered normal space as Captain Belin arrived on the bridge.

"What do we have?" he asked the bridge officers.

"Sir," the tactical officer replied, "we're at the designated coordinates and there's nothing on the sensors."

"Any trace of the signal?"

"Nothing."

"Did Command send a copy of the distress signal?"

"No sir," the communications officer answered. "They just sent the coordinates and that it was a corporate freighter in distress."

"I see, did you contact Freeholm to tell them to reschedule the handover?"

"Yes sir."

"And?"

"They acknowledged the message."

"Okay. Helm start a sweep pattern at full burn. Let's do a quick search. Tactical, deploy a sweep of recon drones on a wide dispersal to half maximum range. When they hit bingo fuel they should auto-recover with the ship."

"Yes sir."

"Comms, connect me with Fleet Command."

"Patching you through, sir."

Belin waited for the few seconds for the channel to be connected and secured. He moved to the rear of the bridge and into a small office to keep the conversation private from the bridge crew. It never looked good for officers to be seen arguing and Belin intended to make his opinion clear. He considered the assignment a waste of time and he wanted to know why.

"Hello *Demeter,* this is Lieutenant Kellerman. What can we do for you, Captain?"

"Put me through to the ranking duty officer."

"Of course sir. What is this regarding?"

"Just put me through."

"Sir, I need to know what the problem is."

"Put me through now."

"Sir, you have to tell me what this is about."

"I'm giving you an order, Lieutenant. Now put the ranking duty officer on the line."

"Yes sir."

Another wait, this one stretched to three minutes.

"Captain Belin, this is Admiral Skinner."

Belin automatically snapped to attention at the woman's voice. He'd expected a commander, maybe a captain. An admiral was too high in the food chain to be the ranking duty officer.

"Yes ma'am."

"Why are you demanding to speak to the ranking duty officer?"

"Sir, it's about the re-tasking of my ship."

"Your ship, Belin? Strange, I'm sure that it's a Laphrian Navy vessel."

"Of course ma'am."

"Sir is fine, or if you prefer – 'Admiral'."

"Yes sir."

"Well, what is the problem?"

"We've arrived at the destination indicated in the orders and there's nothing here."

"So, have you searched the area?"

"We're executing a sweep of the area now, sir."

"Good, although I'm still waiting for you to explain the problem."

"Sir, there was no source of the signal and we didn't detect it on our approach either."

"It was a burst transmission, Captain, and we don't explain orders to you. We send them to you and you execute them."

"Yes Admiral."

"In case it wasn't clear to you, we expect a full sweep of the region. We are developing improved relationships with several mega-corporations and we need to demonstrate how seriously we will protect their investment within our system."

"Of course, Admiral. We're supposed to be providing an escort for a trader leaving Freeholm."

"That's not your concern, Captain."

"But sir…"

"Not your concern, Captain. Conduct a full sweep of the area and then return to base."

"Return to Laphria, sir?" The crew would be happy to hear that news.

"Yes Captain. I have some good news for you. You will be taking delivery of one of the first new ships from the Gutamaya shipyards."

"Sir?"

"Commend your crew, Captain. You have all done a

wonderful job on this and on your previous patrols. You and two other crews have been selected to become the vanguard of the Laphrian fleet."

The news stunned Belin.

"I don't know what to say, Admiral."

"Keep up the good work, Captain, and we'll see you at Fleet Command in two days. Admiral Skinner out."

- 18 -

Piotr increased the Viper's thrust to maximum and put full pips into the engines. No doubt there was a speed restriction in the station's approach paths but he didn't care. He was furious and convinced that Julia Cavus had deliberately avoided telling him about the visitors. If he hadn't asked, he was sure that she wouldn't have told him at all.

His rage lessened slightly when Freeholm's flight control opened a secure connection and fed his system with tactical data from their data net. It flared again as he realised that the ships were three hours ahead of him. It couldn't be a coincidence that three ships of that configuration visited the station with a family of the name 'Cavus'. They had to be the trio of assassins he'd hunted for so long.

The feed from the station indicated that the three ships were heading towards the far edge of the belt. It was a longer journey than to the inner border, although from the system map it looked like a less-monitored route to jump out of the system.

Accessing the network, Piotr requested data on the three visitors. He discovered that his access was limited and he could only see the public registration information for the ships. They were the correct types, but beyond that he couldn't be sure.

He connected with the Pilots Federation database and fed the three ship registrations into the system. Hyperspace comms were low-bandwidth compared to the local communication channels, but even so the search results were returned within a few minutes. They provided a summary of the systems the ships had been tracked in.

According to the list, they'd passed through only three systems, a fact that Piotr considered unlikely.

The pilots he chased must either be using fake ship registrations, or were able to edit their history somehow. That required top level access within the Pilots Federation, or a high order of hacking ability, or enough credits to buy either of the first two options. For Piotr this made it even more likely that these were the trio he'd hunted all this time.

If they were and there was a connection to the station, then why had Julia allowed him to pursue? Perhaps there was a deeper game at play that he couldn't see. Or maybe too deep for the young woman to comprehend.

From the data net he also learned that two of the Sidewinders followed the three ships. Now he wondered why Julia had sent the patrol after them. Were they providing protection? The connection also provided a secure datalink with the two Sidewinders and, even better, a narrowband signal so contacting them wouldn't alert his prey.

He considered contacting the Freeholm pilots, until he realised that if there was some trick at play then they'd already know of his presence. He asked what their orders were and their reply informed him that they would track the departing ships to confirm that they did leave the system.

This eased his suspicions of Julia's motives, although it didn't remove them completely. His ship's computer plotted the course of the five ships ahead of him. The three ships burned at maximum thrust and were almost at the outer border of the belt already. The Sidewinders followed at a more leisurely pace. They would have to cease their pursuit at the belt's edge, unless Julia had ordered them to cross the legal boundary.

Piotr considered that unlikely.

He, however, was not so constrained.

The computer provided intercept estimates. They indicated that the Sidewinders couldn't catch up with the three ships before they left the belt. They didn't need to, their mission was to ensure that the ships departed Freeholm space.

Piotr wondered what the defence force pilots would do if the departing ships changed their minds and turned around. They should have been grateful that Piotr had joined them. On their own they wouldn't stand a chance. For that matter, even with Piotr's help the three of them would be hard-pressed to survive an engagement.

Which presented Piotr with his own dilemma. If they did return to the belt and attacked the Sidewinders, then Piotr would leave the Sidewinders to their fate. On this case, simple mathematics forced the decisions. No, the more pressing problem was for when the three ships entered interplanetary space.

From the interception estimates, he knew that he would catch them some time after they departed the belt. His was the faster ship, the expensive upgrades and improved power distribution capability provided the extra thrust he needed to overtake them.

What would he do then?

That posed a problem. Even with the two Sidewinders and his own custom-enhanced Viper, he couldn't defeat two Vipers and a Fer de Lance. His sensors couldn't resolve any more than their heat and power output at this extended range. He'd be willing to bet that their ships were extensively modified as well.

The best case scenario would be that the three ships jumped once they were no longer mass locked by the asteroids. If they assumed him to be part of the Freeholm defence force then they'd believe that he couldn't follow them. He could then trace their jump destination with his hyperspace cloud analyser.

He still had the problem though. What to do when he caught them?

Even with the perfect scenario, the timing would be critical. If he pursued too closely then he'd leave himself vulnerable to a counterattack. On the other hand, if he was too cautious then he might not get a solid trace for their jump destination. That wouldn't be a total disaster as long as he was close enough to catch the vector of the jump. He called up the galaxy map and saw that this wasn't a densely populated region of space so it should be easy to compute the destination.

He then remembered that they could easily change vector in supercruise which would throw his calculations out of kilter. He could track them, but only if they didn't jump before he entered supercruise himself.

An opportunity like this wouldn't come again so he had to take a chance. They'd almost certainly change vectors. If they were who he suspected then they'd make sure to disguise their trail as much as they could. The following Sidewinders had run hot trying to keep up with them and he'd done the same so they would know that they were being pursued. He maintained maximum burn, pushing his engines beyond their stated capacity.

The three ships exited the belt. The following Sidewinders broke off their pursuit and entered a looping patrol course as they watched what the departing ships would do next.

The three ships could jump at any moment, while he wouldn't be clear of the gravitational effect of a nearby asteroid cluster for several minutes. Piotr cursed, knowing that if they jumped now he'd have to rely on the hyperspace cloud trace. A trace that would become more diffuse with each passing minute.

The ships didn't enter supercruise immediately and for a moment Piotr thought that he might have a chance to catch them. That chance vanished as he burst out of the belt and the three ships frame shifted. He cursed loudly. The timing made him think that the three pilots were taunting him.

When a ship jumped, it created a cloud of energised particles from the transition. The alignment of the particles provided a vector for the jump's destination which the computer could resolve into a destination. The cloud dispersed quickly and the time window to get a decent lock was small, so he maintained full thrust until he approached the jump point.

As he arrived, he cut the engines so that the ion exhaust wouldn't interfere with the cloud. He activated the analyser and waited for the computer to complete the calculations. The computer took longer than usual to finish the scan and Piotr feared that he'd been too slow to reach the cloud.

He waited impatiently until the name of the Crevit system popped up on the holographic display panel.

Piotr knew full well that the three pilots could ambush him in the next system. He couldn't wait though as it was just as likely that they had jumped again. The easiest way to break a hyperspace trail was to jump several times in quick succession. It took longer to locate and scan the cloud than it did to perform the jump.

Piotr locked the destination and watched the frame shift drive charge up until the ship snapped into supercruise. Seconds later, he arrived next to the star in the Crevit system. He set his power distribution to maximum shields and the rest into engines, ready to manoeuvre if he was attacked.

He breathed easier when no incoming had struck his ship. He checked his scanner and saw nothing. It was remotely possible that the ships were out of range, but to have done so they would be at maximum thrust which would have lit them up for everyone to see.

The scan revealed no cloud remnants either. Maybe he had missed them somehow. He couldn't imagine how he hadn't arrived well within the decay limit.

There must be a problem with the hyperspace cloud analyser. Strange that it wasn't reporting a malfunction. He'd arrange for the technicians at Freeholm to service the module when he returned to the station.

With most of the day wasted, he wasn't in the best mood when he hyperspaced back in to the Artemis system. He ignored the Navy patrol's offer of an escort to the belt. In the mood he was in, he'd have welcomed a pirate attack. Piotr realised that he had an appearance to maintain so didn't rush back to the station when he arrived at the belt from hyperspace.

He flew at a leisurely pace through the asteroids. The lazy manoeuvres helped soothe his anger at losing the three ships. His first real lead since the hunt began and it had slipped through his fingers.

On the plus side, it at least proved that the connection with the name had some merit after all. It had seemed like a long shot after months of fruitless searching. Piotr didn't think that it was a coincidence that they had turned up when they did. There must be some connection between them and Darik Cavus. Or maybe Julia.

Either way, he needed to involve himself more in whatever was happening at Freeholm. He'd kept himself aloof from the others as he expected to just pass through this backwater system. He didn't feel comfortable with the idea of having to stay and involve himself with the people here. After the years alone on the hunt, the habit of being with people had slipped away.

To avenge Sahiba he would undergo any discomfort.

Flight Control granted him clearance as he arrived at the station and as soon as he docked he contact station services, who connected him with someone to check the cloud analyser. If the opportunity arose again, he didn't want a faulty module to ruin his chances of following them.

Piotr also realised that if they operated as a team,

he'd need backup. From his years as a bounty hunter he had a long list of contacts for capable pilots with equally capable ships. Before leaving the ship, he sent a few messages to see who might be available at short notice. He'd need to spend some credits, but that didn't bother him.

He made sure to set the ship security to allow access for the technician. He also set the system to log any changes made. If the technician tried anything unexpected then Piotr would know about it. As he left the ship, he enabled the remote operation link.

With the ship secure, he took a lift from the docking bay up the administration level. Piotr intended to start making himself more useful immediately. First he'd see what developments had occurred during his absence and then he would see how he could enhance their efforts. This was a nothing system in the middle of nowhere. Whoever was making some sort of play against Freeholm would likely be some small-time player. Finding whoever it was and stopping them should ingratiate him with the station and more importantly Julia.

If he could gain her trust then maybe she would reveal the connection with the three pilots. And if that didn't work then he could always take more extreme measures.

When he arrived at the security offices, the lack of Julia or the pilots surprised him. An even bigger surprise came as he almost walked into a woman and recognised her as he turned to apologise. He saw recognition flash across her face too, although she reacted swifter than he did and pushed him into an empty adjoining office.

"What the hell? Marcie?"

You could never forget a woman like this. She looked different. But some things you couldn't disguise and disguise was an important tool of the trade for an Imperial Intelligence operative.

"They know me as Dee Callum here."

Piotr looked confused for a moment before he realised

what she meant.

"Of course."

"I recognised your name on the flight control computers. I wanted to speak to you in less public surroundings. I didn't expect to see you so quickly."

"I don't understand."

"I think you do, Piotr Vanchenko. If you don't, then need you to understand."

His brain couldn't be working, but the penny finally dropped. Perhaps there was some advantage to be gained here.

"Naturally, your real identity is safe with me."

"Of course it is. As is your secret with me."

Piotr returned to a state of confusion. Dee happily aided his understanding.

"I didn't remember who you were at first. However, there have been a few new faces around here recently so I ran your name through the system. Some interesting facts came back, including our previous encounter."

"Okay, but what are you doing here? Have you left the service?"

"My purpose here is of no relevance to you. More importantly I know why you are here. You aren't here to help these locals, you have your own quest. Now, I can be a big help you and I'm sure you understand that without any unpleasantness."

He nodded, an Imperial Intelligence agent could be a very useful ally. "And I'm sure you can be of use to me."

"Of course. I'm always happy to help a man on a quest."

- 19 -

Once they departed the station, Mervan wondered what Julia would do next. Considering how angry she'd been the night before, she would most likely make sure that they left the belt. He'd hoped that the first meeting with his niece would have gone more smoothly. Clearly he'd handled the encounter badly. Things always looked clearer with hindsight. As his father would say, "You can't change what has happened. You can only turn it to your advantage."

So how to turn the situation to their advantage?

Mervan wasn't as confident of his reading of Julia as he needed to be. Two things were clear though. She planned to avenge her father and she wanted the three siblings away from her station.

She'd hired the bounty hunter, and the big guy in the bar wasn't a local. When Mervan returned to their lodgings, he ran a search and learned more about Mark Lamon. Julia now had two heavy hitters on her side along with the local defence force, although they weren't much to brag about. The details on Lamon revealed not only his call sign of 'Hammer' but some of his history as well. This 'Hammer' had a history of fighting pirates. He drifted from system to system and took on pirate gangs on his own.

His ship was the beat-up looking Anaconda docked in Freeholm's docking bay. The profile indicated that he was a successful pirate hunter, in an Anaconda that meant he took on pirate hideouts, or he played a Trojan horse. The latter option seemed more likely and with that information Mervan suspected what Julia's plan would be.

And there was something he could take advantage of.

Seline and Lee flanked him as they set course towards the outer rim of the asteroid belt. During previous visits, he laid a series of surveillance and recon drones in the belt around Freeholm. He couldn't risk exposing this network so he was forced to rely on his ship's sensors.

He flew at half thrust, which with the performance upgrades to his Fer de Lance meant that the two Vipers alongside had to push their engines to remain in formation.

Not long after their departure, two new targets registered on his scanner. His system identified them as two Sidewinders. The profiles matched those he'd tracked from the station before. He throttled back a bit and his brother and sister followed suit.

For his ruse to work he needed Julia to believe that they had left the system. He had no intention of doing so. To jump out would mean having to jump back in and pass through Laphrian space and that would inconvenience them.

They flew a direct path as they weren't trying to hide their presence. Around them the asteroids passed by. This was less densely populated area compared to the region around Freeholm so they didn't even need to make any real effort to avoid them.

Naturally Seline bitched throughout the journey. When her voice grated too much, he muted her transmission. Lee didn't and Mervan wondered where his brother got the patience from. She might be his sister but any length of time Mervan spent with her swiftly became a test of endurance.

In the short time since she learned about Darik's death, she'd grown worse. Seline had always possessed an abrasive personality, always eager to wound those around her with derisory comments. When not attacking others, she liked to complain. Over the years she'd developed the ability to complain to a fine art.

He understood that he should be more patient. He'd been the eldest and supposedly the sensible one of the three for all these years. The family had been more balanced before Darik left, even with the family business. His departure fractured the bonds between them. Their father's domineering discipline and Mervan's constant attention kept them together. It had taken its toll on Mervan and only in the past few days had he come to realise that.

A new contact blinked into view on his scanner. It flashed for a few minutes, the point dancing as the computer attempted to resolve the target. To be visible at this distance meant it was throwing out considerable heat.

Only a few ships besides the defence force Sidewinders were docked when the three of them departed the station. An old Cobra Mk III which Mervan assumed to belong to a local trader. There was the big guy's Anaconda and the bounty hunter's Viper. Julia's Eagle was also docked although neither that or the Anaconda would generate a heat signature like the one registered by the scanner.

The Cobra was a possibility. Maybe a local trader picking a different route to avoid the pirates. The other option was Vanchenko's Viper and if he was responding to a call then this wasn't the fastest way out of the belt.

He warned his brother and sister that they might have more than the local law following them and that they would be changing direction for a while to see who shook loose.

They changed bearing and the two Sidewinders altered their course to match. As did the unidentified signal. Twenty minutes later the target resolved into the Viper. Mervan couldn't be certain that it was the bounty hunter but it seemed like a reasonable assumption.

While they continued towards interplanetary space, Mervan pondered why the hunter chased after them. His thoughts led him to two possibilities. The first and probably the most likely reason was that Julia had sent them to back up the defence force pilots. It made the most sense from her perspective at any rate. The two Sidewinders couldn't handle the three of them if they decided to return to the station.

Would they have even tried to stop them?

Vanchenko and his Viper didn't even the odds, but it did tip the balance enough to make it something other than swift annihilation for the Sidewinders.

Mervan considered the other possibility to be unlikely, although with more troubling potential. He wondered if the bounty hunter was chasing them rather than simply helping the defence force. His father paid substantial bribes to ensure that bounties were never applied to the family's ships. That took more than a huge number of credits, it also required the right contacts.

When they reached the outer edge of the belt several hours later, the Sidewinders turned to stay within the asteroids. Mervan had familiarised himself with the local treaties and had expected the defence force fighters to remain within their territory.

He also expected the Viper to do the same.

It didn't and that worried Mervan.

They would need to perform the fake jump earlier than planned. He informed Lee and Seline of the change in plan. They manoeuvred into position as if they were slipstreaming his jump. He initiated the frame shift drive and they entered supercruise. He deployed a jump drone.

The drones were incredibly expensive. Mostly due to the drone's ability to mimic the jump signature of most small and medium-sized ships. The energy required disintegrated the drone and left no trace except the hyperspace cloud wake. On its own the device wouldn't complete the deception, they would either have to disguise their presence in supercruise or drop out without being detected.

Stealth in supercruise was practically impossible. The energy required to keep in frame shift lit a ship up across a star system. Dropping out without being detected was equally difficult except in a few specific circumstances. The most important of which was having the people watching you on a single vector and preferably to their rear.

Mervan had planned for just that circumstance and with the Sidewinders confined to the belt, that would have been simpler to execute. With the bounty hunter chasing them into open space, the manoeuvre became a bit trickier.

They were committed now in any case, so when Mervan deployed the hyperspace decoy drone they all performed an emergency stop. The moment they dropped into normal space, Lee and Seline deployed their cloaks behind them.

The cloaks were another expensive item that could only be purchased from a few select shipyards. With the decoy and the cloaks this mission was costing the family more than most of their usual operations and without a payoff.

Family business had to be completed, no matter the cost.

For all of its expense, the cloak was a simple device. An ultrathin material deployed in micro-seconds into a giant sail behind the ship like a drogue parachute. The cloak was comprised of two layers. The inside was a smart material designed to reflect energy. The outer layer did the opposite and absorbed energy. It also contained microstructures that flickered with minuscule heat readings to emulate the tiny region of space it hid.

In essence the cloak provided a barrier to block a chasing ship's view. The million-credit price tag was so steep because of the deployment speed needed to work. Even deploying in micro-seconds, an observant watcher could catch the flash of energy from the crash stop before the cloak deployed.

It also had a tactical disadvantage. It not only blocked a following ship's view of the deploying craft, the reverse was also true.

So the three of them were blind after they crashed back into real space. They immediately shut down their systems to reduce the heat generation of the ships. Their heat output stabilised and then fell so they were safe to button up their heat vents for a longer period than normal. At the same time they deactivated their flight assist so their ships coasted along without automatic input from the ship's computers.

They couldn't remain buttoned up for long. Eventually the heat build inside the ship would start damaging their ships' systems. They waited as long as they could and then, at his command, they feathered their thrusters to move them out of the protection of the cloaks. Of all the moments in their plan, this one was the most likely point of failure. If Vanchenko hadn't followed the fake jump and lingered in the area then he would detect them.

To his relief, Mervan detected no other ships as they crept along. They couldn't use active sensors as they would give their position away, so it was possible that the bounty hunter lurked somewhere waiting for them to make a move.

In operations like this it was too easy to fall victim of paranoia. You had to keep confident and trust the plan and your own abilities.

They'd discussed the likely point for a pirate ambush and the previous attacks provided the hints to guide their deliberations. The attack would be near the edge of the asteroid belt. Mervan anticipated that Julia would be waiting nearby. All they had to do now was make their way through the belt and wait for the action to start.

Travelling without being detected took care and above all, time. Over the past few months, he'd placed an extensive network of surveillance and recon drones around Freeholm and the surrounding belt. As well as keeping him up to date with ship movements around the station, it allowed him to map the station's own sensor network. Not all of it of course, but enough that a tactical program could predict the unseen placements with what he hoped was a decent degree of accuracy.

The same network confirmed his suspicion that Julia would set up her own trap. It also revealed that her piloting skills included the ability to fly her Eagle in a stealthy fashion as it lost track of her soon after she left the station.

The three siblings employed the same skills to make their way through the belt undetected. Their ships were upgraded in a way that made their task easier although it still required skill.

The network was based around passive sensors except for the ones that monitored the immediate space around Freeholm and the cleared passage through the belt. That meant they had to keep their heat emissions low, or at least unseen by using asteroids as cover to block line of sight. It also meant that they had to travel slowly to reduce their heat build-up. Alongside these measures they needed to maintain EM silence. Any transmission of energy, especially on electromagnetic frequencies, would reveal their position.

They could still communicate with the laser comms system, as this point-to-point transmission was almost impossible to intercept. Naturally his sister filled the channel with complaints about how this would all be over by now if they'd done it her way.

He muted the channel.

Perhaps Darik had the right idea after all. Not about the work, Mervan enjoyed the job. But about going it alone. His father would never allow it, not for a second time.

It took all day for them to cross the width of the belt. Julia's ship had appeared on a few occasions, revealing her route and allowing him to refine their destination. Unknown to Julia, she would have the three siblings waiting behind her for the moment to strike.

- 20 -

For the first time in as long as he could remember, Hammer woke feeling the effects of the previous night's excess. He'd toured every bar he could find, bragging about his sweet cargo run. Julia wanted enough time for a message to get through to the pilots so at least he managed a few hours sleep before having to leave the station.

Julia wasn't as fortunate as she had to be in position near the expected ambush point before he arrived. She had to get there without being spotted which meant taking a circuitous route through the belt and taking it slow to keep her heat signature low. They all considered it likely that the bad guys had at least some remote surveillance drones near to the station.

She left at midnight and followed the same path taken earlier by Piotr and the two Freeholm defence force Sidewinders. Halfway to the edge of the belt she looped back, coasting between clusters of asteroids for cover. It was eight hours of slow and stressful travel and Hammer didn't envy her one bit.

Stealth had never been Hammer's strong suit. He preferred a more direct approach, or at least to pretend to be a victim until the moment came to unleash hell upon those foolish enough to take the bait.

As he settled into the pilot's chair, he increased the oxygen mix for the ship's atmosphere. While that provided an effective way to help clear his head it also violated several safety protocols, so as soon as the thumping in his head calmed he restored the original mix.

He took his time running through the pre-flight checks. The ship's computer handled them all automatically; even so, he always checked the computer's results for himself. Throughout the evening's festivities he'd pondered what he would do next. This would be a milestone mission for him. What had started as drunken maudlin musings became a certainty as he prepared to launch.

He completed the regular checks first, and all systems were operational. Along with the normal flight and ship's systems, he reviewed the status for his custom extras. First was the cargo spoofer. This incredibly expensive piece of kit would fool a cargo scanner so that it reported whatever Hammer programmed the device to return. It was important for attacking pirates to believe that they were about to earn a big score.

The technicians had inspected the extra armoured bulkheads that filled what was once cargo and fuel space. His ship could barely carry any real quantity of cargo and lacked the range of even a shipyard standard model. It could, however, withstand damage that would destroy even smaller warships like the Imperial Cutters and Federation Corvettes.

He spotted movement in the docking bays to the left and in front of him. The pads rose and turned in place revealing two Sidewinders in the faded green and tallow livery of Freeholm's defence force. These were the ready fighters who would scramble the moment that he was attacked. They wouldn't reach the battle in time to take part, but instead formed part of the deception.

Flight Control passed along a message from the Laphrian Navy vessel due to escort him once he left the belt. Captain Belin wanted to change the rendezvous time. Julia's voice intruded over the communication and informed them that she was in position and that they should proceed. Hammer shrugged and voiced his agreement. Flight Control concurred and granted him permission to launch.

The passage through the docking port was as tight as always. He'd flown through these ports so many times it had become second nature to him. The trick was remembering that the bridge was high up on the ship and that most of the length lay in the front of it.

They didn't expect to encounter the opposition until near the edge of the belt, which made sense. If the attack went wrong they wouldn't want to be too far into the belt and so unable to supercruise away. That was what they expected, even so Hammer had to play his part throughout the whole journey.

He kept the active scanner offline. At the flick of a switch, the system would change over to the advanced tracking system. The electronic fingerprint on systems like this were distinctive even in standby mode. It meant a delay of a few seconds but he couldn't afford anything giving the game away.

Of all the tricks he employed, this frustrated him the most. The standard scanner paled in its capabilities compared to the military scanner. It made him feel almost blind as the ship travelled through the cleared passage. Julia had provided him with the access codes for the network of surveillance drones around Freeholm. They did use tight-beam communications, but even so there would be a slight risk of detection.

He flew at half power. The engines had a carefully engineered leak to make them appear poorly maintained. The shields were up, but they were the cheapest available for this class of ship. They wouldn't survive even a weak assault for long, so he'd have to rely on the ship's armour. There he felt more confident.

At the halfway point in the journey, his posture changed. He leant forward in his chair and focused on the scanner in front of him more closely. In his HUD a blue waypoint marker indicated where Julia would be waiting.

The agreed plan was simple. He'd fly along the transit corridor into open space. Outside the belt he expected to meet with the Laphrian Navy escort. That part of the plan had already gone wrong, but that worked in their favour as a patrolling warship would likely scare the pirates away.

Word of an easy score should have reached any watchers quickly. The attacks so far had indicated that the pirates might not be after simple loot. On the chance that the attacks were aimed at Freeholm itself, the decoy cargo was one which was key to the Freeholm economy. A separate rumour had also been spread by some of the security team that the cargo was supposed to be payment for a contract to hire a mercenary squadron to join the defence force.

Providing the bait was taken, Hammer would wait and let the attackers chew on him for a while. Once he led the attackers close enough to the waiting Julia, he'd reveal his capabilities and take all but one of them out. It would then run, and Julia would follow and track the fleeing pirate's jump.

Hammer's vessel couldn't chase a fleeing ship so he was relying on Julia sending him the jump destination. It was a risk and one he didn't agree with. He suggested that she deploy with the defence force fighters and with Piotr. Hammer wasn't a fan of the bounty hunter, but he knew the man's reputation. From what he'd heard he was a skilled pilot and ruthless. Exactly the wingman you needed for an operation like this.

Julia insisted on doing her part alone. Piotr had been missing for the day and she refused to leave the station undefended. Hammer had spoken to the other pilots after Julia departed and they agreed to come as soon as he called. They would be too far away for the initial engagement but as long as he could pass along the jump destination then they could at least provide backup.

They'd have to leave the belt to jump, but Hammer

assumed that as long as they didn't engage anyone in Laphrian space then it should be okay. The defence force pilots didn't care anyway. They'd fly through hell to help Julia avenge her father.

Not for the first time, Hammer wondered what Vanchenko's game was. It seemed obvious that he was here for more than a simple bounty. The way he took off when he heard about the strange visitors indicated that there was more at play here. He'd heard a few rumours about Vanchenko. He was supposed to be some badass bounty hunter. He'd hit the newsfeeds a few times after taking down some big bounties.

Freeholm seemed a bit low-key for that level of bounty. Unless it was linked with the attacks somehow. There was something weird going on, but Hammer didn't care. He left the politics to those interested in such things. His part in the business was simple, he acted as bait. An anvil in sheep's clothing.

Hammer paid even closer attention to the scanner as he entered the final third of his route to the inner edge of the belt. Even with the range set to maximum, he saw nothing on the holographic display except rocks.

That wasn't unexpected. They wouldn't jump in and attack. The new generation of drives meant that jump arrivals were within the local star's gravity well.

He might not involve himself in the politics of the situation but that aspect did strike him as odd. The attackers had to arrive at the star and from there travel to the belt where they waited in ambush. The second part could be done stealthily by skilled pilots. Arriving at the star wasn't, especially one as well-patrolled as Artemis. This might be a backwater system, but the local navy appeared to take their job seriously and do it well.

It smelled wrong to Hammer.

He loosened his shoulders and forced himself to sit upright. He placed his hands near the controls, allowing the muscle memory to guide his fingers into the required positions. If the attack came, it would come soon.

Time slowed as he entered a hyper-alert state. Many pilots used stims or implants to maintain this state longer than the body could normally manage. He preferred not to, as did Julia, or at least that's what she'd told him. The trick to maintaining the state was to keep a level of calm, otherwise your adrenaline would burn through it in no time. The other trick he'd learned was to not fixate on any single thing. Sure, the scanner was the key indicator at the moment, but while you should trust your instruments you also had to keep your eyes open.

Sometimes sensors could be fooled where the human Mk I eyeball wasn't.

It seemed that the bait wouldn't be taken as he approached the edge of the belt. The window of opportunity was closing and he'd have to complete the jump and return in a day or two so they could try again. Of course, if he returned without a mercenary escort then anyone who'd picked up on that rumour would know it had been a ruse.

Four points of light blossomed on the scanner and Hammer smiled. The thrill of combat started in his stomach.

Hammer had his part to play so he waited.

When the four targets resolved into four Sidewinders on the scanner, he increased the power to the engines as if trying to run. Although he felt no fear for himself, he hoped that Julia waited where she said she would be.

He transmitted a distress call in the clear to Freeholm and discovered that the comms channel was jammed. He heard only static on all channels. Even more surprising was the failure in the hyperspace comms system. The computer reported no malfunction.

This was unexpected, but he could handle these four ships alone.

The Sidewinders arced into an intercept course and chased Hammer towards open space. He was happy to allow them to think their manoeuvring was successful and continued his dash away from them.

He kept his engines at three-quarters thrust with his goal to allow them to catch up to him as he approached Julia's position. The screech of laser fire against his shields announced they'd entered weapons range. His Anaconda couldn't out-turn or outrun them and they knew it, so pretending otherwise might give the game away.

Instead he limited his changes in direction to present the angle of the ship with the strongest remaining shields. He also powered up the point defences. These low-powered pulse lasers provided some all-angle protection against missiles and ships that strayed too close.

They remained wary at first. Nibbling at his shields but keeping out of range of his defence turrets. After only a few passes, they stripped his shields to tatters and grew bolder as they realised that the lasers hitting caused little damage to their shields.

He continued to flee. His turrets continued taking ineffective pot-shots at the Sidewinders who now focused their fire on his turrets. One by one they were destroyed. The lasers were the cheapest Hammer could find, usually from spare part auctions at shipyards. The incoming fire caused very little damage to the layered foam metal and composite ceramic armour.

The armour contained pockets of pyrotechnics as part of the deception. Every so often, laser fire would ignite one and sparks and fire would burst creating an illusion that the ship was actually being damaged.

Within a few minutes, the last point defence laser disintegrated into molten slag. Hammer reviewed his position on the scanner and decided that he was near enough to Julia's position for the charade to end.

He changed the Anaconda's operating profile and hidden hard points all over the ship deployed. The ship's power management profile increased energy to the weapon systems. The omni-directional targeting scanners also popped out and immediately began tracking the four hostiles.

Beam lasers slashed against the Sidewinders' shields, burning through them in a single pass. By that point the targeting system had locked onto the four targets. Hammer cancelled one of the locks to keep one of the Sidewinders alive so that it could flee to wherever its home base was located.

Several new targets appeared on the scanner as the systems expanded range and resolution kicked in. The first resolved as an Eagle and positioned near the waypoint marker. The target glowed brighter as the Eagle powered up and moved to chase the four Sidewinders.

He launched a barrage of missiles at the three targeted Sidewinders. The missiles leapt from the launchers and streaked towards them.

Another target appeared on the scanner along a similar vector the Sidewinders had originated from. The target resolved into a Cobra and the computer analysis indicated it was a missile carrier. A warning from his heads-up display indicated that the Cobra had a missile lock on him.

He quickly reassigned his point defences to engage the incoming missiles at the same time as his own missiles tore into the Sidewinders. Hammer swung the Anaconda round to head towards the Cobra. Julia's Eagle accelerated in the direction of the remaining Sidewinder who couldn't believe its luck and now ran with all pips in its engines away from the belt.

Three new targets lit up on the scanner and chased after the Eagle. The jammed communications prevented Hammer from warning Julia about the three ships.

Lasers lanced out from his Anaconda to intercept the incoming missiles. Hammer targeted the Cobra with his missile batteries, and as soon as the lock indicator flashed he unleashed a full magazine at the other ship. Even though the Cobra still had full shields and missiles were more effective against hulls, twenty missiles should take the ship clean out.

The Cobra's own barrage smashed into his ship, the destructive force absorbed by the armour. He tracked his own missiles towards the Cobra who now weaved to try and dodge. Plasma fire from the Cobra's own point defences took out a few of the lead missiles. Another three detonated before hitting the shields and then the Cobra disintegrated under the storm of the remaining missiles.

He returned his focus to Julia. Her Eagle blazed as she chased after the lone Sidewinder. The three ships chasing her remained unresolved and had caught up to her quickly. Hammer feared the worse and was surprised when the three flew past her and towards the fleeing ship.

- 21 -

Waiting formed a large part of the siblings' routine. Contract killers tended to be ambush predators. The best ones would engineer a suitable situation and then wait for the right moment to strike. This shouldn't feel different to their other jobs, but it was.

Even Seline's bitter complaining had quietened to a sullen silence.

They hadn't determined Julia's exact location so Mervan decided to play it safe and positioned them farther back from the expected ambush point. They'd probably have more ground to cover when the action took place, but that couldn't be avoided. Better to have to chase for longer than reveal their presence.

The network of sensors informed them when the Anaconda departed Freeholm. The waiting continued as they tracked the ship's progress through the cleared passage in the asteroid belt. To pass the time, Mervan analysed the data and was impressed by the illusion he saw there. If he hadn't already researched the pilot then he would have been fooled by the appearance of a slow and poorly defended trader.

Despite expecting the attack, Mervan was surprised when it came. Whoever they were, they were good. Even more of a shock was the hardware. Four Sidewinders and a Cobra seemed an underwhelming force for the attacks. Mervan considered it almost insulting that his brother had been defeated by such a small group. A decade of rogue miners and the occasional pirate had obviously degraded his skills.

He experienced a third surprise when he realised that his hyperspace communications were down. The computer reported no malfunction. It just couldn't establish a connection. He'd not heard of anyone developing an effective jammer for hyperspace communications. This couldn't be a coincidence so maybe there was more to these attackers than met the eye.

Mervan suspected that might be the case. For pirates, they weren't keen on collecting the spoils. There was also the question of how they were able to reach the belt without attracting attention despite the regular patrols of the Navy. Fooling the local defence force was one thing and Mervan didn't consider that a major challenge. The Navy was another matter though. Their ships might be old tech, but they kept a close eye on arrivals near the system's star.

The attack developed quickly and Julia revealed her position as her Eagle's engines lit up. The Sidewinders discovered how outmatched they were when the Anaconda unleashed a firestorm upon them.

The time had arrived to intervene. After communicating with his brother and sister, they all accelerated to maximum thrust.

The Cobra attempted to help and disintegrated under a barrage of missiles. The remaining Sidewinder fled and they chased after it. The decoy Anaconda tried to join the chase but couldn't react quickly enough. The fleeing Sidewinder sped with every newton of thrust it possessed away from the belt.

Mervan told Lee to enter supercruise so they had someone ready if the Sidewinder jumped. Moments later his brother reported that his frame shift drive had failed. Seline tried the same without success and then so did Mervan. All three ships' drives failed without any meaningful error message.

The chances of three simultaneous failures were

beyond belief. Had they been sabotaged back on the station?

The chase continued in normal space. All four ships were now past the Anaconda. Mervan's sensors detected a brief communication between the Anaconda and Julia's Eagle. It was encrypted and Mervan doubted that it contained anything of significance. Even so, he tasked the ship's computer with decrypting the transmission.

As they passed Julia's Eagle, he opened a channel to her as they passed by.

"What the hell are you doing here?"

He didn't blame her for being angry.

"I said we would take care of whoever killed your father."

"This is my revenge."

"Oh. And what was your plan when this slippery fish jumps back home?"

"I'll follow him."

"I'm sure you would and then you would be dead."

"I can handle myself."

"That may be so, but this isn't a game."

"I know that, damn it!"

"Sorry, that not what I meant. I know you're taking this seriously, but you have no idea what will be at the other end of the jump. These guys aren't working alone."

"What do you mean?"

"Well, have you tried to enter supercruise?"

"No, I'm going to trace his cloud when he jumps."

"Try it."

"Why the hell would I do that? I'm in pursuit and I'll jump when he does."

"This isn't a trick. We're on his tail and we won't let him go. You won't be able to enter supercruise anyway."

"Of course I will. We're not mass locked this far from the belt."

"Well why hasn't our little rabbit jumped then?"

"I don't know."

"Because he can't. And neither can we. Go on, try it."

The channel went silent for nearly a minute and they continued their chase after the lone Sidewinder.

When her voice returned it managed to sound angrier than before.

"What have you done? Why can't I engage the frame shift drive?"

"It's not our doing. We can't frame shift either."

"This is a trick of some kind. Did you sabotage my ship?"

"I was going to ask the same thing. No, Julia. We are not here to harm you. I know you don't believe me, but we are family and as such we would never seek to harm you."

"Then why are you trying to hinder me?"

"We're not. We are here to assist you in your revenge."

That last statement wasn't true. Originally he'd planned to disable her ship with an energy bomb before following the survivor. The discovery of not being able to jump caused him to rethink the plan. Julia was clearly a competent pilot and while the Eagle wasn't as capable as his Fer de Lance or Lee and Seline's Vipers, it did add another ship to their force.

Another factor came into play when he heard Julia's voice. She sounded so much like her father. He also considered how he would feel if his father was killed and others deemed him unworthy to enact revenge.

Lee didn't comment when he informed them of the change in their plan. Seline argued, although it seemed a token argument as if just for the sake of it.

"Wait a minute," he said cutting off another comment from her as a new target appeared on the scanner. "We have a new ship ahead."

"I don't see anything," said Julia.

"You will. We're running out of time. We can argue as much as you like once we're done. Now will you work with us? Or shall we leave you here?"

"You have no right."

"Right has nothing to do with it. Do you want to avenge your father or not?"

"Of course I do," she spat back at him.

"Then you have no choice."

He took her silence for acceptance and they continued into interplanetary space. The fleeing Sidewinder changed course slightly, bringing it in line with the unresolved contact. Mervan worried that his choice might impair their effort. Julia's Eagle was significantly slower than their ships. Faster than the Sidewinder, but they wouldn't reach it before it joined the ship it now headed towards.

In response he sent Seline and Lee ahead at full burn to flank the two ships. He also launched a recon drone in a direct line after the Sidewinder. With stealth no longer an issue, they activated their active sensors to gather more data on the mysterious ship ahead.

The two Vipers pulled ahead while he remained alongside Julia's Eagle. They fed their sensor data back to his ship and the contact soon resolved into a Panther Clipper.

"Mervan." Lee's voice on the comms channel.

"Yes."

"I'm detecting some strange energy readings from the Panther."

"What sort of readings?"

"I'm not sure. Look on your display."

Mervan did as his brother instructed and saw an unusual pattern radiating from the large trader. Waves of energy pulsed in concentric circles from the ship and seemed to fade into nothing. As the Sidewinder neared the ship, the pulses ceased.

"He's warming up."

"I see it. He must be preparing to jump."

"How can he? Our frame shift drives are failing."

"Maybe they know something we don't. Can you be close enough to slipstream before they jump?"

"I doubt it, Seline might be able to. Her ship is faster."

"Seline?"

"Yes."

"Can you make it?"

"At full burn and all pips in engines I can. I'll be vulnerable though."

"Do it and fire a salvo of missiles at them."

"With shields up the missiles won't do any damage and they'd be lucky to hit at this range."

"It doesn't matter as it will give them something to focus on other than you."

A Panther on its own would be very vulnerable to an attack and the Sidewinder wouldn't be able to put up of a fight either. If they could run then they would have to do so and soon.

With some relief he noticed that the hyperspace comms were active again.

"Seline. Hyperspace comms are back up. Send us the jump location as soon as you are through."

"On it."

"Lee, you stay in real space in case this is a trick. As soon as Seline sends the system, jump in after us. If she doesn't complete the slipstream then analyse the hyperspace cloud and get us a target. "

"Yes Mervan."

"Julia. You need to stick with me."

"Okay."

"We'll enter supercruise now and follow the vector at minimum speed until we have a confirmed destination and then we'll jump. Now we don't know what will be waiting on the other end so be prepared for anything."

"I will."

"Let's do it."

The heat build-up on the Panther reached an incredible level. Mervan wouldn't have thought it possible. He wondered what was on the ship that could generate so much energy.

Mervan engaged supercruise and immediately throttled back as he entered. Julia joined him seconds later. Tense moments passed while he waited for the Panther to jump. He breathed a sigh of relief when he saw the Panther tear into existence. It blazed like a fiery comet and behind it Mervan saw the lesser light of the Sidewinder.

The two ships shimmered as they prepared to enter hyperspace. Almost too late, another blazing spear chased the two ships. Seline arrived with less than a second to spare. Conscious that she would be alone against whatever waited in the next system, Mervan aligned his ship in the vector the others had departed in. Julia followed his actions.

A minute passed before Seline's voice rang over the hyperspace comms channel.

"NLTT 8065. And hurry!"

A day of firsts, there must be more waiting there than he'd expected for Seline to show any degree of concern. He repeated the message to the others as he plotted the jump.

Moments later they passed through an ethereal nebula. Shadows of dust added depth to the scene flashing before his eyes and then a snap as he entered the new system. The dull red sun cast an almost bloodlike pallor across the system. He dropped out of supercruise into normal space and entered chaos.

The scanner filled with contacts. One of them blazed brighter than the others, he assumed that was the Panther. His targeting system sorted through the array of contacts, prioritising them by threat. A flash to his left appeared as Julia entered the fray.

He switched his power distribution profile to favour shields and weapons and engaged the nearest target. The computer counted a dozen fighter-class ships, a mix of Sidewinders and Eagles. It also identified the Panther and a much larger ship. As the computer classified them as non-combatant, he concentrated on the fighters first.

Several of the fighters chased Seline's Viper. It looked like they were falling for her favourite trick. She liked to run away and as the enemy followed her she would turn off flight assist, flip the ship and blaze merry hell upon her pursuers. It was a good trick against two or even three ships, but it was a risky move against five.

Mervan fired his beam lasers at the Sidewinder in his sights and stripped its shields away in a single burst. The target jinked before the beams sliced through its armour.

As he chased the other ship, he kept his eye on the scanner to see how the others fared in the fight.

Julia found herself mobbed by a pair of Eagles and pulled a series of evasive manoeuvres while taking the occasional pot-shot whenever an enemy crossed her forward arc.

Another flash as Lee arrived in the system and the chaotic battle took a new turn. Individually none of the ships could have beaten the three siblings. Julia was a different matter, although she'd kept herself out of serious trouble so far.

Seline's manoeuvre hadn't been as successful as it usually was. She'd reduced two of her pursuers into shredded hulks, but in doing so she'd emptied her multicannon magazines and missile racks. The remaining ships took advantage of the reload and stripped away her forward shields. She flipped the ship again and boosted away, using the Viper's superior acceleration to her advantage.

Lee came to her rescue, moving into her rear quarter and reducing one to a lifeless husk in a single pass.

Mervan clipped one his targets with a missile, causing it to spin out of control. The pilot managed to eject before the ship exploded. Lining up on his next target, Mervan then noticed a strange thing. The ships he chased all wore a similar livery. The ships in the ambush earlier had a dissimilar scruffy look common to pirates, but these had a more uniform appearance.

Rapid laser fire from a Sidewinder weakened his shields before being blown apart by a fusillade from Julia's Eagle. She swept past him and engaged the target he just locked onto. He glanced at the scanner and saw the four of them were now mopping up the scraps. As they seemed to have the fighters under control, he locked onto the Panther and throttled up to close the range.

The Panther lacked active shields which seemed very odd for a ship involved in this type of business. Perhaps it had experienced a malfunction. The ship was running for its life. The crew on board must have realised the futility of their effort.

One of the fighters escaped into hyperspace. Seline wanted to follow but Mervan told her to form up on him. They had almost completed what they had come here to do. However, a fresh opportunity now presented itself.

On his targeting system he scrolled through the subsystems and selected the hyperdrive. Without shields and having the manoeuvrability of a dead whale, the Panther offered no effective defence. His beam lasers sliced through the fat ship's flimsy armour and destroyed the hyperdrive. He repeated the process with the thrusters so the Panther lay vulnerable.

The others formed up alongside and they throttled back so they all hung in space facing the stricken freighter. He opened a channel to the other three ships.

"We've taken care of the mercs here," he said to them all.

"Not quite all," Seline replied. "You let one of them get away and there's another one here. Tell me why we aren't reducing it to molten slag?"

"Well, we can make some real money here."

"I'm only here to kill those who murdered my father,"

Julia said.

"And we have done that. However I believe these mercs were utilising technology that is worth a fortune."

"I don't care," Julia said. "I want this ended."

Seline added, "I agree."

Mervan tried to convince the others that this was a golden opportunity for them. His efforts ended as a flash which eclipsed the local star for a moment flooded their cockpits. The Panther vaporised in the explosion.

"What the hell!" Julia exclaimed.

"Well, that solves that dilemma." Seline's tone was smug.

Mervan sighed, it didn't matter now.

"I'm returning to Freeholm," Julia said. "You three are not welcome there."

"Wait," Mervan said. He still hoped to bring her into the family. "We need to talk."

"There is nothing to discuss."

Julia's ship accelerated and vanished into supercruise.

"Ungrateful bitch," Seline observed.

- 22 -

In the days following Julia's return, the mood of the station improved considerably from the echoes of her father's funeral. The renewed positivity didn't suit Dee Callum's plans at all. Unfortunately for her she couldn't change the plan. She'd advised her superiors that the locals refused to follow the more sensible approach she proposed before her insertion at Freeholm.

Dee worried even more when Julia returned to the station with the news that she'd hired two pilots. Thankfully they'd lucked out with one of the hires. Vanchenko was a man devoted to a singular cause and he'd already asked her for a favour.

He was tracking three ships and only had sketchy energy signature and silhouette data along with probably fake registration data to go on. He'd asked her to run the information through her agency's database. She wasn't comfortable with him knowing she was an Imperial operative, but she believed he could be kept in line as long as he thought she was useful to him.

His knowledge posed a risk though. She'd worked hard and taken months to establish her cover here. The position provided her with excellent access while also keeping her in the background. People didn't tend to take much notice of data technicians.

Dee saw no downside to processing his request. Compared to the news about the disaster in NLTT 8065, a data request on three unknown ships wasn't likely to cause any problems.

How wrong she'd been with that assumption.

The news triggered the call and unnecessary communications presented the greatest risk in any covert operation. As part of the Imperial Intelligence apparatus, Dee operated the latest in covert communications technology. She was certain as she could be that the equipment at her disposal was superior to the countermeasure systems available to the locals. Even so, any transmission by its very nature left a trace, no matter how small.

Unfortunately, her superiors could not be ignored. She set the signal up to masquerade as Freeholm's navigation beacon. Once the handshake protocols completed, the youthful face of her case officer swept into view. The hologram cast pale orange light in the supply office she used. If the signal did get traced sometime in the future then at least it wouldn't be traced to her own office.

Major Waterson wasted no time with preamble.

"What the hell is going on? You were given two very simple tasks. Both of which you are failing."

"Sir…"

"No, agent. You will just listen for now. I will indicate when I require your input."

This wasn't her first chewing-out from a superior and she'd learned over the years it was best to just nod and accept it. So, she nodded.

"Now let me see. The first mission was simple. You had to bring this backwater system into the Imperial fold."

He paused for a moment and she made the mistake of thinking that this was an invitation to speak.

"Sir…"

"I haven't finished."

She needed to be more careful with this one. This officer wasn't a career Intelligence officer. He had much loftier ambitions. She took his slight incline of his head as a signal for her to speak. "Sir, the Laphrians were too aggressive in their plan. They tried to move too quickly and Freeholm was able to gain outside help."

"You should have prevented that."

"Yes sir. The bounty hunter and the trader were unexpected developments as neither of them have operated in this region before. The bounty hunter, a Piotr Vanchenko, may be of use to us."

"How so?"

"He doesn't care for the locals. He is after one thing and that is the identity of those who killed his friend."

"He was the one who requested the ship data?"

"Yes sir. Were you able to find out any information about the three ships or their pilots?"

"We'll come to that later. What about the trader?"

"Mark Lamon, or 'Hammer', isn't really a trader. He's more of a crusader."

"Will he be useful?"

"No, as I said, he's more of a crusader than a mercenary."

"Then get rid of him. Now we need to get your original mission back on track."

"Yes sir. Their plan was flawed and they refused to listen to my advice. We should have followed a longer term plan using rogue miners to stretch their defences rather than the quick hits their hired mercenaries engaged in."

"You're their contact so it was your responsibility to make sure they made the correct decision. Based on your previous mission performances, I believed that you were the best fit for this mission. I'm sure you intend to remedy this situation."

"I have a plan already, sir."

"There's no need. Our Laphrian contacts have deemed that your approach isn't aggressive enough. They plan to use the new hardware they are receiving from us as part of the diplomatic arrangement to conduct an assault on the station."

"Sir, is that wise?"

"The ships will be crewed and owned by the Laphrian Navy. Your role is to make sure that Freeholm doesn't learn of the attack."

"Yes sir."

This wouldn't be easy but what else could she say?

"More important was the device tests. This system provided an ideal opportunity to test the frame shift inhibiter. We're far enough away from prying Federal eyes and the Laphrian Navy's sensor systems are advanced enough to capture meaningful data for the tests. The idea to use the tests to help the attacks has provided useful information for improving the system."

"The Laphrians failed to provide adequate protection for the system. They used the same mercenary company to provide escort and attack Freeholm. There were insufficient assets for both tasks and they were caught off-guard when the Freeholm forces tracked their staging system."

"This should never have happened. You were the point person on this."

"I reported my findings on their preparations several weeks ago, sir."

"I see. So this isn't your fault at all."

"No sir, but I will fix this."

"You won't."

"Sir?"

"That was the sole prototype for the small scale version of the device. The tech team are working to construct another while the loss of the first is investigated. They won't be able to investigate fully until you are pulled out of the field."

"Wait. You're pulling me out? You can't insert anyone with a deep enough cover in time."

"We won't, however the timeline has accelerated considerably. Your only responsibility is to ensure that the Laphrian Navy achieves strategic surprise. For tactical superiority they'll have the new ships and we'll provide one of the remaining prototypes."

"I thought the only one we had was destroyed?"

"The only small version we had. Fitting the device in a ship as small as the Panther Clipper was a technological miracle. Instead we have to supply one of the first generation as part of the loan of a bigger ship."

That could mean only one thing and that wouldn't be easy to keep hidden from Freeholm.

"When is the operation planned for?"

"The Laphrian crews will need a few weeks to shake down their new ships. The attack will take place in a month."

"Yes sir, I will make the necessary preparations immediately."

"Make sure to perform a better job than you have thus far."

Dee bit back her immediate comment. She'd been sent here with inadequate support and a distinct lack of cooperation from the locals. And now she faced an investigation because they didn't listen to her advice.

Up until this point she'd followed her orders without thinking about their source. She now wondered how much Major Waterson had invested in this operation. He was a bright youngest son from a family wealthy enough for a little respect, but lacking the contacts to climb as high as he wanted in the Emperor's service.

If this operation formed part of his plan to elevate his station then he would be even keener to distance himself from any failure. She would have to complete the operation and then face the dissolution of her own career. After a lifetime of service, this was a hard prospect to contemplate.

"Now about the three ships you sent the data on."

Maybe some good news at last. She'd already formulated some ideas for disguising the military build-up at Laphria and Piotr would be useful for that plan.

"Do we have an ID for any of the pilots?" she asked.

"Not specifically, although we do know the ships."

"What can I tell Piotr, the bounty hunter?"

"Nothing."

"Sir, I need to give him something. At the moment he's the best asset I have on the station."

She hated to admit it, but that was indeed the case. She owned a few low-level contacts in the internal security team. They provided access to some of the areas that her cover job didn't allow and at a pinch could provide a little muscle if needed.

Since her insertion into the station, she'd sent several requests for a covert operations team to provide local support. Each request had been denied by Major Waterson as their Laphrian contacts had promised whatever support the mission needed.

That had worked out well.

"Sir?"

"The ship's data came back and all three were red-flagged as part of a four-ship wing. The other ship was an Eagle, but the three matched the ships you sent."

"What were they red-flagged for?"

"Apparently they formed the team that took out an Imperial Courier as it was ferrying a client on a diplomatic mission."

"Who was the client?"

"That's need-to-know only."

Dee guessed that probably meant that Major Waterson didn't know either and that indicated that it was something other than a regular diplomatic mission.

"What does matter," he continued, "is that the pilots for these ships need to receive Imperial justice."

"Is a team being sent to deal with them?"

"We have nothing available in the region. They have been tracked by other operatives to a smuggler's station within your area of operations. Which makes them your responsibility."

"Sir, I have my hands full. Especially if I have to hide

an impending invasion."

"Considering your recent performance, I would expect you to grasp any opportunity to demonstrate your usefulness to the service."

"Of course, sir. Why can't I give Piotr this information? After all he is a bounty hunter and if these are the people he'd hunted all these years, he would owe us."

"Or he could decide that he has no need to be in the area anymore. He would also be outclassed on his own and if he tried to assemble a larger team they might discover the fact and flee. For the moment they are waiting at the hidden station, so you'll need to strike quickly."

"With respect sir, I don't have the assets to do that without involving someone."

"We're providing the Laphrians with a lot of support. They have already agreed to send a hit team to deal with these three assassins. You will provide their contact with the relevant details which I am transmitting to you now."

"Sir, they have already demonstrated their lack of competence. I'm not confident they are capable of pulling this off."

"Even their forces should be able to handle three pilots at a low-rent smugglers base."

"Sir…"

"You have your orders. If you're worried then make sure they go in heavy-handed. As long as they are killed and it doesn't trace back to us, it doesn't matter how messy it gets."

"Yes sir."

Shit.

She was being set up for a fall. She needed a plan out of this situation. Somehow she would need to make sure everything went right with the invasion and the hit. Both scenarios she had little control over. Beyond that, she needed to save her career. She could run, but that would betray the life she had devoted herself to.

Besides, no matter where she ran, they would find her. What was about to happen to the three pilots was proof of that.

- 23 -

Captain Belin considered the Imperial Cutter to be ship of deadly elegance. He admired the sweep of his new ship's lines as he approached in the shuttle. The crew were already on board. They had begun their training when they'd docked the *Demeter* at the Laphria shipyard three days ago.

Belin would have preferred to accompany the crew in exploring their new ship. They shared a bittersweet feeling, particularly those, like Belin, had served on the old Anaconda for many years. They all experienced excitement in deploying in a new ship, especially one as magnificent as the Cutters from the Gutamaya shipyards.

On the other hand, the *Demeter* had served them faithfully. She was slow and handled like a drowning whale but she was sturdy. As well as being well armed she had, up until now, been the pinnacle of the fleet.

While the crew settled into their new ship, Belin spent three days in conference with the other captains of the newly formed flotilla. He'd assumed the conference would be a briefing for the shakedown cruise. Seeing Admiral Locke, one of the fleet admirals and his staff in attendance surprised Belin.

For three days they remained secluded in secrecy and maximum security while Admiral Locke revealed the details of the forthcoming mission. The invasion of Freeholm represented a massive change in Navy policy towards the station. Belin didn't understand why such a reversal of policy was being announced to them by just one of the admirals.

There'd been no hint of such a change in policy from the government and even stranger was the lack of emphasis in the press. Sure, the same diehards that supported the old regime spouted their usual nonsense. No matter how their world improved since the coup, there always seemed to be those who wanted to return to old – and as far as Belin was concerned, imagined – glories.

Something didn't feel right with their orders, although he admitted to himself that his unease could simply be because he disagreed with the plan.

To try and assuage his disquiet, he dug into the intelligence supporting the mission. He experienced a fresh shock when he learned that the Navy already had a pretext for the attack. One of the Freeholm defence force fighters had left the confines of the belt, thus breaking the treaty.

As far as Belin knew, the only Eagles stationed at Freeholm belonged to Darik Cavus and his daughter. With Darik dead it had to be Julia. The report stated that she joined forces with three ships and after failing to file a flight plan as required by the treaty, then jumped to NLTT 8065 and attacked a Navy recon flight searching for the pirates who'd attacked the traders from Freeholm.

Which made no sense at all.

Data on the ships which accompanied the defence force Eagle was restricted. The tags indicated an ongoing Navy Intelligence operation. The data log of the engagement had also been heavily redacted. Enough remained to show the attackers tearing the defenders apart.

Captain Belin struggled to fit the pieces together. The defenders were a small force of Eagles and Sidewinders protecting a Panther Clipper. He wondered what a covert Navy Intelligence unit was doing in the remote system. That information wasn't available.

Even more difficult to comprehend was why Freeholm

would make such a bold move, seemingly unprovoked. Unless they believed that the unit was responsible for Darik Cavus's death. Which made even less sense and how would they know the operation was in the system?

And the deceased head of security's daughter had returned to the Artemis system within an hour of the attack. So why had the Navy allowed her to continue back to Freeholm?

Too many details didn't fit.

The doubts faded a little as the practicalities of the attack occupied more of Belin's time and focus. The Navy had prepared an accurate estimate of the station's defences. As one of the few captains who patrolled the belt border on a regular basis, Belin agreed with their assessment. During his time stationed near the belt he'd developed his own intelligence brief on Freeholm and he felt pride as he recognised his own work in the briefing one of Admiral Locke's aides presented to the assembled officers.

The core of the station's defences came from a small number of Sidewinders. These were cheap fighters used by local militias and defence forces throughout human space. The ships showed little sign of upgrades although it was difficult to tell as they rarely left the confines of the belt.

With the two Eagles, they had a little more information. Especially on the young woman's as she had travelled out of the system on many occasions. Only one of the Eagles remained now of course.

As well as the small force of fighters, the station provided a home to several independent traders. The one's who'd been identified were low-level, operating Cobras and similar class vessels. The small number of larger ships tended to be transport vessels like the Lakon Type 7 with little combat capability.

There were indications that an Anaconda was currently docked at the station. No-one knew for sure whether this ship was a mercenary hired by the station or simply a trader passing through. In either case, the Navy's experience with their own enhanced Anacondas made them aware of the threat one of these ships could pose.

The Anaconda had passed through Laphrian space some days previously, and while it registered no indications that it contained any significant upgrades, the Navy planners took no chances. An opposition force that the strike fleet would use to train against comprised of the *Demeter*, although now manned by a different crew.

Comparable ships for the other Freeholm assets formed the reminder of the opposition force. It would feel strange to be manoeuvring against his old ship. It seemed unlikely that the three unidentified ships had returned to the station as they would have had to pass the Navy patrols. Even so, the opposition force contained representations for them as well.

A greater surprise had also been revealed in the briefings and now lay in view of the shuttle. Shrouded in the stark shadow of the shipyard, Belin saw the outline of a *Majestic*-class Interdictor. These massive capital ships formed the core and the pride of the Imperial Navy.

At two kilometres in length, only the shipyard and the planet itself were larger in his view. The ship looked grand, coloured in Imperial white. Its delicate curves and toroid habitation ring belied the deadly potential of the warship. Only the Federal *Farragut*-class battlecruisers could match these elegant behemoths.

Just a single one of these awesome ships matched the firepower of the entire Laphrian fleet as it currently stood.

Only the closest of allies were granted access to these magnificent ships. That fact, more than the rumours of fresh treaties and agreements, confirmed the closer ties with the Empire. The ship's presence provided an additional clue to the occurrences near the belt in recent weeks.

In the final briefing, the captains were warned that no frame shift activity was possible or permitted within the defensive zone of the shipyard. As one of the chief centres of the Laphrian Navy's activities and once the source of the planet's wealth, the security of the shipyard had always been high. More so even than the arrival region around the orange star as no unpermitted ships were allowed access.

As well as the newly assembled strike fleet, several of the old converted Anacondas patrolled the volume of space around the shipyard along with extensive fighter patrols. While this presence didn't remove his fears for the plan's legitimacy, it did calm his worry about whether this was a rogue operation. After all, a deployment of this magnitude couldn't be achieved without the knowledge and consent of the upper echelons of the Navy.

For the remainder of the journey to his new command, Belin admired the giant warship while focusing his thoughts on the challenges ahead of him.

He'd known that the Navy planned to invest in Cutters for some time, so Belin had read everything he could find about the ships. They were available to favoured pilots so finding information on the basic model didn't prove too difficult. He also discovered a number of virtual cockpits and even full holographic representations of them, which allowed him to familiarise himself with the basic layout.

The other big change was that of tactics. The light cruiser model Anacondas were sturdy and while they appeared crude compared to the Imperial ships, they did have their strengths. The extra armour and shields made them formidable opponents.

They also carried a decent level of firepower, although their lack of manoeuvrability meant that they tended to rely upon turreted and gimballed weapon systems. Those mounts ensured that they had fire arcs which protected every aspect of the ship.

That flexibility came at the cost of firepower.

That provided the most obvious advantage with the Cutters. Their increased speed and dexterity not only provided their own inherent advantages, it also meant that the ship could utilise fixed mount weapons which had greater destructive capability than the turreted or gimballed equivalents.

Compared to the Anacondas they lacked the extravagant armour, but their more modern shields and extra power capacity compensated for that.

The Laphrian shipyard prided itself on the quality of the upgrades that they provided. Up until now they didn't have access to the latest in Imperial technology. It might be true that it wasn't the full extent of that technology, as the export variants tended to be of lower quality than those used by the Imperial Navy themselves. It still represented a major increase in the capability of the Laphrian Navy and Belin looked forward to testing it out.

The Cutters also came equipped with hangers for two short-range fighters. As part of the deal the Navy would receive three squadrons, each containing twelve ships. Two squadrons were to be deployed on the Interdictor, with the remaining squadron being divided amongst the Cutters.

The plan for the assault had been kept simple. As any experienced officer understood, plans always changed at the moment of execution, so the simpler the better. The attack would be led by the *Laphrian Pride*, the *Majestic*-class Interdictor. Deception and covert operations would create strategic surprise. Details on those weren't forthcoming from the planning team although hints were made about having operatives on the inside.

Tactical surprise would be provided by the frame shift inhibiter capability of the *Laphrian Pride*, preventing any support being provided from outside the colony. The rest of the Navy would be placed on high alert and increased patrols around the star would block any attempts to assist Freeholm.

The actual assault force would comprise of the *Laphrian Pride* with three Cutter escorts. The Navy had so far received six Cutters. The other three would remain at the shipyard in supercruise as a strategic reserve.

Nothing fancy was planned for the actual attack. The fleet would supercruise to the belt and then use the Freeholm's own cleared channel to approach the station. The Cutter escorts would suppress any mobile defences that were deployed, like the Sidewinders.

The one big unknown in the intelligence assessment of the station's defences was the station itself. When the Laphrians operated the colony, they had installed a small number of point defences. There was little need for anything more as the Navy held the surrounding volume secure.

The Navy knew almost nothing about what upgrades had been affected since the rebellion. The intelligence note reported that the existing defences had been maintained and the surrounding area contained an extensive sensor network. Freeholm would realise what was happening as soon as the battle group entered the belt. Alone, the Cutters might have managed a stealthy approach but with the Interdictor that would be impossible.

The best case scenario of an immediate Freeholm surrender had been rated as unlikely with less than a two per cent probability. Belin agreed with that assessment. He knew from the interactions with the traders and defence force that memories of their previous life ran deep in the station. They wouldn't give in without a fight.

However, the forces that would be arrayed against them far outnumbered and outgunned any defence they could mount. It wouldn't be a battle, a massacre seemed more likely. Belin hoped that they made the sensible choice.

The plan assumed that they wouldn't, but what the

actual response would be was difficult to determine. Two options seemed likely. The first, and the one that Belin believed would be the case, was that the defence forces would conduct a hit and run campaign throughout the invasion's route through the belt.

If this occurred, then the short-range fighters would be deployed and engage any attackers. The Cutters would remain with the Interdictor, providing close protection.

Here Belin raised an objection. He believed that the Cutters should be used more aggressively to sweep the belt for anyone lying in ambush. The fighter screen could then support the Cutters or the Interdictor as needed. Considering the power of the Interdictor, it was likely that nothing the defenders had could threaten it with any serious damage anyway.

Despite the support of the other captains, the Admiral's staff refused to alter the plan. They deemed it more likely that the defenders would hold back and stage a close defence of the station. That way they'd receive support from the station's weapons as well. Belin argued against this assumption as the defenders would lose their single advantage of manoeuvrability by following such a course.

Once at the station the Interdictor and the Cutters would suppress any defences and protect the armoured shuttles that would deploy the first battalion of Navy infantry. A full regiment would be deployed eventually, unfortunately the Navy only had enough armoured shuttles to deploy a battalion at a time. They didn't anticipate any serious opposition once a foothold had been established.

Belin mused about how things often appeared simple in the briefing room's holographic projectors. Reality rarely turned out that way.

It didn't matter in any case. Orders had been given and it was his job to ensure that his crew and new ship executed those orders. He felt confident as the small shuttle docked in one of the fighter bays and moments later stepped onto his new ship.

- 24 -

The certainty that the three ships were the ones he'd hunted for so long prevented Piotr from leaving the station. Almost a month had passed since he'd chased and lost them. It angered him even more when he returned to Freeholm to discover that they had been spotted outside the belt. He'd scrambled and flown to the edge of the belt, but even with his upgraded equipment, establishing a trace hours after a jump was impossible.

He'd returned to the station and waited impatiently until Julia arrived. News of her victory spread throughout the station and a feeling of jubilation and relief settled upon the population. Her anger appeared at odds with the news and she adamantly refused to answer any of his questions about the three pilots. That proved to Piotr that there must be a connection between them. That connection had to be through her father.

With an effort, he resisted the temptation of kidnapping her to extract the answers he wanted. The cautious hunter part of him counselled that a more tempered approach would gain better results. It also warned that there was a possibility that she didn't have all the information he needed and to act prematurely would give the game away.

Over the past few weeks, he'd suppressed the frustration and played nice with the hero of the hour. He made himself useful to the defence force. He flew patrols around the station. He even escorted traders. It was all demeaning work for a bounty hunter of his calibre but it paid dividends in the end.

The first indication came from a quick conversation in the briefing room. Then a few drinks with the other pilots. There he discovered that putting up with Hammer's boisterous drinking created a special kind of hell – one he endured with a forced smile, until the moment seemed right and he invited Julia to dinner.

Piotr had no romantic intentions, and the age difference made that unlikely. He hadn't desired any type of romantic entanglement for a long time. He'd be willing to follow that path if needed but he believed that what she needed was a friend. Maybe an older brother. Someone she could confide in. Piotr would do everything he could to make sure she would confide in him.

And so he now waited in the most exclusive restaurant in Freeholm. Usually obtaining reservations for a place like this took connections, and on this station it wasn't any different. He dropped Julia's name and a table became available.

The décor appeared to be faux Imperial chic although of a style a few decades out of date. No doubt the style would become fashionable again at some stage, although even if it did, it still wouldn't look the part. His job didn't put him in the upper echelons of society very often. That didn't bother him, it wasn't the water he liked to swim in.

On a rare occasion that he did, he wanted to be impressed. Sitting at the fake wooden table of the Grand Bistro, he felt anything but. Still, it was the best Freeholm had to offer so he waited with a smile on his face. He allowed the smile to broaden as Julia entered the room. She made quite the impression and several minutes passed before she reached the table because everyone stopped her and wanted to shake her hand.

"As popular as ever," Piotr said as he rose and helped her into her seat. "You look stunning." And she did. She'd dressed for the occasion and while her outfit was as out of fashion as the restaurant décor, she wore it much better than the building did. It was rare to see her in anything other than her flight suit.

"Thank you."

Her smile dazzled him for a moment. Even in a platonic relationship, women enjoyed being complimented.

"Have you been here before?" he asked.

"Yes, but it was a long time ago. My father brought me."

"It doesn't seem his type of place?"

She laughed. "It wasn't. There was some fancy dinner in his honour. I remember him grumbling when he had to find something resembling a dress uniform. As you can imagine, the defence force doesn't provide one as standard."

"No, I imagine not."

They slipped into small talk until a waiter approached in what appeared to be an inaccurate historical uniform. He hoped it was inaccurate, to have to suffer wearing such a uniform would be an embarrassment. As the waiter left with their orders, Piotr steered the conversation into a more meaningful direction.

"Did you speak to Mayborn?"

Julia had dodged the question of whether she should take over her father's duties since returning to the station. Piotr learned of this soon after he began his campaign to ingratiate himself into her trust. He immediately saw the benefit to her officially holding the position she was already filling anyway.

"I did and thank you for your advice. I'll admit that I wanted to run off, and to head into the deepest sector of space. I've been considering that for a while anyway. I just didn't know how to tell him."

"You still have that option. You can take the time to prepare and then when you leave you can go in style. Maybe I'll come along with you."

She laughed at that.

"I wanted to go anyway, but my reasons for leaving

now aren't the same. You've helped me see that and for that I'm grateful."

"That's what friends do."

"I know. Lina has told me the same thing."

Lina Mater had proved an obstacle in his campaign. She also turned out to be smarter than she first appeared. At first they clashed. Piotr had become too used to bullying his way to whatever he wanted. With Julia, he knew that he was smarter and more experienced than her. He'd made a tactical error in assuming he could do the same with the older woman.

Realising his error, he shifted tactics and charted a more delicate path. On the few occasions he shared Lina and Julia's company together, he supported the old woman's advice, but balanced that by empowering Julia's choice for her own determination.

More than once he considered hunting Elite-ranked pilots an easier task.

The tactic worked. Piotr assumed that a great part of that was due to his being a stranger. As odd as that seemed at first glance, in dealing with her grief and changing circumstances she needed someone who didn't remind her of her father. That fact that he'd already lived her dream (or so she thought) endeared him to her further.

He pulled himself from his thoughts and concentrated on the young woman sat before him. She provided a means to an end and nothing more. Or so he told himself. Something about her on this evening sparked something he hadn't felt in a long time. He cast the distraction aside. She was a link to the bastards that killed Sahiba and nothing more.

The distraction lingered at the back of his mind.

"So you told Mayborn that you would take the job as head of security?" he asked the question as much to put his mind back on track as much as wanting to know the answer.

"I did."

"That's good. Your father would be proud."

"Do you think so?"

"Of course and not just because you would follow in his footsteps. I feel sure that you will continue to keep this station safe."

"I hope so. The threat is over now."

"Yes, and that is due to you. And your mysterious friends of course," he added with a smile, but the smile masked his desire to know more. Since her return she'd said little about the actual events and even less about the three ships that assisted her.

The lurking feeling hid as the impulse to smash her face in, in front of all these people that thought they were hot shit, until she told him what he needed to know.

Maybe that would be the better option.

He drank the tepid water. Why was it tepid? Just to make it different from the cool and filtered water available to everyone? The random thought was an old trick of his to distract the anger.

"I think we owe those guys a favour. Not just for helping you get the bastards that killed your father, but also for making sure that you came back to us."

Yeah, he was laying it on thick. It wasn't his natural style but apparently that's what she responded to.

"I'm sorry. I can't tell you anything about them."

"What are they? Superheroes that need to keep their identity a secret?"

"Of course not," her laugh mingled with his.

"So why the big mystery? They should be applauded as saviours."

"They insisted that I don't say anything about their help."

"I'm sorry too. I don't mean to pry. I genuinely want to thank them."

"You're not the only one."

"Oh?"

That comment came as a surprise. As far as he knew, Freeholm had accepted her as the sole saviour. The scuttlebutt of the station made no mention of any assistance.

"Yes. Lina keeps asking me who they were as well. I wish you'd both just drop it. I really can't say anything. I don't know them anyway. They were something to do with my father…"

Realising her mistake, she grabbed her drink and tried to drown the words she'd just spoken. Piotr suppressed the smile at hearing just that little bit of confirmation. He spoke quickly to cover her embarrassment.

The long game was definitely the right approach here.

"You're right. It's probably just our old heads. Us oldies always want to know things we shouldn't."

"You're not that old."

Was that a twinkle in her eye?

That stumped him and he didn't know why. Thankfully the waiter arrived with their starter course before the pause developed into something uncomfortable.

Satisfied with that minor revelation for now, Piotr relaxed and he didn't press Julia any further on the topic. Instead he concentrated on making sure she enjoyed the evening. In the process he discovered that he also enjoyed the company and the chatter. The food wouldn't pass muster in a decent restaurant but it was adequate, as was the wine although Piotr ensured that he didn't feel any of the effects from the consumed alcohol.

They chatted through the evening. Julia clearly wasn't suppressing the drink's effects. Amidst the chatter, she flirted with him. Nothing untoward or improper within the inflated character of the setting, but enough to catch his attention.

As the end of the evening approached, he paid the bill and she suggested visiting some of the livelier bars. He demurred so instead she requested that he walk her home. Now he wondered if she did feel an attraction towards him. It didn't matter really, although maybe it would provide a more reliable angle to pry information from her. He'd have to play such a ploy with the utmost delicacy.

He pondered the situation as they walked through the commercial district towards her quarters. Many of the stores remained open throughout the whole 24 hours. Some of the smaller venues, typically those owned and operated by a single person, closed during off-hours. But even these closed and opened at the whim of the owner or the demands of the customers rather than an established timetable.

As a child, he'd grown up on a prosperous outdoor world. He vaguely remembered a pastoral life which followed the passage of the sun's light. After so long in space it felt wrong, almost unnatural not to see some life at any time of the day.

While he possessed the guile to appear sociable, that was far from the case. For him, the solitude of the hunt provided one of the key draws to becoming a bounty hunter. He preferred to live apart from other people, but that was countered by the joy he received by watching them. Yes, people were stupid and did ridiculous things and despite that he appreciated what they had.

He'd known since an early age that the life he saw in others wasn't one he would ever experience for himself. For some the thought might seem maudlin, but not for Piotr. The separation between him and the rest of humanity provided him with the edge to be a better hunter. Normally such introspections occurred deep in space with no-one around.

As they strolled through the late night crowds, Julia chatted merrily about inane topics. The latest gossip about the defence force pilots appeared to be her favourite. Every pilot learned that multitasking was an essential skill for surviving in space. Especially for those who ventured into dark or anarchic systems. That skill proved just as handy as he contemplated his existence while processing and responding to Julia's chatter.

For the briefest moment, he didn't realise that they had stopped in the deserted corridor outside of her apartment. She turned and the light appeared in her eyes. She leaned forward and he responded, kissing her lightly on the lips.

It was a bold move, but also a measured one.

He didn't allow the kiss to linger, but he saw from the change in expression on her face that he'd made the right choice. Now it was time to depart and allow the act to linger in her thoughts. The odd presence lurking in his mind nodded with satisfaction.

"I've had a lovely evening," he told her and he continued quickly before she invited him in. That wasn't part of the plan no matter what the lurking desire thought. "I have an early patrol, so I need to get these weary old bones to bed.

We will do this again."

Indecision crossed her face and then acceptance. He made sure to turn and smile at her as she left and, as he expected, she watched him leave from her door.

All in all, a satisfying evening. He'd received some confirmation of his hunch. And he might not want to do anything about it but knowing that you have the attention of an attractive young lady always felt good.

So good in fact that he decided to wander back through the commercial district and savour the ambience of people enjoying the night. He meandered past the shops and bars, people of all ages chatting, with the hot topic still being Julia's victory. Word of her taking the role of head of security for Freeholm had already started to spread.

Piotr lingered near some of these conversations to gauge a feel for the station's reaction to her appointment. The comments were primarily positive. For most people, she had proven what she needed to. A few dissenting voices suggested that she was too young and inexperienced for the job.

A familiar face caught his attention and he recognised Dee drinking tea at a table in the causeway. She was watching him, so he nodded in her direction before crossing and joining her. She offered him tea from the pot brewing in front of her. From the scent of the steam, it was an exotic brew. He accepted and sipped at the hot liquid.

"I was hoping you would come this way," she said.

"That seems unlikely."

"You're right, it was. However, you had such a pleasant evening that I anticipated that you would take the scenic route back to your quarters."

"So you're spying on me?"

"That's what I do."

He raised an eyebrow at the open admission and she laughed at him.

"We're in a privacy field. Ultrasonic and EM, no-one is eavesdropping on us."

"Isn't that suspicious?"

"Actually they're quite common in crowded public areas like this. Mine is a little more sophisticated than most."

"I see. Have you received any information on the ship details I gave you?"

"Not as yet."

"Why the delay?"

"What do you mean?"

"A database search takes nanoseconds."

"It's not as simple as that," she replied.

"I'm sure it isn't. I don't particularly care how simple or complicated it is, I just need the data. If you can't provide it then I'll look elsewhere."

"Don't bluff me, Piotr. If you could get the data elsewhere then you would have done so by now rather than waiting for me. We both know that no other system you have access to contains the information you need. Not even that contact of yours in the Pilots Federation."

She'd surprised him again.

"You forget I have access to all communications from and to this station."

"I didn't…"

"Yes of course you didn't send it through the station's system."

"Then how?"

"You can't expect a lady to reveal all of her secrets, now can you?"

He waited for her to continue, his earlier good mood spoiled.

"Now don't get pensive with me. There is a way we can help each other out."

"I'm already helping you by not revealing to the Freeholm authorities that they have an Imperial agent working in their flight operations."

"Oh and how would you prove that exactly? And who would you tell? That lovely young head of security you've just enjoyed the evening with? Now I wonder why you've been spending so much time with her recently."

"That's none of your business."

"Quite right. So let's not make it my business. Besides, I didn't come here to argue with you. I need some help and if you provide it then that provides me with the pretext I need to convince my superiors to rerun the search."

"What do you mean?"

"Well, I did hear back on the search. The response told me that the data was classified and above my clearance level. Now do you know what that means?"

"That there is something very peculiar about those ships."

"Yes."

"Could they be Imperial operatives?"

"Possibly although I doubt it. We're usually given a heads-up if there's another operation in the area."

"Okay. So tell me how do I get access to the data?"

"Help me out and I'll re-request but also letting my superiors know that you have been instrumental in the operation here."

"And I should just trust you?"

"Who else are you going to trust?"

He ignored that question. "And what would I have to do?"

"I need that oaf Hammer, as he likes to be known, to leave this station."

"Hammer? What is he to you?"

"Nothing. It's some of the equipment on his ship that poses a risk to my operation here. I had hoped that with our new head of security's victory against the pirates that he'd head off for a new adventure. It seems like she likes having the two of you around."

"He's been here for weeks without causing you a problem, so why the problem now?"

"If it had been up to me, he'd never have been allowed here in the first place. Unfortunately the choice isn't up to me. The equipment he has is used to disguise his payload. After the battle in the belt, that secret is long gone. However the same equipment can be used to trace some of my own devices."

"So why hasn't he?"

"I don't know. He probably doesn't even know that his equipment has that capability or what he would have to look for. Now the chances are he never will. Unfortunately for him, I can't take that chance. Which means neither can you."

"What exactly do you want me to do?"

"The next time he leaves the station he cannot come back."

"You want me to kill him?"

"I don't care as long as he doesn't come back."

Piotr considered the proposal. He didn't like Hammer and he assumed the feeling was mutual. Still, Piotr didn't generally kill people without cause. Although tracing those three ships provided a good reason.

The method would be tricky. Combat in open space was Piotr's speciality but that would be too open. He needed to maintain the good relationship with Julia and she wouldn't appreciate losing one of her two additions to the team. No matter how temporary they were.

A possible avenue to be explored opened in his thoughts. Hammer's ship was essentially a flying arsenal. Perhaps some form of malfunction would do the trick.

"If I kill him then you'll get the data?"

"I will do what I can."

"Good, then I'll see what can be done."

- 25 -

The controls on the Cobra Mark III felt sluggish compared to the old Eagle that Julia usually flew. For a trading ship it handled well and also possessed decent straight line speed. In fact it was much faster than the small fighter. She might have learned how to fly in the Eagle but it was in Lina's Cobra she first ventured into space.

Lina claimed that her ship had been handed down through four generations. The first generation being one of the famous Jamesons who plied the space lanes decades ago. To Julia it seemed that there had been so many Jamesons that there must have been a clan of them. Besides, Lina wasn't above telling a tall story for the fun of it. Her ship was old no doubt, but one of *the* Cobra Mark IIIs seemed unlikely.

The memory made her smile and she glanced out of the cockpit. Despite how spacious it was compared to her normal ship, the view felt restricted. She hated to think what flying a really big ship would be like. During her idle imaginings of flying off to the frontier, she'd examined the different ships she could take and the Cobra Mark III had been near the top of the list. It was small as trading vessels went, but the hold was big enough to make a living with and it handled well enough to be able to put up a fight against most opponents. The four hard points also allowed a decent selection of firepower.

They usually relied on passing traders to transport the monthly quote of minerals to Laphria. Part of the treaty obligations included delivering a fixed quota of metals and the rare minerals required by the Laphrian shipyard. They paid a fair price for the goods so it provided a steady income for the station. For this run, Julia piloted one of the station's reserve fleet of transports.

The news of her father's death had scared away many of the regular traders and while news of the success against the mercenaries (although she still referred to them as pirates to avoid unwelcome questions) was slowly spreading, they had to do this run themselves.

Luckily, Lina offered her help with the run. Although her company provided both a blessing and a curse. She valued the older woman's advice and Julia didn't know how she would have coped over the past weeks without her support. On the other hand, Lina did like to pry into Julia's business a bit too much for comfort.

She could have done the run alone in the battered old Type 7 but Julia drew the line at flying a box with engines. Since the battle in NLTT 8065, things had remained quiet but even so, if something did happen she wanted at least a fighting chance of defending herself.

As they pulled away from the station and flew along the cleared flight path, the hail request blinked.

"Yes, Lina?"

"That's the thanks I get for accompanying you on your boring trip?"

"That and the credits on your balance."

"Well that true, but it's not the reason I agreed to come along."

"I know and your presence is appreciated."

"Of course it is. Now I hear you're developing a taste for older men?"

"What?! Of course not."

"Really? So you haven't been going out with Piotr then?"

"Only as friends."

"I hear you looked quite spectacular. I don't think I've

ever seen you in a dress."

"That's not true and you know it."

"When you were twelve doesn't count."

"There's nothing going on."

"So you say, but be careful with that one."

"I know you don't like him."

"Liking him has nothing to do with it. I don't trust him. He's a cold one."

"He seems friendly enough to me."

"Oh he's very good at hiding it, but behind those eyes there's a real hunter."

"Of course there is. He is a bounty hunter."

"You know what I mean. That man always keeps his eyes on the prize. To be honest I'm surprised he's still around."

"I don't see why. I asked him and Hammer to stay for a few more weeks."

"It's why he agreed to it that puzzles me. He's a driven man and I don't understand what drives him." Lina laughed, the sound rich even across the comms channel. "Maybe he's fallen for someone."

"There's nothing going on. Anyway Hammer stayed and you don't seem to be bothered by that."

"Hammer is very different. There's nothing hidden there. Vanchenko is a different matter."

"I think you're wrong."

"It's possible, I guess. It is an infinite universe after all."

"Ha ha."

"All right, if you won't tell me about your new boyfriend, are you settling in with the new job?"

"There's a lot more office work than I expected."

"After all the times your father complained about it, you're really surprised by that?"

"Well, to be honest I don't think I believed him. It just seemed to be something he complained about."

"Have you hired an assistant?"

"Not yet."

"You should. They would take a lot of the load off you. Your father didn't because he had a masochistic streak and wanted to deal with everything himself. Just accept that there's parts of the job you can hand over. You're the head of security, not the whole team."

"I suppose you're right. Who would you recommend?"

"I don't know. I'm not an administration-type person, I use an expert system to keep track of all my stuff."

"Maybe I should do the same."

"I wouldn't recommend it. The expert system is fine for dealing with the other automated organisations like Gal-Net and local duties. But for your job you need someone who can work with other members of the team."

"I don't really know the administrative staff that well."

"To be honest, neither do I. Although, what about the new girl in flight operations?"

"New girl? There's no new girl in flight ops."

"Yes there is. The young one. You know the one I mean, the redhead."

"Dee? Dee Callum?"

"Sounds about right. I've heard some good things about her. She seems quite organised."

"She's not new. Dee's been at the station for almost a year."

"Whatever. I think she'll be good. You need to be on top of your game in flight operations, even in a station as quiet as Freeholm. I hear she also gets on with the pilots and the technicians. Even the engineers and you know what a grouchy lot they can be!"

"You could be right."

"Of course I'm right. Engineers are famous for their short tempers."

"Very amusing. You should do a live show."

"So what else is going on? Did you hear anything from the people that helped you?"

"You know I can't tell you about that. What is it with

you and Piotr about them?"

"I don't know about Vanchenko but I'm worried about them. You haven't told any of us who they are."

"I can't, Lina."

"Well they worry me. You, and by association us, owe them a debt. Could you have avenged your father without their help?"

"Probably not. It's not a problem though, they had their own reasons for being involved."

"Which you can't tell me."

"Sorry."

"I'm not stupid, you know."

"I never said you were."

"There were three of them, weren't there?"

"I can't say."

"You don't need to. The sensor network tracked three ships during the battle in the belt. They also tracked the same three ships and yours jumping out of the system. It seems an unlikely coincidence to me. Especially as those three ships match the ships that departed from the station the day after your father's funeral. Wait a minute. Didn't Vanchenko go dashing after them?"

"Well yes, but he explained that he was concerned for the patrol of Sidewinders I sent. They would have been outmatched if they had decided to return."

"Hold on Julia, you can't have it both ways. I know the same ships that left were the same ships that helped you. While I can't prove they were same three strangers from the bar on the night of the funeral, it does seem like a reasonable assumption."

"Can we just drop it?"

"No we can't. You're the head of security now. I don't blame you for wanting to use any help you could to kill the bastards who murdered your father. I'm fairly sure that I would have done the same."

"And that has been dealt with."

"Yes it has, but what if they come back?"

"That's not going to happen."

"How can you be so sure?"

"Because I know."

"What do you know? That first meeting with them was hardly a pleasant one. You damn near threw them off the station. Do you know why Vanchenko is after them?"

"He isn't."

"Julia, you need to see the bigger picture here. Doesn't he keep asking about them?"

"No more than you do. Less in fact."

"Okay then. What was his reaction when you returned to Freeholm? Was he happy that you had achieved the vengeance you'd set out for?"

"Well…"

"Indeed. He tore off to the spot where you all jumped from. And now he's hanging around because you are a connection to them."

"That isn't true. He's been helpful in keeping the area around Freeholm secure."

"Of course he's made himself useful. He would hardly do otherwise. He might be many things but he doesn't look like a stupid man. And now he's taking advantage of you…"

"He is not taking advantage of me. I'm not twelve anymore. I do understand the ways of the world."

"I'm not saying you don't. I'm just asking you to be careful. There's more than just your own life at stake now."

The conversation petered out in a strained silence between the two of them after that exchange. Julia found it so frustrating that Lina refused to acknowledge that she was capable of making decisions. She's been chosen to be head of security, after all. She knew the station council. They wouldn't have asked her to do the job just because of the memory of her father.

The argument had become a familiar one over the past few weeks. One that only seemed to rest when Lina left on a trade run. Julia loved the woman dearly. She just wished that she would accept Julia was now in charge of her own life.

Dwelling on the argument just made the feelings worse, so she focused her thoughts onto the plans she'd begun to formulate for the development of Freeholm's defence force. She hadn't spoken to the council officially yet, but the individual members she had encountered indicated that they were serious about preventing similar problems in the future. That required investment, but also a plan.

The station operated too few ships and too few pilots to keep even the immediate volume around the station secure. She'd discussed the options with Piotr and he agreed that developing the capability for longer range patrols and rapid response would be a worthwhile investment for Freeholm.

When they approached the inner border of the belt, Lina offered the olive branch and broke the silence.

"Did the Laphrians say anything about your incursion outside the belt?"

"No, why?"

"Well we're about to meet the esteemed Captain Belin for our escort to the planet to deliver their minerals. Do they know you're piloting one of the transports?"

"No. I sent a message to Captain Belin yesterday to arrange the rendezvous. He didn't respond although one of the staff officers did and informed me that another vessel would be providing the escort and would meet us at the usual departure point."

"Check your scanner."

"Shit. There's two ships there!"

"Indeed. I should have thought of this earlier. You technically broke the treaty and there's been no reaction to that yet. To be honest, you should have thought of this as well, Miss Head of Security."

"Not now, Lina."

"You're right, that was a cheap shot."

"What do we do?"

"That's your call."

"I'm reading two contacts, but they're not resolving. We'll need to leave the belt to determine the ship types."

"I could go ahead. They won't be after me."

"Do you really think they want to act for me crossing into their space?"

"I don't know, but it's possible. Have they ever ignored a breach before?"

"Not that I'm aware of. I guess I assumed that Captain Belin had smoothed things over. He did get along with my father."

"They respected each other, that's for sure."

"I don't want to appear weak."

"That doesn't mean it's a good idea to walk straight into a trap."

"If they had a problem then they would have contacted the usual diplomatic channels, wouldn't they?"

"I would have thought so. This isn't my particular area of expertise though. I do know that some of their press have been spewing their usual bile a bit more vehemently than usual."

"They've not mentioned any incident though, just the usual nonsense about us holding their economy to ransom."

"And that's what worries me. They should be having a field day about it."

"Maybe that's why the Laphrian government haven't mentioned it. There's no reason why they wouldn't want to maintain the status quo."

"Perhaps."

"There's no way to know for certain and we won't find out what's happening here without completing the trade. So let's get it over with."

"All right, but I'll take the lead. You be ready to run if there's trouble."

"I don't need you to run interference for me."

"In this case you do." For the first time since she was a teenager, Julia heard anger in Lina's voice. "Holding you in custody would be big deal for the colony. Our people have been through enough recently, don't you think?"

Her first instinct was to argue, and respond to the tone of Lina's statement rather than its content. Before she opened her mouth she realised that Lina was right, so she simply agreed and took up formation behind the older woman's ship.

She flew steadily, ready to divert all power to her shields and engines at the smallest sign of untoward activity. As they exited the belt into open space, the first contact resolved into an Anaconda, one of the light cruiser conversions that formed the mainstay of the Laphrian fleet. The second contact was a Lakon Type 9, a heavy transport and that did seem odd. Why would the Laphrians bring a transport?

The comms channel blinked indicating an incoming hail and she opened the channel.

"Freeholm vessels, this the Laphrian Navy cruiser *Sito*."

"Where's Captain Belin and the *Demeter*?" Julia asked.

"Captain Belin has been deployed elsewhere, ma'am. My name is Captain Wirral and will be responsible for future escort duties."

"Ma'am?" She couldn't help but laugh. Lina's chuckles on the private channel indicated she felt the same.

"My apologies, ma'am. Is there an honorific you would prefer I use?"

"Julia is fine."

"I'm to inform you that the procedure for the treaty quote transfers is changing as of today."

"I wasn't informed of any change."

"No ma'am and I apologise. It looks like there's been a mix-up with Flight Command. They should have informed you yesterday."

For a supposed mistake, the captain had an excuse at

the ready. Julia wondered what was really going on.

"I'm also authorised to request that these shipments are increased in size and frequency."

"Wait a minute. You can't summarily change the terms of the treaty."

"You misunderstand, ma'am. The treaty obligations aren't being changed. We will buy the extra resources from you at market price plus five per cent. We will also continue to pay the shipping charge, although from now on we will send a transport to collect the resources."

"Why didn't you send the request through the usual trade channels?"

"I'm sure you are aware that elements of our political establishment are not happy with our trade with Freeholm."

"I've seen the newsfeeds."

"We want to expand our shipyard operations to cover a wider variety of ships and that means we need more materials. We'd rather do that without causing any political upset."

"Why is the Navy involved in this?"

"We're just a facilitator, ma'am. We provide escort for the deliveries anyway and communications between the station and Navy patrols are common so won't raise untoward attention. They are also more secure than commercial channels."

"I see. That makes sense I suppose. What is it you want and how often?"

"I'll transmit the specifics, but in broad terms it's quadruple the current shipments on a weekly basis."

That was a sizeable increase. It was well within the station's production capacity and the price was more than fair. With the increased quantities, they would need the Laphrian transports. It saved them a boring trip to the planet as well. The deal looked like a winner.

"I'll need to confirm with the station council, but I

don't anticipate any reason to refuse the request."

"Thank you ma'am. I'm sure you'll understand that with some of the recent events, we will need to insist on an escort for the transport to and from the station. The Navy will continue to do the same in our territory."

"That won't be necessary, the trouble has been dealt with."

"That's good news, ma'am. Fleet Command will be pleased to learn that the pirates are no longer a threat. Do you have confirmation I can provide for your claim?"

"I'm afraid not."

"I see. Then I'm sure you'll understand that we will still require the escort?"

"Yes Captain. What about our current consignment?"

"Please escort the transport to Freeholm and deliver the new shipment. The captain is authorised to transfer payment upon delivery."

"That's fine. We'll escort the Lakon to the station."

"Thank you ma'am. And I have been advised to urge you to keep this deal confidential. We don't wish to antagonise some of the factions on the home planet."

"I'm sure you don't, but that's fine with us."

"Thank you ma'am. I'll be patrolling this region for the next month so as soon as the new shipment is loaded, inform me and we'll arrange the hand over."

"Will do."

They watched the lumbering Lakon change course towards the path through the belt. The pair took position on the flanks of the freighter and over the private comms channel, Julia spoke to Lina.

"So much for your worrying. We've just made the colony richer!"

- 26 -

Pulling escort duty wasn't how Hammer preferred to spend his time. In all honesty he still wasn't sure why he remained at Freeholm. After her success in dealing with the attackers, Julia had asked him and Piotr to remain in case there were any further attacks. So far that didn't appear to be the case and now, almost a month later, Hammer would usually have been long gone.

Yet he hadn't left.

The damage to his Anaconda during the battle meant that he couldn't have left immediately anyway. The big drawback to his style of ambush was that it tended to result in a lot of damage to his ship. He'd worked with the local engineers and technicians and they'd repaired it to his satisfaction.

The unusual makeup of his ship meant that extensive repairs were problematic for most stations because of the large amounts of raw materials needed to restore the armoured plating and extra bulkheads. He usually needed to take the ship to the nearest shipyard. As Freeholm extracted and refined the materials used for ship manufacture, they provided all the materials he needed.

Repairing his ship also allowed him to spend time with the maintenance crew. Working with them counted as a different experience to drinking and fighting with them. A few were once prisoners when the station had been a penal colony. He struggled to believe some of the tales of cruelty they told him.

Aside from the stories told over a few beers, he discovered that he enjoyed spending time with the crowd that kept the ships operational on Freeholm. It was a strange sensation. Hammer got on with people but that tended to be on the surface only. Even when working planetside, he rarely interacted with the other farmers. 'Farmers' being a relative term on most agricultural planets. Technicians would be more accurate as robots did most of the actual growing and tending to the crops. It was outdoor technician work though and the vast size of the farms meant little human contact.

Something had changed him since arriving at this out of the way station. For the first time in many years, he cared about something other than his revenge. That revenge that had been completed some time ago, but living the life didn't fade away so easily.

Seeing Julia live through the same experience as him no doubt aided the transition. It was easier to spot something in others than identify it in himself. The fact that she had gained her revenge so quickly pleased him. He knew all too well what effect the simmering rage could have if left too long to fester.

He liked the people here. Their society was to some extent an insular one, similar to the villages he lived in before. They all knew each other and each other's business. Yet unlike those farming villages, the people here maintained a more cosmopolitan approach to strangers. That attitude no doubt stemmed from the regular contact with traders from the neighbouring systems.

The minerals and ores mined here were valuable but not so rare that it was worth extended travel for. That meant their trade was by necessity with the local systems only and Laphria in particular. If rumours were to be believed then the expansion of the Laphrian shipyard business would bring more business to Freeholm which would surely be a good thing.

He wondered if newfound wealth would change the people here.

He hoped not.

As much as he'd come to appreciate the people here, and that had resurrected his desire to settle somewhere, he understood that this wasn't the place for him. The open skies of an outdoor world called to him once again. He's always honour these people in his thoughts as they'd taught him that life could perhaps be lived again.

He tried to explain it to one of the maintenance engineers in the Dockers bar on the lowest level the night before. And that was another thing. The beer no longer satisfied as it once did.

As much as he didn't want to admit it to himself, he knew the answer. His routine of finding the next target, playing possum and then killing whoever was foolish enough to attack him had grown stale. More than that, drinking all hours and fighting whoever was foolish enough to stand against him had grown stale as well.

Hammer did not appreciate this turn of events and there lay the irony.

It wasn't as if it had been a gradual process. At least then there would have been some warning. Or perhaps the signs had been there all along and he hadn't noticed? He cast that doubt away easily. He knew the catalyst for this change and she had finally agreed to take her father's place.

The developing relationship between her and Piotr also surprised him. And while it wasn't his place, he didn't approve. Over the years he'd encountered many bounty hunters. Like in all walks of life you met all sorts, and Hammer had learned to spot the dangerous ones. Piotr hid it well and as far as Hammer was concerned that made him all the more dangerous.

It also surprised him that Piotr remained at the station as well when Julia asked. Perhaps there was some genuine attraction there but Hammer couldn't or didn't want to believe it. And that provided him with another reason for staying and an excuse for holding off making his own decision for a little while longer.

That was reinforced when Lina asked him to stay after Julia had done the same. Her reason was different though. She disliked Piotr as well, more than that she didn't trust him. He'd agreed to her request.

This run with the Laphrian escort was a simple trip to the edge of the belt. He kept a close eye on the scanner of course, his job was to protect the slow freighter after all. There hadn't been any trouble since Julia had returned so he didn't expect it to happen now, but any experienced pilot kept an eye on the scanner even in a secure system.

Julia remained tight-lipped about the battle, which didn't bother Hammer at all. If the girl wanted to keep secrets then that was her business. Lina and Piotr appeared to think otherwise. Although they'd both backed off on the subject recently.

Now Lina... There was a woman worth thinking about.

And from a seemingly ongoing series of shocks, that perhaps was the strangest. Or was it? It could be a symptom of the changes in perception that had ambushed him recently. He discovered something that he didn't know existed and that was a hole in his life.

He wondered if Lina could fill that hole.

Now that almost embarrassingly corny thought was indeed a strange one and one that challenged the return to outdoor life. She didn't seem the type to want to live under the influence of gravity. He'd encountered others like her on his travels. Loners who preferred the company of their ships to people. Although was he any different?

The comparison with the other traders he'd met wasn't completely accurate. She had close friends here on the station, some like Julia so close they might as well be family. And that posed another possible problem – would she be interested in moving elsewhere?

Hammer smiled to himself. Even the idea that he was

considering such possibilities felt alien to him and it brought about an unsettling union of doubt and hope. He understood that this would be a pivotal moment in his life. Where it would lead after that point he didn't know, but he would be at the station for a few more weeks, so he would take the time to get to know Lina better and who knew where that would lead?

The undercurrent of euphoria tinged with a little fear of the unknown buoyed him throughout the journey to the rendezvous. The escort should have been provided by Piotr until earlier that morning when a ship malfunction grounded him. Although Hammer had been looking forward to a day tinkering with his ship, he'd agreed to fly the escort readily enough. It wasn't an arduous task and even with all his personal changes he loved to fly. There was something powerful about piloting such a large ship on his own.

Alongside him the Laphrian Type 9 flew in close formation. Hammer had spoken to the ship's captain before departure and they'd agreed a tight formation pattern. The freighter carried a full load of minerals and refined ores. With a fighter escort or even a faster ship the escort could sit farther away, and so be better able to react to any incoming threat. With all the armour's extra mass, Hammer's Anaconda was only just quicker and more manoeuvrable than the other ship so he considered a close defence to be the best tactic.

Not that anyone expected any trouble. There hadn't been any attacks since Julia's return and a few traders had passed through without incident. If any pirates lingered in the area then such a prize as the Lakon might provide sufficient temptation.

The other captain proved to be polite, but tight-lipped so there was little conversation during the flight. Hammer kept a close watch on the scanner. Focusing on space around him also diverted his thoughts from the more troubling questions regarding his future.

The occasional small rock posed little threat to his ship or the accompanying Lakon for that matter. In that regard his ship had changed. As it seemed unlikely that he'd need to pull the 'limping decoy' act in the near future, he invested in new shield generators. Ones more worthy of the Anaconda. In all likelihood his ship was now tougher than the military upgraded Anaconda waiting for them at the edge of the belt.

At the handover, the warship confirmed that they would return in a week's time for the next shipment. Hammer advised them to contact Freeholm's flight control to arrange an escort. With a few more polite pleasantries, the two ships vanished into supercruise.

Hammer changed course to return to Freeholm. He considered whether to invite Lina for dinner that evening. He knew that she was on the station as he'd seen her Cobra listed in the docking bay manifest. One part of his mind scoffed at his indecision. After all, he wasn't known for being shy. The majority of his thoughts focused instead on the possibilities. He hadn't been on a date for a very long time. There had been encounters over the years, little more than drunken fumbles between lonely people sharing the same space for a few hours.

This was something different and the novelty of it caused him to break the cardinal rule. He paid little attention to the scanner or the ship's system until a strident alarm and female voice announced that his ship was overheating.

First he wondered when the hell he reactivated the ship's voice. There was something unsettling about having it speak to him. Probably something to do with the scary stories of AIs his father told him as a child that hadn't quite dissipated as he grew up.

The alarm repeated and he realised that there was a threat. Not outside, but inside the ship. He scanned the holographic consoles and saw that the ship was indeed overheating.

It hadn't reached critical levels and while he still cursed, he did so thanking whatever error had triggered the change in alarm protocols. A bigger problem became apparent. The ship shouldn't be overheating in its current operating profile. The engines remained balanced at the sweet spot that enabled maximum manoeuvrability while maintaining a decent speed. Weapons were enabled but weren't firing. Shields were up, but shouldn't cause this level of overload.

The alarm shrieked again as the heat build-up increased. At any moment it would start to cause damage to the internal systems. As an experienced pilot, he kept a fire group dedicated for the heat sinks launchers only. These cheap devices stored ship's heat in disposable heat sinks. They not only provided a quick means of dumping heat but also acted as effective decoys during combat.

The released heat sink extracted a substantial amount of the heat out of the ship's system and the alarms quietened. The mystery of the malfunction remained so Hammer cycled through the ship's systems to determine the cause.

Thirty seconds later the heat spiked again and the alarm filled the bridge. He dumped another heat sink and continued to scan the ship's systems until the alarm screamed again.

He couldn't maintain this cycle for long. His supply was limited.

Another heat sink launched and then a sinking feeling in his gut.

He couldn't be that stupid, surely?

He checked the most obvious control on his consoles and there it was. The heat vents were closed. Ships, especially those as large as Hammer's Anaconda, generated a lot of heat. Generally ships kept their vents open to radiate the heat into space.

In the absolute cold of space, heat was a hard thing to

hide. If they wanted to be less noticeable then they could close the heat vents. Pilots called this 'buttoning up'. It was also a common mistake for rookie pilots to button up by mistake and damage their ships without realising it until too late.

He'd made that same mistake soon after taking command of the Anaconda. While embarrassing, he was at least mildly relieved to have discovered the cause. He'd just have to make sure that no-one else learned of the incident. That would be a difficult one to hold down in the bar.

With some relief, he selected the button and opened the vents. The vent status flashed to open but the heat continued to climb. He was too slow in launching the heat sink and the ship's voice informed him that communications had been damaged.

He cursed again. Even if he could call for help, at this rate of heat build-up there wouldn't be enough time for rescue from Freeholm. He ejected another heat sink and then started switching off all the systems he could. First he disabled the flight assist and powered down the engines – he could coast along for a while without danger. The scanner showed no asteroids in his immediate path.

The heat signature continued to increase.

That didn't make any sense. The engines accounted for most of the ship's heat generation unless the weapons were being fired. He took the weapons offline. No change, although as they weren't being fired he hadn't expected any.

Where was all this extra heat coming from?

He ejected another heat sink to buy himself a bit more time. He had three left and at the current rate that gave him a minute and a half until the heat began chewing through his hull and key systems.

He shut down the sensors and his scanner went blank. No change.

He ejected another heat sink.

He shut down the shields.

The heat dropped by a fraction and then rose again.

He flicked quickly through the systems menu turning off everything he could.

Still the heat continued to rise and he only had one major system left.

He launched another heat sink.

The life support system was only active major system on the ship and he turned it off. For a moment the heat level held and then began to fall.

Hammer cursed.

Life support systems were designed to be as energy efficient as possible and to generate as little heat as physics would allow. Without life support he had no air or heat.

Turning off the life support systems wasn't immediate death. The air would remain breathable for a few hours and the ship was well insulated so it wouldn't get too cold until after he ran out of air. Presumably the ship's designer's deemed that suffocation was preferable to freezing.

There were few options. The first was to try and contact Freeholm, they didn't have a tug but hopefully they would be able to send help. The comms system had suffered a heat-generated malfunction but maybe it could be repaired.

He could just eject. The RemLok escape capsule would return him to the nearest station and he could salvage his ship later. That one was definitely on the last resort list. He didn't like the idea of leaving the ship drifting unattended, even this close to the station.

His remaining option was to locate and fix the malfunction in the life support system. Like most ship systems, it was a modular design to allow easy repair and modification. The manufacturers loved selling upgrades to their basic and even not-so-basic models.

If fate was with him then he could trace the fault,

switch out the broken module and be on his way again before he ran out of air. That assumed that the fault lay in one of the key components that he kept spares of. On that front he was well prepared. He often travelled in deep space and through dangerous star systems and in those situations it was wise to carry spares for anything your life depended on.

He checked the internal sensors to ensure that it was safe to leave the bridge. As he did so, he noticed that the temperature in the cargo hold was much higher than the rest of the ship interior. Apart from that anomaly it looked safe so he unstrapped himself from the chair and headed out of the bridge.

Each major compartment of the ship contained an emergency toolkit and the RemLok safety gear was unobtrusively stored within the collar of his flight suit, so he was unencumbered as he moved through the ship. The lack of gravity aided his movement.

Reaching the main cargo lift, he accessed the ship's systems through the panel built into the wall by the access hatch. Like the battleships of ancient times, each compartment in the Anaconda could be sealed airtight. This prevented fire and atmospheric contaminants from spreading and catastrophic atmosphere loss in the event of a hull breach.

The main life support unit was situated next to the cargo hold. In a regular Anaconda, the cargo hold was a huge cavern ready for transporting goods of all types across human space. In Hammer's Anaconda the space had been mostly filled with extra bulkheads and armour as well as magazines for the missile launchers.

He realised how lucky he had been to have had the cargo hold resealed at its smaller size. Not only did that mean less energy was required to maintain atmosphere but if the missiles had been stored there, the soaring temperature could have caused them to cook off.

With all the safety systems on advanced munitions

that wouldn't have resulted in an explosion. No, it would have been a more insidious danger of noxious chemicals in the air. The ship's computer should detect that type of threat but as with anything in space you couldn't take it for granted.

From the panel, he ran a diagnostics trace. This pulse contained a software agent that traversed a system by providing its own energy, to determine damage even if it was powered down. It couldn't diagnose higher order issues, but could determine physical damage.

The trace revealed a variation in the life support system's configuration in the cargo hold sub-system. With no other faults revealed, he started there and quickly discovered the cause of the malfunction. Underneath the access panel, he found an override circuit board attached to the sub-system control board.

The circuitry on the board revealed its simple but deadly purpose. It created a feedback loop between the life support system and the cargo hold. The hold came with a built-in refrigeration unit which was set to maximum. Meanwhile the sensors reported to the refrigeration unit that it needed to keep the cargo hold cooler while simultaneously telling the life support system that the cargo hold was too hot.

The two systems battled each other without realising it, consuming large amounts of energy and thus generating a lot of heat. With the problem identified, the fix didn't take long. As a precaution he also ran a software diagnostic on the system to check for any other hidden surprises.

He returned to the bridge and on the main console the self-diagnostics reported a minor change in the heat management software. The margin of error built into the system had been modified, not by a lot but enough to approach critical levels before the alarm was raised.

He restored the manufacturer's backup for the routine

and then reactivated the life support system. As it powered up he tensed, ready to shut it down immediately at the sign of anything untoward. The system came online without error and after a few minutes he brought the other systems back online.

The trip back to the Freeholm took longer than the outward bound journey. He no longer thought about what a date with Lina might be like. He didn't care why they had sabotaged his ship. He just wanted to know who.

- 27 -

Julia watched as the team assembled in the briefing room. She stood at the podium ready to provide the briefing. Beside her sat Dee Callum. Julia invited her to join her staff, or rather to be her staff, and Dee had agreed. The young woman had proved to be a godsend for Julia. The paperwork for the head of security position had mounted at an alarming rate. Thankfully Dee approached the problem with efficient determination and now the office ran smoother than it had even in her father's time.

In front of her, the four defence force pilots formed a not-so-subtle barrier between Piotr and the left and Hammer on the right. Since his return to the station after escorting the Laphrian freighter a week ago, Julia had noticed a rising tension between the two of them. The change was more apparent with Hammer. He'd become withdrawn and seemingly suspicious of everyone. He rarely spoke to anyone on the team and in fact had to be dragged off one of the station's technicians after discovering him working on his ship. Once well-liked by the maintenance and engineering crew, they now avoided him as much as possible.

Julia had tried speaking to him without any success. He'd evidently spent too many years alone, even Lina could get barely more than a few words from him.

As for Piotr, he claimed that he didn't know the cause of the problem. Julia noticed that the bounty hunter avoided Hammer as much as possible. Piotr had proved to be as much of a boon to her office as Dee had. He had helped by providing contacts for new ships which meant she at least had some good news to start the briefing with.

"Good morning everyone."

All except Hammer responded. He continued to frown into the distance. Not aimed at her, she noticed, but he was definitely brooding over something. She made a mental note to investigate further and this time she would accept no refusal on his part.

"There are just four items for this morning's briefing and we even have some good news to start with."

She smiled at the assembled pilots.

"First item is new ships for the defence force, which at the moment means you four." They responded with hopeful grins. "The station council has agreed to the budget increase for the new ships and thanks to Piotr we have sourced six Eagles at a reasonable price. Naturally you four will be the first to receive the upgrades."

The four cheered. The sound was far too loud in the small room. A few staff in the neighbouring office looked to see what the commotion was about.

"The new ships will arrive in two weeks. In the meantime my ship will be available to you for familiarisation flights and training. The station's maintenance team have agreed and increased their schedule to keep her flying for more than the usual daily flight."

She received appreciative nods from the four pilots and a confident smile from Piotr.

"The current Sidewinders will be retasked for training purposes."

"Will new pilots be joining us?" Rob Deacon asked. He had carefully placed himself next to Hammer as the only person in the room even comparable in size to him.

"I was just getting to that. We've had a couple of young volunteers. They're already flight qualified, although only in small traders. Piotr has agreed to assess their potential on a few training flights in the Sidewinders. If they work out then we'll assign them to the Eagles and we'll divide the training up between the four of you."

Less enthusiastic nods greeted that news.

"You have all met Dee Callum who has joined my staff. There will be others coming, but I'm ready to announce one of the other key placements for the team."

They all looked at her expectantly. Except for Piotr who already knew who she'd chosen as they discussed the role over dinner the night before.

"We've never had an official lead pilot for the defence force. We've had pilots who have assumed the role but have never been acknowledged for it. Well, I would like to change that right now."

It hadn't been an easy choice. Not so much for her selecting someone to fill the role, but more the distance she now needed to enforce between herself and the flight operations. Her father had managed both only due to the small size of the force, but also because Julia had shared the role. This first expansion was modest in comparison to her ultimate plan for a full squadron of fighters. They would then need officers and assigning a lead pilot was the first step in that process.

"Rob, will you stand up?"

He did so with a wide grin on his face. The others applauded their approval. They all respected Rob as a pilot, and he also took charge of situations when needed to. Lina and Piotr both agreed that he would make a fine lead pilot.

Julia stepped down from the podium and fixed a pair of wings she'd printed onto his tunic.

"Rob Deacon, by the authority assigned to me by the elected station council, I grant you the rank of lead pilot."

Julia stepped back to the podium and waited for the excitement to calm down.

"Next item of business is the latest Laphrian trade. They're sending another Type 9 this afternoon to pick up their latest order. Despite the fact that things have been calm here for a few weeks, they still want an escort for their freighter. The cargo is worth a lot of credits so naturally we're happy to oblige. It's this new business that is helping us fund the new ships."

Her original plan was to assign Hammer to these runs as long as he was at the station. His ship had by far the most firepower and demonstrated the station's commitment to the deal. With Hammer's abrupt change in attitude, she was now wary of trusting him with the responsibility. However, she faced a dilemma of too few resources, especially with the news that she would shortly announce.

The regular pilots needed to get up to strength on the Eagles as quickly as possible. And to match the escort that Hammer could provide, she would need all four pilots which would restrict the station's ability to respond if anything happened elsewhere. For now she would have to rely on Hammer and hope that nothing went wrong.

"Hammer, I need you to provide escort for the freighter. You need to cover the inward and outward journeys."

He didn't seem happy about the assignment. "Why not send the bounty hunter?"

"Because it's my call and I need you to do it."

Hammer looked ready to argue then shrugged his shoulders and nodded.

What the hell was going on with him?

"There is another reason and that is because I have a mission for Piotr."

The bounty hunter sat up in response to her statement. This was news to him. She had been tempted to discuss the matter with him during dinner. Dee advised that he had the right skills and ship for the job. Lina simply warned her about placing too much trust in him.

In the end the decision was a purely practical one. As an independent operator, he provided a veneer of cover if he was caught. She certainly couldn't do it herself. The Laphrians had already covered up one breach of the treaty, an incursion this deep in their space would be difficult to cover up if she were caught.

Again the two women had disagreed over whether she needed to act at all. Dee argued that the information was clearly suspect and probably intended for her to make a wrong decision, thus jeopardising their relationship with the planet. Lina was less sanguine about it. She could believe that the information was false, but she insisted that they needed to be sure.

And now the team needed to be informed of the information she had received.

"Now for the final piece of business and I have to stress that what I'm about to say cannot be discussed with anyone outside of this room. Nor can it be discussed outside of a secure area even with the people in this briefing."

That caught everyone's attention and they all leaned closer. Even Hammer.

"Two days ago, I received a communication from an ally on Laphria. They claim that their Navy is preparing some sort of strike against us."

"That doesn't make sense," Rob declared. "What would they have to gain?"

"I agree that it seems nonsensical. Trade with them has increased significantly with the new deal."

"But they won't let you near the planet to deliver it," Hammer entered the conversation.

"True and that is one of the reasons we need to confirm whether this information is correct."

"Who is your source?" Piotr asked.

"I can't say."

"This room is secure, surely?"

"Even so I can't name the source. It doesn't matter anyway as we can no longer contact them."

"Why not?"

"We don't know and that concerns me."

"It might just be coincidence."

"Maybe, but we cannot take that chance."

"You mentioned one of the reasons. What are the others?" Rob asked.

"It's mostly circumstantial. Our media monitoring of their local newsfeeds has shown a marked increase in the hard-line rhetoric against us. Traders aren't being allowed to the shipyard."

"Has that been confirmed?"

"Yes. Lina detoured on her last flight and was denied access. They've set up a temporary trading outpost well beyond Laphrian orbit. Visiting traders have to report there and none are allowed to approach any closer to the planet without authorisation and official escort. From her sensor logs, we were able to discern a large number of transports ferrying goods to and from the planet."

"That must be costing them a fortune," San Kira commented. "Have they provided an explanation?"

"To the traders they said only that there was a security exercise in progress."

"That's one hell of an exercise," San Kira responded.

"Agreed. The council's diplomatic representative has contacted the government and the Navy and were told the same thing. However, a back channel contact told us that the extra security is part of the deal with the Imperial Navy."

"What do you mean?" Hammer asked.

"Well, from the newsfeeds and local sources we know that they are buying new ships from the Gutamaya shipyards. Cutters and short-range fighters from what we can tell. As part of that deal, the Laphrian shipyard is being upgraded to provide service and maintenance facilities for Imperial-type ships."

"I wouldn't have thought that there are many ships in this region needing servicing?" Rob said.

"As far as we know there aren't. However the Laphrian Navy are supposed to be replacing all of the Anaconda light cruisers with Cutters and they'll want to service those ships themselves. We're also not that far from the Empire although the jump route is a bit convoluted. Having a local shipyard will provide a stepping stone for more activity in the region. Apparently the upgrades to the shipyard require some Imperial technology that they don't like sharing without significant security protocols."

"And is that true?"

"We don't know. No-one here has had any dealings with the Empire. Or at least not enough to be familiar with how they conduct this level of business."

"So the reason might be genuine?"

"It might. However, we need to be sure which is why I want Piotr to fly a recon mission to the shipyards and provide data on what the Laphrians are up to."

"On this evidence?" Piotr replied. "You've heard a rumour and nothing more."

"If the bounty hunter is afraid to go then I will fly to the planet and trade and see what is going on," Hammer interjected.

"No Hammer, you already have your task. Anyway, you wouldn't get close enough for the data we need. We need someone who can sneak close enough to get a breakdown of the operation in progress. Piotr has the skills and the right ship for the mission."

"I do and if you really want me to recon the shipyard, I will. You know I will help out in any way that I can."

Hammer snorted in disgust at Piotr's statement.

"Thanks Piotr. Now here's the limited information we have…"

- 28 -

Even on a quiet station like Freeholm, you could usually find someone in the pilot's ready room. This early in the morning Piotr had the room to himself, and the guards at the door also helped to ensure privacy. He doubted that he should handle the present mission. Julia had been correct on two counts. He did have the skills and the ship for the task. However, this mission brought in a political dimension that he didn't want to get involved with. On top of that was the risk. If the Laphrian Navy had increased their security then this wouldn't be easy.

It would help secure his trust with Julia. On that front some progress had been made. She still wouldn't reveal any details of the engagement with the three targets, but she did talk about her past and of the years growing up on the station. He learned more about their history and from that he gleaned that she knew little, if anything, about her father before he came to the station.

He had hoped that she would provide some connection he could follow to find the three. That now seemed unlikely and he felt unusually calm at this. Maybe the older woman, Lina, knew more about the father's history. Developing the trust with Julia had proved a relatively easy affair, it just required time and the ability to listen. Lina, on the other hand, proved a cannier adversary and he knew that she didn't like him, let alone trust him.

The door behind him opened, disturbing his thoughts. Dee entered the room and waited for the door to close before greeting him.

"Preparing for your mission, I see."

"Of course."

"We should talk before you depart."

"I thought you might want that. I expect you'd rather I didn't complete this mission."

"On the contrary. I want you to complete the mission. I have the latest patrol data for you. They're from long-range scans so you'll need to plot your own course when you get in close. And luckily for you, this area has had the surveillance package disabled as part of the security on this mission. Otherwise our head of security would be very curious in how we know each other."

Piotr shrugged. "I know many people."

"Indeed you do. That doesn't seem to have helped you much."

"What do you mean?"

"I expected that Hammer would no longer be at the station anymore."

"I sabotaged his ship, he shouldn't have been able to return."

"I relied on you for that single task. You claimed to need my help and for that I asked a single favour from you."

"I will deal with him."

"How do you intend to manage that? You will be gone for several days and he's suspicious after your failed attempt. We will have to factor his presence into our plans."

"What about the information you promised?"

"Your memory appears to be faulty. The information was in return for dealing with Hammer. You failed so why should I provide the information you seek?"

"You have it?"

"As I explained, the information is compartmentalised by security clearance. You need to provide me with something I can trade with my superiors for the data."

"All right. What can I do?"

"You need to do a lot better than your last effort."

"I get the message."

"Do you? I am your only link to the information you need to end your quest. If you fail this time then you will never find the people who murdered your friend."

"I understand! Now tell me what you want."

"You have to complete the mission."

"Really?"

"Yes. You will complete the recon and when you return you will provide this data to our head of security." She handed a tiny data chit to him. "Load this software into your sensor manager. It will merge the data we want into your flight record."

"I still have to fly the mission?"

"Of course. The data must appear genuine, there are subtleties that can only be introduced by actually travelling through space. Don't worry. The Navy knows you will be there and have been ordered not to interfere."

That didn't fill him with confidence. How many people knew about this? A secret like this left him vulnerable here on the station.

"When I return you will get me the data?"

"Of course. Just make sure that you complete the mission this time."

"I will."

"Then you had best get on with it."

She turned and left the ready room, leaving him alone once again.

He completed dressing in his flight suit. All pilots wore a similar suit. Skin tight, it protected from the three great dangers to those who operated in space. The inner material adapted dynamically to help the human body withstand the forces generated from high-speed manoeuvres. Medical treatments also enhanced this ability and some pilots took it to extremes, undreamed of in the early days of space flight, through implants and augmentations.

269

It also provided protection against environmental threats such as extreme heat and cold. Like many bounty hunters, Piotr upgraded the suit with body armour in case of face to face encounters.

The third protection was against atmosphere loss. Combined with the RemLok safety system, in an emergency Piotr could survive hard vacuum for several minutes. For planned excursions into space, the suit provided attachments for helmets and active micrometeorite protection.

The ritual of putting on the suit calmed his thoughts. He didn't like the situation at all. Clearly he was being used by the Imperial Intelligence operative. However she held the key to the data he needed so he had no choice but to follow her instructions. He lacked any influence or other contacts in Imperial circles. With those stuck-up idiots, face and prestige were everything and he had little of either. Not in their eyes.

He flew out of the station in his Viper. His preferred the ambush predator method of hunting so his ship was tailored to allow stealthy travel and hiding in space, and the unleashing of maximum firepower once his prey crossed his gun sights. He'd sacrificed armour and protective capability to push its stealth capability to the limits of human technology.

Even with a thousand years of technological development, stealth in space was difficult to achieve. Especially when you had to cross a third of a star system with no occluding objects to hide behind. For such journeys, the trick was to drift while maintaining minimum heat and radiation emissions.

Ordinarily a job like this required a long build-up as travelling in supercruise lit a ship up half a system away. That meant approaching the target in real space. Crossing this much distance under normal power could take months, time that Piotr didn't have.

He did know of a short cut although it was quite risky.

Piotr didn't want to be on this mission. Any time away from Freeholm meant that he risked not being there if the three ships returned. That would be unacceptable. Dee's interference in the mission indicated that the Laphrians had something to hide and would be aware of his approach anyway.

That provided him with some latitude. He didn't need to take all of his usual precautions. He just had to make the appearance of stealth. As long as he returned with the data then his part in the mission would be complete. And then Dee would provide him with the information he needed.

Amongst his electronic bag of tricks was a specialist software module that created a deliberate malfunction in the frame shift drive. Normally the device was used to create a misjump. These changed a destination after a jump was initiated and were a dangerous but effective means to escape a foe tracking your vessel.

Not as commonly known, and only available in specialised and extremely expensive disruption devices, was a function that worked while in supercruise. When triggered it would force the ship out of supercruise while generating a jump cloud, leading any pursuers away on a false trail.

Piotr knew from his previous trips through the system that the Laphrian Navy maintained a patrol in supercruise. That enabled them to respond to any incursion with little delay. They would no doubt detect his approach and if the reports were true then they'd also have more eyes watching than usual. He only needed enough time to get close enough and then perform the fake jump.

As plans went, it lacked his preferred precision, but it would get the task completed. Once clear of the asteroid belt, he activated the ship registry disguise so they wouldn't be able to identify his ship, then engaged the frame shift drive and transitioned into supercruise. His sensors detected two Laphrian Anacondas on patrol at extreme range. The first was positioned near the star in the usual position. The second orbited near the shipyard, no doubt watching out for ships attempting to do what Piotr was about to.

He glanced at the system map and calculated his window of opportunity. It was close. This far from any real point of mass, he would move much more quickly than the ship just outside the planet's gravity well. Piotr accelerated hard from the belt and travelled at incredible speed across the gulf of interplanetary space.

It crossed his mind that the Laphrians could see his actions as a pretext for anything they might be planning against Freeholm. If that were the case then maybe this was a set-up. For a moment he considered just leaving the system. Perhaps there would be another way to find the data he needed. The moment of indecision passed quickly. He had a concrete line of investigation here. He would take care not to rely on the Navy's good graces – just in case.

The Navy vessel reacted and its signature flared as its frame shift drive powered against the planet's gravity towards Piotr's ship. On his comms panel, Piotr read the other ship's message demanding to know his identity and purpose. Piotr ignored the communication and continued towards his target.

As he travelled he continually calculated the convergence points. Another flare on his sensors appeared as a second Laphrian light cruiser entered supercruise and vectored towards him. A quick calculation provided some relief when he realised that he still had time. The sensation lasted only a few more seconds until another contact appeared. This one between him and the Laphrian shipyard.

Piotr cursed as he examined the configuration of ships on his scanner. The Navy had positioned the ships well, and they would prevent any easy access to the shipyard. To complete the mission he would have to drop out sooner than he'd anticipated.

So much for returning to Freeholm in good time.

If either of the ships approached within interdiction range then Piotr's deception wouldn't work. He could avoid the nearest ship, but would then be bracketed by the other two. The only other option was to vector away and seek another approach angle. He guessed that wouldn't work as the Navy would simply put more ships in his path.

He was committed to the direct path or to abandon the mission all together. With another curse, he angled his course towards the closest ship. His timing would have to be perfect. Every second in supercruise reduced his travel time by days and he had to return to the station as quickly as he could.

More bad news as he realised that the nearest contact was accelerating faster than it should have been. A decades-old Anaconda, even a military upgraded one, shouldn't be able to pull out of the planet's gravity well like that. He remembered something from Julia's briefing. The Navy were due to be replacing their Anacondas with Imperial Cutters.

Piotr hadn't factored those into his plan.

He then wondered about his other assumption.

Just because Dee wanted him to fake his mission's findings, did that logically mean that the Navy was also aware? He'd quite naturally assumed that they were, but what if the Imperial support was more covert?

If the approaching ship was a Cutter then in supercruise it would be upon him before he'd reach a point close enough to perform a recon run. It would also be able to manoeuvre quickly enough to block any move Piotr made. He didn't even have the option to turn and run now.

He'd had close calls on hunts before, but not since the early days of his career had he put himself into such an obvious trap as this. He preferred to be the one causing the fight or flight decisions, not making them.

In this case, fight was to complete the mission and to do that he'd need to perform the fake jump within the next two minutes. He'd return to normal space much farther away than he'd planned, but then at least he could rely on his own skills to even the technological mismatch between his and the Navy ships.

If he left it any longer then the Navy Cutter would interdict him and pull him into real space. Then he'd have little chance of escape. The alternative was to run. He could plot a jump before being interdicted and then leave the system.

Running wasn't an option. He had to complete the mission to get the information he needed from Dee's superiors. He knew the choice was made for him.

He triggered the device.

Frame shift drives not only provided the mechanism for shifting between spatial dimensions, they also dampened the effects of the shearing forces involved in such changes. A large part of the energy flared into the fake departure cloud. The rest slammed his ship back into normal space.

The momentum he carried on his entry into supercruise continued when he returned into normal space. He needed that momentum to move him away from his re-entry point. As he drifted, he shut down all of the ship's systems so that he generated no heat or electromagnetic transmissions.

He sealed his suit so that he could turn off life support. He couldn't run like that indefinitely but he could travel for a few hours in this fashion. It proved a fortuitous precaution when several minutes later, an entry cloud formed and the Cutter entered normal space. Piotr could only watch on the scanner as the Cutter began its search.

Had the fake cloud failed? Or was this just a ship's captain being ultra-cautious? It didn't really matter either way. Piotr could only watch as the other ship entered a search pattern as he drifted along his course towards the shipyard. He hoped that their pattern would take them far enough away that he could risk re-engaging the life support system.

The other captain clearly wasn't listening to Piotr's wishes as his first turn brought him towards Piotr's drifting Viper. The move sparked fresh concern as he watched his safe air window count down. The Cutter's next turn at least quashed the worry that they had detected him.

Like submariners of ancient Earth, Piotr's ship registered the sweeps of energy from the Cutter's active sensor scans. Piotr felt reasonably confident that his hull's absorption capability was enough to prevent it registering on the Cutter's scanners.

Piotr was powerless to do anything except watch. Any action on his part would reveal his location. Two fresh contacts on his scanner elevated his concern to alarm. Their movement patterns indicated that these were fighters deployed from the Cutter. Without any active sensors, the ship's computer lacked the data to identify the ships.

The two fighters took station on either flank of the Cutter and so extended its active scanner range. The next turn in their patrol brought the ships heading towards Piotr again. His ship's momentum had moved him a considerable distance in the intervening time and he breathed more easily once they turned away.

For the next three hours, the Cutter and its escorts maintained the patrol. The pattern and Piotr's own vector meant that the two parties separated at a slow, yet steady pace. Despite the gradual separation, the Laphrian ships remained close enough that he didn't dare risk engaging his life support. His air should remain acceptable for a further two hours but the temperature was starting to affect him.

The air in the cockpit was now cold enough to freeze his skin. The suit kept the worst effects at bay but only for a short time. He shivered inside the multi-layered suit. He would need to engage the life support soon but he couldn't do that until the Cutter moved far enough away.

He watched the movement of the ships on his scanner, the bright dots in the hologram the sole focus of all of his attention. They were finally moving away from his course but not as quickly as Piotr would have liked.

The cold reached beyond pain. Hatred's bitter warmth kept him strong beyond the point that others would have re-engaged the life support and run for it, or even surrendered themselves to the Navy. He never even considered the option. In the grip of the cold, he understood that he existed for only a single purpose.

The realisation comforted him. He'd known that the quest had consumed him throughout the long years but he'd never accepted the raw truth of it. He might die in the chill of his cockpit, but that would be better than giving up on the slim chance of the information from the Imperial Intelligence network.

Eventually his patience was rewarded and he could switch the life support back on. The pain he'd suffered in the cold paled compared the agony as feeling returned to his limbs. It lasted for several hours despite the best efforts of his suit's medical system to ease his torment.

All the while, his ship continued its course and when his faculties returned, exhausted from the repair of his body, he saw what Dee Callum wanted to hide from Freeholm's residents.

- 29 -

Everything about the new Cutter pleased Captain Belin. It had lived up to the promises from the saleswoman from the Gutamaya shipyards and more besides. The crew had adapted to their new ship quickly and the brief shakedown cruise had almost ironed out the wrinkles in their new operating procedures. As pleased as he was with their progress, Belin still would have preferred a few more weeks of familiarisation.

The approach of an unidentified ship several days ago had shaken Admiral Locke's planning team. One of the patrol ships around the Laphrian shipyard had detected an incoming vessel and intercepted. They'd believed that the ship had thought the better part of valour and jumped out of the system. Even so the patrol had searched real space for the intruder to be certain.

When another unidentified ship jumped out of the system a few days later, they realised they had been duped. Despite the assurances from the intelligence officer that the fly-by had been part of a deception plan, the command crew appeared nervous that the element of surprise had now been lost.

The possibility that the intelligence and command elements weren't synchronised worried Belin enough for him to raise it at one of the briefings. He knew from the attitudes of his fellow captains that they shared his concern although didn't speak out.

His concern was played down by the command staff although they brought forward the date for the attack.

While he saw the sense in the change, he worried that the whole plan was ill-conceived.

Belin was confident that his crew would be up to the task and the same seemed true for the other Cutters assigned to the battle group. However, scuttlebutt indicated that the *Majestic*-class Interdictor which formed the centrepiece for the fleet might not be as ready.

Belin again raised his concerns which were brushed away by the command staff at the previous planning meeting. Worryingly, they didn't deny the rumours of the faults in the flagship. They considered the ship to be powerful enough to take on anything the forces at Freeholm could throw at it. Belin agreed that should be the case, but he also believed that you took extra care when dealing with a cornered animal. The residents of Freeholm remembered all too well life before their insurrection and wouldn't return to that life without a fight.

He tried to convince the staff to follow standard Imperial protocol to stand off the Interdictor and secure the station using the Cutters and fighters. Again his suggestion was dismissed. The fleet would bull its way in to the station and they expected that the show of force alone would suppress most of the resistance without a shot being fired.

They were correct on one count. The new ships should make short work of any defence that Freeholm could mount. The latest pick-up of ores and minerals from the colony had also brought new intelligence to light. Plans were in motion to expand the station's defence force and to improve its equipment.

Rumour indicated that the force's Sidewinders would be upgraded to Eagles. A significant improvement on their current capabilities, but not enough to pose any real threat to the attackers. Yet still he experienced a nagging doubt.

He brought his attention back to his new quarters. The

captain's quarters reflected the importance of rank in Imperial society. They were larger and better appointed than those on his previous ship. The form of the furnishings looked expensive and provided a pleasing shape to the room. He'd always felt at home on his ships but this was something different. He'd never experienced opulence in any form, but he felt that he could get used to it if it meant comfort like this.

A beep on the control panel embedded in the wall indicated an incoming message on his private comms channel. He looked at the identity and upon seeing it was an old friend from the academy, he accepted the call.

"Davies. How are things in operations?"

"The same as ever. Too much bureaucracy."

"I can imagine."

"And your new ship?"

"A delight. She handles like a dream and the crew have adapted well."

"That's good to hear. We don't get to play with new toys like you line officers."

"You made your choice when you graduated."

"You know that's not exactly true."

Belin nodded his agreement. They'd both been involved in the coup that toppled the sitting government of the time. Belin had formed the very public spearhead of the coup.

Few officers involved in the operation escaped retribution and Commander Davies had found his career blocked by unseen, but not unknown forces. To some extent Belin suffered the same. Thankfully for him, he had reached the rank he'd always wanted – the command of his own ship.

Davies hadn't been so fortunate.

"We couldn't ignore what was happening," Belin said.

"No we couldn't. Some of us have paid a higher price than others though."

"I know and I tried what I can…"

"I'm sorry. I didn't mean to imply…"

"It's okay."

"I'm afraid it's not."

"What do you mean?"

"You know what I mean."

And Belin did.

"I thought information on the operation was restricted?"

"It is. I might not have risen above the rank of commander but I've been in the Navy long enough to feel the pulse of what's going on. Besides, you can't put together an invasion force like this without logistics being involved."

"I guess not."

"Well, that choice we faced ten years ago is back again."

"Their head of security broke the treaty."

"So we invade Freeholm. It's an excuse and you know it."

"They were also responsible for the reconnaissance mission near the shipyard."

"Hardly an act of war."

"It's still a breach of treaty and besides, I'm a Navy captain and the orders are clear."

"Our orders were clear back then too."

"Things are different. The fleet is going into harm's way and I cannot make their mission harder."

"Freeholm's forces are barely a match for a single Cutter let alone the battle group preparing to leave orbit."

"You forget the mercenary forces helping them."

"Two ships and yes, the Anaconda might put up a reasonable fight. Even so, the fact that they can mount a minimal defence doesn't justify attacking them."

"I don't disagree but the orders are not ours to question."

"And where would we be if we'd thought like that ten

years ago?"

"It was different then."

"So you've said, but do you really believe that?"

"I'll admit I have my doubts. We don't have the full information on why we are attacking the station. It may be a justified action."

"In what circumstance would it be justified?"

"You don't understand. As a ship's captain my responsibility is to my crew. If my ship is going in to combat then I owe it to my crew to be with them and provide the leadership they need."

"You're evading the question and what of your responsibility to the Laphrian people?"

"I've seen the newsfeeds. Public opinion against Freeholm has never been so low."

"Thanks to the vitriol of extremist groups. The public are being manipulated. They certainly wouldn't accept this course of action. More concerning is the fact that they are not being given the choice."

"And what do you expect me to do?"

"You must stop this war before it starts."

"I am just a single captain. I'm an escort for the main assault. If I did pull my support for the attack, they would simply arrest me and replace me and the attack would still go ahead. So you tell me, what am I supposed to do?"

"You've changed, Stefan. When you were an ensign, we didn't even need to discuss what had to be done. We just acted."

"As ensigns we risked only our own lives. Now we have the lives of others who depend on our decisions."

"It seems to me that you'd rather hide from your responsibilities."

This comment stung Belin and he retorted angrily, "And what have you done? How have you tried to prevent this attack?"

"I am contacting you. I have little influence in Navy command."

"I see. So you're passing the buck?"

"No, I am doing what I can."

"Are you?"

"What can I do?"

"In honesty I don't think there's anything you can do. And it's debatable whether you should try. We don't have to like our orders but we do have to follow them."

"What about ten years ago?"

"Then we didn't disobey orders. Well, not initially at least. The rebellion wasn't of our making and the revelation of what happened at the penal colony for so many years. Our population was shocked when they discovered horror of life on the colony and of the secret activities of the government and some of the industrial concerns."

"So we come back to why is this attack taking place?"

"And on that point I do agree with you. However that doubt isn't enough to challenge our orders."

"I take it that means you won't do anything?"

"I can't."

"Then I hope you'll keep our conversation private?"

"Of course, and I hope you won't do anything foolish."

"I will do whatever is needed. I do know other officers in the battle group."

"Be careful. You are treading close to treason with this message. You're lucky that my personal channels use a different encryption scheme to the standard military channels. I've not changed so much that I forgot our previous protocols. Others might not be so cautious or able to keep your word to themselves."

"And you be careful too. And I hope that you'll return to the person that I once knew."

The transmission terminated and Belin continued his preparations. In three days, the battle group would depart Laphrian orbit and head to invade Freeholm.

- 30 -

Despite the conviction that had cemented during the approach to the Laphrian shipyard, Piotr experienced pangs of doubt. They continued right up until the moment he presented the false data in the briefing. His escape from Laphrian space lacked elegance and he knew for sure that they'd tracked his escape as he jumped out of the system. He'd then jumped through several systems just to make sure he wasn't followed, then re-established his ship's identity and returned to the Artemis system.

There was a risk that the Navy had built a detailed enough profile of his ship that they'd recognise him when he arrived in supercruise by Artemis. He wasted no time in plotting the course back to Freeholm.

Throughout the journey, he worried about the rightness of his course of action. He'd seen what the Laphrian Navy had in store for Freeholm and quite frankly it was overkill for the forces that the station had available.

The enormity of the lie helped him rationalise his decision. Even if they knew the truth of the force arrayed against them, would that really help them? No, it would surely be better for them to be surprised and hopefully that shock would enable them to make the right decision.

It also meant that Piotr would need to leave the system before the action started. He couldn't do that until Dee provided the information he needed. He didn't get the opportunity to speak with her before the briefing. Even though it was late in the evening, Julia insisted that the pilots review the information he'd obtained at once.

Dee took the data chit from him and placed it in the briefing room's console. Dee and Julia quickly reviewed the data as they waited for the rest. Hammer was the last to arrive and to Piotr's surprise he didn't scowl at the bounty hunter.

Perhaps the reason for the big man's mellowing came in the form of Lina who arrived at the same time. Piotr wondered if the two had finally got together. Well, they wouldn't have long to enjoy their new relationship unless they left the station soon.

A moment's indecision interrupted Piotr's thoughts as he watched the couple settle into the seats. From observing Hammer's body language, Piotr realised that something had soothed the foul mood that sparked confrontation between the two of them. For a while Piotr feared that Hammer had learned that he had sabotaged his ship.

It rankled Piotr's pride that Hammer had somehow survived the malfunction. Well, it wouldn't matter now.

With everyone ready, Julia indicated that Piotr should conduct the briefing. He took his place at the podium with a holoscreen displaying his flight path around him. Everyone in the room waited expectantly for him to start.

He could still change his mind and tell them the truth.

He crushed the doubt.

The choice had been made and his efforts for the past years would count as nothing if he didn't get the information from Dee. If he crossed her now, she would never reveal the data on the three ships. Everything he had worked for rested on this moment.

With a sweep of his hand to start the sensor playback, he began the briefing.

"It would have taken weeks to get close enough to scan the shipyard without being detected so I took a chance. I calculated that a quick dash with a bit of deception would get me in close.

"As you can see it didn't go quite to plan. The patrols

around the shipyard were more capable than I expected. The visible ships were the Anacondas you're all familiar with. What I didn't expect was the Cutter they had in real space ready to respond to an incursion.

"Their quicker than expected response meant that I had to drop out of supercruise earlier than I anticipated and coast to the shipyard. That's why it's taken longer than I predicted to get back."

"How did you manage to drop out unseen?" Hammer interrupted.

"As you can see, I didn't. I tried a little misjump trick but it didn't work." A bit of brutal honesty to help sell the big lie. "The Cutter followed me out but I was able to keep cold long enough for them to lose me."

"How long did it take?" Hammer followed up.

"Let's leave the questions until the end," Julia interjected. "Please continue, Piotr."

Piotr resumed the sensor playback.

"I'll admit that when I started the mission, I doubted the point of the run. While I drifted in towards the shipyard I wondered at the extra security. As I neared, more targets appeared on my scanners. You can see by their deployment that the Laphrian Navy had the area tightly buttoned up with patrols in close with fighters and at range with two Cutters and six converted Anacondas."

"So there was something there after all?" Lina remarked.

"Yes, at least that what's I thought at first."

"What do you mean?"

"Well there was certainly a lot of hardware in the region around the shipyard so they had to be protecting something. At that range my sensors only detected the ships moving around. It was only as I drew closer that the sensors were able to resolve anything around the shipyard itself."

"And what did you find there?" Lina asked.

"If you look at this configuration of the shipyard, you

will see that it has changed from the historical record provided to me before I left. Two of the assembly bays are being converted into something different. There are two different ships there. I believe they are Imperial Couriers although I'm not sure what that means."

He presented the lie as Dee had ordered him to. It tasted dry in his mouth. Throughout his quest he'd committed many dark deeds, but this one outweighed them all. He'd seen the *Majestic*-class Interdictor and the lines of shuttles ferrying fate knew what to the massive warship. He'd condemned an entire starport.

"I think I might know," Dee continued the deception. He didn't know what story she would weave to lull these poor bastards into accepting the lie.

"What do you think?" Julia asked.

"I've seen something similar before and while I'd need to check the details to be sure, this looks like a Gutamaya shipyards development team. I wouldn't be surprised if some of the patrolling Cutters were owned by the shipyard as well. They take a technology transfer like this very seriously."

"How can you be certain?" Julia wanted to know.

"There are a few sources I can check with. It will take a day or so."

"I would like to be more certain there's no hostile intent before then."

"Well, we can run a tactical analysis on the deployment. The expert systems will have a rundown shortly. I submitted the data as soon as it was downloaded."

"All right," Julia said. "Let's break until the results come in. In the meantime, let's review the sensor logs individually, then Piotr can answer any questions and Dee can go through the tactical analysis if its finished by then."

Hammer looked like he was about to object but a light touch from Lina forestalled his question. The rest nodded and split into smaller groups as they headed to the outer office to use the terminals. Piotr remained to speak with Dee although he waited for the others to leave.

"I've done what you asked."

"Not here," she hissed in response. "I'll come to your quarters two hours after the briefing is finished."

He'd waited this long, a few more hours wouldn't be too bad. So he thought, at any rate. He tried but failed to disguise the impatience in his voice as he answered queries from the pilots about the recon run. He hoped the others believed his shortness to be tiredness and stress from the mission.

Not that he really cared what they thought, since as soon as he had the information he needed, he would leave this station to its fate.

Dee then presented her tactical analysis which created more questions. For three hours, the team went through every detail over and over again. Finally the questions and discussions ceased. The crew seemed content that the extra security around the shipyard wasn't intended to harm them.

A final moment of doubt assailed him. It faded as everyone left the briefing room and he followed them before heading towards his own quarters. There he discovered that waiting alone was far worse than suffering the endless questions had been.

The irony of it didn't escape him. Here he was, a famed bounty hunter whose speciality was waiting in ambush, pacing his small quarters waiting for Dee to arrive. She added to his torment by arriving over an hour late.

"Where in fate's name have you been?" he demanded.

"Nice to see you too."

"Well?"

"Hey. Let me make something clear – I am not your errand girl. Not only am I busy as our head of security's only staff officer, I'm also trying to hide a half-assed invasion in an attempt to minimise some of the inevitable bloodshed."

"Without me that would have been impossible."

"And to top it all, I'm having to play nice with my superior officer to get you the information you want on those three hostiles."

"Do you have it?"

At this she sighed and sat down in one of the two seats in the living area of the quarters. "Can I get a drink?"

"I guess so. I don't have anything special, just the standard issue dispenser."

"Station coffee is fine. At least it's actual coffee here."

"Yeah, they spare no expense for their guests."

"Well, I've been in worse places."

"I'm sure you have and to be honest I have too. How do you take it?"

"Black and sweet."

"Here you go. Now are you going to make me wait even longer?"

"No and I'm sorry."

"Don't be sorry, just tell me what you know."

"I've been ordered to tell you to forget about them."

"That's it? You had me deceive these poor bastards for that? There's no way I can forget them."

"I know. I checked you out after your arrival and I discovered the reason why you're hunting these people."

"Then you know I won't stop searching for them."

"I also know that you no longer need to."

"What do you mean?"

"I realised that you wouldn't take my word and drop the matter and to be honest I don't blame you, so I pressed for more. I explained the situation to my superiors and even called in some favours so at least I could tell you something."

Dee sipped some of the bitter brew and Piotr waited for her to continue.

"You should forget about them because their termination has been sanctioned at the highest level. Wherever they are, they will not survive for long."

"Why?"

"The details are classified but I was able to find out the basics. The three ships were part of a larger team of assassins who murdered an Imperial citizen some twenty years ago."

"So they killed one of your people. Does the Intelligence Service usually hold a death warrant for killers this long?"

"Of course it does. No-one is ever safe from Imperial justice. No matter how long it takes."

"Fine. I'll happily kill them in the name of the Emperor for you."

Dee shook her head.

"It's not that simple, I'm afraid."

"Of course it isn't. You've been happy to use bounty hunters before. Why is this different?"

"The citizen was a client of a well-connected patron and had been marked as someone who would rise high in the service. His death was more than the killing of a citizen. It proved embarrassing for other, more important parties. The timing of the killing was also more than a little inconvenient."

"So they pissed off the wrong people. Again I can deal with that for you."

"I knew you'd make the offer so I've already suggested that. The offer was politely declined."

"I'm sure it was."

"Your help in this local matter has been appreciated though and I have been authorised to transfer two hundred thousand credits to your account."

"I didn't do it for the money."

"I know that, but you have helped our operations here and I'd like to make sure that you receive something for it. Even if it wasn't what you hoped for."

"Do you know where they are?"

"I don't. That information is classified higher than my clearance. A team has been despatched to eliminate them."

"Wait a minute. You said they were part of a larger team?"

"There were four ships in the attack. They took out an Imperial Courier with the client and his staff."

"And do you know who the fourth attacker was?"

"No, although intelligence did indicate that the attackers were a family unit."

"Now that's interesting. I think I know who the fourth person is. Or was."

"Who?"

"I think you know the price for that information."

"The operation is already in motion. There's no way for me to stop it."

"I think for Imperial justice to be true it needs to include all the guilty parties, don't you?"

"Okay. I'll see what I can do."

"I don't think so. I will need to meet with your superior. I like you, Dee, but it seems that you don't have the juice needed to make this deal."

"They won't agree to that."

"That's fine with me. You have the three and I'll have their leader to myself." Piotr hoped that they wouldn't figure out that he suspected that Darik Cavus was the fourth man. The assumption was slim, but the family connection provided an inkling. It also seemed obvious that he wasn't the leader. The suggestion that it was a family team did provide some hope for eventual retribution. Every family had a head after all.

"All right, I will speak to them once this operation is finished."

"You'll speak to them now."

"Not a chance. I'm on a communications blackout until the invasion is under way. That is the priority now and until that mission is completed they won't even consider speaking to you."

"All right then. I'll wait somewhere local until it's all

over and then we'll talk again."

"I don't think so. I cannot allow the possibility that you leaving the station will tip the locals that something is about to happen."

"And how do you intend to stop me?"

"I'd rather you chose to stay through your own choice. I've made arrangements to make sure that you're kept safe when the time comes. If not I can make sure that station security keep you safe and out of the way until everything is done."

"I don't like the sound of that."

"You don't have to. You're part of this now and you'll need to play your role. Don't worry when the fighting starts, your ship's identity has been given to the Laphrian Navy so you'll come up as friendly on their IFF systems."

"And I should just take your word on this?"

"You don't really have any choice. You're in this as deep as I am, in case you're trying to think of a creative way out of the situation. Do as you are told and it will work out for you. And it won't be long until all this is over."

"How long exactly?"

"Not long at all."

- 31 -

You could find bars like these all over the galaxy, assuming you had the right contacts. You could find similar places, bars full of lowlives, anywhere. For the real deal you had to visit anarchy systems or find the right contacts to locate hidden bases who were ever-watchful for law enforcement or bounty hunters.

In his younger days Mervan enjoyed the ambience of places like this. He liked the people you found here. In a universe full of dangerous characters, you could find most of them here. Small ponds full of big fish and the Cavus family considered themselves the ultimate predators.

Seline and Lee still enjoyed the atmosphere of these places and the thrill of courting danger. Seline loved to play the wide-eyed innocent surrounded by a world she knew nothing about. Those more experienced recognised the look in her eyes, something even her talent for disguise could never quite hide. The younger or more foolish, however, often fell for the act and usually paid the price.

Lee was a little more direct. He was ever eager for engaging in physical confrontation. To satisfy these urges he often entered the dome for the no-holds-barred zero-G combat that one often found in these places.

On both fronts, Mervan knew that if their father ever discovered their games then he would be furious. Their livelihood depended upon not being noticed. Of course they never used the same identities wherever they went, but still the old man insisted on a paranoid level of security.

He took another sip of the cocktail in his hand. A local invention that was reputedly so strong that it burned the hairs from your nostrils. It certainly had a kick to it although the culture in his system ensured that no ill effects would occur from drinking the cocktail.

Mervan wondered how his father would react beyond the obvious if he ever discovered the truth about his children. Of the four of them, Darik had been the most honest in accepting that this wasn't the life for him. Darik's skills were more than sufficient for the role and he was a capable pilot and fighter. Murder, however, wasn't something he wanted to spend his life practising.

Lee and Seline were thrill junkies. A fine trait for the merely violent, but their work required a little more finesse. As his eyes scanned the assembled pirates, mercenaries, smugglers and their respective groupies, Mervan couldn't help but think that he no longer wanted to be part of this. The constant attention to keep his siblings out of trouble had wearied him recently.

Perhaps Darik had the right idea after all.

They'd all been surprised when their father had simply let his son leave the life. Although really, what other option had there been? Despite Seline's claims to the contrary, none of them would have welcomed the death of their brother. Keeping him imprisoned would have hidden the problem for a while, only to allow the resentment to ferment within the family.

No, their father had made the correct choice as he seemingly always did. But Mervan had grown tired of the life as well. The years of watching his younger brother had infected him with the desire for something approaching a normal life.

An impossible dream.

Unfortunately he saw no way that he could leave. The act of leaving might have been easy enough, but the consequences of such an action were too heavy for him to bear. He knew all too well that he held the siblings together and with his father's retreat from the action end of the business, it was up to him to act as team leader.

A change in circumstance would be more than welcome, although he couldn't see any way that would happen without tragedy.

They'd been at this smugglers' outpost for three days now. Since destroying the killers who murdered their brother, they'd completed two more contracts. En route home, they'd received a cryptic message from their father to meet him here. That had struck all of them as unusual. He rarely left their home these days except when really needed to.

The communication contained no reason for the out of character rendezvous so they'd flown here and waited. Spending too long in a place like this without being local tended to attract attention. Even more worrying was that Seline and Lee were getting bored and that usually meant trouble for somebody.

Some of the unwanted attention was looking in their direction at the moment. He nudged Lee's elbow and whispered in his ear.

"It looks like we've gained a follower."

Lee knew not to look and just nodded.

"On the table in the far left by the central bar. I can see three of them. They're doing a reasonable job of hiding it."

Lee nodded his understanding again and when a scantily clad woman walked by, he used the excuse to allow his eyes to wander across the crowd. Mervan used the same excuse although he was momentarily distracted by the elegance that the young woman moved with, despite the need for magnetic boots.

Convention in a place like this tended to be that everyone used magnetics. Free-floating wasn't welcome in a serious drinking place. There were other more specialist places for that type of action. Zero-G stripping could be a thing of beauty although it could also be painful to watch if the dancer hadn't performed without the aid of gravity before.

Seline downed her drink and noticed her brothers staring. She took one glance and laughed.

"She is pretty, boys, although the three in the corner appear to have a hard-on for all of us. One each seems fair enough to me."

"I don't think they're alone," Mervan replied.

He reached under the table and placed a microbug so that it faced the three watchers. Wireless comms in the bar were jammed to prevent eavesdropping. These bars were considered sanctuaries and suitable places to talk business. However for those who knew the right people, such as Mervan, the tables and other furniture all had contact points that allowed physical communications throughout the bar.

The secure channels had to be rented and Mervan had already placed a camera above the front entrance and by the bar to better keep an eye on the patrons. The video stream was transferred through his skin touching the table and to his implants. With the faces recognised, the system replayed video of the men entering the bar.

As Mervan expected the men came in separately, except for the middle one. He had come with a lithe woman who had moved out of shot. The camera didn't have a good enough angle to get a lock on her features so Mervan now scanned the crowd manually trying to find her.

The others kept their hands against the table so he could talk to them using the comms system.

"There's a woman here. I'm sending you the image that I have. I'm sure she's part of the team."

"So which us gets two to play with?" Seline quipped.

"I'd like to know who they are before dealing with them."

"Let's just flush them out," Lee suggested. "Lead them somewhere out of the way and find out what they know."

His visual search failed to find the woman who had entered and the software claimed that she hadn't left, but with such a poor image it was difficult to be certain. He'd rather wait for a bit longer, but he also realised that his brother and sister were itching for some action. At least this way it would be away from a busy bar.

"I'm willing to bet that there's more than four of them. There's something about them. They operate as a team."

"Like us?" Lee asked.

"No. For them it is training."

"Police?"

"Maybe. If they are then they've got some balls on them."

"Even the girl."

"Especially the girl. You know what the locals would do to her here if they caught her."

"Military then?"

"Possibly. Again it's a hell of a risk."

"It doesn't matter either way. Let's get out of here and then we can find out what they want and who they are," Seline said.

"All right," Mervan replied. "Let's go, but keep your eyes open. And take care. We can't get thrown off this station. Father would freak if we weren't here to meet him and we'd attracted that level of attention."

"Understood."

"Then let's go. Lee, you go first. Seline, you watch our backs."

"Yes big brother," she replied while Lee simply stood and walked slowly towards the entrance.

Mervan followed her a moment later but kept part of his attention focused on the feeds from his cameras. He watched the reaction of the three in the corner as they left the bar. They didn't move until the siblings departed.

"Where are we going?" Seline asked.

"Head to our quarters," Mervan responded.

They maintained a loose spacing as they wound through the many corridors to their quarters on the outer level of the station. Unlike many stations, this starport was hidden inside an asteroid. While similar bases were spun to generate a gravity for its inhabitants, this one couldn't do the same without attracting attention. This base wasn't within anarchy space, it was kept hidden within a Federal system and so couldn't afford to attract the notice of the Federal Navy patrols.

Mervan counted five individuals leaving the bar to follow them. The family's contracts over the years included many important and powerful people so they had tackled with various military and covert operations units over the years. Mervan felt sure that these were the same here. He ran the faces through his database connections. Not surprisingly, no identities were confirmed. It would have been useful to know who was attempting to track them, but it didn't matter. Somebody wanted to kill or capture them and they would have to stop them. Quietly if possible.

At suitable locations along the walk, Mervan placed additional cameras to observe the team following them. Outside the bar he could rely on wireless communications to transmit the feeds. Only one extra person joined the group bringing the team's strength up to six – four men and two women. All moved with the same deceptive grace even in mag-boots. They looked different but moved the same. They had to be a military unit.

Now he had to decide when and where to ambush the followers. Their quarters were away from the busier areas. Security on stations like these wasn't as tight as in more civilised systems. Though while their response times were slower they did tend to go in heavy-handed. Pacification was more important than taking prisoners here.

That provided them with some time to play with and any trouble would be cleared up with judicious spending of credits, or handing them over to the locals if they turned out to be law enforcement or bounty hunters.

Mervan assumed that the team intended to kill or capture the three of them in their quarters. It made the most sense and would be what he would do in their place. It also worked for them as the battle would be out of sight.

"Lee, Seline. We'll take them in our quarters."

"How many?" Lee asked.

"Six."

"Great, now we have two each," Seline replied. From the timbre of her voice, Mervan sensed she looked forward to the encounter.

"Don't get carried away. I want to know who they're working for so keep them alive if possible. I'd also rather not have to pay the tax for corpses here. It would be one more thing for the locals to remember us by."

"I promise nothing," she told him.

They slowed their pace and allowed the team to get closer. They must have had their own monitoring devices as they slowed their pace as well. Mervan checked the sensor packages he'd positioned around their quarters. The sensors indicated no other presences in the area and so the three siblings entered their quarters and prepared to defend themselves.

As they entered the reception area, the lights snapped on but too bright. Brighter than a sun. As his eyesight failed, Mervan perceived four shapes moving towards them.

So the team following them was really ten strong.

The flash burst did its job and dazzled their optic nerves. Fighting the daze, Mervan focused his implant screens on the sensors only to discover a white noise of interference. The assault team were jamming their sensor packages. He didn't see the armoured soldier charging him across the short distance of the room. The first he knew was the weight of the man crashing into him.

His boots detected the sudden shift in weight and disabled the mag lock with the floor to prevent his ankles from pulling apart. The impact smashed him against the wall and he lashed out blindly, the edge of his hand striking a glancing blow. He heard the grunts of his siblings as they were attacked as well.

With a thought, he activated the ultrasonic subdermal implants which immediately began pulsing high frequency sound throughout the room. The returned waves were analysed in real time, building an image of edges and shapes of the fight around him.

Now able to see the outline of his attacker, Mervan aimed his blows with greater precision. The relatively slow update of the sonar made following quick movement confusing. The sonar provided only approximations of the man he fought and when he had practised with the view after the surgery, he had found it distracting. Now in the heat of combat, the low resolution aided him. The dead areas indicated gaps in the armour his assailant wore and provided targets for his blows, and he smiled as he heard the man cry out.

The struggle was desperate, far from the measured moves of training. He grunted as the man returned the blows, attempting to subdue his resistance. He saw the constantly changing shapes of two other fights nearby. His brother and sister lacked the same implants as Mervan. They preferred their own methods and they were proving just as able to respond to the ambush.

His eyesight shifted from the bright piercing light to a confused mosaic of light and shadow. He detected movement but little else. He pushed his attacker away, now a dark form in his returning vision. From the small of his back Mervan pulled a small knife and thrust into the neck of his attacker. The soldier's layers of protective fabric slowed the blade's progress, but with an effort fuelled by a furious howl, Mervan drove it into the man's carotid artery.

Through his sonar sight, which gave him 360 degrees of vision, a hole appeared in the wall beside him. Mervan rolled away as the following team entered the room to aid their comrades. He ignored the scream of the second soldier to die, his blood filled with a terrible agent which set his nerves on fire. Seline kicked the shrieking form to the floor as she leapt towards Lee who strained to free himself from two of the soldiers.

Ranged weapons weren't allowed to be carried openly on the station although they weren't banned outright. Mervan reached for one of the handguns they'd stashed after their arrival and opened fire on the team entering the room. Even at such close range, he missed with the first shot.

The leading soldier, a blonde-haired woman, turned and aimed her weapon at him.

He fired again before she stopped moving. The magnetically accelerated flechette pierced her armour through the shoulder. She grimaced with the sudden pain but continued to bring her gun into line. He fired a three-round burst. The sabots punched through armour twice more. The last smashed her helmet's visor.

She didn't make a sound from the first hit until she collapsed to the ground.

Beside him, the struggle continued. He had to trust that Seline and Lee had the situation handled as the next soldier charged through the door. A laser hissed past Mervan's face, the energised air hot against his skin. He fired again. The gun throbbed indicating the magazine was now half-full. The flechettes worked well against even the soldier's armour, but they lacked stopping power and it took the rest of the clip to put the solder down.

In that time, two more soldiers jumped over the bodies of their fallen comrades. Lee's bellow of rage followed by an agonised howl and the snapping of bone mingled into the same terrible song, indicating another soldier down.

With his gun empty, Mervan fell forward to grab the weapon from the woman he had shot. He missed and knocked it in the air, making it spin away in a lazy fashion. A dragon roared with fury as the lead soldier opened fire with his assault weapon. Mervan grabbed the woman's body and twisted it, using it as a shield. The force of the impacts battered him against the floor.

Temporarily suppressed, Mervan could only watch as the next soldier leapt into the room and aimed at Seline who had just slit the final ambusher's throat. The blood jetted into globules in the air and she turned to face the soldier as he pulled the trigger. The burst slowed his motion and Seline's chest disintegrated under the hail of fire.

Mervan shouted an unintelligible word of rage, pushing the corpse into the line of fire and grabbing the floating weapon. He unleashed a storm of projectiles into the standing soldier and the last two as they entered the room.

A howl of enraged grief accompanied Lee as he sprang from the floor and grabbed the soldier who'd killed Seline in mid-air. He yanked the gun from the soldier's hands. He then continued to bellow his anger he crushed the man's throat.

A full magazine of automatic fire cut down the soldier who'd fired at him from the doorway. A few bullets struck the final two but only causing light wounds as their armour absorbed the impacts.

Mervan cursed as his gun clicked empty and lunged for another fallen weapon. Two bullets struck his shoulder, most of their force contained by the smart fabric of his suit. The bullets pushed him from his destination leaving him open to the two remaining soldiers.

They turned their weapons towards him.

He looked for another body or something he could

use as a shield.

He found nothing.

Movement caught his eye and Lee charged into the two soldiers. One managed to fire off a shot but it failed to stop Lee who was howling like a beast. Mervan thought he might tear off a soldier's head as he twisted at the man's helmet. The brutality of Lee's assault distracted the other soldier.

Taking advantage of the man's mistake, Mervan grabbed him from behind and locked a choke hold around his throat. He watched as Lee tore off the soldier's helmet and with it much of his face. Hands dripping with blood, he reached for the soldier Mervan held.

"No!" Mervan commanded. "We need answers. When we know who sent him and why, then you can do what you will."

He didn't need to check Seline's vital signs to confirm she was dead. Her ruined torso told him that even an advanced medical facility couldn't restore her and no such facility existed on this station. Even knowing that, he told his brother to check on his sister. The sound of his brother's weeping was something he'd never expected nor wanted to hear. He would need a target suitable for his brother's fury and it couldn't wait until their father arrived.

News of the Laphrian fleet deployment spread through Freeholm like wildfire. As her father had done while he was head of security, Julia liked to walk through the commercial levels to show her face and capture the mood of the populace. This morning everyone's conversation revolved around the fleet approaching the belt.

Flight Control had detected the battle group's movement twelve minutes ago. She heard the news while dressing in her quarters. She'd contacted the Navy and demanded to know what was going on. They'd responded immediately, explaining that this was merely a rapid deployment exercise. With recent events, the Navy felt that they should show greater commitment for security in the belt and their support for Freeholm's sovereignty.

Julia thought that was a pile of shit.

This was clearly a show of strength for something, especially when she'd seen the disposition of the ships in the group.

She'd told Flight Control to keep the news quiet for now. That didn't stop the news from spreading. Traders loved to gossip, after all. They didn't know the whole story though and that was why she now heading to the office. She should have taken the direct route, since as she passed through the busy promenade, she was delayed by concerned citizens or those trying to show their support.

Most of the questions were the same – what was going on? She promised them that she would let everyone know as soon as she had the full information. Others insisted that they stood with her.

From the older citizens in particular she was told that they would fight if needed.

Julia hoped that it wouldn't come to that. She knew what was coming and with the forces they had, it wouldn't even slow the Laphrians down. She wanted the Navy's statement to be true or at most that this was just a show of force.

It took her over twenty minutes to reach the briefing room. By the entrance to administrative level, extra guards held a crowd away from the door and she had to force her way through. Most allowed her past once they realised who had pushed them out of the way. Feelings were running high and the guards had to help her through.

She had never seen the population like this. There was fear in these people, but more than that she recognised their anger too. She felt the same blend of emotion herself.

The others had taken the direct lift to the deck and waited for her in the briefing room. Dee busied herself at the projector setting up the latest sensor readings for the approaching fleet.

"How the hell did you miss a two-kilometre long warship?" she spat at Piotr as she entered.

"It was not there," he replied.

"We all reviewed the data together," Dee intervened. "If it was there then we all missed it."

"Then where did it come from?"

"I have no idea," Piotr replied. "Maybe it has just arrived?"

Dee shook her head. "We haven't detected its arrival. When it departed the shipyard is the first we've seen of it."

"Maybe I should talk to him further," Hammer growled.

Piotr glared at Hammer and reached for his sidearm.

The holster was empty of course, personal weapons weren't allowed on the station.

"No," Julia declared. "This isn't a witch hunt. Dee is correct. We all reviewed the data, and the ship wasn't there. I spoke rashly and Piotr – I'm sorry. We will need your help." She turned to Dee. "Have we heard anything new from the Navy?"

"No, they're just repeating what they told you earlier."

"What is the latest?"

"There are four ships in supercruise heading towards us. One Interdictor and three Cutters. They will arrive at the border within thirty minutes."

"Where did they get an Interdictor?" Hammer asked.

"We don't know, presumably the same place they received the Cutters."

"The Empire doesn't just give these things away," Hammer said. "And I doubt that the Laphrians could simply buy one."

"It doesn't matter," Julia replied. "Our immediate concern is what their intentions are."

"Is there any chance that they're conducting an exercise as they claim?" Lina asked.

Dee shrugged. "It's possible, although there's no way of knowing."

"Is there anything on the newsfeeds?" Julia enquired.

"Nothing as yet."

"So what do we do?" Lina asked.

"Well we don't want to provoke anything but we can't just stand by either," Julia declared.

"Why not?" Dee said.

"What do you mean?"

"If this an exercise and we have a patrol nearby then there's the potential for an incident."

"You just said that you didn't believe this was an exercise. If we are about to be attacked then I'd prefer to fight away from the station."

"The station possesses more firepower than all of the

ships that we have."

"And that provides our last line of defence against an attack. We would need to hold them in the belt, I don't want to put the population in danger."

"I hate to be the one to raise this, but if they are here to attack then wouldn't we be putting the population in danger? What type of defence could we mount against this force?"

"That's what I want to determine. We'll need to be certain of the Laphrian intentions before any operations. The decision also rests with the station council and the population." She paused for a moment. "Okay, so what do we know about how these ships would operate?"

"We can't match them in a straight fight," Piotr stated.

"The coward is correct," Hammer replied.

Piotr reacted instantly to the insult. Lina and Rob stepped in between them.

"All right," Julia snapped. "What's going on between you two?"

"This snake has been working against us all along," Hammer declared. "He sabotaged my ship and has deceived us all with his fake recon run."

"This is a lie," Piotr retorted.

Lina whispered to Hammer and placed her hands on his shoulders, gently trying to move him away from the bounty hunter.

Julia couldn't believe what she'd just heard.

"Hammer, these are serious accusations. Do you have any proof of this?"

The fury in his face faded as he realised that he'd spoken without thinking.

"I am investigating and there are some…"

"See," said Piotr, "the oaf lies to you. I risked my life getting the data to you. As for sabotaging his ship – why would I do such a thing? It's madness."

"We don't need this," Julia told them both. "Piotr has shown no reason to be a threat. We need you both if we are to tackle this thing. Did you report the sabotage?" She indicated towards Mayborn, the station's head of internal security.

"No."

"You can't investigate an issue like that on your own. If your ship was sabotaged then it's not just an attack against you, it's also an attack on this station. At the moment you possess the most powerful ship we have. Now did you find any evidence of who might have sabotaged your ship?"

"The ship's cameras recorded Piotr in the area of the ship on the night before the system failure."

"My ship is berthed next to yours. Of course it would see me!"

"Piotr, please. Hammer, is that all you have?"

The big man nodded.

"Okay. Well that's not enough to go on and certainly not enough to make rash accusations. I'm also not happy that this is the first I'm hearing of this." She glanced at Lina as she said this. "We could be at war at any moment and I need to know that everyone here is one hundred per cent."

Piotr looked like he was about to say something and she forestalled him with a raised hand.

"I appreciate that neither of you signed up for a shooting war and unlike the rest of us you don't live here, so while I really want you both to help in the fight if it happens, you do have the option of leaving."

Without a pause Hammer declared, "I'll fight." Julia saw Lina place her hand on his shoulder. She then looked at Piotr. Again he seemed about to say something, but after a glance at Dee he simply nodded.

Now that surprised her. She wasn't aware that there was anything between Piotr and Dee. Sure, she'd noticed them conversing on their own occasionally, but she'd assumed that had been work-related and not something romantic.

For a time she'd considered the same. There had been a few moments when it seemed as if something would develop between her and Piotr. With all the changes recently, it didn't seem the right time so they'd remained friends. She trusted him. Hammer's accusation just didn't sit right with her. He had to be wrong.

Surprising as it seemed, she thought it might be a good thing. Piotr did seem an odd person at times. Perhaps more so as she got to know him better. There was a secret about him that Julia hadn't managed to grasp but even so he had proved very helpful in her work to expand the station's defence force. A relationship between him and Dee might keep him at the station which would be a definite boon.

She also wanted Hammer to stay and maybe the developing relationship between him and Lina would help on that front as well. Although she knew from Lina that they had talked about moving to an outdoor world somewhere. Julia didn't think that Lina would agree to that. She had been very close to her father and had lived at the station longer than Julia had. She hadn't said no outright to Hammer, though.

There were more immediate concerns, of course. The Laphrian task force would arrive at any minute and she need the two hired guns to be focused on that and not each other.

"Mayborn, can you investigate the sabotage?"

"Of course."

"Hammer. As soon as you get some time, which might not be for a while, sit down with Mayborn and give him all the details. I won't have sabotage on this station. Do you understand?"

Hammer nodded his agreement, but his face was still set firm and Julia knew that she'd have to keep the two of them apart in any operation until the matter was cleared up. That would weaken her position as they represented two of her most combat-capable assets.

"Let's get back on topic. Has anyone here encountered Imperial ships in operations like this?"

"Not quite like this," said Hammer. "But I do know a bit about Imperial fleet tactics."

"Where from?"

He actually looked a bit embarrassed. "Er. Well in a past life I was a bit of a history buff. One thing about working the land planetside is that you get plenty of time for reading. To be honest, hunting pirates leaves a lot of time on your hands as well."

Julia wasn't sure how this helped, but as no-one else appeared to have anything to offer this seemed the only option.

"Dee, can you bring up historical records in here?" Hammer asked.

"Of course."

"Bring up the Beaumont insurrection from 3294."

A map of a star system appeared from the holo-projector.

"The Beaumont system was a frontier world far below Achenar. No official reason or explanation was provided but Federal newsfeeds claimed that a bureaucratic oversight put a pirate clan captured during an Imperial Navy sweep of the area into the same mine where they'd been sent for hard labour. The mining base was positioned in a rich cluster in the asteroid belt around two AUs from the populated planet."

The parallels with their own position weren't lost on Julia, or the other pilots.

"Slave revolts in the Empire are rare, however the mine used a higher proportion of penal slaves. They were slaves who had been sentenced rather than bonded. Usually criminals or deserters and in this case pirates. Security at the mine was higher than usual for this type of operation but it backfired. The new prisoners overwhelmed their guards on arrival and were able to release the other slaves. Most wanted nothing to do with the rebellion, but there were enough who joined them to make use of the hardware available at the station.

"Naturally, Imperial authorities didn't reveal much about the action. Fortunately for us there was an independent trader in the area who filmed most of the recapture operation before he jumped away and sold his story to the newsfeeds.

"Anyway, the base had a short-range fighter squadron. The same class as what the bounty hunter supposedly encountered. They're standard issue on the *Majestic*-class ships at any rate. They can have up to eight squadrons stationed on them."

"How many ships in an Imperial fighter squadron?" Julia asked.

"It can vary, but usually twelve or sixteen. The colony had a fighter squadron and a single Cutter deployed which the rebels were planning to use to escape. However, the local Imperial forces reacted quickly and were able to deploy before the rebels escaped."

"What forces did they send?" Lina asked.

Hammer indicated the newsfeed video. "As you can see they deployed a single *Majestic* with six Cutters. The *Majestic* stationed away from the mining colony and launched fighters who went in supported by four of the Cutters. The other two Cutters deployed nearby to provide support if needed or run down any that tried to escape.

"As the Imperial forces moved in, three fighters attempted to escape. The short-range fighters don't have jump-capable drives so were quickly run down by the Cutters and destroyed.

"The others made a stand at the base deciding to fight rather than surrender. They didn't last long. Once the fighters and Cutters secured the area, the *Majestic* deployed a Navy infantry battalion with dropships and recaptured the mine."

"How does this help us?" Piotr wanted to know.

"It tells what we're up against."

"It also tells us what we aren't," Mayborn commented.

"What do you mean?" Julia asked.

"They were Imperial forces, well-trained and supported. They were also familiar with their ships. The Laphrian forces have only just received these new ships so won't be as familiar with them. That might provide us with some small advantage."

"Maybe," she replied. "So based on what you've told us, you'd expect the Laphrians to hold the Interdictor back and deploy the Cutters and fighters within the belt."

"Yes, they won't want to bring the pride of their Navy into the belt without securing it first."

"So we might have the opportunity to engage the smaller forces before they reach the station?"

"Yes, but don't underestimate the Cutters. They are far more capable ships than the converted Anacondas they used before."

"The fleet is entering real space," Dee interrupted.

"Show us."

Dee switched the holoscreen to show the sensor readings from the station's sentinel probes along the asteroid belt's border. A single Cutter arrived first, followed seconds later by the *Majestic* and the other two Cutters. They looked tiny compared to the Interdictor. The three Cutters moved to assume defensive positions around the huge warship.

As they moved into position, a swarm of fighters deployed from the Interdictor and spread into a loose formation towards the asteroid belt.

"Well they're here and we don't have a plan," Julia said.

"Wait," Hammer replied.

"What for?"

"Just wait. Something isn't right here."

"What do you mean?"

311

"The Cutters are in too tight with the Interdictor."

"So?"

"Just watch."

They watched while the fighters continued to move into the belt.

"We're now at war, they've crossed the treaty line," Mayborn declared.

No-one replied.

The *Majestic*-class Interdictor stopped moving as it reached the edge of the belt and the Cutters maintained position on its flanks and to the rear. The fighters continued into the belt and the first sentinel feed blinked out as it was destroyed.

"They've made a mistake," Hammer grinned.

Piotr nodded.

"What do you mean?" Julia asked.

"They've deployed the fighter screen without support."

"So? There's over fifty fighters there."

"Indeed, but would you rather engage fifty fighters and the Cutters as well?"

"Of course not."

"Then this is our opportunity to cause some damage before they get to the station."

"You're right. Look, the fighters have formed two groups." She noticed that Dee looked pensive. "It's okay," she told her aide. "We can use this mistake."

"Yes we can."

"They're sweeping either side of the transit corridor. Maybe that means they're bringing the Interdictor in close and that would be their next mistake."

"Let's not get carried away. We don't know what they'll do next, but we can take advantage of what they're doing now."

"What are your orders?" Rob asked.

"Hammer – how many fighters can you engage?"

"I can take on one of the groups. Assuming there's no

more treachery." He cast a glare at Piotr.

"I'll cover him," Lina said.

"All right. You two take the left flank. Don't follow the fighters when they disengage, come back to the station if that happens."

They both nodded their agreement.

"The rest of you are with me. We'll take the right flank and don't pursue if they run. Let's hit what we can but keep near the station."

"What if this is a ruse?" Dee asked. "We need a reserve force."

"Damn it, you're right." Julia paused for a moment to think. "Okay. The new Sidewinder pilots will stay in orbit around the station."

"They're all green," Rob commented. "They'll need someone experienced to be with them."

Her lead pilot was right, but who to choose.

"Piotr could lead the reserve," Dee said.

Julia thought about that. She'd rather have him in the combat group with her, but there wasn't much choice. Lina covering Hammer's rear made perfect sense and she wasn't a combat leader despite her years of experience. That left herself or Rob. Rob had trained with the main force pilots for years, as had she.

"That's a good suggestion. Thanks Dee." Hammer snorted. Lina frowned at him and hissed in his ear. He nodded and returned his focus to Julia.

She would definitely need to keep the two of them apart, Julia thought.

"Piotr – you lead the reserve force. Be ready for my word if we need you."

"Of course."

"All right, let's get moving."

"What about the council?" Mayborn asked.

"We have to deploy now and they've already granted me the authority I need to respond."

"Even so."

"You brief them, and then make sure the station's defences are active and ready."

"Of course."

"And Mayborn?"

"Yes?"

"Initiate a full communications lockdown. There are to be no communications from the station unless expressly authorised by myself or a council member."

"I'll arrange it immediately."

"Then let's go."

- 33 -

Of the small fleet, Hammer's Anaconda departed first from Freeholm, with Lina's Cobra close behind. The remaining fighters took several minutes to form up and by then Hammer was accelerating into the belt. Rather than following the more open transit corridor, he set course along a more direct path.

Hammer's anger at himself for the rash accusation against Piotr in the briefing still simmered. He'd promised Lina that he wouldn't say anything until he found proof. So far all he'd discovered was circumstantial at best.

Piotr hadn't been a suspect when Hammer returned to Freeholm. He'd had no contact with Piotr before and little direct interaction after coming to the station. Their modes of operation differed immensely. Their idea of fun didn't converge in any way. He'd taken a dislike to the bounty hunter when they'd first met solely on the impression of a secret darkness within him.

When he returned, it had taken all of his will to suppress the rage he'd felt. Only the fact that he didn't know who tried to kill him allowed him to bury the fury.

Initially he suspected one of the maintenance team from the station. They were the only people beside himself with access to his ship. So he'd checked the ship's sensor logs for the previous evening. After an extensive search he discovered an anomaly. He found twenty minutes of what appeared to be fake data. It didn't tell him who, but at least he now knew when.

A judicious bribe bought him access to the station's

security recordings for the docking bays. Although they only recorded access to the bays, he discovered that Piotr had been there. While reviewing the feed, something else struck him as strange. The maintenance team didn't enter the bay for the whole evening. They had been scheduled for overtime on the ship to complete the upgrades.

Further investigation revealed that the scheduled team had been shifted to perform some emergency repairs on the bounty hunter's Viper. Suspicion enough for Hammer, but not enough to prove Piotr's guilt. He continued his search and when Lina persisted in wanting to know why he behaved so pensively all the time, he told her of his suspicions. She agreed that the evidence indicated something might be amiss, but urged him to be absolutely certain before acting.

And now he'd blown it by publicly accusing Piotr.

He cursed his stupidity but what was done couldn't be changed, so turned his mind to other things.

This asteroid belt presented an anomaly. Most belts were extremely diffuse collections of asteroids following a similar orbit around the star. You occasionally found clusters, denser areas where groups of asteroids clumped together. They didn't tend to survive for long in astronomical terms, but for human operations they were usually stable enough.

When they weren't, such as some of those around Freeholm, powerful engines were placed on them to nudge them into more favourable orbits. As he flew past one of the local clusters, he noticed the bright flare of some of those engines as they moved several billion tons of rock and metal.

Most mining operations were mobile and relocated when they neared the end of the mineable stores within an asteroid. Some operations like Freeholm had developed into cities and became impractical to move or the local population had little interest in doing so. In these circumstances, the asteroids were moved to the mining facility rather than the other way round.

Beyond the clusters the density of asteroids plummeted, providing Hammer and Lina with little cover between them and the approaching fighters. Hammer noticed that their progress had been slow. They seemed more interested in hunting down the recon and surveillance drones scattered throughout the volume. The main difference between this zone and the cleared transit corridor was the amount of dust and small debris which floated in space.

That dust now sparkled against his ship's shields as he powered towards the fighters. They hadn't reacted yet and he doubted they would. He was surprised to see that the main force hadn't changed their position. The fighters could defeat his Anaconda but they'd take heavy casualties and the outcome would be uncertain. Even though they didn't know about his modifications, he'd expected the Laphrians to deploy the Cutters against him.

On the scanner, he noticed that the second group led by Julia were advancing quickly. He believed that they'd have a harder time against the fighters than he would. His ship was designed to engage multiple smaller targets. Even so, he was pleased that he'd reconfigured his ship for straight combat rather than his usual ambush tactics.

There were enough fighters arrayed against him to make the battle a challenge. His armour wouldn't be enough this time. He'd need his shields and the upgraded point defence systems.

He also watched the blip on the scanner which represented Lina's Cobra. Now there was perhaps the greatest surprise of all.

When he had returned to the station he didn't know who to trust, so kept himself to himself and paid close attention to those he interacted with. The sudden paranoia came as an unpleasant change to him. His normally open nature didn't sit well with the need to be ever-vigilant. In space that was always the case, you could never be too careful. But outside of the cockpit he liked to live a little.

Lina approached him a few times and despite his developing feelings for her, he brushed her off.

She persisted though and eventually wore down his defences until they spent an evening together.

He smiled as he remembered that first evening together. It had been like something from a soppy romance vid. In the comfort of her quarters they enjoyed a light meal and some wine imported from Panem in the Kappa Fornacis system.

And they talked.

They talked all through the night. Hammer had been reluctant to reveal too much of himself at first and simply listened to Lina. She told him of her past, life on the station and even trivial gossip. Their shared dislike for Piotr proved to be the key that unlocked Hammer's tongue and the story of his life poured from him.

Lina switched from chatty to attentive listener without him realising. Occasionally she would ask a pertinent question that prodded him into revealing more. At one stage he panicked, realising how much of himself he had revealed. He had never spoken to anyone so openly and it frightened him.

Even in the memory he felt a little ashamed at how daunted he'd been by revealing his past. He'd battled pirate gangs alone and here he was, afraid to share his life.

Yes, just like a soppy romance vid indeed.

As morning chased away the night, he discovered that actually he enjoyed sharing his feelings with someone. It felt right. He was still him, that didn't change, but having that other person by your side made the world seem brighter than it did before.

This simple, if profound, revelation staggered him. Along with the other changes in recent weeks, he felt unsure of how he should proceed.

They finally arrived at the topic of the events on his ship during his return from the escort run. He told the story in fragments, still angry and reluctant to delve into the subject. He knew that he would kill whoever had tried to kill him. There couldn't be any other way and he didn't want to involve this woman in the repercussions of what would follow when he did.

It took some time and piece by piece Lina coaxed the full story from him and what he'd learned so far. When he faltered in the telling, she told a story of her own to lead him onward. When he finally finished, she insisted that she would help him. He refused at first and she kept at him until he agreed. He was a stranger in Freeholm and while he'd learned a few things on his own, she had a much wider range of local contacts.

Even harder to agree to was her insistence that they take it to station security when they had something more than suspicion. As far as he was concerned, he would deal with the matter as he had done for so long. Lina reminded him that he wasn't alone in this situation. She wanted to go to Julia and Jon Mayborn immediately, but he drew the line at that point.

Pointlessly it seemed, as he'd been unable to keep his mouth shut.

Now Piotr knew that Hammer was gunning for him and he didn't know how the bounty hunter would react. Piotr denied it of course, that was to be expected, but how else would he do next? Would he try again? And as Lina had asked, why did he want to kill Hammer in the first place?

Hammer lacked answers for those questions and that frustrated him. At least with the combat ahead of him, he knew who he faced and was equipped to fight them. For someone who relied on deception for his trade, Hammer wasn't really suited for covert operations and investigations.

Lina also complicated things. Maybe it would be better to focus on the future and build a life which contained her. They'd skirted around the subject and on the face of it wanted different things... He desired to return planetside and live under the open sky whereas she still wanted to live in space.

These questions could be put to one side for now. In combat you didn't need any distractions. He was confident in his own skills and the capability of his ship. Even so, you didn't enter any fight blindly.

The scanner now showed that the fighter squadron had noticed their approach and were forming up. He opened a channel to Lina.

"They've spotted us."

"I see and it looks like they want a fight."

That had been a worry for him. If the fighters decided to run then there would have been no way for the defenders to capitalise on the mistake. The enemy fighters vastly outnumbered the two ships and while they would have been foolish to ignore the potential for an Anaconda, especially as their Navy's primary combat vessels were Anacondas, they obviously felt they could handle the two ships.

Good.

"Well, let's give them what they want."

"I'm with you all the way."

"Thanks."

And he meant it. Not just for covering his rear, which was the Anaconda's main weakness. It moved well for such a big ship but a skilled fighter could all too easily sit on his tail and avoid most of his weapons' fire arcs. She'd also brought something new and out here in the cold of space, he decided that he definitely wanted something warm in his life.

No matter what it took.

"All right, let's get ready. Remember just keep on my tail. Don't let them separate us or we'll be in trouble."

"And such a handsome tail it is."

"Well, feel free to admire it as much as you want. Just make sure to stop anyone from scratching it."

"Will do."

"As we approach weapons range I'll slow down so I can volley fire as many targets as I can. My turret weapons will chip away their shields as they close but I'll still overkill with the missiles."

"You told me this back at the docking bay."

"I know. I usually fight alone so I want to make sure we're together on this."

"Oh we're together all right and you best never forget that."

"This isn't the time for that," he said, although he couldn't hide the smile in his voice.

"It's always the time and I'll follow your lead. Just give me a heads-up if you're about to do anything drastic."

"Will do."

The Laphrian fighters formed into four flights as they approached. Each group contained eight fighters. One group arched upward and Hammer guessed that they would dive in from above. The second swept out to Hammer's left and would strike on his flank. The third flight dived low.

"Lina."

"Yes."

"The group diving low will try and hit from the rear. Keep your eyes on them. Most of my launchers are built into my upper armour so I won't get many shots on them. I'll roll as they pass underneath to try and at least get a few as they pass."

"No problem."

"Ten minutes until firing range."

"I'll head up to catch the group diving in, hopefully take down some of their shields to leave them open for your missiles. When you engage them, I'll drop back down for the bottom group."

"Sounds good. It looks like the fourth group is acting as a reserve."

"Makes sense."

"I'd rather they just piled in. It's going to be tricky keeping an eye on them when we're in a brawl with the rest."

"I'll keep my eyes on them too."

"Appreciated."

The fighter groups continued along their paths and separated, creating space between the individual ships. This would slow the tracking system's response as it moved from one ship to the next.

Not for the first time, Hammer congratulated himself on upgrading his targeting system. Most non-military ships could track and target a handful of targets at once. His could handle over a dozen simultaneously and the battle management software automatically sequenced targets via a range of priorities.

"Moving up now," Lina reported.

Hammer saw the stalk on her contact on the scanner lengthen as she flew up to target the incoming group of fighters. His own weapons also opened fire. Turreted pulse lasers blazed at the upper and flank groups. The Anaconda supported a variety of hard point classes and they all blasted away with their impacts flaring against the incoming fighters' shields.

"Slowing down now. Match my speed and keep to the rear."

"Throttling back," Lina responded.

The fighters now entered their own engagement envelopes and concentrated their fire on the Anaconda. They were at the extreme end of their weapon range so their weapons lost most of their strength before hitting the shields. Blue energy sparked across the bow and upper regions of his ship.

With his own weapons starting to run hot, Hammer diverted energy from the engines into the weapon systems and a single pip into the shields. With this many attackers his shields wouldn't last long, but the only way to survive the engagement would be to take some of these fighters down quickly and then find space for another run.

"Keep your boost ready, Lina, as they pass I will boost forwards and then turn to face them as they come around."

"I'll be ready. This upper group are in range for a salvo and I'm dropping down below."

"Okay."

The targeting system chirped as it confirmed locks on the upper group and Hammer unleashed six missiles from each launcher at the group. They streaked from launchers in a cloud of fury and charged towards the fighters. On his scanner, the line of new white contacts swept to the group.

"Rolling to the left."

"I'm engaging down below."

As the Anaconda rolled to face the flanking group, they unleashed their own storm of laser fire which splashed against his shields. Since they'd moved closer than the upper group had been, the hits caused more damage to the shields. The outer blue ring of the three shield indicators disappeared.

The reduced distance worked in his favour as well. His pulse and burst lasers ripped through the shields of the fighters and a moment later, when the launchers indicated they were ready, he unleashed another salvo of missiles.

He continued the roll to engage the bottom group who were now almost level with his ship. On the scanner, the first salvo of missiles reached the upper group of fighters. They scattered as they fled, breaking the unit's cohesion. One of the more skilled pilots switched off flight assist and spun in place to gun down the pursuing missiles.

The remnants of the wave blinked out of view almost

in the same second as most struck their targets and others were shot down in the last instant. Although there appeared to be several explosions, Hammer couldn't be certain of how many kills as he had to pay attention to the below group who would pass through his weapon's fire arcs within seconds.

"I'm taking hits," Lina reported.

"I'm turning now. When I fire this next salvo, boost straight ahead and we'll turn and re-engage."

"They'll turn faster than we will."

"I know. We're faster in a straight line though."

"What about the reserve group?"

"Let's charge them."

"We can't get too close to the main force."

"We won't, they'll scatter out of our way."

"All right. I'm still following your lead."

"If only that were true all the time."

"And now who's being inappropriate?"

"I have no idea what you mean. Firing now. Boosting."

He put all pips into his engines and shields. The shields had collapsed to their last ring. The extra power would help them regenerate before they engaged the three groups. Without the extra power, his energy weapons would cool down slowly. He'd have to rely on missiles alone for the reserve group.

The Anaconda and the Cobra accelerated from the engagement zone and charged the reserve unit.

"How's your ship?" he asked Lina.

"Systems are all fine. Multicannons are reloading. Some minor hull damage and I'm waiting for the shields to recharge. How many did we get?"

"I'm not sure. Checking now. It looks like two kills from the upper group with a possible damaged ship. It's moving erratically. Only one from the flanking group. I thought we'd get more on the first pass. They won't fall for the same trick so easily."

"What about the bottom flight?"

"We did better there. Half of them are destroyed."

"So we're not doing too badly then."

"No, but we need to do better on the next pass."

"Do you think they'll want another round?"

"It looks like they're up for it as they're turning already. We'll be in weapons range of the reserve group in two minutes. Focus your fire on the two on their right flank. I'll smash through the centre and put everything back in weapons and shields."

"What about the rest?"

"We have a few minutes before they get here, let's take out this group on its own if we can before they arrive."

"Shields are coming back up."

"Good."

"Engaging."

Hammer targeted all of the ships in the group and fired another barrage of missiles, as the eight fighters tried to manoeuvre close to the two larger ships. While the missiles sped towards their targets, Hammer fired the retro thrusters to slow his ship and turned it in a wide arc to face to returning fighters from the first engagement.

The reserve group reacted slowly to the attack and five fighters exploded from the onslaught of laser fire and missiles. The remaining three turned and ran.

"I got one."

"Nice work."

Hammer checked his weapon load-outs. He had less than half of his missiles remaining. The fighters formed a single mass as they surged towards Lina and Hammer. There was no tactical finesse in their approach. They were going to try and overwhelm the two ships in a close-quarter brawl.

"This will be the last pass," Hammer told Lina. "I don't have enough ammo for a long fight so we need to be through them as quickly as possible. I don't think they're going to try anything clever. They'll move in close and try to wear us down with numbers."

"I'm ready."

"Good. When we pass through, disengage flight assist and spin and fly backwards towards the station."

"We're retreating?"

"No, we're going to fly backwards. They will try and mob us. Let's see how far they're willing to follow us."

"Let's do it."

- 34 -

Julia's small squadron of Eagles departed Freeholm several minutes after Hammer and Lina. The small fighters lacked the thrust of the larger ships, and Julia and the defence force pilots watched from afar as they charged into battle against the fighter force.

On both sides of the transit corridor, the fighters had destroyed many of the sentinel sensor packages, reducing their ability to monitor the enemy fighters' actions. The lack of sensors and extreme range provided Julia with little reliable information to determine how Hammer and Lina fared in their battle.

She just saw a confused mass of heat signatures, some transient so probably explosions. Others cooled as they drifted away from the battle. She assumed those to be debris from destroyed ships.

They had their own foes to face. The enemy squadron was slightly smaller than the group which Lina and Hammer faced with twenty-four ships. With the four veteran defence force pilots and herself, they were severely outnumbered.

Their Eagles were individually more capable than the Imperial fighters that they faced. The Eagle was designed as a jump-capable multirole ship intended to operate in small units across vast distances. It was tougher, faster and carried a bigger punch than the smaller Imperial fighters.

Their advantage lay in numbers and manoeuvrability. Advantages that Julia knew couldn't be discounted.

Unlike Hammer's Anaconda and Lina's Cobra, the Eagles weren't fast enough to keep the smaller ships at bay. They also lacked long-range firepower so they had to dogfight against the more numerous enemy.

The flashing comms panel attracted her attention and when she accepted the incoming message, Mayborn's face filled the small screen.

"Julia. I've just come from the council."

"What did they say?"

"They supported your decision. They do want to speak to you when you return."

"Of course. How's morale?"

"Most of the population are aware of what's going on. We've had a couple of volunteers from visiting ships, but most want to leave. We're holding them here for now."

"That's the right call. We'll get into it once we return."

"Okay."

"What about the residents?"

"They're angry more than anything. Again there are volunteers but also a few who want to leave but don't have transport."

"How many?"

"I don't have a clear picture yet. There have been a dozen so far."

"Try to keep them calm."

"The council are speaking to everyone now. They want you to speak at a public meeting after you've briefed them on your return."

"I don't see what more I can tell them."

"Well, hopefully you'll bring a victory back with you."

"I'll try. Is the communications lockdown in place?"

"Yes, all comms into and out of the station are blocked. We're buffering the incoming messages. I think I should release those we deem safe."

"Agreed."

"We're maintaining the ship-to-ship links for the deployed ships and of course Flight Control."

"Good. Have you started the defence preparations?"

"Yes. The rail guns and point defences are all active. We also have a reserve store of rail guns that I wasn't aware of."

"Oh. Where from?"

"Your father, apparently."

"What?"

"He stashed some in one of the shut-down mining camps."

"How did you find out?"

"I was informed by the council."

"They knew?"

"Apparently."

"Do you have a full inventory?"

"I've sent a small team over to investigate."

"Have a report for me when I return."

"Will do. How's it going? We can see that Hammer and Lina have engaged their targets."

"They're too far away for my sensors to be able to resolve the details."

"Understood. Good hunting."

"Thanks, Mayborn."

At full thrust, the Eagles covered the distance to the invaders quickly. The encroaching fighters responded by forming a wall of pairs and they changed course to intercept.

"Eagle Two to all Eagles."

Eagle One had been her father's ship designation. She would never assume that call sign.

"All Eagles form up on me. Arrowhead formation."

The Freeholm defence force were primarily trained for patrol and escort duties. This type of mass combat wasn't something they had prepared for. She knew that she couldn't allow her pilots to be separated. Alone they would die, together they had a chance.

"There's too many of them to fight individually. Maintain formation and engage targets of opportunity as they appear. Follow my lead."

The four pilots all radioed their understanding.

She checked their position relative to her own. "Stagger your height intervals and do not cross each other's line of fire."

The four following ships adjusted their height.

"They're coming straight at us. We'll angle to the right and strafe targets as they cross our sights. When we reach the end of their line, concentrate your fire on the two end-pairs. We need to focus our firepower whenever we get the opportunity."

The two forces collided in a sudden burst of laser, cannon and missile fire. The pilots followed her lead as she banked left. She'd anticipated that this first pass would be the worst. All of the enemy fighters had a firing solution and blazed away. The Eagles' shield strengths dropped alarmingly and their return fire appeared to have little effect on the wall of fighters.

The weight of fire lessened as the two forces intersected and the Eagles reached the end of the Laphrian line. The Freeholm ships' own fire now started to cause its own damage. The four Imperial-model fighters disintegrated under the concentrated barrage and the Eagles flew through the debris of their enemies.

Julia led her force in a sharp turn but the smaller Imperial fighters out-turned them and she led her ships into a second hail of fire. Her shields were already weakened and, as the lead ship in the formation, she suffered the bulk of it. Her shields collapsed and the shots chewed into her hull.

"Rob. Put everything into your shields and take point."

"Roger that."

She retreated behind her lead pilot. The other ships in her flight blazed a fresh volley at their enemy.

"Combine your fire," she reminded them.

They followed her lead and two more Laphrian fighters exploded and scattered their comrades. The fighters reformed quickly although by the time they did, Julia's flight had passed through.

"Full burn until our shields restore and then flip and straight back at them."

The Eagles possessed a few advantages. They had greater firepower on an individual basis, and a greater ability to withstand damage along with better straight line speed. The opposition had numbers and better manoeuvrability on their side. Advantages which they needed to nullify.

"We'll hit and run. When we turn, head straight at them at full speed to cut down the time they have to fire. Concentrate all fire on one target and then all switch to another if we get the chance on a pass."

Everyone acknowledged her order.

The enemy fighters hadn't demonstrated any tactical finesse so far. They'd relied on their innate advantages, so she hoped that her forces would complete at least two or three runs before the opposition reacted.

The first pass went as expected, they destroyed one fighter and severely damaged another. The damaged fighter limped towards its mothership and she saw an escape pod amongst the wreckage. As Julia pulled into a tight turn to re-engage, the enemy ships separated into two formations. The first rolled upwards intending to hit them from above while the other went wide and low.

Julia lacked the forces to meet each formation directly. The move also meant that the enemy fighters would bring more guns to bear and for longer. The Eagles would take longer to recover between each pass which also gave the opposition more time to recover.

"They're splitting up. All fighters follow my lead and target what I target."

The lower formation appeared to be diving deeper than the upper group were climbing, so she took a chance and angled her ship to intercept the upper fighters. With their extra speed, they would be through the formation before the lower group attained a firing solution.

They concentrated their fire on the two central fighters, blasting a whole which they shot through. The remaining fighters spun on the spot while their drives thrust against their inertia to put them in the chase again.

The lower formation of fighters pushed themselves wide, still below the Eagles but approaching from the flank.

Julia checked the angle of their approach and the status of her ships. Everyone lost their shields on the previous pass. Rob's ship and her own had taken severe damage to the hull as well. They would need a couple of minutes for their shields to recover.

"San – you take point."

"On it."

With the enemy split into groups, Julia's opportunities for engagement were lessened as one group would leapfrog the other. However, the smaller numbers in each group did present another option.

"Everyone else form a loose arrowhead. Rob - you and I will take the outermost wing positions. When I give the word, disable flight assist and flip to face the enemy. Slow to allow them to approach and then select individual targets and pour it on. Maintain speed so their fire window is limited. Hopefully we'll take a few down before they realise what's going on."

The ships adjusted their positions and then followed her instructions. As soon as the Eagles engaged, the fighters boosted to bring their own weapons into range. Julia had selected the arrowhead formation to reduce the fire on her and Rob's ships. It also meant that for a short time only, San's Eagle was in range of their guns and they poured all of their firepower onto her.

"San – pull back. Everyone return to flat wall."

The order came too late as San's shields collapsed in a flare of energies and her nose cone and cockpit disappeared for a moment under a storm of impacts.

Gimna and Delvin responded by decelerating and blocking the incoming fire with their ships. It provided enough of a respite for San to flip her ship back into their direction of travel. The combined fire of the incoming fighters quickly stripped Gimna and Delvin's shields and they manoeuvred to reduce the volume of fire and to try and bring their own weapons into line.

On the flanks, Julia and Rob thrust forward to bolster the collapsing line. Their stream of shells annihilated two more fighters but the others didn't let up on their targets. They had the two Eagles in their sights and had no intention of letting them go. On her scanner, Julia noted with some alarm that the other formation now arched in to their rear.

She didn't like to admit it, but this fight was over. They'd taken too much damage to last long in a firefight. Their advantages were nullified and it was time to head home.

"Eagle One to all ships. Retreat to base."

"But Julia…"

"No discussion. Return to base now."

"Acknowledged."

But it might already be too late.

The attacking formation angled their attack to herd the Eagles closer to the flanking group. They weren't quite cut off yet but they would pass close enough to the fighter to receive fire.

And San was already on her own heading towards them.

"San – throttle back and allow Gimna and Delvin to catch up with you. Then angle away on your course. Put everything into your shields. Delvin and Gimna do the same. You three are going to have to cover me and Rob as we pass."

Delvin and Gimna broke from the formation and boosted towards San. Rob and Julia unleashed everything they had against the pursuing group. Another fighter limped from the formation, trailing fire and sparks from damaged systems. They burned their retro thrusters to increase the separation between them and the fighters and, by the slimmest of margins, pushed themselves out of range.

The reprieve only lasted a moment as the fighters boosted their engines and surged forward to re-engage. Another hail of fire spat at the retreating Eagles. Rob and Julia transferred more energy into their shields. That reduced their offensive capability as they had less energy to manage the heat that firing their lasers generated.

"Let's angle further away," Julia told Rob. "We can increase the divergence so at least we don't get caught cleanly between the two formations."

It would help but the move meant that the Eagles now formed two separate units and neither unit was in a position to effectively engage either of the attacking formations.

"San, lead Delvin and Gimna wide of the flanking squadron. Do not engage directly. Skirt past them and let them chase you."

She could only watch as San and the other two Eagles angled away from the flanking fighter group. At least they weren't in a position now to turn and engage Rob and herself from the rear. If that had happened, they wouldn't have a chance to returning home.

With the energy from their boost decaying, the fighters slipped out of weapons range. Her sensors indicated that the enemy had used more energy into their drives so that they could boost back into range more quickly.

When they did, they pushed that energy into weapons and shields. The returning fire from Rob and Julia now caused little damage. When a fighter lost its shields, it pulled back and another took its place. At the beginning of the engagement, the fighters had operated in a disorganised fashion. Julia didn't know what had changed but they now presented a much more effective fighting force, which didn't bode well for their long fighting retreat back to the station, or the future and more desperate battle to come.

- 35 -

That was quick thinking on Dee's part, Piotr thought as he flew into position five kilometres from Freeholm's docking port. The five trainee pilots formed up around him.

"Power everything down and maintain radio silence. Flight Control will pipe their sensor feed through laser comms to us."

He didn't wait for their acknowledgement and closed the channel.

This was not where he wanted to be. He'd come to this miserable station at the arse-end of the galaxy for one reason only. That reason was now null and void, but thanks to Dee and her mission, he was stuck here.

Worse than that, his long quest to avenge Sahiba's murder was over. For years he'd dedicated his entire existence to that single goal and now it had been snatched away from him. His life lacked purpose. He still had his trade, of course. Hunting the scum of human space provided some small satisfaction and enough credits to maintain his ship and himself in comfort.

It wouldn't be around here, though. Reading between the lines, it appeared that this backwater system and the nearby systems would soon fall under Imperial influence. He preferred not to work in Imperial space. Their stratified society offended his Federal tastes. He'd grown up in the slums of an industrial world at the heart of the Federation. He believed the reports of the Federal feeds broadcast.

He'd even visited Sol once.

He would give anything to kill those who murdered Sahiba. If that option was no longer available then he wouldn't wallow in that. They were dead and that's what mattered.

Except that he knew that to be a lie.

A fresh concern surfaced. What if Dee had lied to him and they weren't dead?

He could easily imagine scenarios why they wouldn't want the targets dead. Perhaps they worked for the Imperial Intelligence services. He would need to be certain. If he could trace the dead then it would confirm that they had been killed. He thought it unlikely they would kill two people just to throw him off the scent.

Unless they were being killed anyway? Killing two birds with one stone, as the saying went. If that were the case then digging into their histories would reveal the truth.

Although what if they created a history to make it seem like they were those he'd hunted all this time?

Another discomforting thought and one that he wasn't sure how to answer. The cycle of deception could stretch on forever. He could only act upon the information he had available. A frustrating truth, but the reality of the situation nonetheless. However, if he didn't get out of this system before the Laphrian Navy reached Freeholm then it might all become a moot point.

The feed from Flight Control provided a real-time update on the situation towards the edge of the belt. On the left flank, Hammer and Lina had already engaged the fighter group. The destroyed sensors reduced the resolution available on the contacts, but they received enough to gain a rough impression of the battle.

Hammer's accusation back on the station had surprised Piotr. It was true that he had sabotaged Hammer's ship, but he had been careful. There should have been no trace. The lack of evidence to accompany the charge provided

337

some room for manoeuvre. And there was another reason to get out of the system. The woman Lina appeared to be preventing Hammer from acting prematurely, although not enough to stop him speaking at all.

The warning was useful though. If he left the system, he needed to be sure that Hammer would or could not follow him. Piotr researched Hammer's background soon after arriving at the station. It had taken a bit of digging but he was fully aware that the man had followed a singular purpose of revenge in the same way Piotr did.

In a normal situation, Piotr would have respected him for that. In fact he did. However, that respect wasn't enough to stop Piotr acting in his own self-interest. It was obvious that Hammer wasn't a man you wanted hunting you down.

He would have to be dealt with.

Perhaps the Laphrians would solve the problem for him by destroying Hammer in the engagement. It was a possibility and Piotr watched the unfolding battle with interest. From his investigation, he knew that Hammer's Anaconda was converted with engaging multiple small targets simultaneously in mind. It could take a beating and then unleash hell upon its opponents.

Pirate forces tended to be small in number. Rarely did you encounter more than a handful at a time. Unless you entered anarchic space and then all bets were off. Piotr had claimed many rich bounties by daring to enter these unprotected regions. This time, however, Hammer faced a more numerous opponent. It might be true that they were only short-range fighters, but they still packed a punch and with what appeared to be two squadrons, Hammer might have overcommitted himself.

Piotr hoped so, at any rate. It would ease the worries that Hammer's continued existence created.

As the minutes passed, he watched the battle unfold in the direction he hadn't wanted to see. The two larger ships were kept under pressure but they were swatting down individual fighters with relative ease.

When the battle between Julia's Eagles and the other fighter wing started, Piotr realised that whoever was commanding these fighter groups didn't know what he was doing. In both cases they failed to capitalise on their numeric advantage and he wondered what the hell the Laphrian Navy was up to.

The comms panel blinked, indicating an incoming request. It was a secure channel from Flight Control.

"Yes."

"Piotr, it's Dee. I have an update for you."

"I see it. The Navy is getting their arse handed to them. I thought there was a plan?"

"There was."

"So what's going on?"

"Somebody has decided that they know better."

"I see. And how does that affect me?"

"Well, that's what I'm contacting you for."

"I hope it's a way out of this mess."

"Not yet."

"That's no good to me. The local ships might be doing well out there but once that Interdictor comes into play, it will be over. And I don't want to be here when it arrives."

"Don't worry, you'll be fine."

"If I'm here then I'm not fine. If the Laphrians come then I'm the enemy. If the locals find out I've been helping you, then I'm equally screwed. And your hit squad took out the reason I came here for in the first place."

"Ah. That's what I need to talk to you about. The hit squad failed."

He laughed at that. "So much for Imperial justice."

"We were forced to use local contacts and they killed one of the family, the sister, but the brothers took out the squad."

"I did offer to do it for you."

"Now isn't the time to gloat."

"All right then. How many?"

"A full assault squad of ten."

"No bullshit now. Were the team any good?"

"Not up to our usual standards, but they were fully trained and equipped special operations troops."

"So they were pretty good then?"

"Yes and augmented."

"It's a shame they failed and still killed the sister. I would have liked to have taken all three for myself."

"I know that, but I had my orders."

"So what has changed?"

"Frankly I need your help."

"With what? Never mind. Just point me at the two brothers and I'll take them."

"No. I need your help in the current situation."

"I don't think that's a good idea. The Laphrians are screwing up their operation, but they'll sort themselves out, they have the firepower they need."

"You're probably right, but I want someone close at hand to tip the balance should it be necessary."

"And that would be me?"

"Smart and handsome."

"Whatever. And by risking my neck and helping you I get...?"

"You get what you wanted all along. We'll let you kill the two brothers."

"You should have let me do that in the first place."

"Maybe, but the decision wasn't mine to make then."

"And it is now?"

"To an extent. The operation here is key to our future interests in this region. Unfortunately I lack the support I'd like for this type of operation that I would have liked for this closing phase. It's too important and I cannot fail."

"I get that."

"It's not just important for me so I have a little more leverage."

"Enough to work out a deal."

"What kind of deal?"

"You provide the support that I need when I request it and when this is over, I will provide you the full intelligence package on the two brothers."

"Okay. Assuming that I trust that you'll keep your word, how will I survive the coming battle to collect it?"

"Arrangements have already been made and I've kept you out of the fight so far, haven't I?"

"Yes you have, although it looks like your side is losing."

"Some mistakes have been made, but that will change."

"You're in contact with them?"

"Of course."

"Isn't that risky with the communications blackout?"

"I've been doing this for a long time, Piotr."

"No need to be defensive. So how do I keep safe?"

"I've provided your ship details to the Laphrians and they've encoded it into their IFF systems. Providing you don't kill any of them, you'll be all right."

"When they reach here, I won't be able to pretend to fight them or the others will recognise it and they'll want to know why."

"You'll need to figure that one out for yourself. The IFF system is robust enough to take a few stray hits against shields before switching you to hostile."

"Is that per ship?"

"I don't know, I'll find out. Don't worry, you won't have to cover for long. This thing should be over in the next few hours."

- 36 -

Captain Belin couldn't believe what he was hearing.

He considered the operation poorly planned and conceived from the first briefing. He'd expected it to be more costly than the Admiral's staff believed, but he'd never expected to lose so many people so quickly. The bulk of the fleet hadn't engaged the Freeholm defence forces yet.

They'd planned the mission for weeks and had practised it for just as long. It had all been for nothing. The Admiral informed them of the change when they emerged from supercruise. Belin protested the order but as before he had been ignored.

With the list of the casualties in hand, he logged into the virtual conference along with Admiral Locke, his staff, the colonel commanding the Navy infantry battalion and the other ship captains.

The first thing Belin noticed was the nervous expression on the Admiral's face and that didn't bode well. He then realised that a new face was present in the assembled officers.

"Thank you all for joining us," the Admiral said. "Commander Reese has been arrested and replaced by Lieutenant Commander Weirman. She now commands the fighter group."

"Sir," Belin said. "Why was Reese arrested?"

"He failed in his orders and will face a court martial when we return. The debacle of our losses against Freeholm was unacceptable, and he alone is responsible for that failure."

In the virtual meeting room, Belin glanced at his fellow officers. None of them appeared ready to defend their deposed comrade.

"With respect sir. The fighters shouldn't have been deployed without support."

"Captain, those were my orders and he failed to follow those orders."

"Sir, may I ask why our orders were changed?"

"You may not." The Admiral hesitated before continuing. In that second of indecision, Belin knew that they were all in real trouble. "The deployment had two objectives. The first was to remove any static defensive measures placed by the station and the second to draw out the defenders to confirm the strength forces they have available."

"Sir, the fighters found no defensive systems, only sensor and recon packages. And without support, the fighters were outmatched."

"Commander Reese should have pulled his fighters back and lured the enemy closer to the main fleet."

"Sir, if we had deployed the Cutters in support, we could have inflicted severe losses on the local forces. As it was, they hit our fighters hard."

He spoke the words in a flat tone, suppressing the urge to shout at the Admiral. This operation was turning into a disaster.

"And that is why Commander Reese is under arrest. He has jeopardised the mission. Now if you're done questioning my orders, Captain, may I continue?"

Belin recognised the threat in the Admiral's voice. Arguing with the superior officer like this verged on insubordination and from the Admiral's recent actions, he wouldn't hesitate to arrest Belin. Then who would lead his crew?

What worried Belin more than anything was the reason for the sudden change in orders. Had the Admiral been afraid? After all, Admiral Locke hadn't seen any combat in his career. He'd commanded a desk since graduating from the academy and seemed an odd choice to command this operation.

"Of course sir."

"Thank you, Captain. Now despite the losses, the mission objectives were achieved. Much of the enemy's electronic intelligence-gathering apparatus has been destroyed. Thanks to our assets, we now know the location of their remaining packages. We believe that they do not include mines, but we will take the usual precautions.

"We have also learned that Freeholm did not deploy all of their forces in the engagement."

That surprised Belin.

"Sir, do we know what forces were held in reserve?"

"Please leave any questions to the proper time, Captain."

This didn't follow the usual Navy command doctrine. Officers were encouraged to question and gain greater understanding of their operations. The Admiral's behaviour reminded Belin of how things used to be before the coup.

"Yes sir."

"The reserve force consists of several fighter-class ships. They are commanded by a notorious bounty hunter. A briefing package has been sent to your personal files."

Belin accessed his data files and isolated the new package. A single Viper and four Sidewinders didn't seem like much of a reserve.

"Sir," Colonel Junesford spoke up.

"Yes Colonel."

"I haven't seen any reports of the operation on the newsfeeds."

"That's correct, Colonel. The operation is sensitive. There are some civilian concerns that would attempt to interfere with the operation. When we have finished, then we will announce our success."

Junesford looked pensive and Belin hoped that he'd follow up with the obvious question. The question that he hoped everyone wanted to ask: was their mission sanctioned by the civilian government?

"Yes sir."

Belin cursed inwardly. It looked like he was the lone voice of dissent in the command group so he would have to be careful. With hindsight, it was easy to see that his old friend Davies had been correct, but what to do now?

He could continue to protest the orders, but what would that really achieve? He'd end up in the brig and his ship placed under the command of another. It wouldn't stop the attack. He needed allies and preferably part of the *Laphrian Pride*'s command-level staff.

"I know that some of you have concerns for the civilians in Freeholm. So there will be another change in timing. We will provide the residents of Freeholm twelve hours in which to leave the station or to surrender."

Belin appreciated the sentiment, although he wasn't convinced that was the real reason. From a military perspective it was madness. They'd already thrown away their advantage in the first battle and were now going to do so again.

"Sir, is this wise?"

"I'm growing tired of your questions, Captain."

"Sir, with respect, we need to go in now and hard." The other captains nodded their agreement, but still didn't speak out. "They may have won the first engagement but they must have taken damage. I'd estimate that all of their ships barring their reserve force suffered damage and now we're giving them time to repair. Sir, I urge you to reconsider. We can go in now and have the base seized within a few hours. There is no reason to delay."

"The decision is mine, Captain. They are relying on mercenary forces to bolster their defence. The civilian population will also now be aware of the situation and will want to leave or surrender. They won't have the stomach for a battle."

"Again, with respect sir, someone in your chair thought the same ten years ago."

"You go too far, Captain. We are here to remedy the mistakes of our past. Within twenty-four hours, Freeholm will be a Laphrian installation again and we will have exclusive access to the belt's resources once more.

"Change is coming, Captain. We are the vanguard of that change and it is our duty to ensure that no possible enemy lurks within our borders to threaten our future."

Once again Belin glanced around, seeking any sign of support from his fellow officers. Surely they could see that this was wrong? They all avoided his glance.

"Captain, you have been a reluctant participant in this operation from the beginning. If you feel that you are not up to the task ahead of you, then step aside. Another will command your ship."

"No sir. I meant no disrespect, I seek only to achieve our mission objectives with a little loss as possible."

"An admirable goal, Captain, and we are in agreement. We will give the residents of Freeholm the opportunity to surrender. If they do not then we will move in full force against them. Even if they do repair their ships, they will not be able to stand in our way."

Belin simply nodded in response. He didn't trust himself to speak.

"Now let us continue. The time will provide the fighter group to repair their ships and for Weirman to assume his command over the squadrons. I do not expect any problem with this." The Admiral stared at the young officer.

"No sir. Repairs are already under way."

"Good. The Cutters will provide close protection for my vessel. Belin, you will protect the rear. Do you have any questions?"

"No sir."

"Good. When the deadline is up, we will move into

the belt and follow the transit corridor to the station. Two fighter wings will deploy in advance and sweep on the flanks ahead of the main group. Using the data from our asset, they will destroy any remaining sensor devices."

Unwilling to give up completely, Belin spoke. "Sir."

"Yes, Captain."

"What if the defenders sally and attack?"

"The fighters will engage."

"And the Cutters, sir?"

"Will remain in close protection. Without the *Laphrian Pride*, we cannot assault the station. The mission imperative is to secure the station. The fighters will handle any response from Freeholm and under Weirman's leadership, they will not be taken unawares again. Will they, Commander?"

The newly promoted officer hesitated for just a moment before responding. "Yes sir."

"Sir," Belin said. "The Cutters' strengths are their speed and manoeuvrability. If we keep them mobile and supporting the fighters, they can respond better to anything the defenders try."

"I have made my decision, Captain."

"But sir."

"That is enough, Captain!" the Admiral almost shouted and Belin realised he had gone too far. Admiral Locke had no wish to discuss the deployment and any question was an attack on his capability. Belin thought that the Navy had operated as a meritocracy since the coup but that clearly wasn't the case here. Belin also realised that he was now causing more harm than good.

He would have to find another way.

"Sorry sir."

"It will be fine, Captain. Every possibility has been analysed and planned for."

Every possibility except the commanding officer not having a clue as to what he was doing, Belin thought bitterly. Although he kept his mouth shut.

"Once we reach the station, the flanking Cutters will secure the surrounding space and suppress any defences. Colonel Junesford's troops will then deploy in the shuttles and capture the station."

It all sounded so simple, Belin thought. And it should be, but it hadn't been so far and with these latest changes to the plan he didn't see why that would change any time soon.

- 37 -

"I don't understand why they're giving us time to prepare," Mayborn said to Julia while walking to the mezzanine overlooking the outer commercial district.

"Maybe they know we can't beat them and think we'll just roll over."

"Will we?"

"That's what we're about to find out."

On the mezzanine waited the station council members, some of Mayborn's security people and her fellow pilots. Hammer stood next to Lina. On the other side, Piotr stood with Dee. Julia was surprised that Piotr agreed to remain on the station. He appeared ill at ease but she guessed that whatever relationship was developing between the bounty hunter and her assistant had grown strong enough to cause him to stay.

Lately, Julia sensed something odd about the bounty hunter and she hadn't forgotten Hammer's accusation. She didn't believe it, why would the bounty hunter want to kill Hammer? It didn't make sense although she didn't think Hammer would be the type to make an unfounded accusation.

In any case, they had bigger problems to face.

She hadn't been as surprised when Hammer agreed to stay. His and Lina's relationship had reached a stage that when Lina said she'd fight he wouldn't leave her to fight alone.

That at least provided some good news. Without Hammer's Anaconda, they lacked heavy firepower except for the rail gun emplacements on the station and surrounding asteroids. She'd spent the morning talking to the team. First with the pilots who'd all agreed to stay and fight. San had sustained some injuries in the battle but convinced Julia that she could still fly. Even though the defence force pilots were obliged to fight, she offered them all the chance to leave if they wanted.

None of them accepted her offer.

Then she'd met with Mayborn. His security teams had received an influx of volunteers as news of the impending attack spread throughout the station. She'd expected the reaction from the older population. They'd suffered under the Laphrian regime and wouldn't want to again. Just as many volunteers came from the younger residents and those who'd moved to Freeholm after the rebellion.

Mayborn put most of them to work helping to construct barricades and defence installations. He also reported that the rail gun emplacements were all almost operational. They would add to the firepower of the station considerably. The downside was that if the enemy battle group was in range of the rail guns then the station would be directly threatened as well.

Her final meeting had been with the station council. They reiterated their support for Julia's decisions. They'd been as surprised as Julia with the ultimatum from the Laphrian Navy. It hadn't changed their resolve although they made it clear that there would need to be a public meeting.

In all of the conversations so far, no-one answered the biggest question of all. Julia didn't know how they were going defeat a fleet that outgunned them by such a huge margin. All were adamant on one point, they would fight and make taking the station as costly as possible.

The demand to surrender also indicated that they intended to capture rather than destroy the station. Why they had decided to now, no-one knew either. Relations with the planet had been strained on occasion, but apart from some newsfeed commentators, things had seemed peaceful.

The station council agreed to stay and defend Freeholm. The message provided another option for the civilian population and ultimately the choice would be theirs. They'd asked Julia to conduct the public meeting. At first she'd refused, but she accepted the wisdom of her being the station's representative as she would be their leader in the coming battle.

Standing now at the balcony above the commercial levels, she could see what must have all of the station's population crammed into every available space. Julia had never spoken publicly to so many people before and she took a moment to assemble her thoughts.

"The last time I spoke to you all was at the funeral of my father. Sometimes that moment seems like an age ago and others only yesterday. In reality, only two months have passed since that day. So much has happened in that short time and over those weeks I have discovered the burden that my father carried for the last decade.

"In the past few hours you've heard rumours and snippets of information. I'm sure many of you are concerned about what you've heard, so I will tell you all plainly what is happening. We can then decide how we will react to this information.

"In the early hours of this morning, a Laphrian Navy group exited supercruise and deployed two fighter wings within the belt. This act is a direct contravention of the co-existence treaty signed by the station council and the Laphrian government a little under ten years ago.

"It seems that the events of previous weeks and this unwarranted attack may be connected in some way although we don't have any details as yet. What we do know is that the Navy fighters entered our space and attacked our sentinel and sensor packages deployed in the belt to monitor the transit corridor. With the agreement of the council, I deployed our station defence forces supported by our allies who have helped us over the past few weeks.

"Leaving a small reserve force in case of a surprise attack from another direction, our forces engaged the fighters and in a close-fought battle forced the fighters from our space. We suffered no casualties in the engagement but our sensor logs indicate that at least twelve Laphrian fighters were destroyed with the same number or more being severely damaged."

"Why can't we contact our families off station?" a figure from the heart of crowd shouted. Julia didn't recognise the man but his dress indicated him to be one of the traders currently docked at the station.

"Upon learning of the incursion we established a complete communications lockdown, which is why you haven't been able to communicate outside the station. This was done for operational security reasons. The situation has changed since then so we will open some free channels to allow people to speak with families and loved ones on Laphria or outside the Artemis system."

"Is it true that the Navy has demanded our surrender?"

This question came from a woman holding a baby in her arms on the uppermost level near the front of the crowd.

"Just under an hour ago Admiral Locke, commander of the battle group, contacted us with instructions to surrender or depart the station within twelve hours."

Hushed comment and conversation spread throughout the crowd.

"Or what?" another man asked when it died down.

"There was no explicit threat, but the ships remain at the edge of territory and it is likely that they will attack Freeholm once the deadline has passed."

"What then?"

"That is what we are here to decide. Those of us here are ready to fight, even our out-of-system friends."

"Can you win?"

"The harsh reality here is that the Navy outnumber us and have bigger and better ships."

"Is it true they have an Imperial Interdictor in the fleet?"

"Yes, they have an Imperial *Majestic*-class warship."

The drone of muttered conversation turned sharp and fearful. A woman from the lower level shouted, "How can we fight a ship like that?"

"With everything we have."

"You don't stand a chance," the previous man shouted. "And in trying you'll kill us all."

A spatter of muttered agreement followed his statement.

"We have stated that we are willing to fight and if my father was still here he would say the same. Many of you were here when this station was a Laphrian penal colony. I was a young child then, but even so I remember the horror of living under the regime. The terrible conditions. The endless work in the mines and refinery plant."

A chorus of agreement rose from many of the assembled citizens.

"The choice to fight is yours. We have three simple choices. The first is that we fight."

"And if we lose?" the man heckled.

Julia ignored him and continued, "The second is that we surrender. And the third is that we run. I call that we fight, but that is the decision for us all to make. Or we all surrender."

"And if we surrender?" the woman with the baby asked.

"Then we revert to ten years ago. We will be prisoners of the Navy."

"What will they do with us?"

"I don't know. Why are they attacking us now after so long at peace? All we know is that they want this station back."

"Then let them have it," the first man declared. "Let us

leave the station."

"We don't have enough ships for a full evacuation."

A hush fell over the crowd.

"Even if we forced the docked traders to transport people off the station, we could only move less than half of the resident population."

"Then it's surrender or fight?" an old woman asked.

"I'm afraid so," Julia replied.

Julia waited for the babble of conversation to die down again.

"There is another option. With the agreement of the docked traders." She glanced at a dozen or so pilots and crew all in flight gear on the deck below. Many had wanted to leave immediately but she had convinced them to stay for the meeting and provide transport out of the system for the neediest. They eventually agreed, for a sizeable commission. "Some of the population can be transported safely from the station."

"Who decides who stays or goes? You?" the man demanded.

Julia nodded. "Yes, I will help decide who should go. The sick, the children and the very old. From our records we can fit those into the trading ships and if those residents with their own transports are willing to help."

There weren't many residents with their own ships like Lina, but there were a few. Mostly small transport vessels that wouldn't be much use for fighting but could get more people away from the station.

"And what of those who want to surrender?" asked a well-dressed woman who owned one of the shops in the commercial district.

"Surrender is an all or nothing deal. We either agree to hand over the station and hope that the Laphrians won't force us into slave labour or we fight."

"How can you stop a two-kilometre long warship?" the man asked. Others shouted their concern in tandem.

"I'm sure you understand that we can't discuss

operational details openly, but we do have some ideas."

And they did. Well, Hammer did. It was a crazy idea and Lina had protested vehemently when Hammer explained the details, but it might work.

The crowd chewed that over for a minute. Some groups began arguing the merits of one option or the other. Julia called for order.

"Time is pressing and we should be thankful we have the time. But we must use it wisely and now we have to make a choice. Do we fight or do we surrender?"

"If we decide to fight then what can we do?" the old woman asked.

Julia glanced at Mayborn, who nodded. She replied "The pilots you see here beside me and their ships are our first line of defence. If all goes well then the Laphrians won't board the station. However, they do need to capture the station so they will try to bring troops.

"Freeholm has its own built-in defences but if the worst happens then it will be fighting within the station itself. Many of you have already volunteered your services to help with the internal defence either in combat or by building barricades. If they do land then they will pay dearly for each corridor they try to pass through."

"And those of us who want to leave?" the woman with the baby enquired.

"My aide Dee Callum will organise the evacuation."

Dee certainly hadn't been happy to receive the assignment. She insisted that she had to help Julia. She'd been quite insistent but Julia overrode her concerns. The people had to see that Julia was taking the evacuation seriously and that mean having someone of importance managing the process.

"The evacuation flights will depart the station within ten hours. Those wishing to leave should register their desire through the ship's management services. You'll be assessed and assigned a ship as needed. Full instructions will be provided."

"And what if there aren't enough places?" the woman asked.

"If necessary, places will be prioritised. As I've already said we'll make sure that the sick, infirm, very young and very old will have a way off the station. We'll try to fit as many others as possible but they will be a lower priority.

"Now we will have a vote."

There'd been some vigorous discussion on how best to conduct the vote. A show of hands had been suggested and while the station's crime tracking software might have been able to count the raised hands, it would have taken too long to set up.

In the end, Lina offered a brilliant suggestion. All residents and visitors to the station were assigned an identity tag. This provided access profiles and personal identity information. More usefully in this case, they were equipped with a distress beacon which would summon station security or emergency responders if they encountered a problem.

"When I tell you to vote, activate the alarm on your ID kit and when I tell you to stop, release the contact. The alarms are all registered and those within the vote window will be counted."

Julia hoped that there wasn't a genuine emergency in the next few minutes.

"Those of you who want to surrender, vote now."

She waited for a full minute. The tense silence stretched as people glanced at each other to see which way they were voting.

"Release the buttons. And we'll wait for a few seconds. Okay then. Those who want to fight should vote now."

Another tense minute passed.

"Release the buttons now. Voting is completed. It will take Mr Mayborn a short while to receive the results."

The level of chatter on the floors increased as they waited and then hushed as Mayborn spoke quietly into

Julia's ear. She smiled.

"The choice is made and with almost ninety-five per cent of the voters decided we fight. Now please return to your quarters. If you need anything, contact security and they will organise supplies or movement as necessary.

"Thank you everyone and now let's move."

No-one moved.

Everyone stood still and stared up at her and she worried for a moment what it meant. Then someone clapped. And then another. Quickly more joined and then everyone clapped and cheered, including those around her on the mezzanine.

The sudden show of support touched her and she hoped she could live up to their hope.

- 38 -

Captain Belin sat in his command chair on the bridge of the Cutter *Tarsis* as the deadline approached. The twelve hours had passed all too quickly. His first order had been to make sure that his crew got some rest and food. He then instructed a full review of the ship's systems. Belin considered the chance of Freeholm surrendering to be as close to zero as possible so there would be fighting.

While the first watch rested, he attempted to contact the other ship captains. They weren't keen on talking to him and it required some persistence on his part before they accepted his call. He assumed that his performance with the Admiral had made him persona non grata with the other captains. If things were returning to the old ways then they no doubt worried about guilt by association.

With a mission of this importance, it seemed likely that the Admiral was destined for great things. That made him someone to tread carefully with. Not that Belin had done so far with any tact. Belin feared that they were returning to what their world had been. And he was making that happen.

He considered options for stopping the attack. He also reflected upon what his old comrade Davies had said and the question from Colonel Junesford in the virtual conference. What if word of the operation leaked to the civilian newsfeeds?

Such thoughts constituted treason. It wasn't up to a lowly captain to decide policy for the fleet, although he'd made the choice before. Then the issue appeared so clear cut, but now he had responsibilities and the choice didn't seem so obvious. What concerned Belin was that in this case the military wasn't implementing policy, but creating it without the knowledge or agreement of the civilian authority.

More problematic for Belin was that he lacked the contacts to investigate discreetly. He could, after all, be wrong. His participation in the coup had marred his career in the Navy. So much so that he wondered why he'd been selected for the mission at all. Although on the flip side, no other captain in the fleet possessed the same level of combat experience as he did. With a decade of peace and occasional pirate incursions, only a few officers had fired shots against an enemy at all.

Part of the joys of spending a career on the border, Belin supposed.

When he did eventually speak to the ship captains, they resisted any attempt to steer the conversation towards anything other than the strict adherence to the mission orders. He couldn't force the issue. Even with circumspect wording, he risked everything if they reported him.

He didn't try speaking to the captain of the *Laphrian Pride*. An officer so close to the Admiral was likely to report the contact. Instead he tried to talk to Colonel Junesford. Of all the officers present at the meeting, he alone questioned the Admiral. Although he'd shut down quickly when pressured, Belin believed that the soldier might prove to be a useful and maybe only ally.

The Colonel proved as deft as Belin in choosing his words carefully. Deriving any useful meaning from the conversation was difficult. The end result was frustration. Even more so in that they lacked sufficient time to evolve their relationship. Belin believed that he'd made his position clear but was unsure what response, if any, Junesford would make.

Tired and frustrated by his lack of progress, Belin slept

for an hour. Like any career officer, he'd learned over the years to snatch sleep where he could. But the short nap didn't restore him as much as he'd like.

Checking the time, he discovered that only two hours remained until the deadline expired. He returned to the bridge to ensure that the ship and his crew were ready for the coming operation.

"Situation report," he requested from his first officer as he entered the bridge.

"It's all quiet at the moment, sir. We've seen a ship depart Freeholm. It was a Lakon Type 7."

"So some are starting to leave the station."

"Didn't you think they would, sir?"

"I wasn't sure, Commander. Anything else?"

"Just some patrols around the station. It looks like two pairs of Sidewinders."

"Any sign of the units that engaged our fighters?"

"Nothing so far, sir."

"They're probably repairing and making the most of the time we've given them, as I thought they would."

"Sir?"

"It doesn't matter."

"Yes sir. What are your orders?"

"We wait. Make sure the crew have eaten before the deadline. Things will move pretty quickly after then."

"Will they surrender, sir?"

"I don't think so, Commander. They fought us before and I can't see them just handing their home over because we've told them to."

"They won't stand a chance, sir."

"I know and that will just make them fight harder."

"Yes sir."

So they waited.

The crew continued to follow their routine around him as Belin studied the long-range scans of the station. He saw little apart from the patrols the Commander had mentioned. Twenty minutes passed and two more ships departed the station. They set course towards the outer system. The scanner identified them as a Cobra Mark III and a Hauler.

Belin hoped that more ships would depart. He anticipated that the battle would be brutal. Their defeat would be inevitable, but as he'd said to his first officer, they would fight hard. Even so, they couldn't win.

Worse would happen when they assaulted the station itself. He did not know what plans were in place for those captured in the battle. At the very least, they would lose their homes and possessions and be shipped out of the Artemis system.

Another ship departed Freeholm as the previous two reached interplanetary space and vanished from the scanner as they jumped out of the system. He wished them well on their journey. They would be the lucky ones.

His thoughts turned to the Admiral. During the initial planning, his staff had been bold and aggressive with their plan to take Freeholm. Too aggressive in Belin's opinion, but their plan would have achieved their mission. Now he appeared reluctant to use the most powerful ship the Laphrian Navy had ever possessed.

It should have been capable of capturing the station on its own.

So why would the Admiral not use his key asset?

On an impulse, he called up the network intelligence system and checked the status of the *Laphrian Pride*. He was unfamiliar with the full specifications of the massive warship and it took several minutes before he realised what had caused his nagging doubt.

The power output of the ship was lower than he'd expected. He'd known from the briefing before leaving the planet that it wasn't at full operational capacity. It seemed that the ship's status was below even what that briefing indicated.

While it might not be operating at full strength, its shields and weapons were way beyond anything the defenders at Freeholm could throw at them. Which led to another conclusion and one that Belin didn't want to contemplate, even if the shadow of the thought had crossed his mind before.

What if the Admiral was afraid?

The Navy selection process and training should have prevented such a trait in their officers, especially ones as senior as Admiral Locke. Belin didn't want to believe the system had failed so badly, but it did explain the Admiral's behaviour.

He had no way to be sure though and accusing an officer of such behaviour would end his career.

Two more transports departed from Freeholm.

Less than an hour of the deadline remained.

"Sir, we have an incoming message from Fleet Command," the first officer reported.

"What do they want?"

"We have to transfer our fighters to the flagship."

Each of the Cutters carried two fighters for local defence and patrols. They provided the Cutters with additional capabilities and reach in combat. Losing them would diminish his strike capability.

"Did they say why?"

"Yes sir. They're using the fighters from all of the Cutters to help rebuild the fighter squadrons. We are ordered to transfer them immediately."

"All right, send the fighters."

Another half hour passed and two more ships left Freeholm. They were the last ships to leave the station before the deadline.

Three seconds after the deadline passed, the Admiral's voice spoke over the shared channel.

"The rebels in Freeholm have ignored our reasonable demand for their surrender. Some of their ships have been detected leaving, but they represent only a small fraction of the population. We now must assume that the remaining population is hostile.

"All ships are ordered to set course for the station. All Cutters to remain in defensive formation around my ship. Fighter wings to sweep the flanks."

"You heard the Admiral," said Belin. "Set course for Freeholm."

– 39 –

It might have been his plan but that didn't mean that Hammer felt comfortable being the point man on it. The entire defence force waited in their cockpits while the deadline passed. As soon as they received confirmation that the Laphrian fleet entered the belt, the ships deployed. Hammer exited the station first and the others soon followed and formed up around him.

He watched the approaching fleet on his scanner. They maintained a tighter formation than the initial incursion. The two fighter groups swept ahead on the flanks but this time they remained close enough to be supported by the main group.

Hammer had expected this deployment when he'd described his plan to Julia and the others. Unfortunately it looked like the Laphrians weren't going to give him exactly what he wanted. He'd hoped that the Navy had learned from their previous error and deploy the Cutters more loosely to directly support the fighters.

This presented a problem for his plan as approaching the Interdictor would be difficult enough without the Cutters being able to add their fire as well. It would be up to the others to try and draw them out. If they didn't then his attack could become very short-lived.

Volunteers from the station residents and even some of the visiting pilots bolstered the defenders. They piloted trading ships but most independent traders carried some firepower and so they were accepted into the small force.

The plan was a simple one but would require judicious timing and more than a little luck.

Piotr formed up on Hammer's left. Hammer didn't trust the bounty hunter but without any proof that he'd sabotaged Hammer's ship, he had little choice but accept his inclusion. As an experienced combat pilot, it made sense for him to lead one of the flanking wings. The rest of his force comprised of Rob and San in their Eagles and one of the trader volunteers in a Cobra Mk III.

Julia led the wing forming up on his left. The small force included Delvin and Gimna. All three of them flew their Eagles and another trader volunteer in a Sidewinder joined them.

Hammer formed his own group with Lina providing support in her Cobra. She also acted as the lead for the final flight which was assembling behind him. These were the key to the plan and were defended by the five reserve pilots in their Sidewinders and another trader volunteer. Hammer needed to smash a big enough hole for the two 'fire ships' to reach their target.

The fire ships were two tugs which usually dragged ore between mines and the refineries. Overnight they had been transformed. Blisters of enriched military-grade fuel had been fixed to their frames and at the centre of the globes sat an expertly modified twenty-five gigawatt fusion reactor, primed to explode.

The maintenance and engineering teams, helped by volunteers and the pilots themselves, worked miracles in the few hours available to them. Not only did they repair the damage sustained in the first battle, they also upgraded some of the ships to arm them with the rail guns stashed by Darik.

These rail guns were the most powerful weapons available to the defenders, besides Hammer's missile salvos. Two had been fitted to Hammer's Anaconda, giving the extra punch he'd need as the point ship in the attack. Others had been fitted to the volunteer traders. They were expected to avoid dogfighting and concentrate on targeting the Interdictor or the Cutters if needs be.

The rail guns on the station itself provided the colony's final line of defence. Those placed on the surrounding asteroids could also cover the station as well as pound the attacking forces as they approached.

Hammer reviewed the schematics of the Interdictor. The lateral weapon arrays presented a terrible risk for his manoeuvre. Assuming he survived the initial onslaught, he'd like to escape the attack. He'd never hear the end of it from Lina if he didn't.

So instead of flying away, he mapped a route following the contours of the ship and programmed it into his autopilot. That would leave him free to manage the weapons and shields so he could continue hitting the Interdictor. Keeping close to the ship also reduced any opportunities for the supporting ships like the Cutters to intervene.

The route didn't take long to create but it provided a welcome distraction, so he reviewed and revised it until the order came over the comms channel to move out.

After setting his speed to half maximum, he watched the scanner to see the other units deploy. The flanking forces leapt ahead at full thrust and then angled outwards. They would aim to hit the fighter groups at their furthest edge and so turn them away from the main attack. While they hoped the attack would pull the fighters and Cutters away, Hammer didn't rely on it. He planned to keep a close watch on any forces that lingered and might try to intercept his own approach.

The most vulnerable group followed in his wake. The engineers had done what they could to protect the fire ships by bolting on armour plating and fitting shield emitters. Despite these efforts, they wouldn't be able to take many hits and they couldn't afford to lose even one of them.

Lina positioned herself above and to the rear of Hammer's ship, ready to engage any approaching fighters. The reserve Sidewinders formed a loose ring around the fire ships to do the same.

A tense two hours passed as the two forces approached each other. The flanking groups continued to spread out wide and eventually Hammer noticed a slight bowing to the Laphrian fighter groups as they attempted to prevent being flanked. The lines broke as the Freeholm forces hit the lines.

To his left, Piotr's flight smashed through the line of fighters and charged towards the Cutter. The line of fighters collapsed into a confused ball before recovering and chasing after Piotr and his flight. This was the response they'd hoped for.

Unfortunately the fighters on the right flank maintained better cohesion and reformed their line after Julia's group. Compounding this, the Cutters flanking the Interdictor maintained their positions, forcing both Freeholm groups to turn away or fly straight into the Interdictor's guns.

Hammer couldn't track their battle further as he now entered engagement range of the right fighter group and they charged towards his ship. His turrets opened fire as soon as they crossed their fire arcs. Laser and cannon fire stabbed into the oncoming swarm. He slowed the ship to maximise the time for engagement by a few more seconds. He would only get one pass against the fighters so he spread his missile locks as thinly as he could. They wouldn't be enough to destroy many, but would help break up the enemy formation. It would hopefully weaken them enough for Lina and following Sidewinders to tackle.

He held off firing the missiles as long as he could to allow his turrets to weaken and in a few cases strip away the enemy fighters' shields. The fighters responded with their own hail of fire which splashed against Hammer's shields amidst a bright display of energy.

Hammer held his nerve and at the very last moment fired a full salvo at the passing fighters. A lucky shot with the rail gun sent one of fighters spinning out of control. The fighters streaked past his ship and some flipped on their axis and continued to fire as they travelled backwards.

His rear turrets continued to blaze away at the fighters as they passed and Lina joined the fray with her beam lasers slicing through shields, tearing a fighter in two. The reserve Sidewinders surged forward to assist her and formed a blocking line to prevent the fighters reaching the fire ships.

The missiles arced up and turned in a swarm to chase the fighters. The backwards-facing fighters managed to shoot several down before the rest intercepted their comrades. A cascade of explosions shattered the fighters' formation.

Hammer fired another salvo from his rear launchers and then Lina and the Sidewinders were on their own as Hammer's Anaconda charged on towards the Interdictor. He couldn't watch to see how Lina fared against the remaining fighters. Every part of his being cried out to turn the ship around. With an effort he pushed the feelings down. To help her, he had to complete the mission.

Fire from the Interdictor impacted in flashes against his shields. On the bow, the massive ship only had light point defence systems and putting more power into his shields kept the fire at bay for now. Charging in at full thrust, he angled down slightly to avoid fire from the main battery if the huge ship attempted to manoeuvre.

He swore loudly, his words echoing back at him in the large bridge as the Cutters on both flanks remained in tight formation. He rolled the ship as they opened fire at extreme range. The manoeuvre dodged one incoming burst but another struck his shields and they dropped to seventy percent.

The weapons on the Cutters were more powerful than he expected and he reacted by twisting the ship back across the Interdictor's bow. He was now close enough to the flagship that it provided some cover from the Cutters. He wondered why the Cutters hadn't moved forward to compensate. Between the two of them and the fire from the Interdictor's forward array, he wouldn't have lasted long.

Maybe fate smiled upon him.

He jinked from side to side, firing bursts from all of his heavier weapons at one Cutter and then the other. He didn't fire any missiles – he would need them soon.

He saw one burst spray against the Cutter on the left and it pulled back into closer cover with the Interdictor. He thanked whatever spirit was making these Laphrian captains timid in the face of fire and focused a concentrated burst of fire at the other Cutter. The burst scored solid hits but he received a full salvo in response and this captain showed no intention of trying to hide.

Another incoming barrage collapsed his forward shields so once again he angled closer to the Interdictor. He was almost inside its shields and then they would protect Hammer from the Cutter for a short time.

The core part of the attack run approached. With a deft motion, Hammer switched control of the ship over to the autopilot. The course was no longer ideal as the nearby Cutter would likely take advantage of his exposed position, but he couldn't pilot the ship and fire the complicated weapon sequence at the same time.

Affording himself a glance at the scanner to see how the battle behind him progressed, he saw that one of the Sidewinders had been destroyed. Lina and the remaining three fought in a close-range dogfight with a dozen fighters. The two fire ships appeared intact.

As his ship rolled, Hammer scrolled through the listed targets and assigned missile locks to all of the shield emitters within his fire arcs. The turret weapons were set to automatic and fired at targets of opportunity including the Cutter and the Interdictor's point defences.

Energies flared on the Interdictor's shields as they responded in kind. Missile locks filled Hammer's vision. He released a full magazine from each of the launchers and cycled through the targets to prepare for another salvo while the magazines reloaded.

Trying not to hit targets after a lifetime depending on deadly accuracy didn't come naturally to Piotr. He'd hoped that Dee would create a suitable ploy to keep him out of the battle. She'd failed him and so he was forced to rely on what she told him.

He wasn't convinced it was working.

The first engagement as they swept through the fighter group lasted only seconds and he received a few hits on his shields, but nothing that worried him too much. The battle became more hectic as he led the charge against the Cutter protecting this flank of the Interdictor.

The angle of his approach provided a distant view of Hammer's Anaconda as it powered through a force of fighters. Piotr couldn't help but be impressed by the firepower the Anaconda displayed as it devastated the fighters around it.

Piotr had objected to Hammer's plan at the briefing. Partly because it put him right in the firing line, but also because there was a slim chance that it might work. Piotr wanted out of this system and assuming Dee kept her word then he had more important places to be. Obviously the station forces couldn't defeat the fleet arrayed against them, but they could slow it down.

He tried to speak to Dee before they deployed from the station. She didn't reply to his hails. Julia informed him that she was busy with the evacuation and assured him that he'd see her when they returned. Piotr noticed that Julia wore a strange smile when she told him. He didn't understand what that meant.

Now flying into the hail of defensive fire, he realised two things. The first was the IFF trick that Dee explained to him wasn't working. The Laphrian Navy targeted him just the same as the other ships in his formation. With that realisation he let his speed bleed off a little so that he wasn't the lead ship.

The other realisation was that he didn't know what to do.

This presented a more significant problem. He understood what Julia expected from him. She'd given him two missions. The first to occupy the attention of the Cutter and fighter group protecting the Interdictor's left flank. The second was to keep the trader volunteer in the Cobra alive so that she could use her newly installed rail guns against the Interdictor.

Assuming that Hammer managed to bring the ship's shields down.

It looked like he he'd failed on the second objective already as his scanner indicated that the trader was being mobbed by several fighters. She wasn't dead yet but probably would be soon.

He'd never known indecision in combat before. That was a sure way to get killed. He didn't know whether Dee had deceived him or if the IFF system had failed in some way. In either case it clearly wasn't working, so pretending to fight while the others were blown from the sky wasn't going to keep him alive.

Streaking towards the Cutter, he saw that it merely orientated itself towards the attack – it didn't leave the Interdictor's side. Accompanying that understanding came a blaze of fire from the Interdictor's lateral weapons array. Bolts of plasma and laser energy stabbed across space towards him.

Charging into the fusillade didn't seem like such a good idea so he pulled his Viper away from the incoming fire. He still didn't know what to do. He could help the

Laphrians although Dee had been insistent that her cover be maintained and Piotr wasn't convinced that the invading forces wouldn't just destroy him anyway.

He could run.

The Eagles wouldn't be able to keep up with him and the Laphrians probably wouldn't chase him down. Of course if he did that then he'd lose any chance of retrieving the information from Dee. That was only true if she hadn't set him up. As an intelligence operative, she would likely prove difficult to track down.

And as much as he'd be reluctant to admit it, the thought of running away didn't feel right. Neither did fighting for a cause that wasn't his. Although in the end, he would do whatever was necessary to survive. And when he returned to Freeholm, he would catch Dee before the Laphrians attacked the station and extract the information he needed from her by any means necessary.

The decision made, he now needed a plan. He turned the Viper tighter and charged towards the melee of fighters harassing the trader volunteer. Moments before, Piotr had been happy to leave the pilot to her fate, however he now needed the Cobra's rail guns.

"What are we doing?" Rob asked over the comms channel.

"We can't take the Cutter on without heavy weapons. We need to rescue the trader and get her into play. Follow my lead."

"Will do."

Piotr rarely operated as part of a team and he wasn't happy to be the leader of this small squadron. As long as they did what he wanted then he'd find a use for them.

He split his weapons into two fire groups. The first were paired beam lasers which he fired at maximum range at the targeted fighter. As soon as the lasers overheated he switched to the multicannons and fired a stream of shells at the same target. The two weapon types provided an effective combination. The beam lasers ripped through shields with ease and the cannon shells tore through ship armour just as easily.

The fighter exploded and Piotr locked onto the next. Alongside him, the two Eagles engaged their own targets. Between the three ships they knocked out four fighters before the enemy responded. Piotr briefly targeted the Cobra to check its condition and saw that it could still fight having suffered only light hull damage.

They sure made the Cobras tough, he mused. That's probably why they were still so popular with independent traders.

The remaining fighters turned to face Piotr and his allies. The fighters flew into a storm of fire and lost another two of their number. They fought back and the inferior Eagles suffered most under their onslaught. With their shields down, they pulled away and left Piotr alone. Half of the fighters peeled away to chase the vulnerable Eagles.

Piotr continued his charge and kept firing. The fighters attempted to mob him and overwhelm with numbers alone. Another fighter exploded as the beam lasers vaporised the cockpit and its occupant.

He allowed his momentum to carry him away from the fighters and continued firing until out of range. His shields needed to recharge so he let his ship drift to where the Cobra waited. The two Eagles weren't faring as well. They hadn't escaped the chasing fighters although they still manoeuvred and fought hard.

Diverting more power into the shields allowed them to recharge quicker. As they did so, he hailed the Cobra and instructed her to follow him. She wouldn't be able to match his twists and turns but she would be able to protect his rear.

He accelerated towards the nearest Eagle. The ship's computer identified it as San's. Four of the short-range fighters harried her as she dodged and weaved between the lines of fire. She flew with skill but that wasn't enough

374

to keep her pursuers from tearing down her shields the moment they reformed. Only through luck had she managed to avoid any serious damage.

The four fighters paid little attention to anything beyond their own personal chase. A trait Piotr had observed in many rookie pilots. Sometimes even experienced ones if they succumbed to bloodlust or even plain old target fixation.

In this case it proved their undoing.

He took out the first and pivoted to engage the second as he flew past. One of the fighters disintegrated as the trader scored a direct hit with the rail guns. They were notoriously difficult to aim and Piotr found himself impressed by the trader's skill.

Maybe he should try to make more directed use of his allies.

San took out the remaining fighter and then formed up alongside Piotr who led them towards Rob. Freeholm's lead pilot flew desperately against the seven fighters trailing him. They'd split into two groups and allowed little opportunity to recover or fight back. His shields were down, his hull rating was way down and occasional malfunctions hampered his efforts.

His flight had taken him far away from the others and it would take several minutes for Piotr's group to catch up with them.

"Barnes," Piotr instructed. "You need to change course towards us."

"I can't. They're herding me."

"You need to try. We can't reach you in time if you don't."

Piotr's Viper led the small group as they raced towards Rob. The Cobra followed closely behind, its powerful drive almost as fast as the Viper. San's Eagle lagged farther and farther behind.

Up ahead, Rob fired his retros and angled a turn away from the nearest fighters. They responded quickly and cannon fire chewed into the Eagle's tail. He pitched and disabled flight assist to gain more precise control of his turn. The chasing fighters matched him easily and the second group cut him off.

"This isn't working."

"All right, just boost and run. We'll catch you."

"You won't get to me in time. I'll keep them busy, you continue with the mission."

Rob's request made sense. Piotr calculated the vectors and he wouldn't reach Rob before the chasing fighters ran him down.

"Acknowledged. Keep ahead of them and try to head back to Freeholm if you can."

False hope.

"We can't leave him," San said.

"We have no choice. The others are attacking the Interdictor and we need to take care of the Cutter."

"I won't leave him."

Turning the Viper back towards the Cutter, Piotr saw the flash of explosions on the far side of the Interdictor. He didn't understand why the Cutter hadn't changed position. If it had followed them then they'd all been killed for certain. Even more puzzling was a third Cutter stationed at the rear of the warship. Why hadn't it supported either of the flanks being attacked?

San pitched her Eagle towards Rob.

"Damn it, you can't reach him in time!"

"I have to try."

Piotr didn't know what to do. He wasn't used to leading people. It seemed obvious to him that the young pilot was making a mistake. Rob would be long dead before she reached him. Worse than that, he was now down half of his small force. Taking the Cutter down would be more difficult than he anticipated.

A thought occurred to him. He didn't need to destroy the Cutter. The Laphrians were proving inept at commanding their ships. They should have redeployed the Cutters to block the attacks, only they hadn't. Whether the Freeholm forces forced the Interdictor back or not wouldn't be decided on this flank.

Which meant that he just needed to make it look good.

He dived and the Cobra followed close behind. The real danger came from the lateral arrays on the Interdictor. If he angled their approach so the Cutter obscured the Interdictor's firing solution, that would reduce the weight of fire. The sheer size of the warship made it impossible to block the fire completely, but it should be enough. They only needed to get in close to fire a few shots and then they could retreat.

The Cobra probably wouldn't make it.

The pilot didn't need to know that. She just needed to keep following. He sent her a message.

"Keep on my tail – we're going to run at the Cutter. Focus everything you have on that."

"Roger that."

They needed speed now more than anything so he put full pips into the engines with the two remaining into his shields to better withstand any defensive fire. The angle of approach was tighter than he'd thought, but he followed the line and the Cobra followed after him.

Plasma bolts from the Interdictor reached out towards them, but the course held true and only slight evasions were needed. That changed when they entered the weapons range of the Cutter. Pulse and beam lasers sliced through the space around them. Piotr rolled and jinked, using every trick he knew to make him harder to hit.

He returned fire. His beam lasers soon overheated so he shifted power from the engines to the weapons. The extra power enabled the lasers to fire for longer and to recover. On his targeting system, the shield strength of the Cutter dropped rapidly. His own shields were taking a beating as well but he kept dodging and firing.

Four bolts from the Cobra's rail guns shattered the Cutter's shields.

His next volley took out their main left weapon mounting.

An excitement surged in Piotr. They could destroy this ship!

Another salvo of rail gun bolts crashed into the Cutter. It shuddered under the impact, casting debris into space.

Caught up the same thrill that he condemned the Laphrian fighter pilots for, he charged at the Cutter, unleashing everything he had. With the beam lasers, he picked out subsystems and took them down one by one. His multicannons chewed into their armour with a hail of shells.

Too late, Piotr realised that he'd crossed the safe threshold. Point defences from the Interdictor flashed against the Viper's shields, knocking them into the red.

"I'm taking hits."

That was the last he heard from the volunteer trader.

He pulled out of his attack run and exposed his underside to a hail of fire from the Interdictor which stripped away his shields and impacted his armour.

The Cutter was out of action. Piotr saw secondary explosions as he banked past but he was now caught out in the open. The point defences quickly bracketed him and his own subsystems starting reporting failures.

He rolled and dived to evade the fire and now crossed in front of the lateral array. Only a quick response on the stick allowed him to dodge the heavy weapons fire. If even one of the ship-sized plasma bolts hit him, his ship would vaporise and Piotr with it.

He arced in towards the Interdictor. It wasn't much cover but at least cut down the number of weapons able to achieve a lock. He could stay still and he'd also run out of space. The moment he reached the stern of the ship, he'd be open for the third and completely fresh Cutter.

There was no real chance of escape here. At maximum burn he would reduce the time the Cutter had to fire. If somehow they missed, he could at least gain some distance before he could follow him. He rolled as he flew past the mighty engines of the Interdictor and straight into the guns of the Cutter.

They didn't miss – the impacts punched holes in his armour and sent the Viper into a spin.

This was it.

He didn't give up though, and manoeuvred the remains of his ship with its damaged systems. More laser fire chopped into his hull and he noticed that the other Cutter was starting to recover.

Two bright flashes on his scanner heralded the arrival of two new ships. He knew these ships. His computer recognised them as well.

These were two of the three ships he'd provided data on to Dee.

The Viper unleashed its weapons on the flanking Cutter and tore it apart.

The Fer de Lance concentrated on the rear Cutter which turned to face the new opponent.

Filled with righteous fury, Piotr wrestled with the controls to bring the Fer de Lance into view. Its shields flared from impacts from the Cutter and the Interdictor. He waited for the black ship's shields to collapse and prepared to fire his remaining weapons. The moment came, then Piotr's ship shuddered and everything fell black.

- 41 -

"We're approaching the fighter line," Julia transmitted to her small squadron. Delvin and Gimna were formed up tight on either side of her. Marc Roland, the trader volunteer, followed close behind in his Sidewinder.

Julia had tried to talk him out of being part of the main attacking force but he insisted. His Sidewinder was much improved beyond factory spec but even so she doubted its survivability in the battle to come. So she positioned him to watch their tails. Considering the number of fighters they were about to pass through, that wasn't a bad plan and she hoped that it would lessen the fire sent in Marc's direction.

He wasn't even a regular trader at Freeholm but had been the first to respond when she'd placed the call to arms on the station's bulletin board.

"Delvin, you target the furthest fighter on the line."

"Done."

"Gimna and Marc, you take the next one in."

They both acknowledged her command.

"Keep on course as we pass through. Pivot as we make contact and if we take the two before moving out of range, then target the third ship in the line. I doubt we'll get a chance for any more."

The three Eagles and trailing Sidewinder tore through the fighter line at maximum thrust. Laser and cannon fire raged from all of the ships and the fighters quickly responded in kind.

"Maintain formation," she said as she noticed Delvin drifting away.

"Roger."

The two formations collided and Julia's group spun to face backwards and continued firing. The outermost fighter disintegrated in a ball of fire and debris. Several of the other fighters turned to fire at them, but both groups quickly passed out of range.

"Transfer power from weapons to shields. Let's get them recharged as quickly as possible."

Julia angled her ship towards their next target, the Cutter positioned on the right flank of the Interdictor. They needed to attract its attention before Hammer started his attack run. Compared to Piotr's group they had a slight disadvantage as none of Julia's ships were equipped with rail guns.

Checking her scanner, she wasn't pleased to see that the enemy fighters had maintained their formation and were already angling towards Hammer and his group. Indecision flickered in her mind. Without Hammer's attack this battle would all be for nothing. Should she chase the fighters?

No. Hammer knew how to fight and his ship was designed to combat multiple fighters at once. While the number was undoubtedly higher than what he was used to, he wasn't alone. She had to think like a leader not as just another pilot.

"Keep your power in your shields and engines until we reach firing range on the Cutter. We're going to be in sight of the Interdictor's guns all the way so jink and weave. When we're close enough I'll fire the missiles."

She rarely wasted a missile mount on her Eagle. With only three hard points, she could ill afford to waste one of them on a weapon which would run out of ammunition within a few seconds. For this battle, though, they were the ace up her sleeve. The two magazines contained a full load of EMP missiles. They were programmed to detonate at a fixed distance from the target. When they detonated a powerful electromagnetic blast would scramble targeting systems, hopefully long enough for Julia's flight to get in close and do some damage.

During the briefing, Rob challenged her and insisted that he lead the attack. As this wasn't just a diversion and they were getting in close, she denied his request. A job this dangerous had to be done herself, and besides she wanted her lead pilot alongside Piotr. She still didn't want to believe Hammer's accusation but that didn't mean she fully trusted the bounty hunter either.

Using her thrusters, she randomly added lateral and vertical movement to make her ship more difficult to target. The others followed her lead. A quick glance at the scanner indicated that the fighters had made contact with Hammer. The swarm of red contacts suddenly bloomed in white when Hammer unleashed a barrage of missiles.

Satisfied that Hammer appeared to have the situation under control, at least for now, she focused her attention on the Cutter. During the briefing, they'd all agreed that the Cutters would be mobile and ready to plug any holes that appeared in their fleet's defence. In fact the attack plan depended on that response.

The Laphrian Navy didn't respond as they'd expected. Instead of coming to meet them, the Cutter stuck stubbornly close to the Interdictor. This made their task difficult on two fronts. The first was that they'd expected to fight the Cutter on its own rather than under the protection of the Interdictor's guns. If the Cutter had been isolated then Julia's ships would have been able to use their greater manoeuvrability to their advantage. She now also worried that the EMP missiles might not get through a defensive barrage from both enemy ships at the same time.

"Okay, we've come far enough, wide turn in and come at the Cutter directly."

The incoming fire intensified as they faced their target. Julia threw her Eagle into more violent evasive manoeuvres but was careful not to impede her forward velocity.

"I'll be in missile range in two minutes."

Their angle of approach now meant that she could see Hammer charging the bow of the Interdictor. His shields flashed under constant bombardment from the warship. She then noticed a lessening of incoming fire. Incredulous, she watched the Cutter turn away from her incoming attack to face Hammer.

The Cutter captain's decision provided Julia with an opportunity. Originally she planned to divide her missiles between the two targets. With the Cutter leaving itself open and its proximity to the flagship, she decided to fire them all at the Cutter. The blast radius of the warheads should include the Interdictor's lateral array as well.

Once the missiles hit, they would have a clear run at the Cutter.

Her targeting system reported that the Cutter was now in firing range and fired all six missiles from the launcher. The reload took a few seconds and then the second salvo followed the first.

"Missiles away. Concentrate everything we have on the Cutter."

"What about the Interdictor?" Delvin asked.

"That's Hammer's problem for now. But we can at least get the Cutter off his back."

"Understood."

They entered firing range thirty seconds later and fired everything they had. The first sustained volley caused little damage to the shields. When viewing the Cutter alongside the Interdictor it looked tiny and it was easy to underestimate the versatile warship. The way it shrugged off their lasers reminded Julia of its capability.

Once again the enemy captain displayed some indecision, as it started turning towards Julia's group and then back towards Hammer again. Julia didn't know what the captain was playing at but she happily took advantage of it.

The Cutter's point defences shot down three of the missiles but the rest struck with great effect. The missiles detonated in beautiful blossoms of blue. The energy from the explosions bathed the two ships in ghostly light for only a second.

The weight of fire aimed at Julia and her allies dropped to almost zero. It was time to take advantage.

"Put all power into your weapons."

All of their ships were equipped with lasers which meant they didn't have to worry about running out of ammunition. They did have to worry about power management. Firing a laser generated a considerable amount of heat. Feeding extra power into the system provided better heat management and disposal meaning that they could fire the lasers for longer.

The damage caused by the lasers also dropped off over distance. With the Cutter's targeting systems down, they could risk flying closer and using the reduced range to good effect.

Their next volley slashed across the Cutter's shields and Julia saw from her readouts that they'd reduced its strength significantly.

"Keep firing."

Movement to the right on her scanner attracted her attention and she looked out of the cockpit and she saw the rear Cutter move into view.

"Contact right."

But the warning was too late. The full volley smashed into Delvin's Eagle, collapsing his shields immediately and blasting through the hull.

"Delvin, what's your status?"

"Everything's down except life support and weapons."

"Can you move?"

"Barely."

"Then get out of here."

"No, you need my guns."

The Cutter fired again. Delvin jinked to try and avoid the fire but a beam laser clipped his wing and cast him into a gentle spin.

"Engines are down."

"I'm coming."

She pulled her Eagle into a tight turn and boosted towards Delvin with the aim of putting herself between him and the Cutter. To her surprise, the Cutter pulled back to its original position. What in fate's name was going on here?

A ripple of bright explosions brought her attention back towards the prow of the Interdictor. Through the clouds of debris, Hammer's Anaconda emerged. It looked battered. Dark rents could be seen in the armour, from which smoke and escaping gases spewed into space.

She re-joined her ships in firing on the Cutter. At point blank range the Cutter's shields fell quickly. When they did so the Cutter turned to face them. Evidently the captain decided his own safety was now of greater importance.

"The Cutter's moving. Keep away from the forward guns."

Even without targeting, a skilled or even just a lucky pilot could still ruin their day.

"Target its subsystems. It will take too long to break through the hull. I'll go for the cockpit. Marc, you aim for the main weapons. And Gimna, take the engines. Delvin, you get the hell out of here."

"I'm trying. My main drive is down."

"Eject if you need to."

"No, I can get it going again."

They continued to pour fire onto the Cutter. It fired blindly and failed to hit anything but continued to pivot.

"Get the hell out of here. This thing will have you in its sights."

"I can make it."

Julia thrust herself in from the Cutter as her lasers attempted to destroy the cockpit, but its armour was formidable. The Cutter fired at her and missed but carried on its turn.

Another blaze of explosions rippled along the length of the Interdictor. She didn't dare look to see how Hammer was doing. She was busy playing chicken with the Cutter. It fired again and a beam laser removed half of her shields.

"Move!"

Her scanner indicated she was causing damage, as were the others, but it wasn't fast enough. In the corner of her eye she also saw the Interdictor starting to roll. She didn't know what that meant but it couldn't be good.

The Cutter fired again. Not at her this time. Delvin hung motionless, easy prey, and his Eagle burst into fragments as the full force of the Cutter's salvo ripped through it.

"God damn it!"

She screamed her rage into the channel and kept firing. Why didn't he eject? She couldn't think about that now. The Cutter kept turning but reversed its direction and fired. She danced easily out of its way.

Her computer erupted with a cascade of threat warnings. She was being targeting by dozens of different systems. The Interdictor was back online.

The massive ship continued its roll. It looked so slow and ungainly. On its flank, Hammer's Anaconda appeared minuscule as it followed a rolling path of its own. Laser and rail gun fire spat out from the few remaining hard points. It dipped under the lateral weapons array but the bigger ship's twist put it back into the fire arcs and the huge guns blasted. Some of them spat fire in Julia's direction but most fired point blank into the Anaconda.

Nothing could have withstood that amount of firepower at such close range and the Anaconda shattered. The blast rippled against the flank of the Interdictor and secondary explosions cascaded along its lateral weapons array, culminating in a single explosion which burst out from its hull.

For a moment, Julia froze in shock. In less than a minute she had seen Delvin and Hammer killed. Her eyes looked at but didn't see the stream of debris pouring from the savage gash in the side of the Interdictor.

The threat alarms ceased their strident call and she was in the cockpit again. The Cutter fired another desperate shot which missed.

"Gimna and Marc – focus everything you have on the cockpit."

The combined fire quickly smashed into the Cutter's cockpit and she saw a lone figure pulled into space by the escaping atmosphere.

"What do we do now?" Marc asked.

To their left an explosion brighter than the sun polarised the screens.

- 42 -

Chaos and disaster.

Captain Belin watched the scanner and that was all he saw. He'd known that the operation wouldn't go as well as it should. Keeping the Cutters static and close to the flagship was ridiculous. If they'd kept out wide they could have intercepted and stopped the attack on the flanks. He could then have assisted the frontal defence.

All he could do was watch the battle around him as it developed.

He contacted the Admiral several times, asking, then demanding and even pleading to be allowed to join the fight. The Admiral denied his requests and eventually stopped accepting his hails. By then the battle had degenerated into an almost hopeless situation.

In the centre, the defenders had succeeded in their counterattack and brought down the *Laphrian Pride*'s shields. A fresh group of ships now headed towards that vulnerable point. Belin remained convinced that Freeholm's forces lacked anything capable of destroying the Interdictor outright.

An hour ago he wouldn't have predicted the current situation either.

On his right, the fighter squadron leader disobeyed his orders and chased after the attacking ships, or one of them at least. The others dived in but were beaten back by heavy fire.

To his left, things went less well. The fighter screen maintained its formation and fell upon the centre attack, although they appeared to enjoy little success. Even worse was that the small force somehow disabled the Cutter and the Interdictor's targeting so were able to fly in close and engage the escorting ship directly.

His tactical officer reported the EMP blast. The bulk of the Interdictor had protected Belin's Cutter from the blast.

Up until this point, Belin's dilemma had been an ethical one. An objection which he overruled with his duty to his crew. It would prey on his mind how long he procrastinated before acting. His duty wasn't simply to his crew but the other crews as well.

He ordered his ship into battle. He would engage the attackers on his left flank. The fighters on the right were holding that flank for now. With little resistance, the attackers on the left had become bold and were drifting around the crippled Cutter firing at will. They engaged the nearest Eagle and hit it with full force.

As the weapons charged for a second shot, the Admiral's aide appeared on the comms.

"Captain Belin. You are ordered back into position."

"Sir, they will be destroyed if I do not help."

"Your orders are to protect the rear."

"There is no threat here. I can help and still be in position to cover if something appears."

His tactical officer looked at him and Belin nodded. The *Tarsis* fired again but missed.

"Captain, this is your last warning. Pull back into position now or you will be arrested."

This was unbelievable. He couldn't imagine why the Admiral wouldn't want him to support his fellow ships. Was he so scared of being wrong? Nothing made sense.

"Yes sir."

That moment of surrender tasted bitter. He wanted to help his sister ship, but to go against direct orders challenged the memory of a life in the Navy.

A life which began by disobeying orders, a stray

thought reminded him.

The battle to the right had become more fractious. The Freeholm ships turned the tide against the fighters, although a force of them chased one of the Eagles away. One chased after in an apparent effort to save his comrade. Belin calculated the distances and thought that unlikely.

Two ships, a Cobra Mark III and a Viper, dived towards the Cutter on the Interdictor's right flank. The Cutter soon reported its shields failing despite heavy fire from itself and the Interdictor's lateral weapons array. Seconds later it reported a kill on the Cobra although it had now sustained heavy damage.

Belin then noticed the Viper flying along the length of the Interdictor towards him. Of course, the Viper had exposed itself to the larger warship's point defences. He ordered the ship ready to attack the Viper the moment it appeared.

Long seconds crawled past as the Viper accelerated. As it flew into view, the *Tarsis* fired and struck clean hits on the Viper. It continued its approach so the *Tarsis* twisted to hold a bead on the Viper attempting to escape. They fired again, clipping the engines and causing it to spin.

Another clean hit and they would have it.

Two black ships appeared on the scanner and quickly entered combat range. The first was another Viper and it angled towards the flanking Cutter with all its weapons blazing. Without any shields, the sudden attack devastated the already wounded Cutter and it had nothing to fight back with.

Not so the Interdictor and it opened fire at the charging Viper.

Belin's more immediate threat was the other ship. The sharp arrow of its silhouette identified it as a Fer de Lance. Fast, well protected and heavily armed, it dived like the angel of death towards the *Tarsis*. Belin's ship fired one last salvo at the stricken Viper as it turned to face its new foe.

The time for standing and fighting was over. The Fer de Lance presented a dangerous opponent and they would need manoeuvrability to be able to take it on. The black ship streaked past and pivoted so that it could continue to fire. Laser and shell impacts sparkled across the Cutter's shields. The *Tarsis's* powerful engines pushed everyone back into their seats as it powered them on a new course after the Fer de Lance.

Fire poured from the enemy ship, although some of it now missed as the *Tarsis* built up speed. Their weapons engaged and struck the vessel. Its shields held under the weight of the first volley.

The pilot of the Fer de Lance was good. He continued flying backwards but in loose arcs so that he kept directly behind the Interdictor where it had fewer point defences. He also managed his weapons well, ensuring that a constant stream of fire pummelled the chasing Cutter.

This close, the Cutter's only real advantage was its weapons. It possessed more hard points than the Fer de Lance and Belin used all of this advantage that it could. The surprise attack provided the enemy with some clear shots, but now as the two ships flew around each other, fewer shots hit.

The duel became a boxing match as much as space combat. They danced around each other firing constant jabs and the occasional hammer blow. Despite the delicate manoeuvres, it was as much a battle of attrition as one of position.

Flying backwards might have demonstrated the enemy pilot's skill and allowed him to maintain fire on his opponent but it did have one drawback. Like many common starships, the Fer de Lance didn't treat all axes equally. Its main thrusters were designed to push forward which left him less power to adjust his motion. Flying forward, the *Tarsis* didn't suffer from the same handicap and moment by moment as the enemy ship lost some of its momentum, the *Tarsis* gained more direct hits.

Their shields collapsed at the same time and in the same moment the Fer de Lance thrust with everything it had and pulled a tight turn, to try and reach the rear of Belin's ship.

It was a risk but Belin stood his ground. The ship pivoted opposite to its direction of travel and the roles were reversed. The Fer de Lance chased the Cutter and they both unleashed everything they had against each other. Here the advantage of a multi-crewed ship came into play. The tactical officer governed the weapons while the pilot concentrated only on flying the ship.

Over the comms, the *Laphrian Pride* reported that the Viper which jumped in with the Fer de Lance was destroyed and that seemed to spur the Fer de Lance to greater efforts. It boosted forward and sat right in front of the nose of the Cutter. For a moment that lasted far too long, the enemy ship was within the cone of convergence and fired unopposed.

The pilot reacted swiftly and twisted into a new course. The enemy didn't react to the manoeuvre as quickly and now the Cutter had a tight angle behind the Fer de Lance. The *Tarsis* fired all of its weapons into the rear of the black ship which jinked and spun to try and avoid the fire. Some of the weapons missed but not all of them.

The Cutter's port beam laser sliced into one of the Fer de Lance's engine mounts and the resulting explosion spun the ship. Another volley smashed into the ship. And then another.

Thrusters flared as the Fer de Lance tried to manoeuvre. Belin paused to allow the pilot to eject, but he continued to wrestle with his controls. The next volley tore the ship apart.

His own ship had suffered damage as well. Belin let the crew handle what was needed while he assessed the situation. He discovered that the Interdictor's forward shields were down and that the warship was rolling to bring its lateral weapons to bear.

A sudden flash illuminated the far side of the ship and the *Laphrian Pride* shuddered as more explosions detonated. Over the comms, they reported a kill on the Anaconda but also failures on the port side lateral weapons arrays. In the distance he also saw the outlines of asteroids. They were nearing the station.

The forces to Belin's right were scattered. A lone Eagle still being chased down by a mob of fighters. Another Eagle followed in pursuit. There wasn't a threat there. On the right side, an Eagle and a Sidewinder continued to harass the damaged Cutter. Belin ordered a course to support them.

They fired as soon as they came into view and hit the Sidewinder. Its shields collapsed but the Eagle's engine's flared as it turned and ran. With both flanks secure, he pulled out wide to gain a better view of the Interdictor's bow.

Huge rents marred the skin around the weapon ports. Missile impacts pockmarked the once-white hull. The ship rolled slowly back to its original orientation. Beyond the bow, his sensors tracked a small group of Sidewinders and a Cobra flying away. They didn't appear to be heading towards Freeholm but were cutting across towards the Eagle being chased.

He wished them luck as long as they kept away from the fleet, or what remained of it at any rate. The Cutter in front of him was badly damaged and he sent a message for them to fall back behind the *Laphrian Pride*.

Two ships from Freeholm remained on course to the Interdictor. His sensors couldn't recognise the types. The silhouettes indicated that each was comprised of a clump of orbs. He didn't know what they were but he was willing to bet that they didn't bode well for the flagship.

He ordered the *Tarsis* forward to gain a better firing angle on the two approaching ships. He fired on the first and its shields flared and collapsed. He prepared to fire again when everything vanished in a white light. Urgent messages jammed the comms channels. The bridge crew's sight returned and they saw another of the strange ships drifting along the flank of the Interdictor.

Belin hesitated. He didn't know whether his fire had detonated the first ship or if it was going to blow up anyway. If he fired now and blew up the second ship, it would compound the damage already done. If it was meant to explode, then leaving it could cause a wider spread of damage if it detonated further along the hull.

He contacted the *Laphrian Pride* and instructed them to turn hard to starboard. For once they listened to him. As the ship turned, the cluster of globes started to follow and Belin fired. With the second shot the spheres exploded, scorching the hull but not penetrating it.

He asked to speak to the Admiral but was told that he wasn't available. The battle appeared to be over for now but they hadn't reached Freeholm yet. He brought the *Tarsis* to the upper deck of the *Laphrian Pride* and scanned the volume of space ahead. The station was situated in a small cluster of asteroids, arrayed like four guardians around the old penal colony.

Belin didn't see the seven blinks on the nearest asteroid as he was busy talking to the comms officer on the Interdictor. On the upper deck of the flagship, three huge turrets contained plasma accelerators capable of melting a ship with a single hit. The one nearest to the prow of the ship sat at an off-angle, its mounting warped from the damage to the structure.

The turret exploded in a storm of released energy and debris as rail gun bolts smashed through its protective armour. The other two turrets rotated to face the asteroid and Belin saw the blinks this time. Only one of the bolts struck the second turret and both turrets fired a beam of bright energy back at their assailants.

The beams struck the asteroids with such ferocity they

melted the rock to slag. The awesome display of power took down only one of the rail gun emplacements and they fired again. Their shots were more accurate this time and peppered the turret although they didn't destroy it.

Plasma accelerators of that size took minutes to recharge for the next shot. The Interdictor started a ponderous turn to bring the starboard weapons array in play to respond to this new attack. Belin brought the *Tarsis* into position as well. His shields were fully restored, but they'd suffered considerable hull damage. These rail guns posed a significant risk to his ship as they'd punch through his armour with ease.

Another volley struck the second turret causing sparks from failures within the mounting. Smoke leaked from the holes caused by the bolts. Belin returned fire along with the Interdictor's starboard guns, but all shots missed their target.

The *Tarsis's* second salvo hit the target but it was well protected amongst the dense rock of the asteroid. It responded with another volley. The two turrets fired and the combined fire vaporised one of the emplacements. The beam from the second turret faltered and then died. It exploded as more rail gun bolts tore through its armour.

"Captain Belin!" Colonel Junesford's voice startled him.

"Yes Colonel."

"Stand down."

"What?"

"This battle is over. Cease fire and return to the flagship. We're recalling the fighters."

"Where's the Admiral?"

"In his quarters. I left him his personal sidearm."

"You stopped him? Why now?"

"The operation had turned into a disaster and I had to do something. So did the rest of the crew, it seems. None of them intervened when I arrested him."

"What about Freeholm?"

"It will remain with its current owners for now. I think they'll see the wisdom in not pursuing their attack."

"Why?"

"We have reinforcements on their way. However, Fleet Command seemed a little surprised that our training operation had actually entered Freeholm space."

And there it was – Belin's shame. He'd known all along of course, but in that instant he understood his failure to act. His old friend had been correct and he'd failed to listen.

"Why didn't they say something?"

"Apparently they did."

"What now?"

"That remains to be seen but for now we withdraw from Freeholm space. There will no doubt be an investigation. I'm sure the top brass will want to know how something like this could happen without their knowledge. I'm sure we'll all see a court martial. Well, the command-level officers for sure, but for now let's just get the hell out of here."

"Yes Colonel."

– 43 –

A tense week passed in Freeholm.

It had also been a hectic week for Julia. The only restful moments were the few hours of snatched sleep and when she watched the remains of the invasion fleet retreat. The moment felt surreal with her alone in the sky, shadowing the damaged Interdictor and the two remaining Cutters.

She kept her distance and ordered the others back to Freeholm. Lina was furious and wanted to continue the attack to make sure that they never returned. Obviously the older woman just wanted revenge. Julia could easily imagine the grief that drove Lina's desire.

As a sensible commander, she should have returned with them, but she had to see the attackers leave. It also reinforced the reality of their victory. Even seeing the damage to the Interdictor didn't quite make it real.

Everyone had sustained severe damage during the battle. Julia's Eagle limped along at far less than its usual capability. As she followed the Navy ships, she scanned the debris. She discovered Piotr's escape capsule amongst the fragments of his ship. The old bounty hunter trick of suppressing the distress signal meant that she thought he'd been killed. She called to Flight Control and they sent a ship to collect his capsule.

The first priority upon their return had been fixing their damaged ships. All around her, jubilant people wanted to celebrate. They didn't comprehend the cost yet. Julia did, but she couldn't allow herself to succumb to grief. She had to cajole the maintenance and engineering crews into making the repairs in a hurry.

Only when the ships were operational again did she let them join the revelry around the station. Everyone celebrated for the rest of the day. All except those who'd actually fought in the battle. They retreated to their own favoured places. Each sought solace in their own way.

They didn't know if the Laphrians would return. It seemed unlikely but no certain information had been received. The station council communicated constantly with the Laphrian authorities. The civilian government claimed that the attack was a rogue operation and that they were investigating.

The council pressed for more details and reparations and a public declaration of co-existence. They received the last item but the responses on the first two were vague at best.

Contact with the Navy had also resumed. They were a bit more open and had sent urgent supplies when asked. They also kept their patrols well away from the belt. They acted eager to resume a working relationship with the station although no-one from Freeholm appeared ready to accept that yet, especially Julia.

Jamming of the newsfeeds stopped and the Laphrian channels confirmed what little the authorities had said, filled with outrage from the planet's population. Although not from all of them. The same channels as before spewed their hate for Freeholm. Some things didn't change.

Amidst the news, they learned that the commanding admiral of the invasion fleet had committed suicide during the journey home. Further investigations were promised into why the Admiral had been allowed to keep his sidearm.

The morning of the second day brought with it grief and sorrow. During the celebrations, people allowed themselves to forget the price that had been paid. Not completely and not everyone, but for most the simple thrill of facing certain devastation and surviving it inspired an exhilarating euphoria.

For Julia it also brought the news that Dee was missing. She cursed herself for not noticing the previous day. The excuse that things had been hectic felt like a poor one. Mayborn initiated a search for her and found no trace in her quarters or anyone who had seen her since the evacuation. He suggested that maybe she had slipped away on one of the departing transports.

That didn't make sense to Julia. Dee had seemed keen to be part of the battle. Why would she then sneak away before it started? If indeed she had. Mayborn checked with Flight Control and no other ships had departed from the station during the battle. Marc departed from the station late the previous day and a Sidewinder was a single pilot ship, so it was unlikely he'd provided transport for her.

Other events required Julia's attention so she left Mayborn to continue the search. As time stretched on though, the conflict of worrying what might have happened to Dee or why she would have left Freeholm preyed on Julia's thoughts.

They weren't able to recover Hammer's body and naturally his death hit Lina hard. Apart from checking her ship was ready for action, she retreated to her room and refused to speak to anybody. Julia visited when she could, but Lina wouldn't answer. Julia considered getting security to force the door in. If she thought that might have helped then she would have done but instead decided to leave it for the day.

Lina came out of her quarters that morning and surprised Julia by finding her in the briefing room. The conversation was brief. Lina wanted to hold a memorial service for Hammer that afternoon. The funeral arrangements were another of Julia's priorities. She'd hoped for more time to put them together.

Ju Reyers's body had already been shipped to her

family. She had died in the attack with Piotr's group. Her family had been traced and informed. A process which Julia struggled with. What could you say a family light years away? Ju had only visited the station a few times over the years on trade runs yet had still signed up for the call to arms.

For Hammer's memorial, Julia wanted something formal that the station could take part in. As much as the population declared them all to be heroes, as far as Julia was concerned, he was the hero. Without his plan and sacrifice, the Laphrians would have invaded the station.

Lina disagreed. Not with the sentiment, even in her grief she appreciated the depth of feeling from everyone. She wanted a private service with just those present at the battle and the few friends that Hammer had made during his short stay at Freeholm.

She didn't get her wish. Word of the memorial spread and when the time for the service arrived, a large crowd assembled near the observation deck. Too many people wanted to attend and crowds gathered as close as they could wherever there was space. Julia watched her old friend crumble and helped her stand. All too easily, Julia remembered Lina's support at her father's funeral.

The wealth of public feeling shocked Lina from her personal despair and she invited those that could to join the ceremony. With the station's solidarity, she realised that the grief wasn't just her own. Hammer had touched all of these lives in some way.

For some they were friends and worked with Hammer closely. It might have been true that Hammer alienated them with suspicion and paranoia after the fault on the escort run, but that didn't matter.

Lina told them all about the man who'd come out of the blue into her life. She related their differences and Hammer's life and dreams. She faltered throughout the eulogy but always recovered to remember Hammer in her own words.

For centuries there was a spacer tradition that if a body couldn't be recovered, then an empty coffin would be filled with small tokens by those attending. The coffin soon filled with patches, glasses and a whole range of small items which provided some connection between the mourner and Hammer.

At the suggestion of the engineering chief, a cargo pod was transformed into an oversized coffin. The mementoes all fitted inside and a memorial plaque laser-etched into the surface. Lina wept openly as the pod launched into space.

The wake proved a sombre affair. Julia remembered her father's wake and how everybody celebrated the life that they'd shared with him. This was different. They'd known Hammer for such a short time that the anecdotes were quickly exhausted. His main contribution to their world had already been celebrated the night before but now the cost of that victory was all too apparent.

Piotr presented a different dilemma. For three days he remained unconscious in the medical bay. He'd received multiple injuries when his ship had been destroyed. The most serious was a head wound which even with the latest medical technology was difficult to repair. His other injuries including a damaged spine, ruptured spleen and a broken arm were efficiently dealt with by med-bots and tailored repair systems.

When he awoke his first words were to ask for Dee.

He became distraught when the nurse informed him that no-one knew where she was. Julia visited him but he spoke little after he determined that she didn't know any more. When she asked him whether she'd have any reason to leave the station without telling anyone, he reacted angrily but without any explanation.

He was clearly still affected by his injuries so Julia left him to rest. A little while later, a security alert announced that he'd left the med-bay. Considering his injuries, the medical staff believed him a threat to his own safety and wanted him brought back. Mayborn's people eventually found him in the morgue although Piotr refused to respond to the security officers who'd found him.

The dead brothers provided Julia with another problem. She hadn't been aware of their presence during the battle. It was only as she searched through the debris she discovered their inert escape pods. Despite the severe damage to the pods, the bodies were still recognisable.

That wasn't always the case with these retrievals.

She recognised who they were after returning to the station and viewing the bodies. She didn't reveal that. They still hadn't been formally identified although the analysis of the battle had revealed their involvement. Without their intervention, Piotr would now be dead.

Julia didn't know what to do with the bodies. Her first instinct had been to conduct a nameless pilot service for them both. It would have been more convenient but they were family, even if she didn't know them. There had to be other family members out there somewhere who would want to hold the memorial. Without any easy way of finding out, she left the bodies on ice.

Piotr's trip to the morgue changed that.

When Mayborn reported that Piotr had been found and was unresponsive, she went down there herself. Piotr stood there and stared at the bodies. He'd opened the sealed body sheathes so that their faces could be seen.

"They saved your life," she told him as she entered.

The silence hung between them in the cold air for several seconds before he turned and looked at her. She couldn't read the tortured expression on his face. It smoothed away as he nodded but the haunted look in his eyes remained.

"You should go back to the medical bay."

"Who were they?"

"We don't know."

Julia remembered how insistent he'd been when

trying to track their ships. There was clearly some history between them and not something she wanted to get into right now.

He nodded again.

"Please, let these guards take you back to the med-bay. Your injuries haven't fully healed yet."

"Have you found Dee?"

"No. No, not yet. When we learn anything new I will be sure to let you know."

He nodded again and, with a final glance at the bodies, shuffled towards the exit. Julia watched him leave and was concerned by how broken he looked. It wasn't just the physical injuries. It seemed like something more fundamental had died within him. This wasn't the bounty hunter who'd arrived at the station two months ago.

The next day a maintenance team discovered Marc's body stuffed into an equipment locker. They tried to keep the news quiet but something like this didn't remain private for long on a small station like Freeholm.

Mayborn's team weren't really set up for a murder investigation but the connections seemed obvious enough. Blood analysis revealed a toxic agent and there were no other signs of injury. Only Dee was listed as missing from the station registry. The conclusion was that Dee had murdered the pilot so that she could use his ship to escape.

The reason as to why she would need to escape after the victory with the Laphrian Navy was unclear, but the possibilities left an unpleasant taste in Julia's mouth. She didn't want to believe that Dee provided support for Laphrian attack but the more she discussed it with Mayborn, the more likely that appeared to be. Her concern then manifested into doubt about her decisions. She'd trusted Dee as an aide and given her access to everything.

Word of Marc's death leaked out, but with Mayborn and the station council's help, most people believed it was an accident. It hit everyone hard; they'd lost another of their heroes.

The following day brought with it news of more death. At least this time it was far removed from the station but still entwined with recent events. The Laphrian newsfeeds reported the deaths of several important people – businessmen, government officials and even high-level Navy officers – sparking a frenzy of accusations and recriminations.

The extremist press accused the government of a cover-up and using the recent events as a smokescreen to put forward their own deadly agenda. The more balanced media simply wanted to know how such tragic events could happen, especially this soon after an unsanctioned Navy operation.

Amidst it all, the government spokesman looked harassed and uncertain. To Julia and many commentators on the feeds, it looked like the government didn't really know what was going on. And if they did they were certainly keeping the information tightly controlled.

The frenzy intensified when it was revealed that all of those killed were persons of interest in the investigation about why a rogue Navy operation had attacked Freeholm.

Worry about these developments flashed through Freeholm as well. Julia joined the council in a virtual conference with several Laphrian representatives to express their concern at these events. The officials went to great lengths to assure Freeholm that the deaths were not of their doing. Full investigations were in progress and they would keep the station council fully informed.

Better news came when the officials stated that a full public apology for the attack would take place the next day and that reparations for the loss of life and damage caused would also be arranged.

It had been a hectic week indeed and happy that

at least it ended on a positive note, Julia retired to her quarters. She wasn't left in peace for long. Flight Control reported a vessel approaching the station and requesting to speak with her and only her.

She asked them who it was.

When they told her the name, she stood up and told them to allow the ship to dock and that she would meet the pilot.

- 44 -

Julia saw the resemblance to his children the moment she entered the room. The similarity with Mervan was particularly strong. He had the same heavy build that strained against the flight suit. His face was heavily lined and his white hair revealed his age.

"Rex Cavus?" she asked although it obviously had to be him. He exactly fitted what little Mervan had spoken of him.

"Yes and you must be Julia."

He approached and offered his hand which she took. His grip was strong and he wore a broad smile that didn't quite reach his eyes.

"Yes. Welcome to Freeholm."

"No need to be so formal. We might not know each other but we are of the same blood. Correct?"

"You are correct. We don't know each other."

He inclined his head.

"I've arranged quarters for you."

"That won't be necessary. I have come here only to collect the bodies of my sons."

"I thought that you would…"

"I would very much like to get to know you better but I am afraid that this isn't the right place or the right time."

"This is my home."

"I understand that but this isn't a good place to for me to be at the moment. Even so, I could not leave my sons' bodies unattended."

Julia remembered the family business.

"You've just come from Laphria?"

"It is best that we do not talk of that. I simply did what had to be done."

"I see. Where is Seline?"

"She is no longer with us." A flicker of emotion crossed his face yet his eyes remained a cold blue. "I suspect that is why my sons foolishly came to this system in so much of a rush that they didn't consult with me first."

"Their timing was fortuitous for us."

"I can believe it was, but not for them. They always did react impulsively, especially the younger ones, Lee and Seline. They were ever happy to rush into trouble."

"I would have liked to have known them better."

"Yes. Mervan spoke highly of you on the few occasions that he mentioned you. I wish he had told me sooner that you existed. Things might have been better if we had known each other."

"My father."

"I know. You might not believe it but I didn't want to separate in that way."

"So why did you?"

"What other way could there have been? The family business requires a certain discipline. It's not something that you can exist on the fringes of. You are either part of it or not."

"I don't understand."

"I think that you do. It's much like your job here as head of security. The job is your life and you are always needed."

"Yes. I suppose that's true."

"It is the same for us. A different job of course but the lifestyle is the same. Although we have to be more circumspect than you."

He offered a small smile to indicate the humour and Julia found herself responding in kind.

"Now I would like to see my sons and make arrangements for their transport."

"Of course. Follow me."

"It would probably be best if I wasn't seen by too many people. My face isn't widely known and I would appreciate keeping it that way."

"We can take the lifts most of the way."

"That should be fine."

She led him through the station. As she said, most of the way was through the lift system which connected all of the station's levels. A silence fell between them which she felt the urge to fill but was unsure how.

As the morgue was situated near the administrative levels, they encountered few people along their journey. She led him into the room and pulled the two bodies from the holding banks.

Rex approached them, opened the seals on the body sheathes and peeled them back. The first revealed the waxy face of Lee and then he revealed Mervan. He stood between the two bodies looking at one and then the other. He touched their cheeks gently.

"Can you provide trolleys or something to move them?"

"Yes of course. I'll arrange coffins as well for their transport."

"Thank you."

Julia reached for her comms unit and then turned to face a noise behind her. An unsteady Piotr pushed her into the room and knocked the comms unit from her hand.

"Step out of the way, Julia," he instructed.

"Wait a minute. What's going on?"

She moved back but positioned herself in the line of fire between the two men.

"This is not your business."

"This is my station which makes it my business. Now put the gun down."

Piotr looked like death warmed up with his sallow skin. His eyes gleamed with purpose and that worried her.

"I knew you would come." He motioned the pistol at the old man.

"Just calm down, Piotr. Give me the gun."

Julia took a step towards him and he snapped the gun to point at her. His body trembled but the hand holding the gun showed no such weakness.

"Stay where you are. Now move back. I don't want to shoot you but I will if I have to."

"You had better do as he says," said Rex.

Uncomfortable but unwilling to make the situation worse, she backed away. Piotr now had a clear view of the older man. She didn't give up trying to talk him down.

"What's this about?"

"I knew you would come. There had to be another. She didn't lie about that at any rate. So I left a camera and waited and here you are."

"Indeed. Here I am, Mister Vanchenko, but I'm not who you're really looking for, am I?"

"What do you mean?"

"I know who you are, Mister Vanchenko, and I know that you've been looking for my children for a long time."

"What the hell is going on here? Do you two know each other?"

Julia reached for her sidearm but Piotr was quicker and the gun was once more directly in her face.

"You are not part of this."

"Look. I'm just trying to stop you doing something stupid."

"There is no choice," Piotr said. Did she hear regret in his voice?

"There is always a choice," said Rex.

"Not this time. I have waited too long and I cannot be sure I will get another opportunity."

"You won't. How many years has it been since Sahiba Mehta's unfortunate end?"

"Do not speak her name," Piotr hissed.

"She was in the wrong place at the wrong time."

"Your children killed her."

"Yes they did. And now you're going to kill me – why?"

"Because you deserve to die."

"I didn't kill her."

"You created the monsters that did."

"My children are not monsters, Mister Vanchenko. I think you have more guilt on that count than I. Especially here."

"What do you mean?"

"You haven't been playing by the rules now have you, Mister Vanchenko?"

"I don't know what you mean."

"Oh, I think you do."

"Will someone please tell me what the hell is going on here?"

"Of course, Julia." Rex reached carefully into his pocket and, without taking his eyes from Piotr, placed a small transparent cube onto the tray holding Lee's body."

"What is that?" Piotr asked.

"This is a portable holo-projector. You can buy them in any tech-market. This one has some interesting information about your activities over the last few weeks."

Piotr swung the gun towards Rex but as he pulled the trigger, the gun was knocked from his hand by a sharp blow from Julia. With a smooth motion, she pulled her own from its holster and aimed it at Piotr. He stepped forward, ready to try and seize the weapon, and collapsed as Julia kicked his weakened legs from under him.

She backed away so that she had both men in sight.

"Now one of you is going to tell what this is all about."

"Of course," Rex replied. "It's very simple really. A dear bounty hunter friend of Mister Vanchenko's was caught in the crossfire of an operation conducted by Mervan and the others. Piotr swore revenge and has hunted them down ever since. The irony of course is that my sons' ill-timed intervention saved this bounty hunter's life.

"With my children dead but not by his hand, the revenge he sought was unsatisfied so he needed to find me."

"You knew all this time that he was looking for you?"

"Actually no. It wasn't until I investigated what had happened here that I discovered the connection with Mister Vanchenko. And he has been a busy man."

Piotr made to stand and Julie knocked him back.

"You had your chance to tell me what was happening and you ignored me. Don't worry, you'll get to speak."

"We shall see."

"What does that mean?"

"It doesn't matter. Now do you remember sending Mister Vanchenko on a recon patrol to the Laphrian shipyard?"

"Yes."

"And he came back claiming that there was nothing suspicious there?"

"Yes. We all saw the sensor data."

"You saw something, but it wasn't the raw data. Here's the raw dump."

A hologram of a *Majestic*-class Interdictor in orbit around Laphria filled the room.

Piotr yelled and lunged for the weapon. Julia stepped back and kicked him back down. Could this be true?

"Not only did he deceive you, he then tried to assassinate Mark Lamon."

"Who?"

"Ah, you probably knew him as Hammer?"

No. That couldn't be.

"Is this true?" she demanded.

And he didn't deny it.

"Is this true?"

He still didn't deny it.

"One. Last. Time. Did you do it?"

"I had no choice…"

Julia pulled the trigger and shot him in the face.

"Well done. I knew you had it in you."

"Shut your mouth, old man."

She couldn't turn away from the mess in front of her.

"I should leave."

"You stay where you. The station's sensors will have detected weapons fire and a security team will be on its way."

"Then I should be gone before they arrive."

"They already know you are here. Don't worry, you haven't committed a crime of the station so it's all on me. I'll keep you out of it."

"What will you tell them?"

"The truth."

"Are you sure that's wise?"

"Maybe not, but it was a righteous kill."

"It sure was. Well, if things go badly then there is another life waiting for you should you want it."

"What do you mean?"

"You're family, my granddaughter, and there is a place for you."

"I am not a murderer."

"Of course not. Sometimes people need killing."

- 45 -

Rex didn't bother looking back at the station as he flew his Viper out of the belt. There was no point. He felt sure that he would see his granddaughter again, but it wouldn't be here and it wouldn't be now.

Julia had kept her word and told the security chief exactly what had happened. She didn't mention her relationship with Rex, for which he was grateful. While not a crime in itself, they may have made a bigger effort to discover more about him for curiosity's sake if nothing else.

He took a chance as they were separated and placed a microbug on Julia. He guessed that while station security possessed the technology to locate such surveillance devices, it wasn't part of their day to day mindset to check. Especially when it was their head of security in the firing line.

She kept calm throughout, did as she said and told the truth.

Once the facts of the encounter had been revealed, the mood changed from one of shock to grim consideration. He would love to have been part of the discussions that followed. Quite naturally they didn't involve Julia. Not until they'd reached their own conclusion.

When they did, she resisted them. Rex felt sure that the misplaced need to take responsibility would fade with time. They decided that there were no charges for Julia to answer to. Not unexpected as far as Rex was concerned. She argued with them although she didn't quite go as far as Rex hoped and resign.

The station didn't seem bothered by keeping her as their head of security. Which meant that she wouldn't come looking for Rex any time soon. No matter, she'd find her way eventually. In the meantime he had other lines to follow. There were other members of the family for him to meet.

He also thought it strange that no-one asked about the source of his information. The intelligence operative was currently being turned into slurry by genetically engineered bacteria. He would dump the cargo pod into space when he was far enough from the station. The process would continue and when complete, a small valve would open and the liquid that was Dee Callum would spray into space, never to be found.